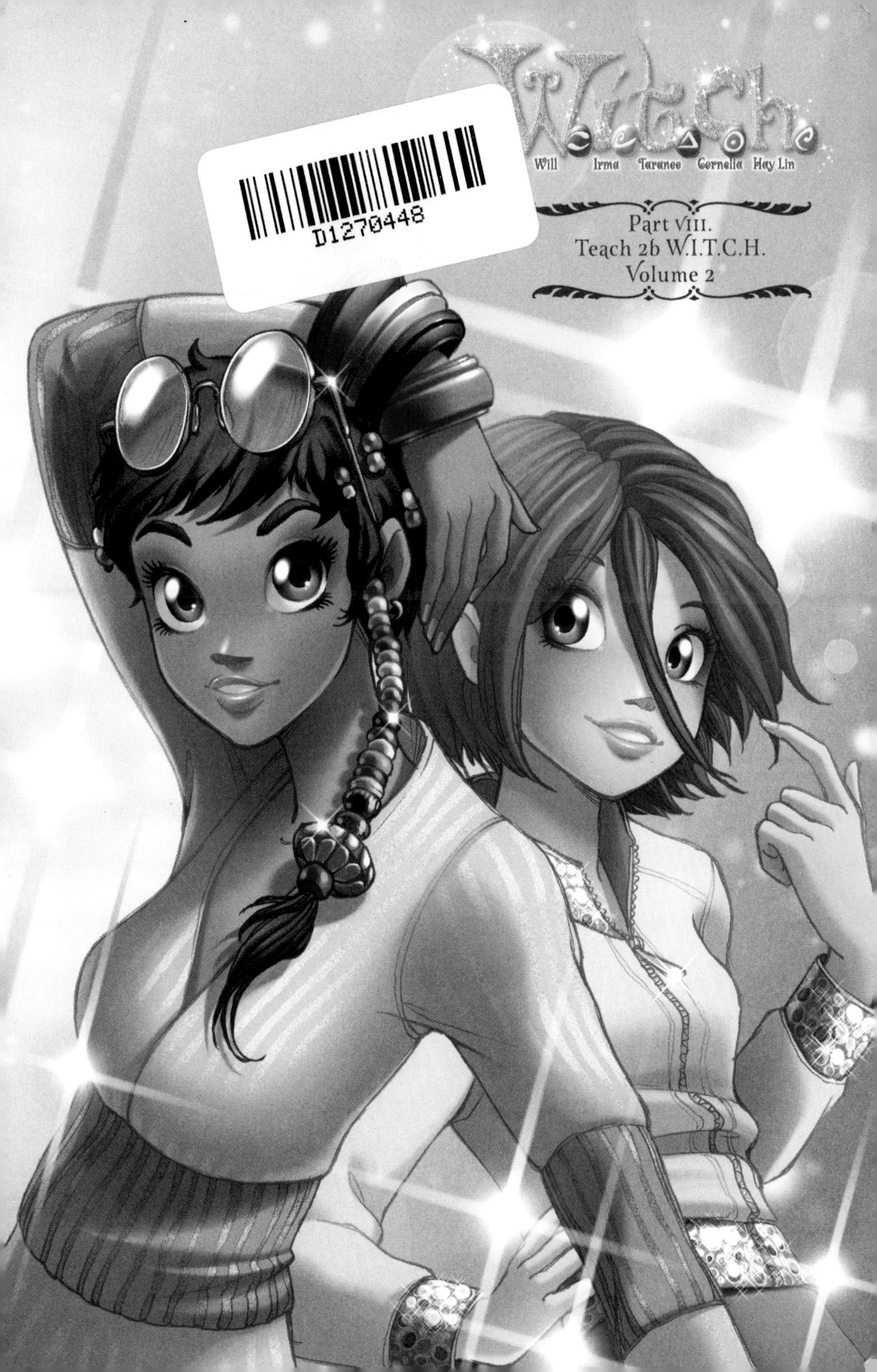
W.i.t.c.h.
Will Irma Taranee Cornelia Hay Lin
Part VIII.
Teach 2b W.I.T.C.H.
Volume 2

W.i.t.c.h.

Will   Irma   Taranee   Cornelia   Hay Lin

Part VIII.
Teach 2b W.I.T.C.H.
Volume 2

CONTENTS

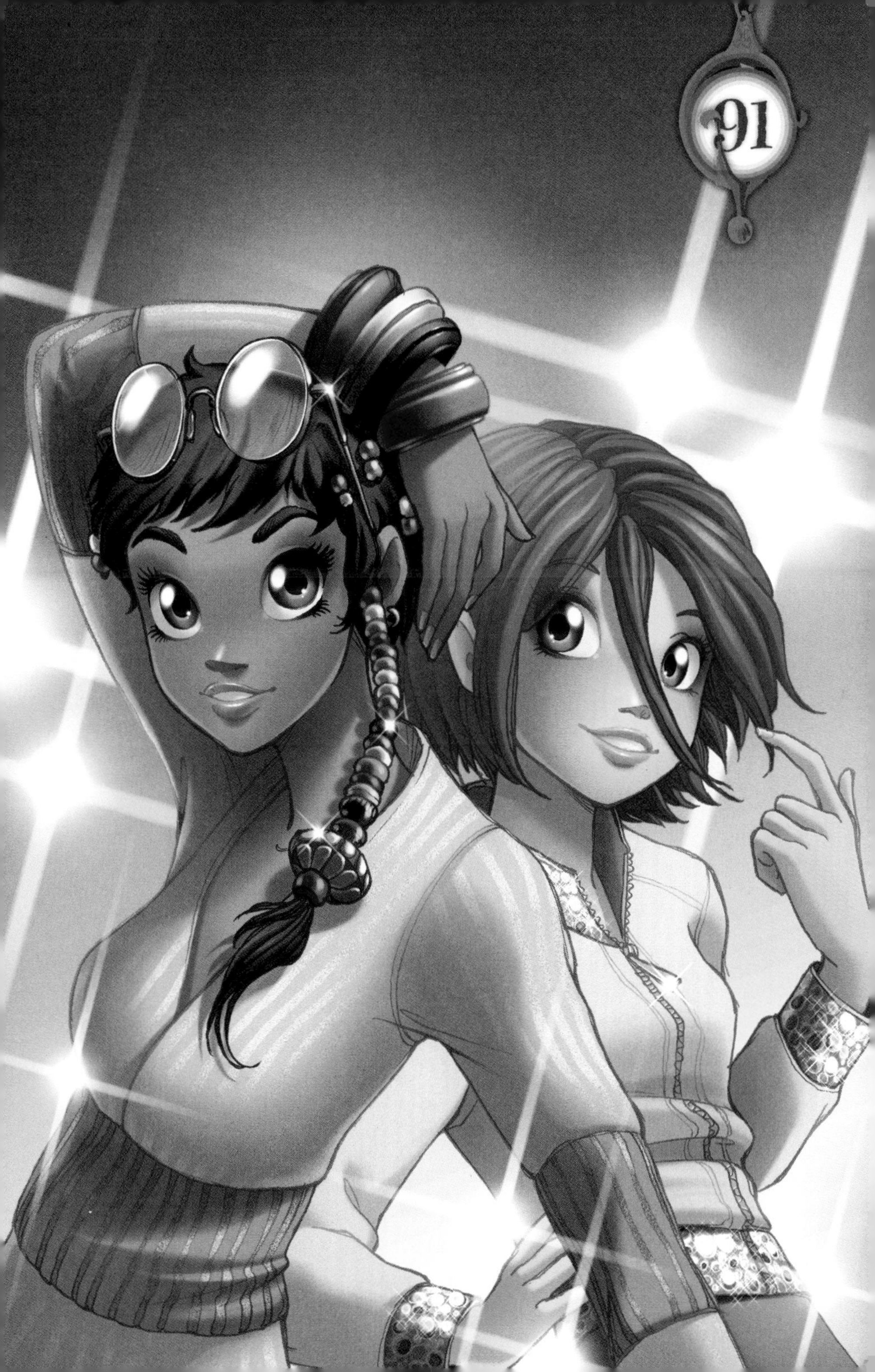
91

More Than Meets the Eye

"You're you! And there's nobody like you in the world."

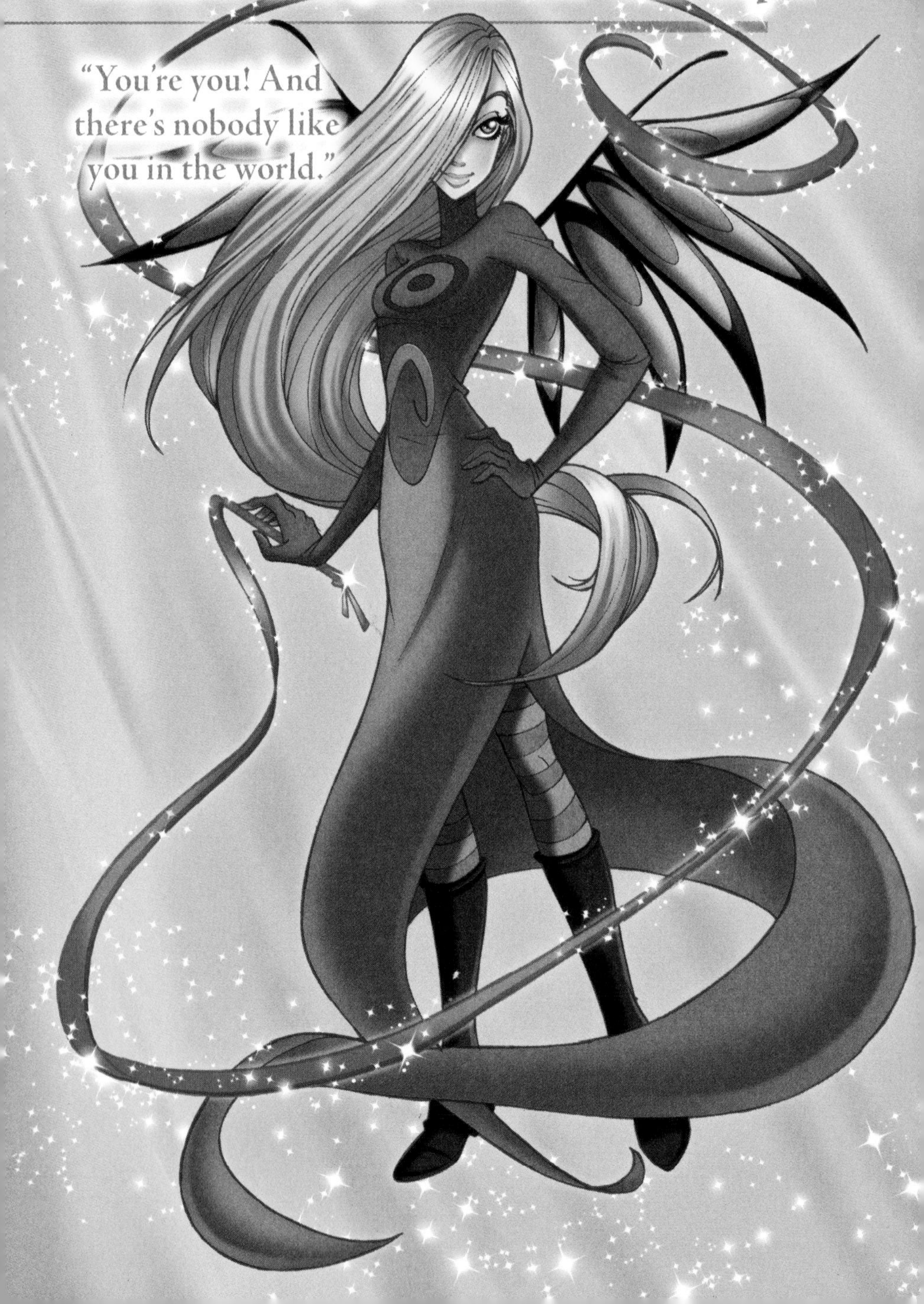

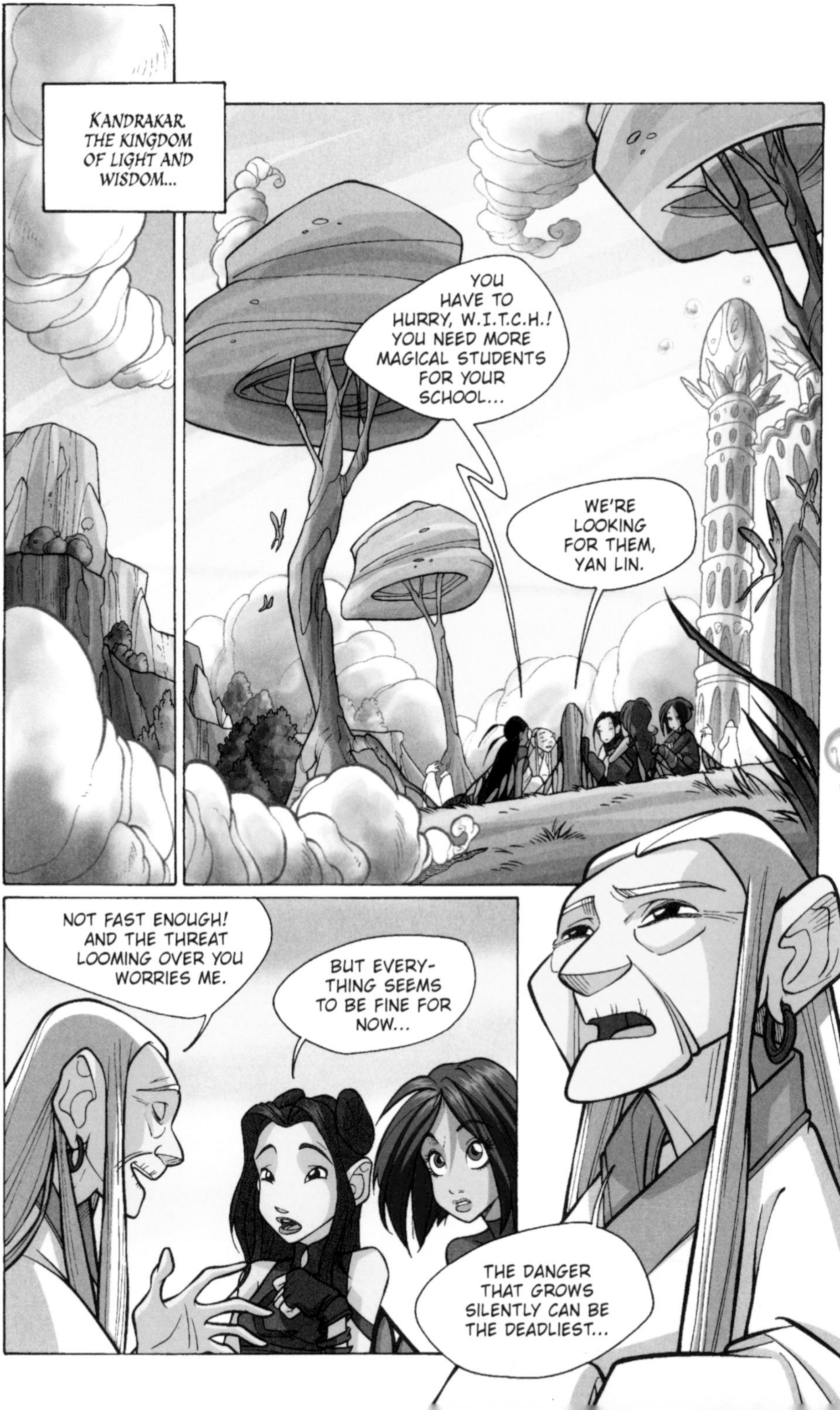
KANDRAKAR THE KINGDOM OF LIGHT AND WISDOM...
YOU HAVE TO HURRY, W.I.T.C.H.! YOU NEED MORE MAGICAL STUDENTS FOR YOUR SCHOOL...
WE'RE LOOKING FOR THEM, YAN LIN.
NOT FAST ENOUGH! AND THE THREAT LOOMING OVER YOU WORRIES ME.
BUT EVERY-THING SEEMS TO BE FINE FOR NOW...
THE DANGER THAT GROWS SILENTLY CAN BE THE DEADLIEST...

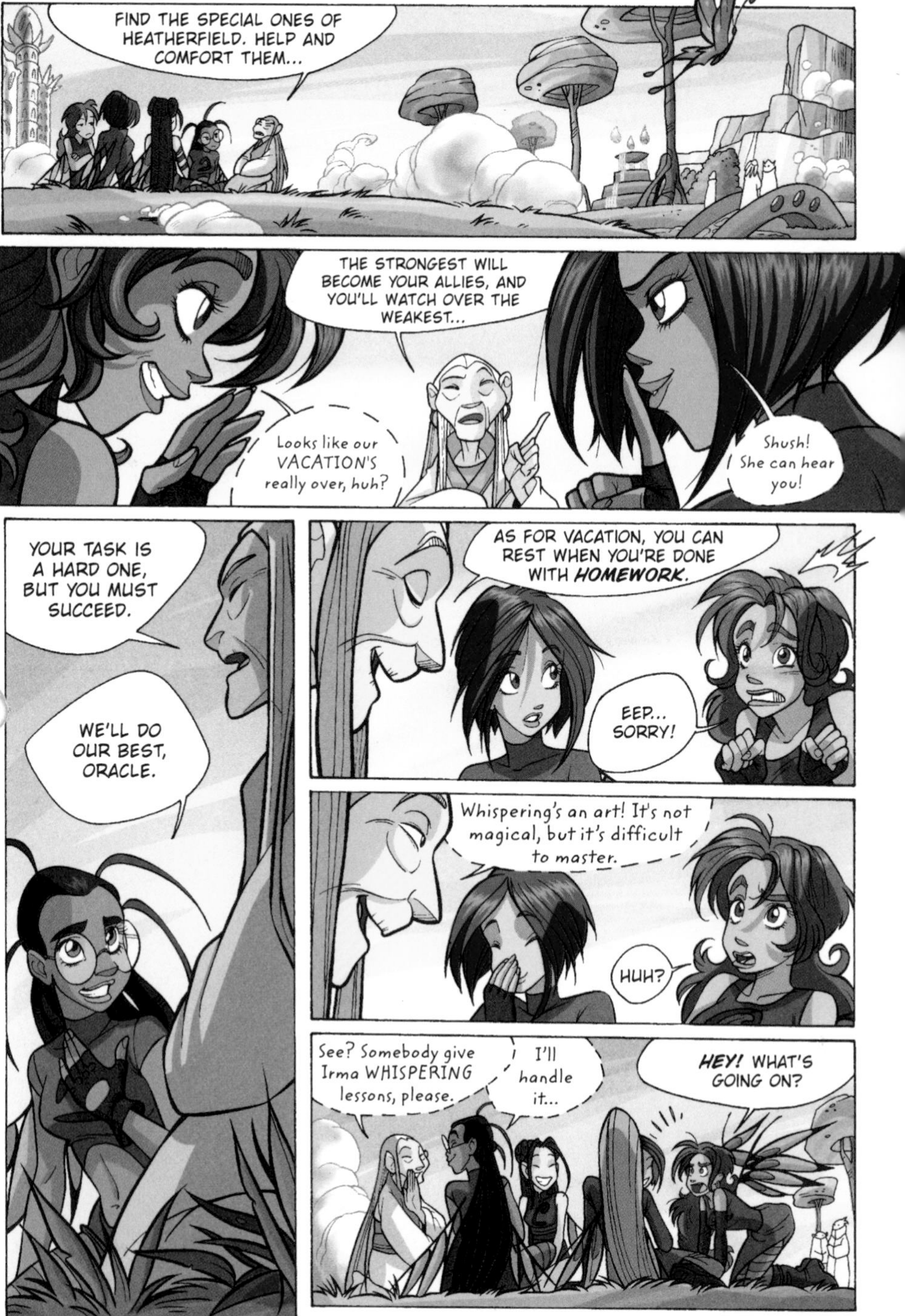
FIND THE SPECIAL ONES OF HEATHERFIELD. HELP AND COMFORT THEM...
THE STRONGEST WILL BECOME YOUR ALLIES, AND YOU'LL WATCH OVER THE WEAKEST...
Looks like our VACATION'S really over, huh?
Shush! She can hear you!
YOUR TASK IS A HARD ONE, BUT YOU MUST SUCCEED.
WE'LL DO OUR BEST, ORACLE.
AS FOR VACATION, YOU CAN REST WHEN YOU'RE DONE WITH **HOMEWORK**.
EEP... SORRY!
Whispering's an art! It's not magical, but it's difficult to master.
HUH?
See? Somebody give Irma WHISPERING lessons, please.
I'll handle it...
HEY! WHAT'S GOING ON?

6

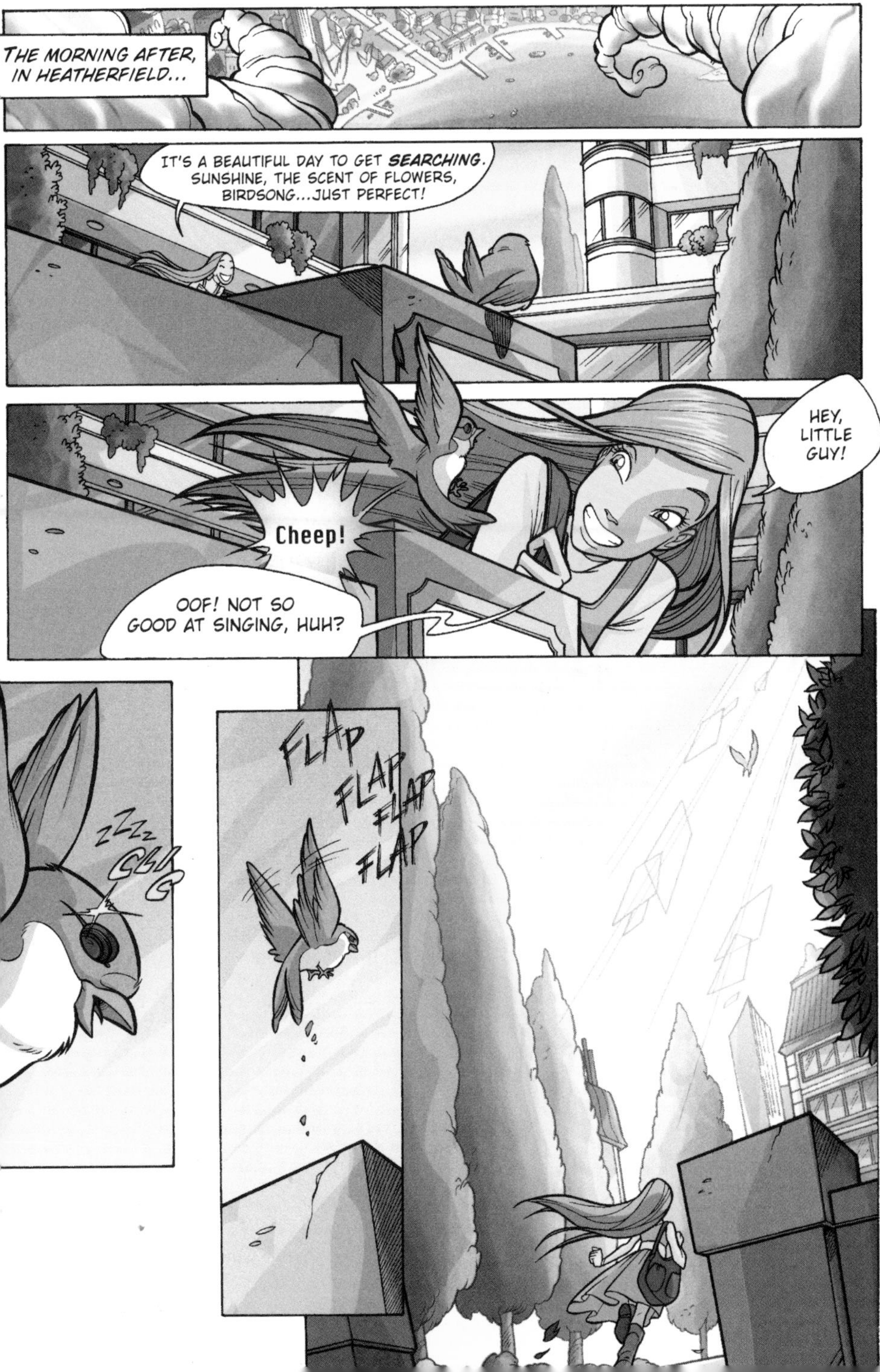
THE MORNING AFTER, IN HEATHERFIELD...
IT'S A BEAUTIFUL DAY TO GET SEARCHING. SUNSHINE, THE SCENT OF FLOWERS, BIRDSONG...JUST PERFECT!
HEY, LITTLE GUY!
Cheep!
OOF! NOT SO GOOD AT SINGING, HUH?
ZZZz
FLAP FLAP FLAP FLAP

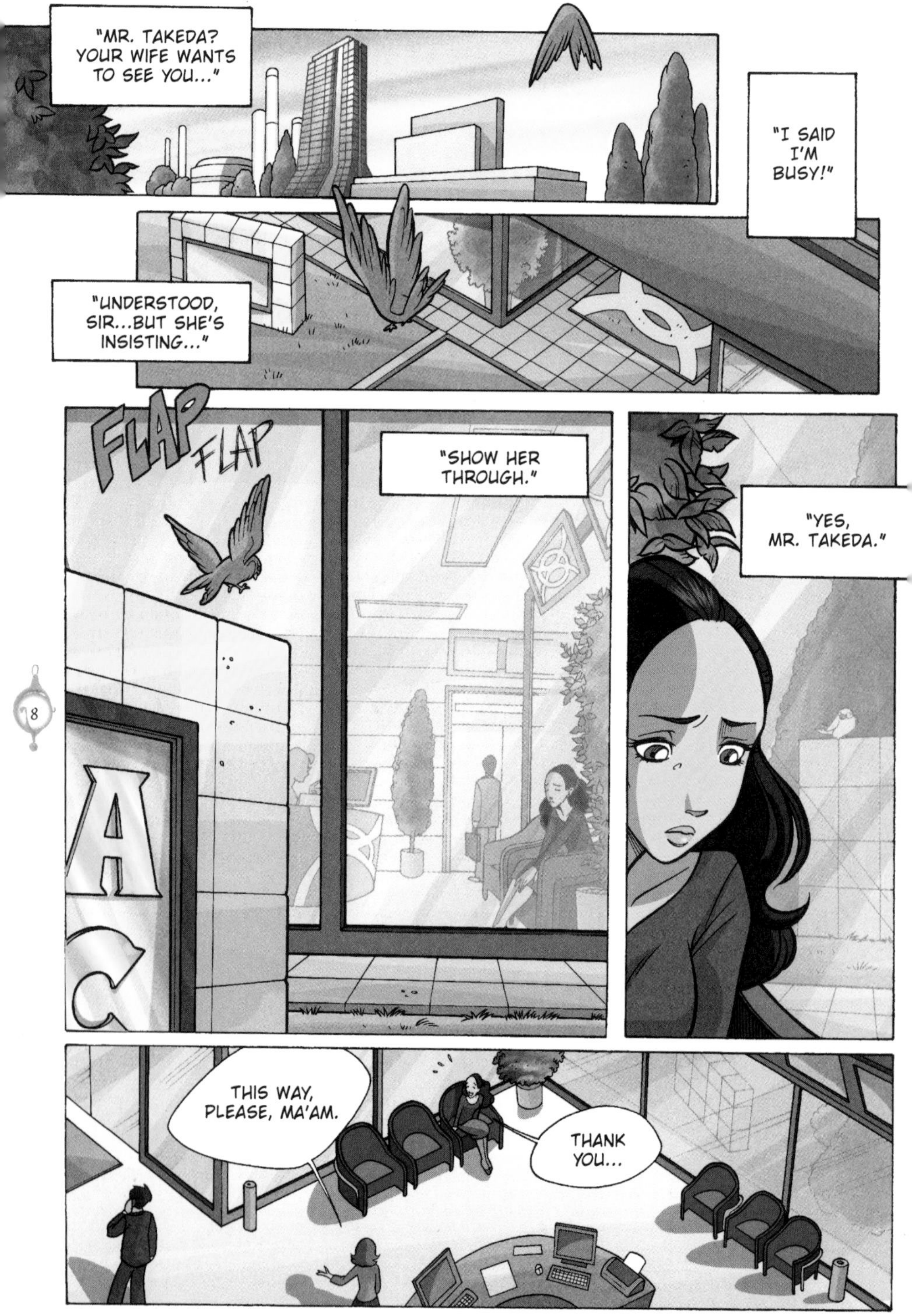
"MR. TAKEDA? YOUR WIFE WANTS TO SEE YOU..."
"I SAID I'M BUSY!"
"UNDERSTOOD, SIR...BUT SHE'S INSISTING..."
FLAP FLAP
"SHOW HER THROUGH."
"YES, MR. TAKEDA."
THIS WAY, PLEASE, MA'AM.
THANK YOU...

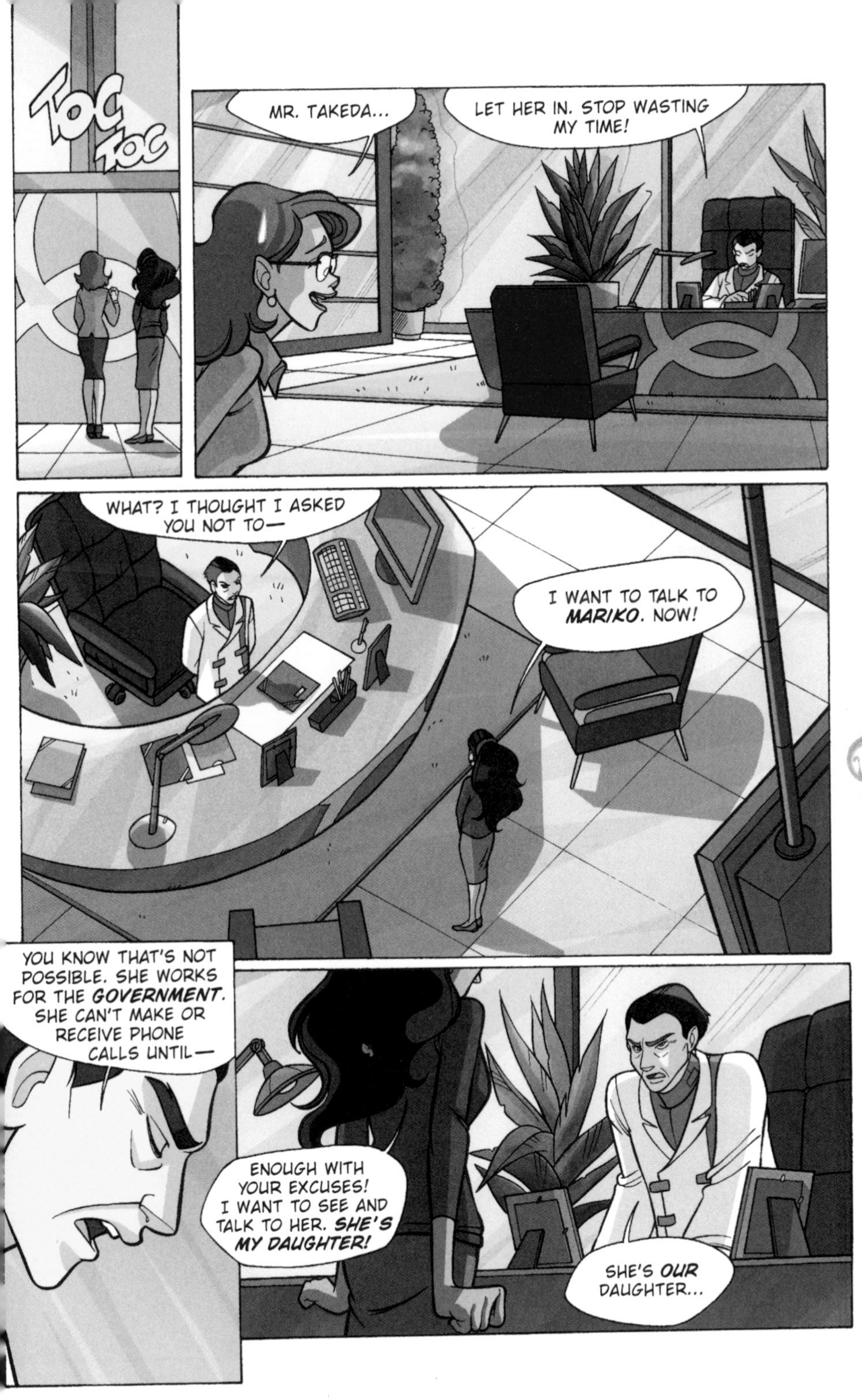
TOC TOC
MR. TAKEDA...
LET HER IN. STOP WASTING MY TIME!
WHAT? I THOUGHT I ASKED YOU NOT TO—
I WANT TO TALK TO MARIKO. NOW!
YOU KNOW THAT'S NOT POSSIBLE. SHE WORKS FOR THE GOVERNMENT. SHE CAN'T MAKE OR RECEIVE PHONE CALLS UNTIL—
ENOUGH WITH YOUR EXCUSES! I WANT TO SEE AND TALK TO HER. SHE'S MY DAUGHTER!
SHE'S OUR DAUGHTER...

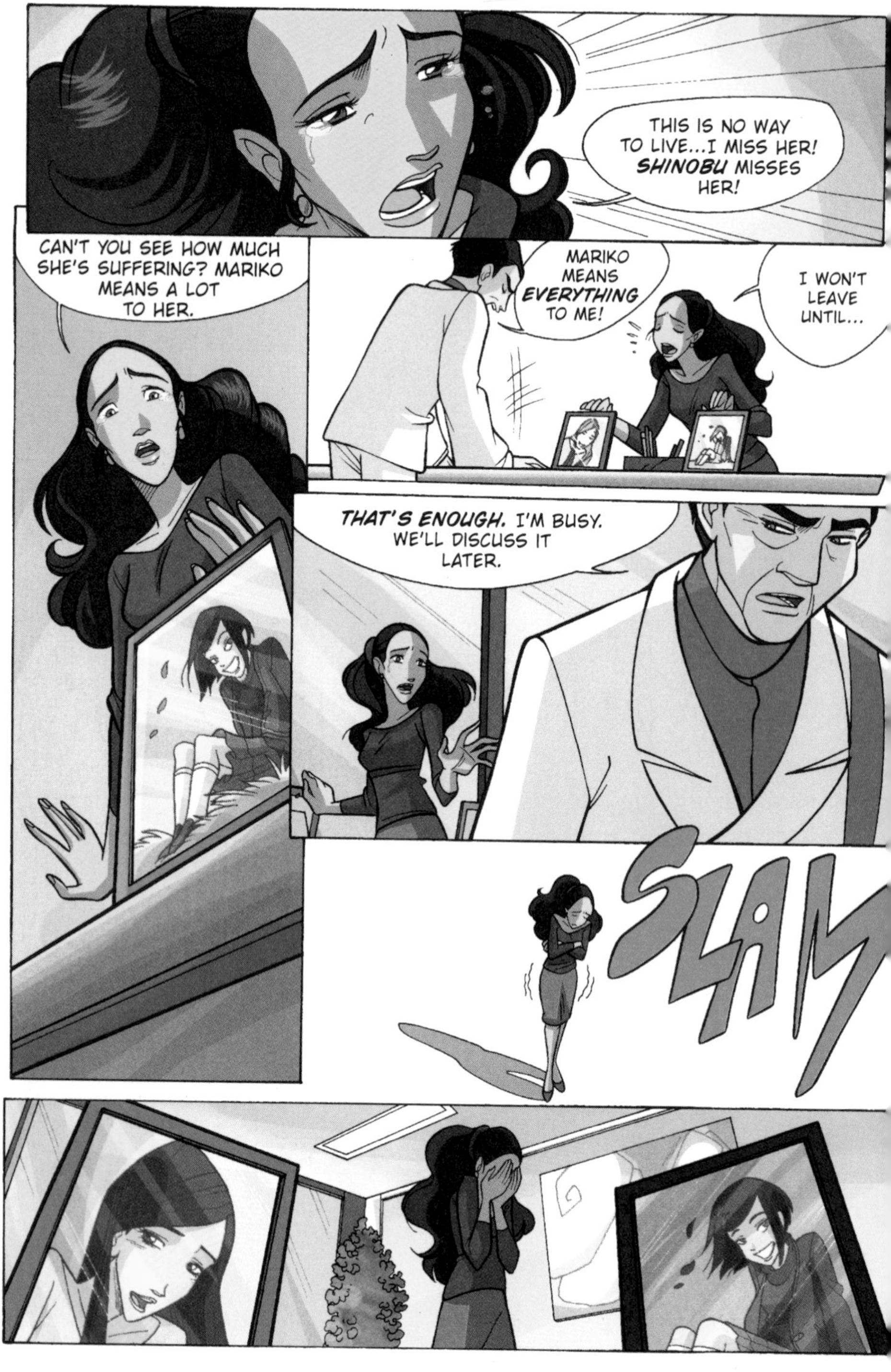
THIS IS NO WAY TO LIVE...I MISS HER! SHINOBU MISSES HER!
CAN'T YOU SEE HOW MUCH SHE'S SUFFERING? MARIKO MEANS A LOT TO HER.
MARIKO MEANS EVERYTHING TO ME!
I WON'T LEAVE UNTIL...
THAT'S ENOUGH. I'M BUSY. WE'LL DISCUSS IT LATER.
SLAM

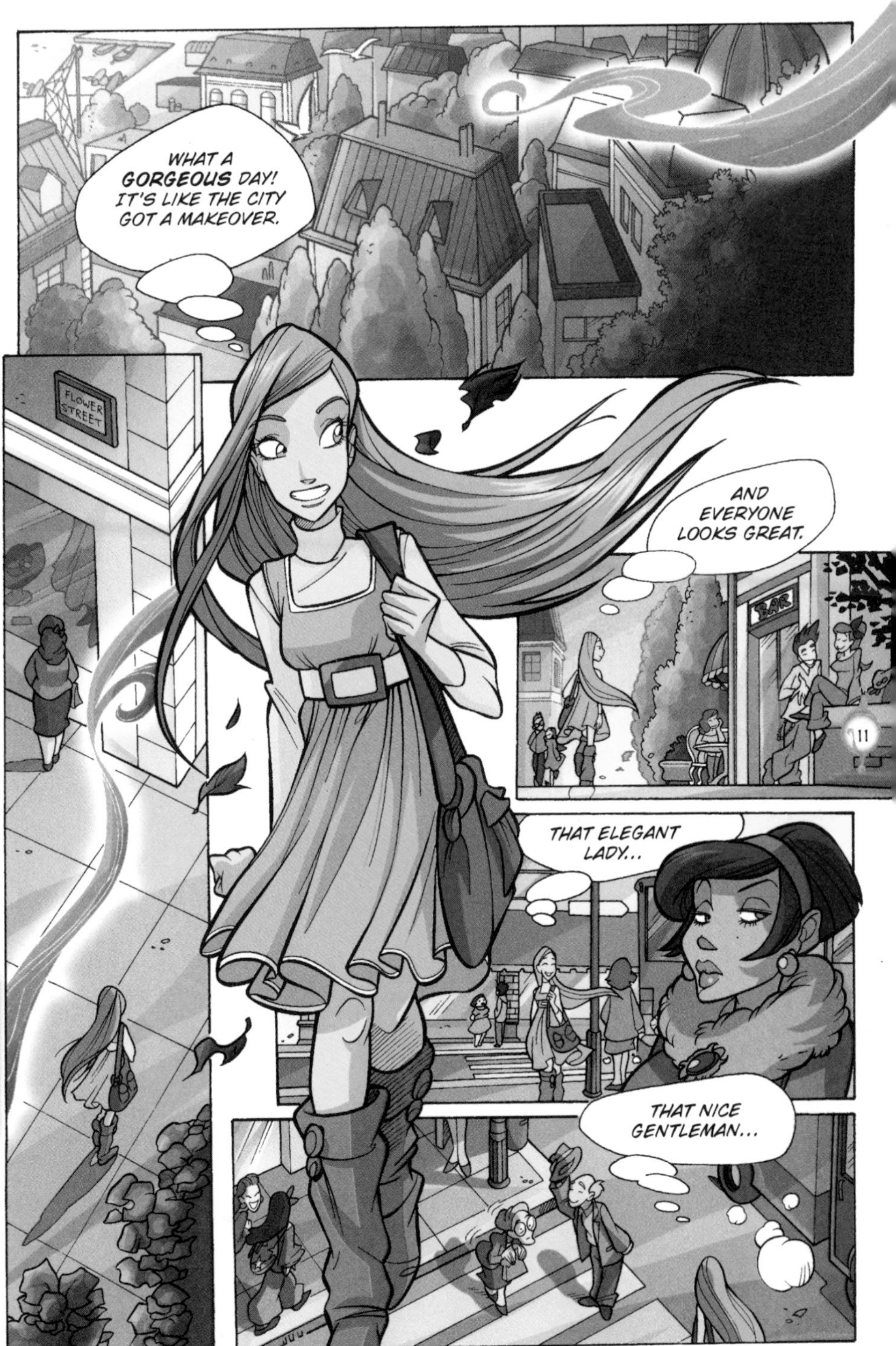
WHAT A GORGEOUS DAY! IT'S LIKE THE CITY GOT A MAKEOVER.
FLOWER STREET
AND EVERYONE LOOKS GREAT.
BAR
THAT ELEGANT LADY...
THAT NICE GENTLEMAN...

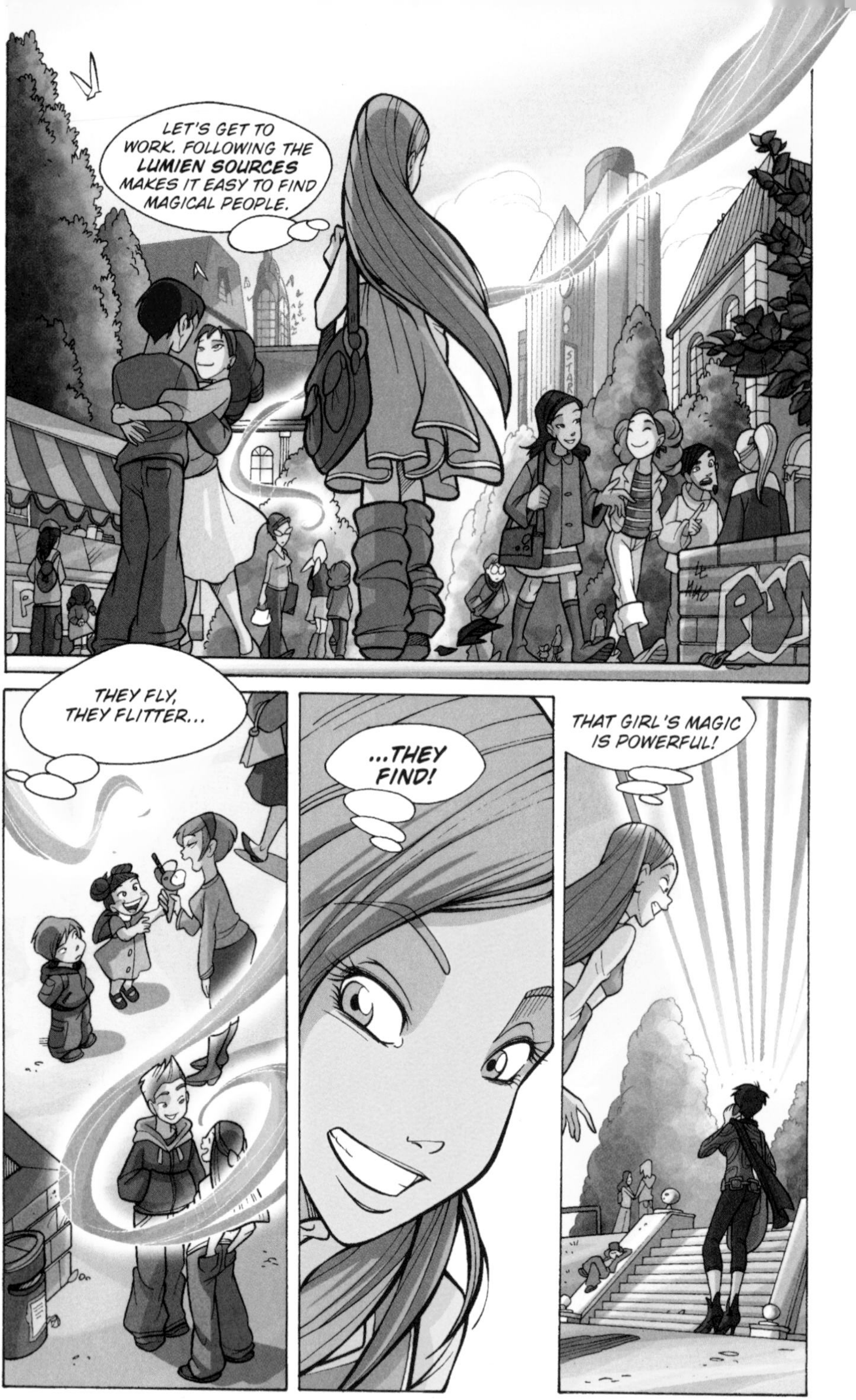

LET'S GET TO WORK. FOLLOWING THE LUMIEN SOURCES MAKES IT EASY TO FIND MAGICAL PEOPLE.
THEY FLY, THEY FLITTER...
...THEY FIND!
THAT GIRL'S MAGIC IS POWERFUL!

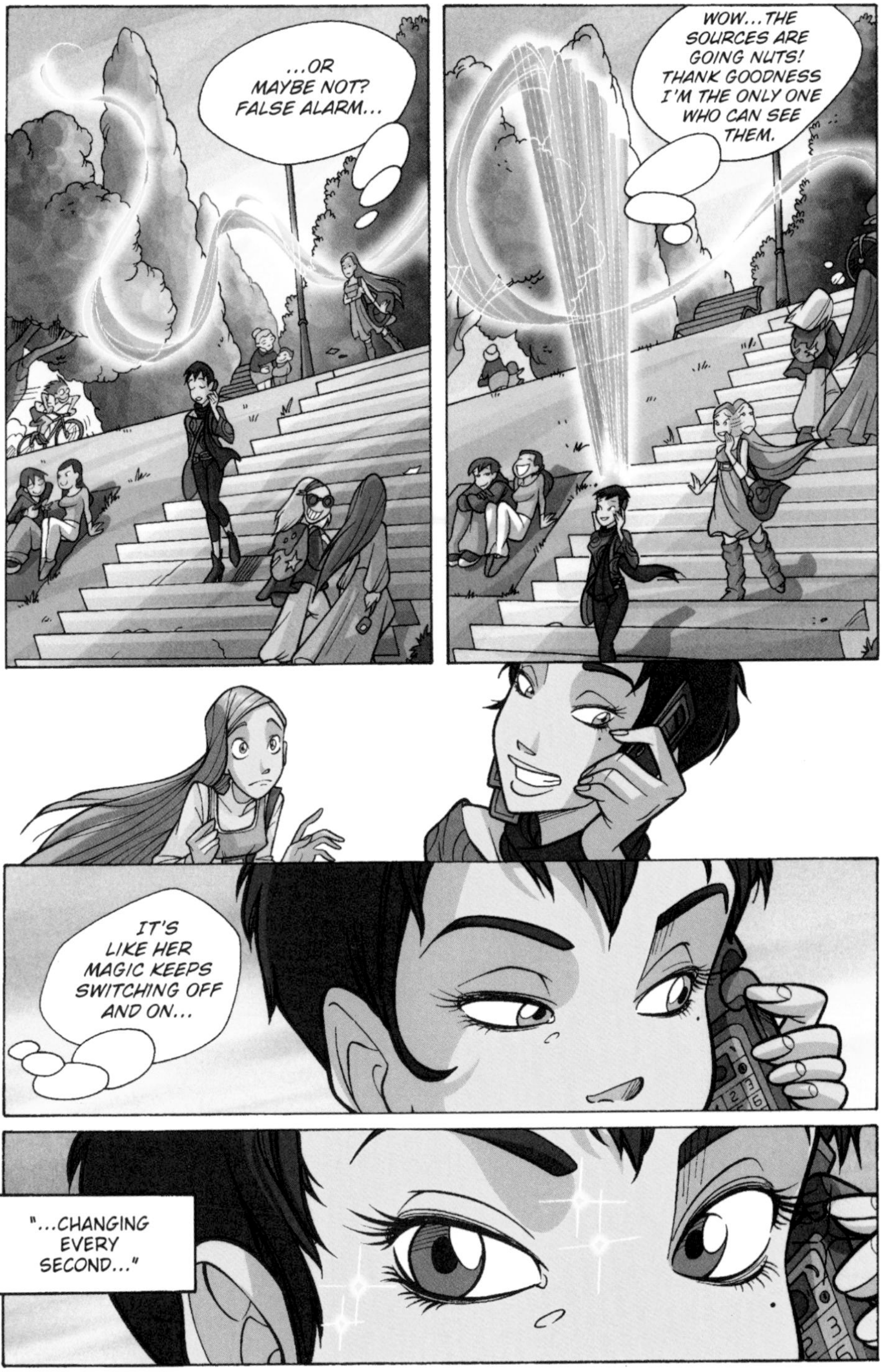
...OR MAYBE NOT? FALSE ALARM...
WOW...THE SOURCES ARE GOING NUTS! THANK GOODNESS I'M THE ONLY ONE WHO CAN SEE THEM.
IT'S LIKE HER MAGIC KEEPS SWITCHING OFF AND ON...
"...CHANGING EVERY SECOND..."

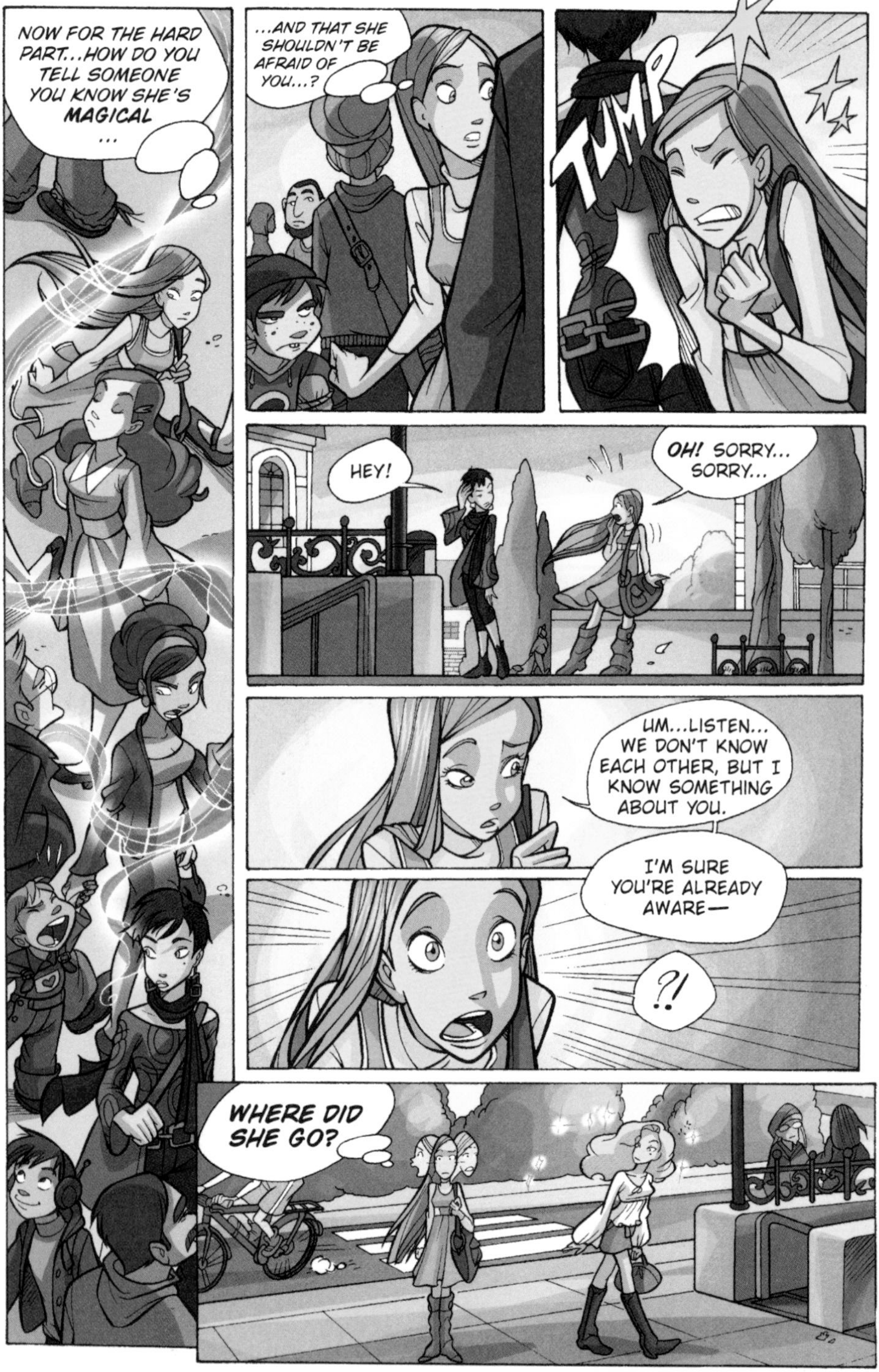
NOW FOR THE HARD PART...HOW DO YOU TELL SOMEONE YOU KNOW SHE'S MAGICAL ...
...AND THAT SHE SHOULDN'T BE AFRAID OF YOU...?
TUMP
HEY!
OH! SORRY... SORRY...
UM...LISTEN... WE DON'T KNOW EACH OTHER, BUT I KNOW SOMETHING ABOUT YOU.
I'M SURE YOU'RE ALREADY AWARE—
?!
WHERE DID SHE GO?

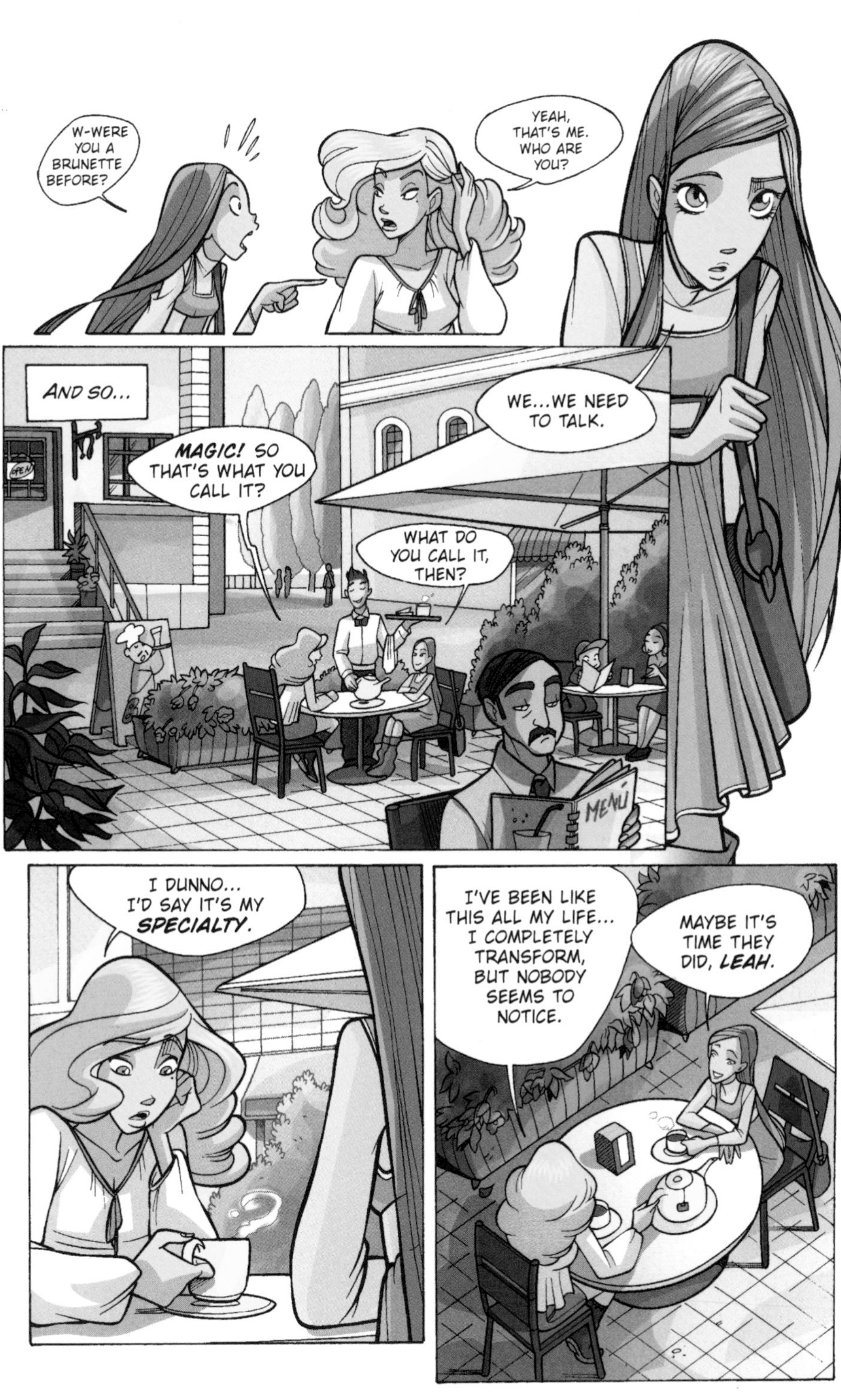
W-WERE YOU A BRUNETTE BEFORE?
YEAH, THAT'S ME. WHO ARE YOU?
WE...WE NEED TO TALK.
AND SO...
MAGIC! SO THAT'S WHAT YOU CALL IT?
WHAT DO YOU CALL IT, THEN?
MENU
I DUNNO... I'D SAY IT'S MY SPECIALTY.
I'VE BEEN LIKE THIS ALL MY LIFE... I COMPLETELY TRANSFORM, BUT NOBODY SEEMS TO NOTICE.
MAYBE IT'S TIME THEY DID, LEAH.

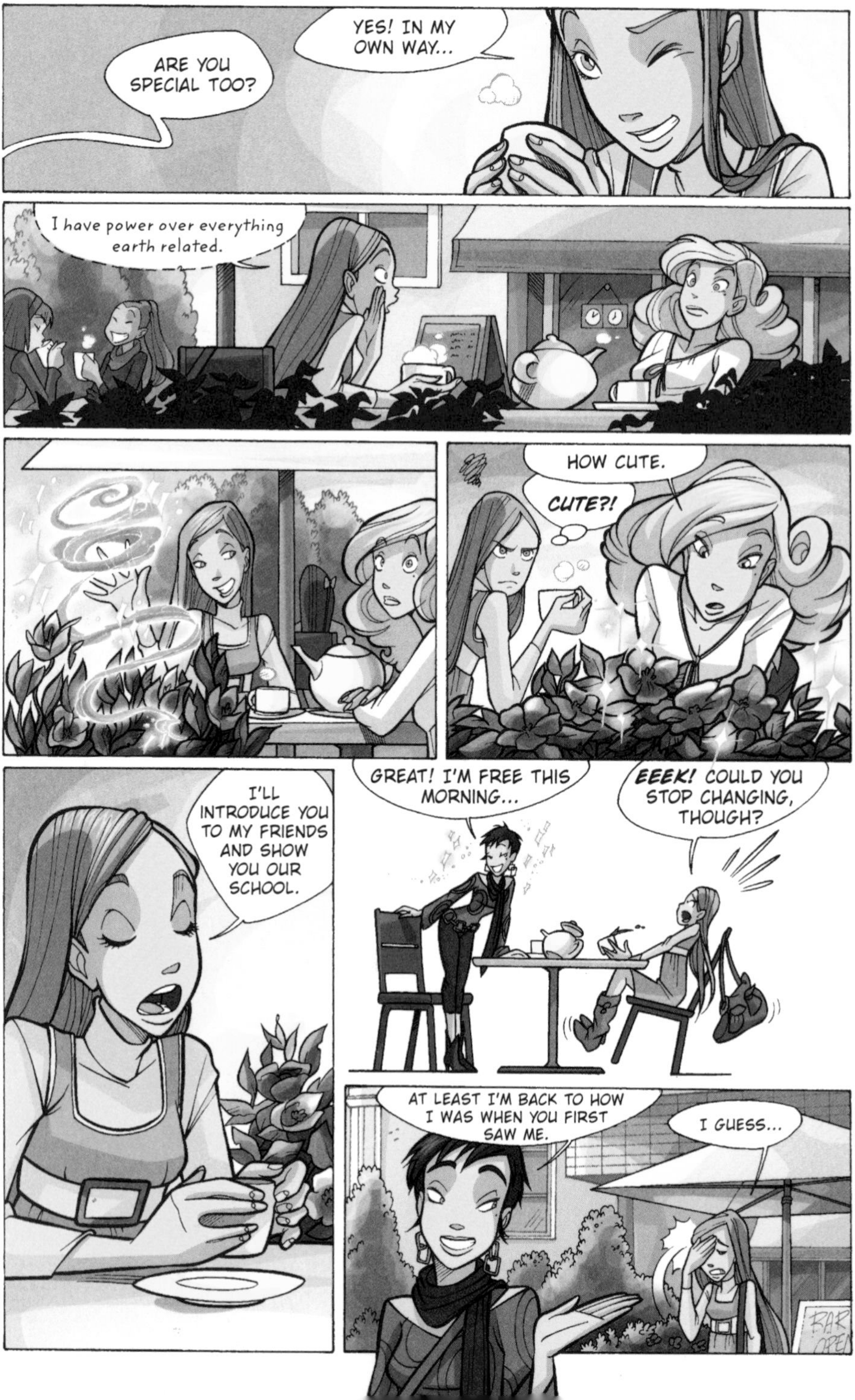
ARE YOU SPECIAL TOO?
YES! IN MY OWN WAY...
I have power over everything earth related.
HOW CUTE.
CUTE?!
I'LL INTRODUCE YOU TO MY FRIENDS AND SHOW YOU OUR SCHOOL.
GREAT! I'M FREE THIS MORNING...
EEEK! COULD YOU STOP CHANGING, THOUGH?
AT LEAST I'M BACK TO HOW I WAS WHEN YOU FIRST SAW ME.
I GUESS...

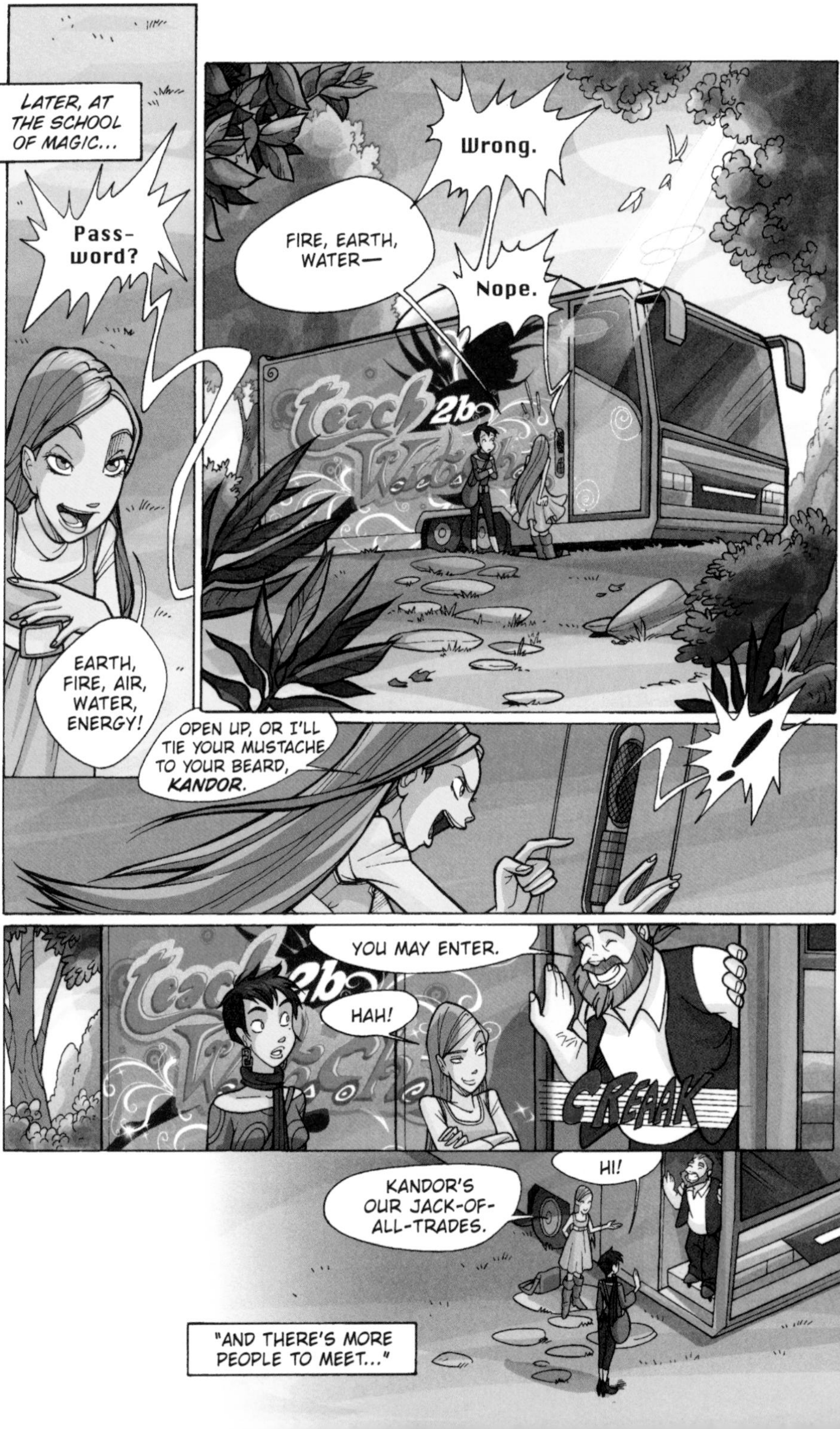
LATER, AT THE SCHOOL OF MAGIC...
Pass-word?
Wrong.
FIRE, EARTH, WATER—
Nope.
EARTH, FIRE, AIR, WATER, ENERGY!
OPEN UP, OR I'LL TIE YOUR MUSTACHE TO YOUR BEARD, KANDOR.
!
YOU MAY ENTER.
HAH!
CREAAK
HI!
KANDOR'S OUR JACK-OF-ALL-TRADES.
"AND THERE'S MORE PEOPLE TO MEET..."

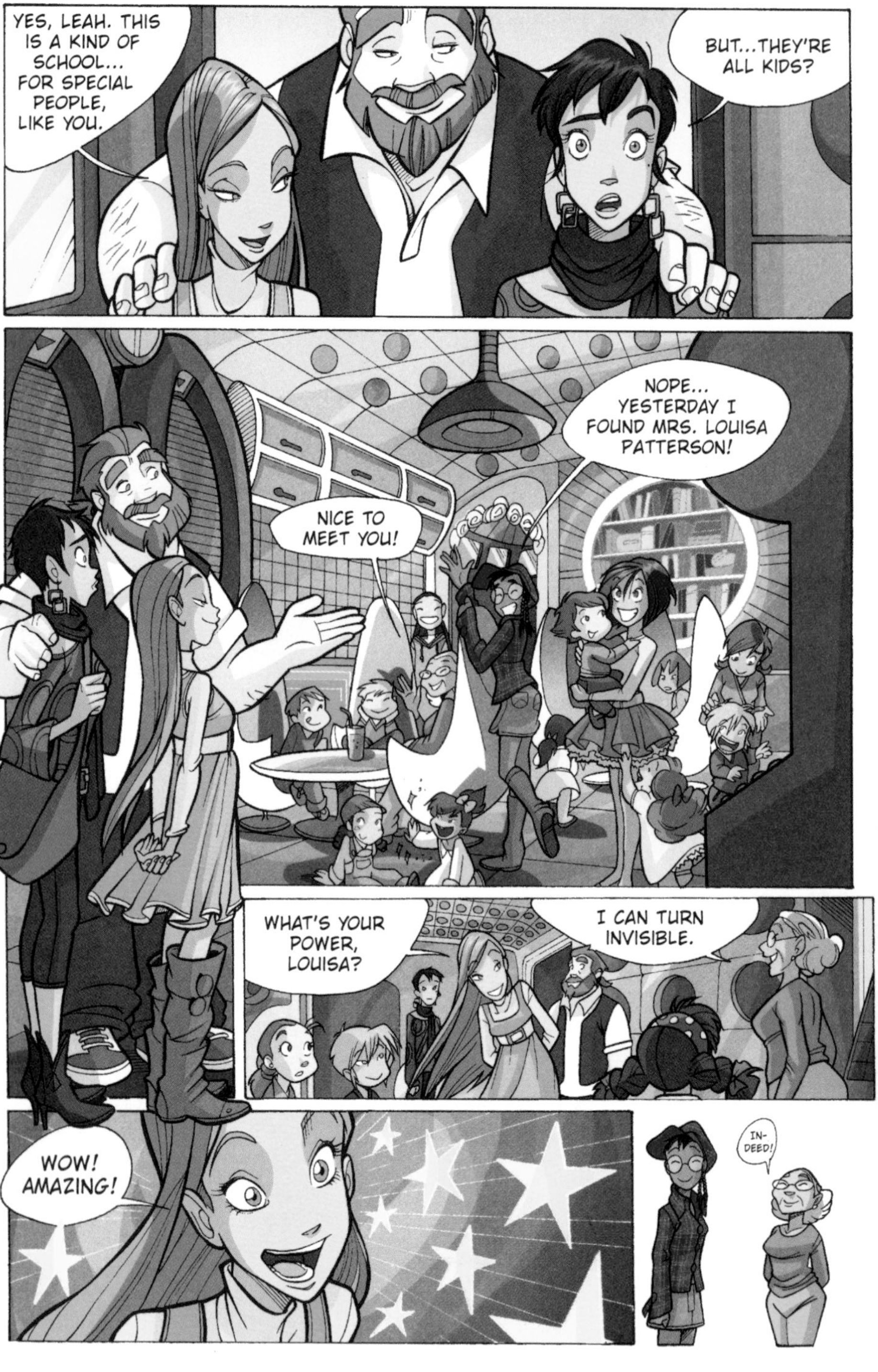
YES, LEAH. THIS IS A KIND OF SCHOOL... FOR SPECIAL PEOPLE, LIKE YOU.
BUT...THEY'RE ALL KIDS?
NOPE... YESTERDAY I FOUND MRS. LOUISA PATTERSON!
NICE TO MEET YOU!
WHAT'S YOUR POWER, LOUISA?
I CAN TURN INVISIBLE.
WOW! AMAZING!
IN-DEED!

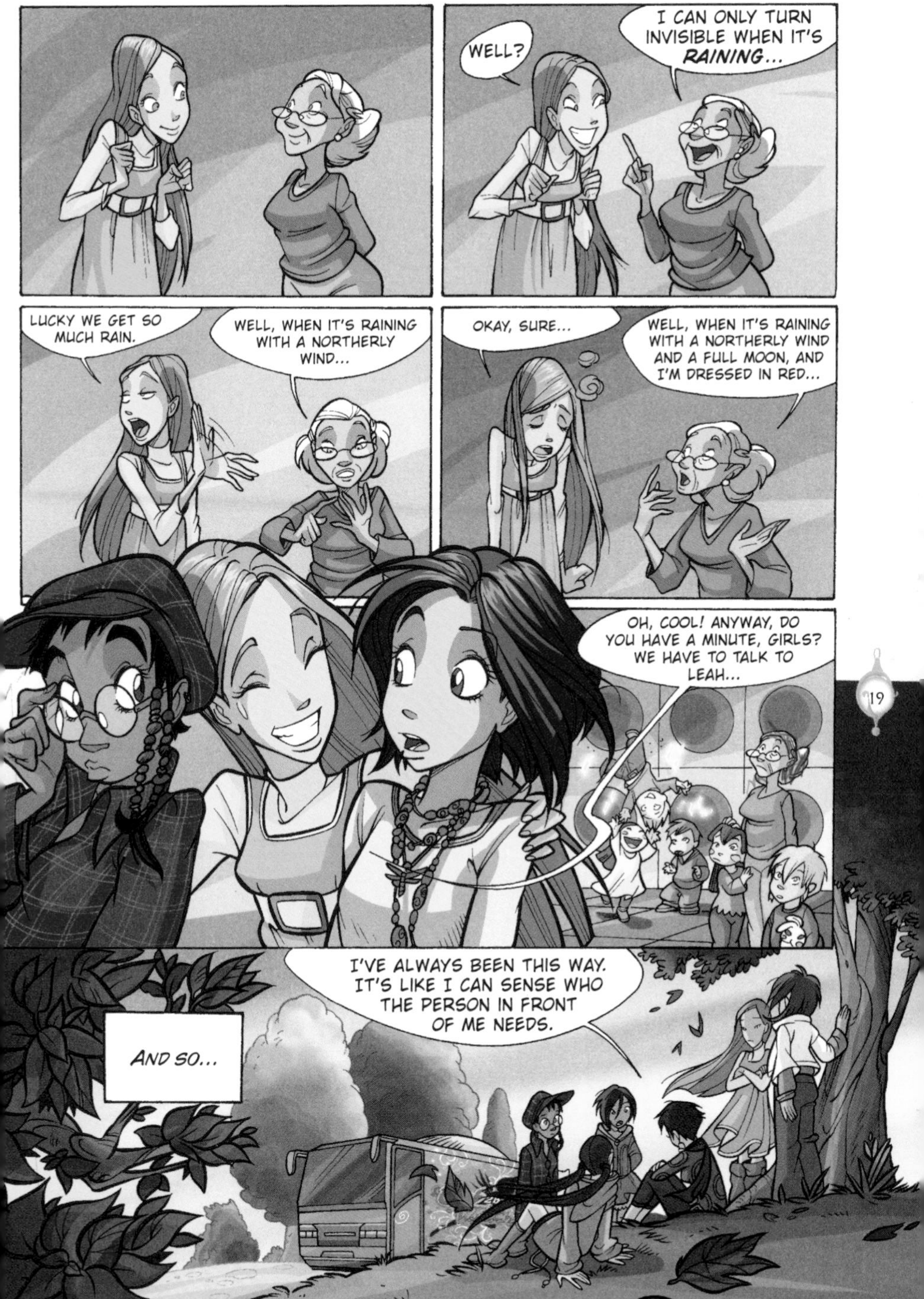
WELL?
I CAN ONLY TURN INVISIBLE WHEN IT'S RAINING...
LUCKY WE GET SO MUCH RAIN.
WELL, WHEN IT'S RAINING WITH A NORTHERLY WIND...
OKAY, SURE...
WELL, WHEN IT'S RAINING WITH A NORTHERLY WIND AND A FULL MOON, AND I'M DRESSED IN RED...
OH, COOL! ANYWAY, DO YOU HAVE A MINUTE, GIRLS? WE HAVE TO TALK TO LEAH...
AND SO...
I'VE ALWAYS BEEN THIS WAY. IT'S LIKE I CAN SENSE WHO THE PERSON IN FRONT OF ME NEEDS.

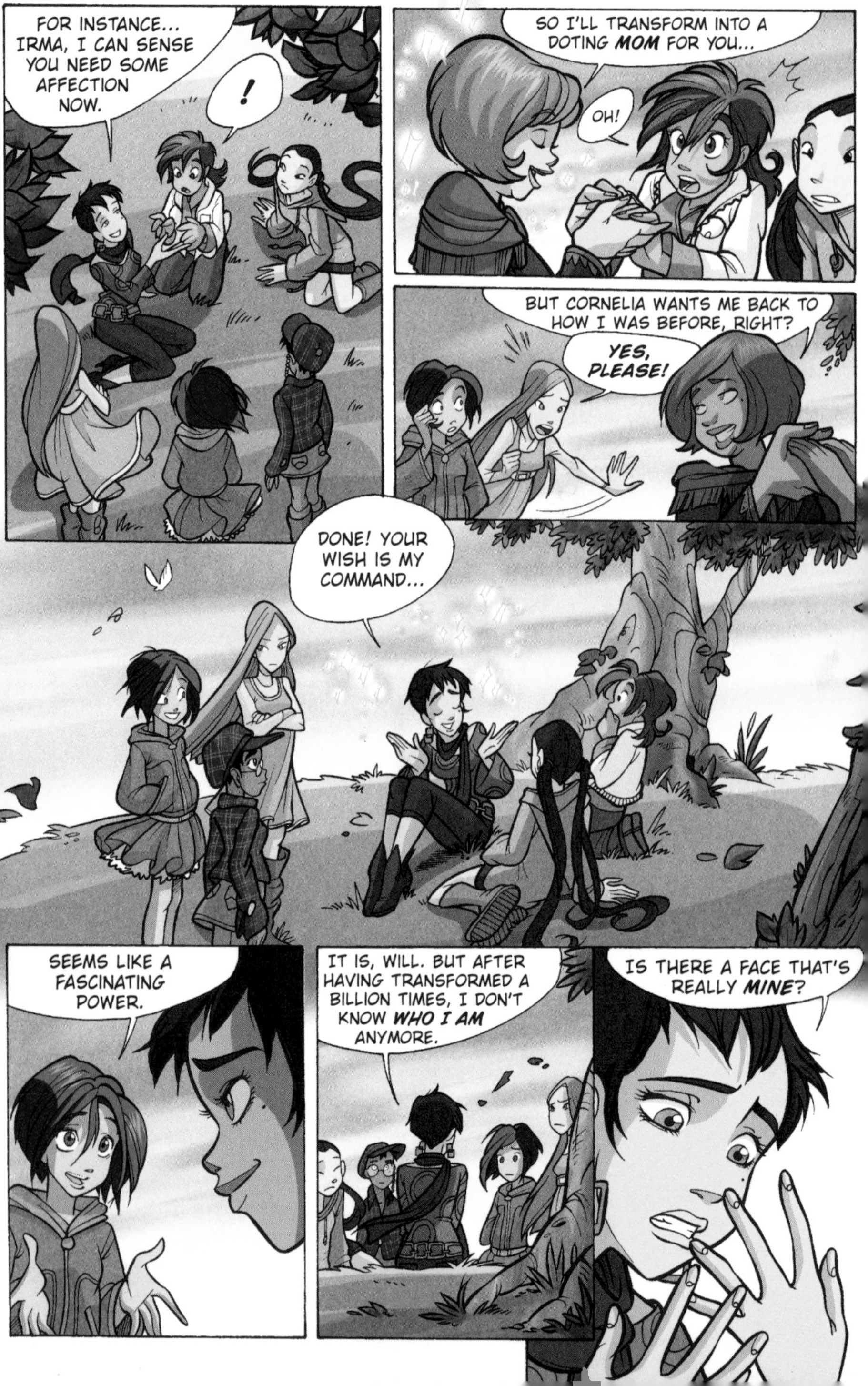
FOR INSTANCE... IRMA, I CAN SENSE YOU NEED SOME AFFECTION NOW.
!
SO I'LL TRANSFORM INTO A DOTING *MOM* FOR YOU...
OH!
BUT CORNELIA WANTS ME BACK TO HOW I WAS BEFORE, RIGHT?
YES, PLEASE!
DONE! YOUR WISH IS MY COMMAND...
SEEMS LIKE A FASCINATING POWER.
IT IS, WILL. BUT AFTER HAVING TRANSFORMED A BILLION TIMES, I DON'T KNOW *WHO I AM* ANYMORE.
IS THERE A FACE THAT'S REALLY *MINE*?

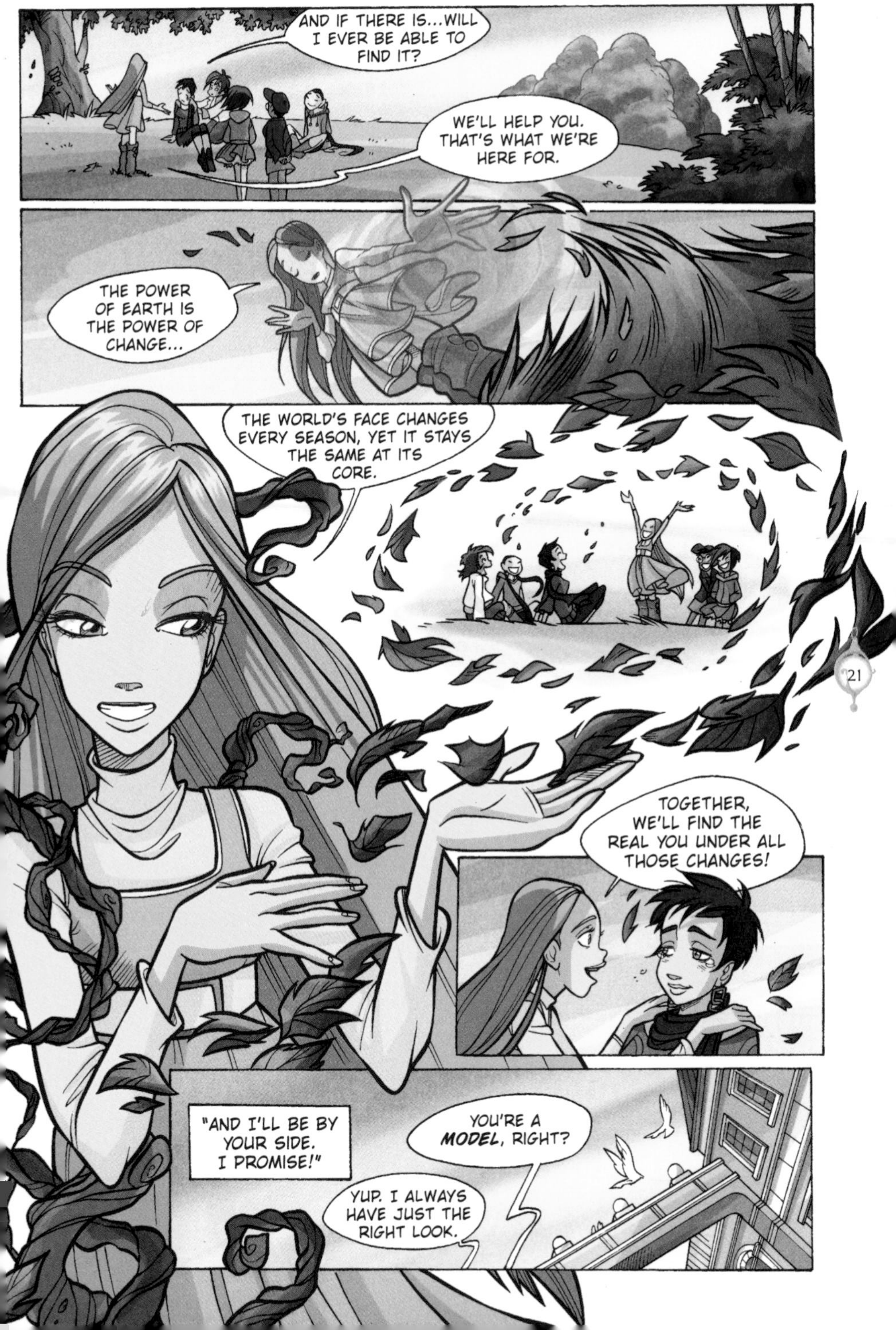
AND IF THERE IS...WILL I EVER BE ABLE TO FIND IT?
WE'LL HELP YOU. THAT'S WHAT WE'RE HERE FOR.
THE POWER OF EARTH IS THE POWER OF CHANGE...
THE WORLD'S FACE CHANGES EVERY SEASON, YET IT STAYS THE SAME AT ITS CORE.
TOGETHER, WE'LL FIND THE REAL YOU UNDER ALL THOSE CHANGES!
"AND I'LL BE BY YOUR SIDE. I PROMISE!"
YOU'RE A ***MODEL***, RIGHT?
YUP. I ALWAYS HAVE JUST THE RIGHT LOOK.

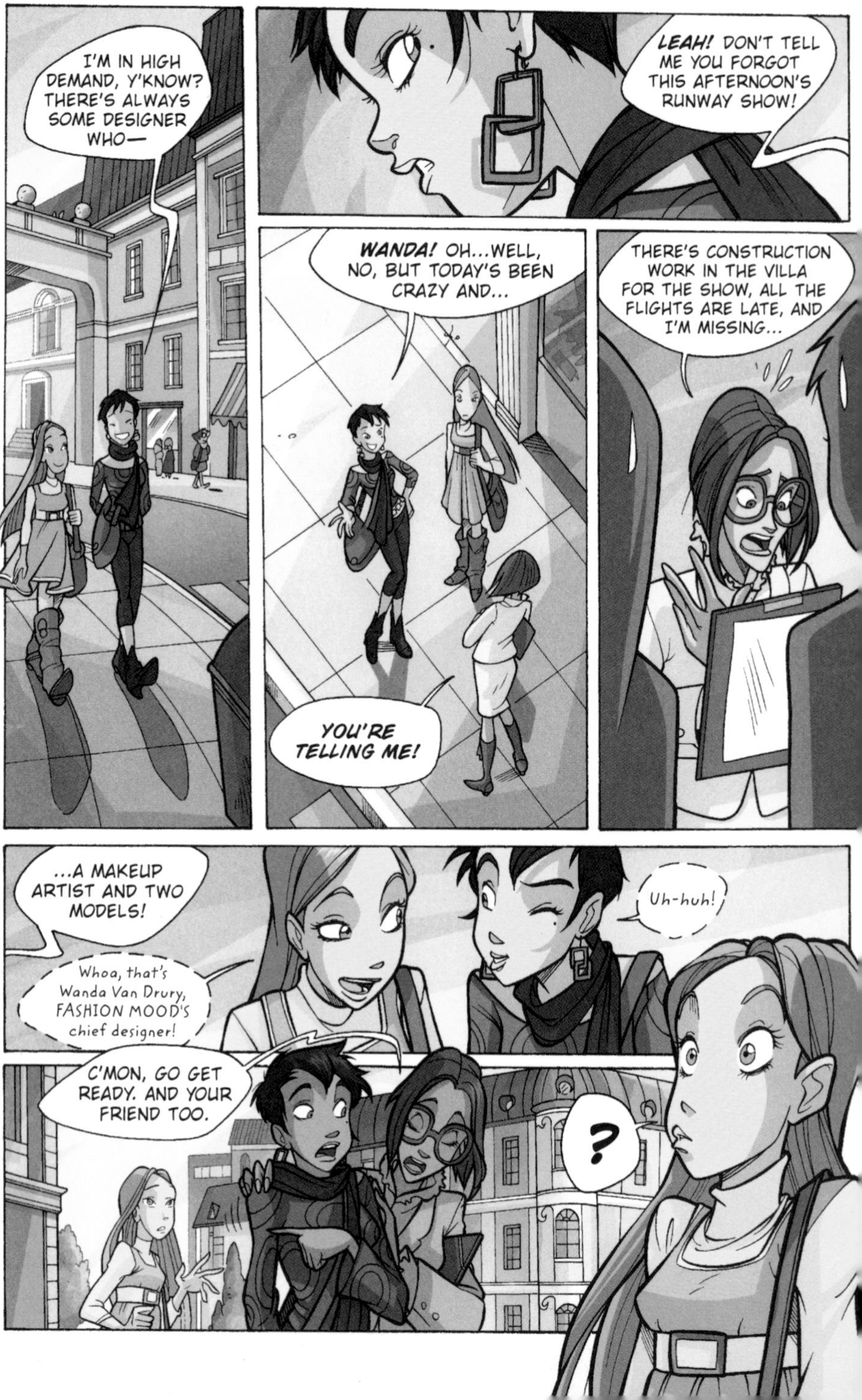

I'M IN HIGH DEMAND, Y'KNOW? THERE'S ALWAYS SOME DESIGNER WHO—
LEAH! DON'T TELL ME YOU FORGOT THIS AFTERNOON'S RUNWAY SHOW!
WANDA! OH...WELL, NO, BUT TODAY'S BEEN CRAZY AND...
YOU'RE TELLING ME!
THERE'S CONSTRUCTION WORK IN THE VILLA FOR THE SHOW, ALL THE FLIGHTS ARE LATE, AND I'M MISSING...
...A MAKEUP ARTIST AND TWO MODELS!
Whoa, that's Wanda Van Drury, FASHION MOOD'S chief designer!
Uh-huh!
C'MON, GO GET READY. AND YOUR FRIEND TOO.
?

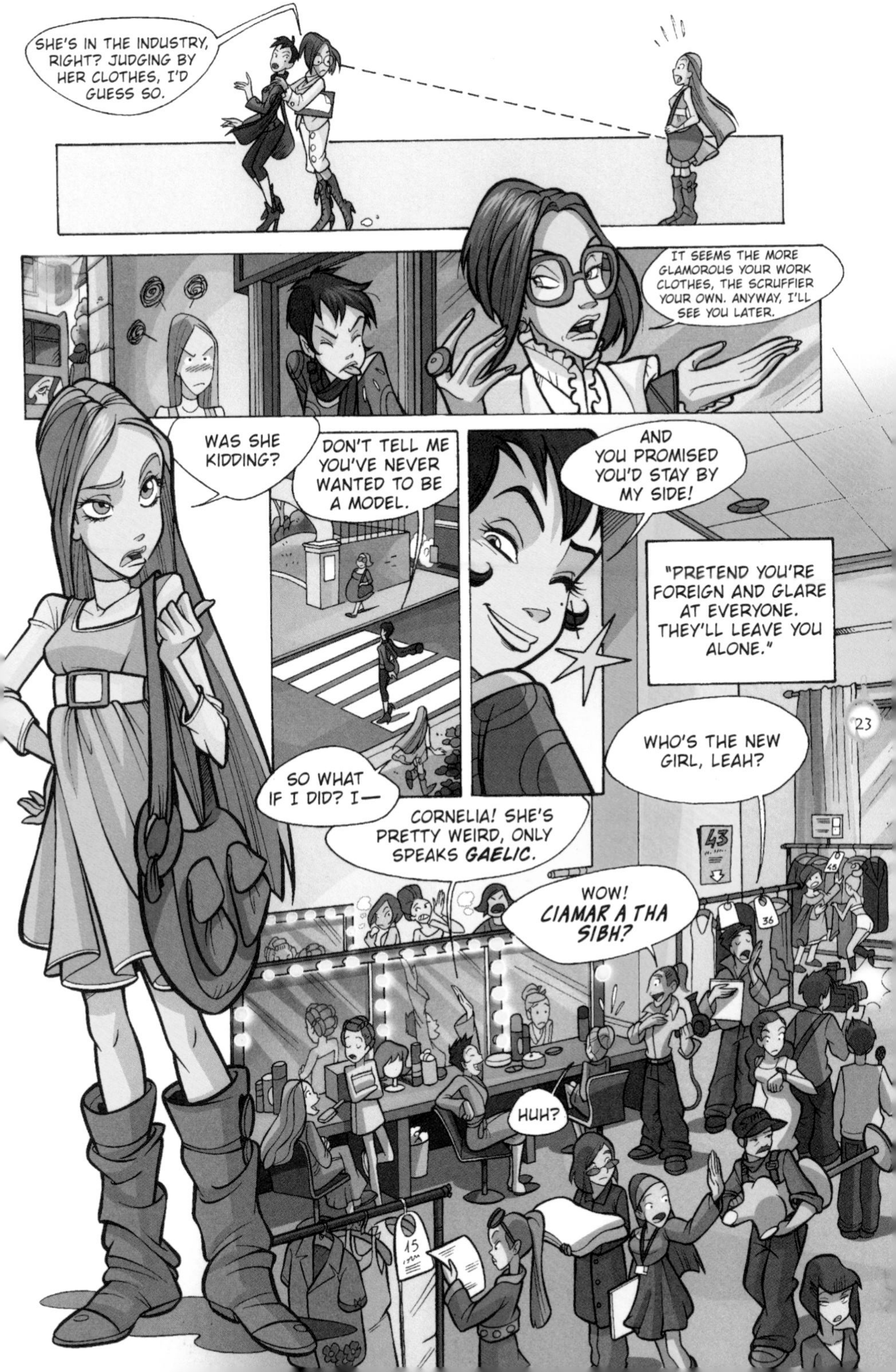

SHE'S IN THE INDUSTRY, RIGHT? JUDGING BY HER CLOTHES, I'D GUESS SO.
IT SEEMS THE MORE GLAMOROUS YOUR WORK CLOTHES, THE SCRUFFIER YOUR OWN. ANYWAY, I'LL SEE YOU LATER.
WAS SHE KIDDING?
DON'T TELL ME YOU'VE NEVER WANTED TO BE A MODEL.
SO WHAT IF I DID? I—
AND YOU PROMISED YOU'D STAY BY MY SIDE!
"PRETEND YOU'RE FOREIGN AND GLARE AT EVERYONE. THEY'LL LEAVE YOU ALONE."
WHO'S THE NEW GIRL, LEAH?
CORNELIA! SHE'S PRETTY WEIRD, ONLY SPEAKS **GAELIC**.
WOW! ***CIAMAR A THA SIBH?***
HUH?

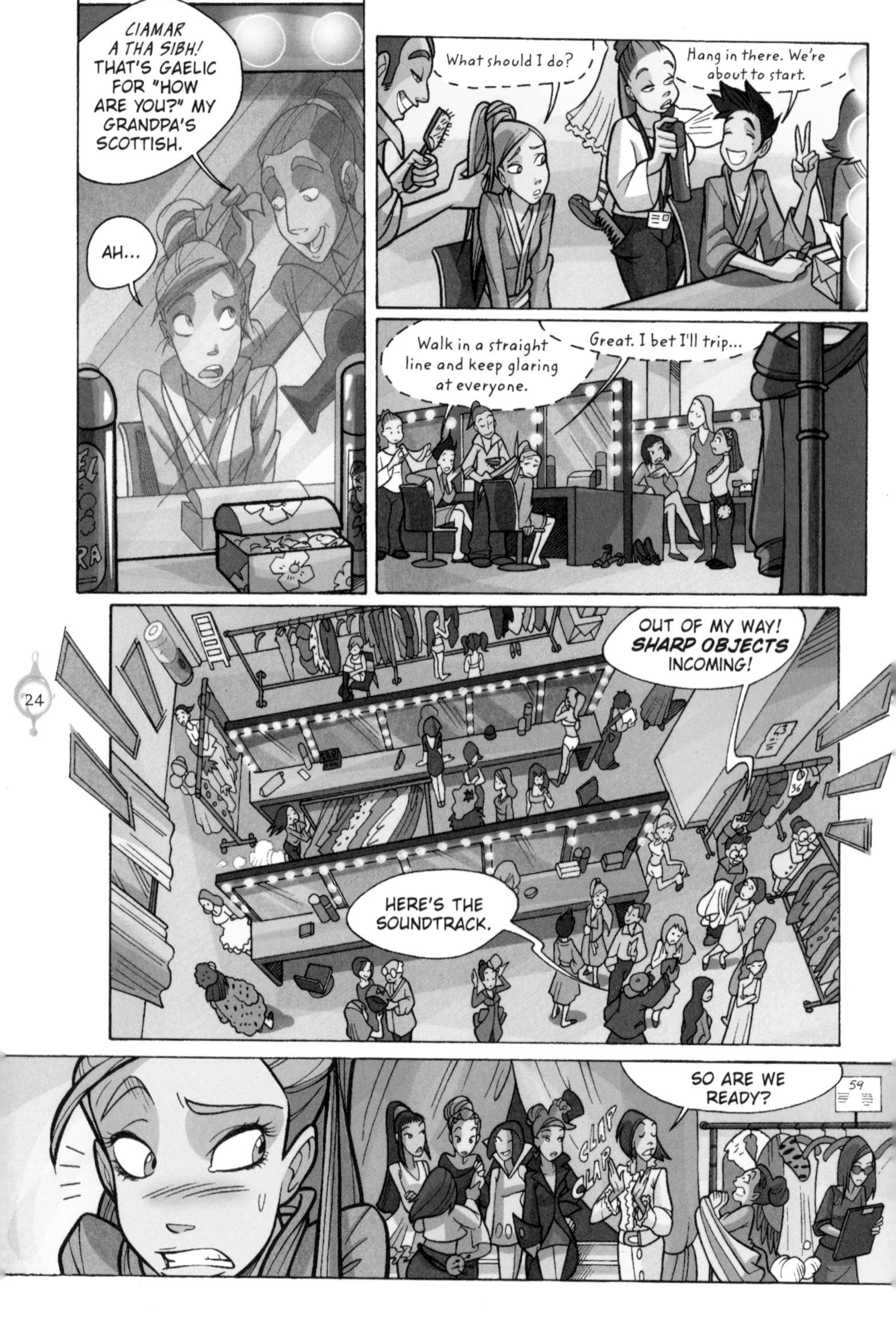
CIAMAR A THA SIBH! THAT'S GAELIC FOR "HOW ARE YOU?" MY GRANDPA'S SCOTTISH.
AH...
What should I do?
Hang in there. We're about to start.
Walk in a straight line and keep glaring at everyone.
Great. I bet I'll trip...
OUT OF MY WAY! SHARP OBJECTS INCOMING!
HERE'S THE SOUNDTRACK.
SO ARE WE READY?
CLAP CLAP

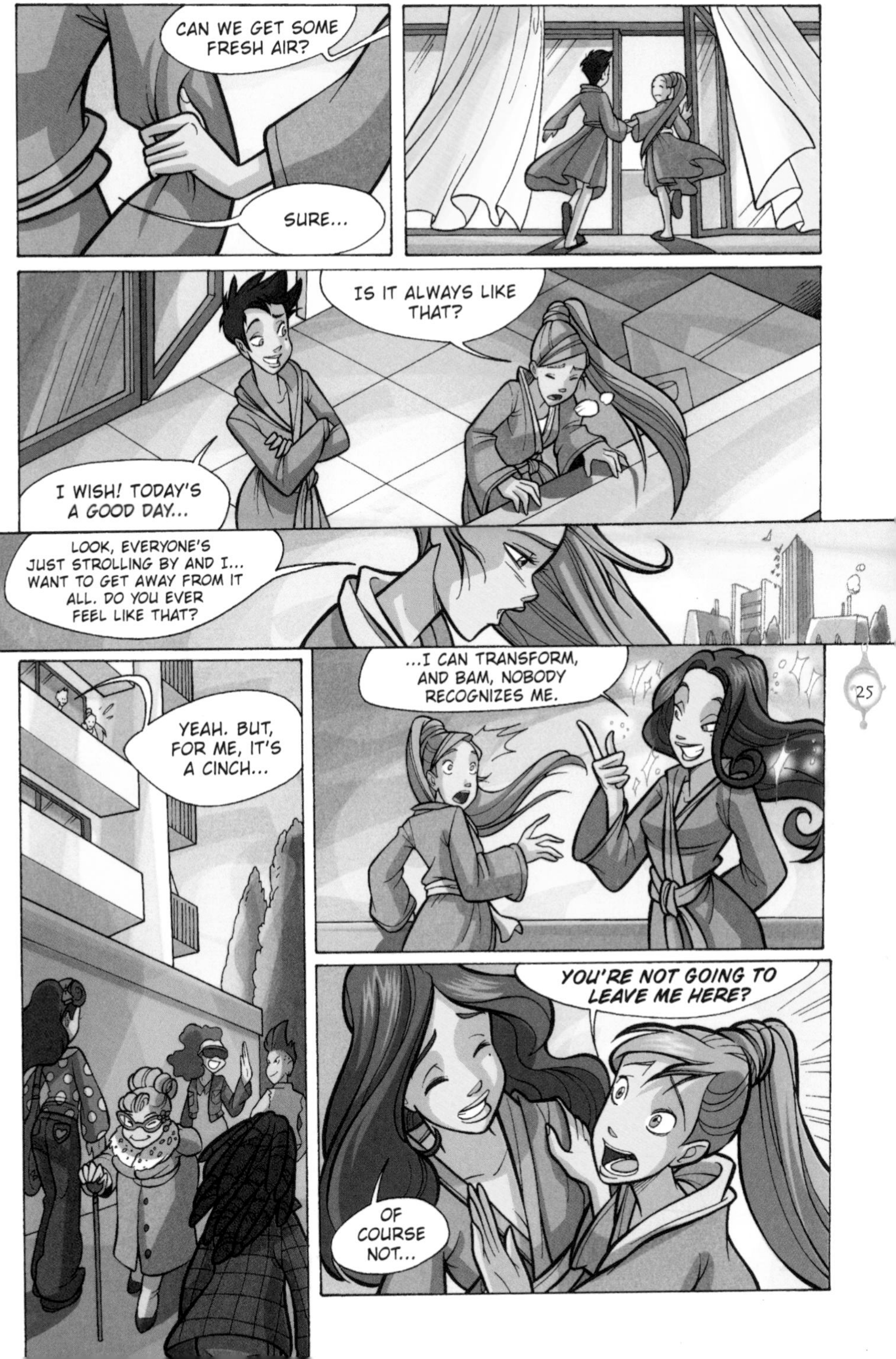
CAN WE GET SOME FRESH AIR?
SURE...
IS IT ALWAYS LIKE THAT?
I WISH! TODAY'S A GOOD DAY...
LOOK, EVERYONE'S JUST STROLLING BY AND I... WANT TO GET AWAY FROM IT ALL. DO YOU EVER FEEL LIKE THAT?
YEAH. BUT, FOR ME, IT'S A CINCH...
...I CAN TRANSFORM, AND BAM, NOBODY RECOGNIZES ME.
YOU'RE NOT GOING TO LEAVE ME HERE?
OF COURSE NOT...

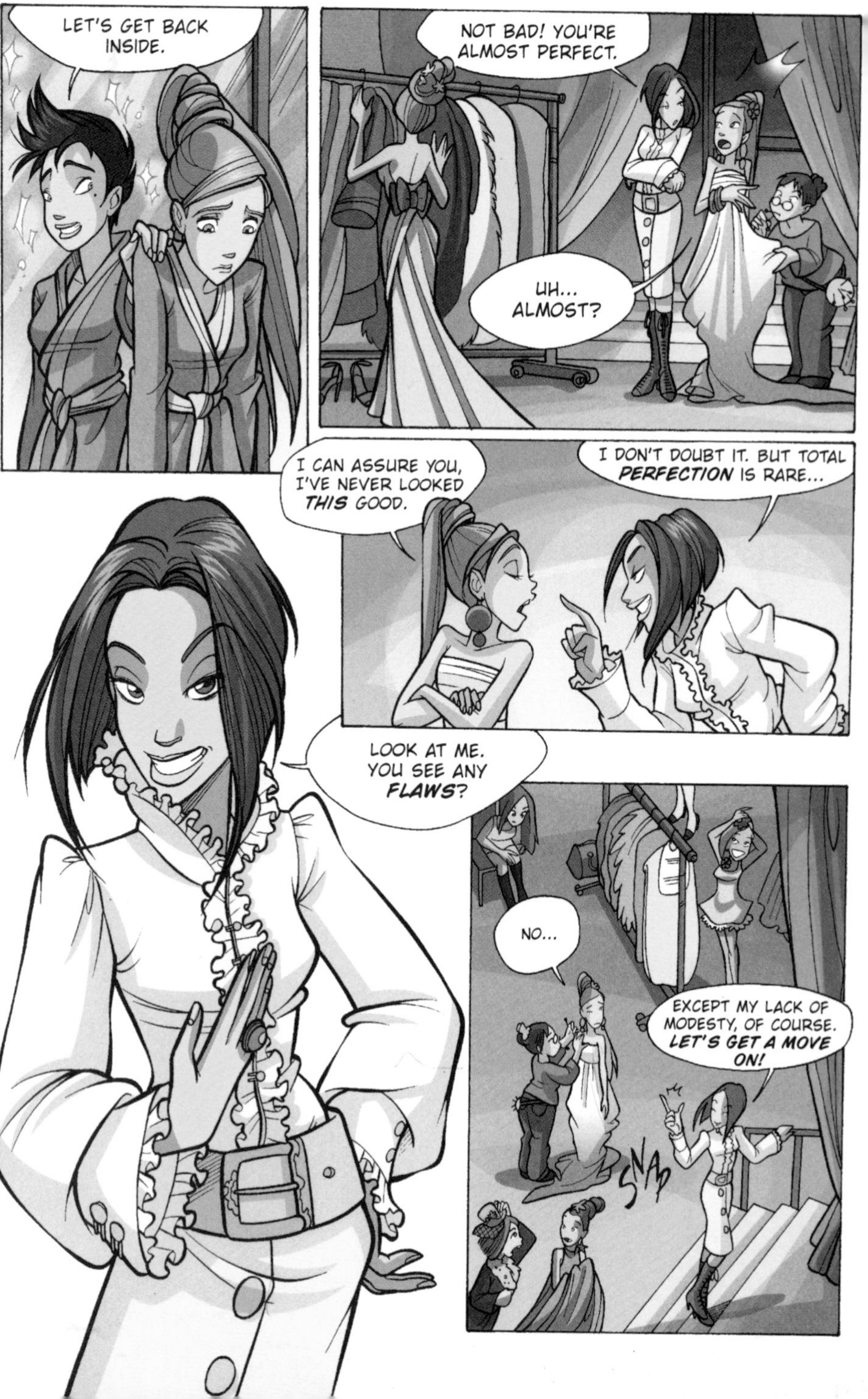
LET'S GET BACK INSIDE.
NOT BAD! YOU'RE ALMOST PERFECT.
UH... ALMOST?
I CAN ASSURE YOU, I'VE NEVER LOOKED THIS GOOD.
I DON'T DOUBT IT. BUT TOTAL PERFECTION IS RARE...
LOOK AT ME. YOU SEE ANY FLAWS?
NO...
EXCEPT MY LACK OF MODESTY, OF COURSE. LET'S GET A MOVE ON!
SNAP

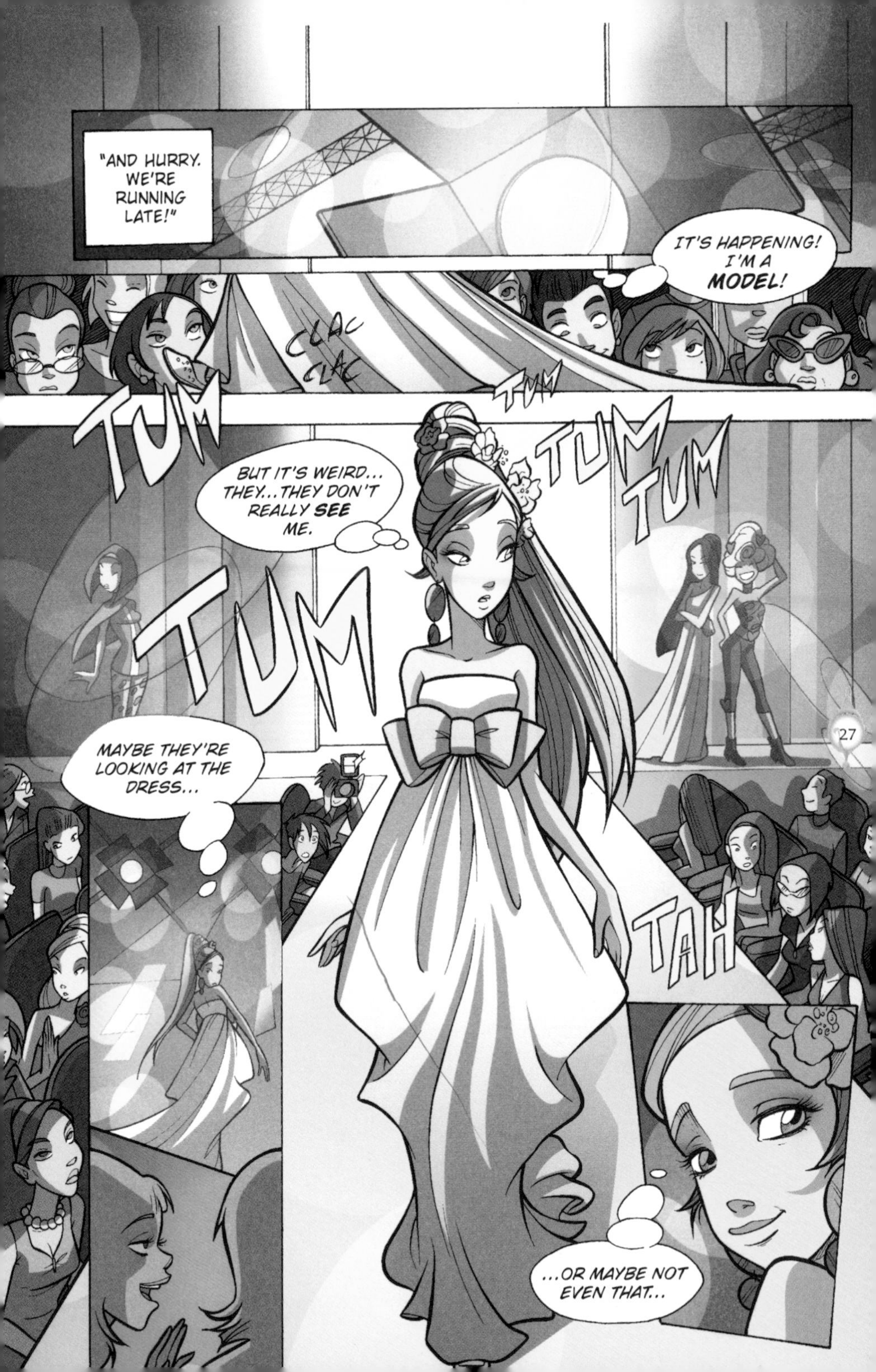
"AND HURRY. WE'RE RUNNING LATE!"
IT'S HAPPENING! I'M A **MODEL!**
CLAC CLAC
TUM
TUM
BUT IT'S WEIRD... THEY...THEY DON'T REALLY **SEE** ME.
TUM
TUM
TUM
MAYBE THEY'RE LOOKING AT THE DRESS...
TAH
...OR MAYBE NOT EVEN THAT...

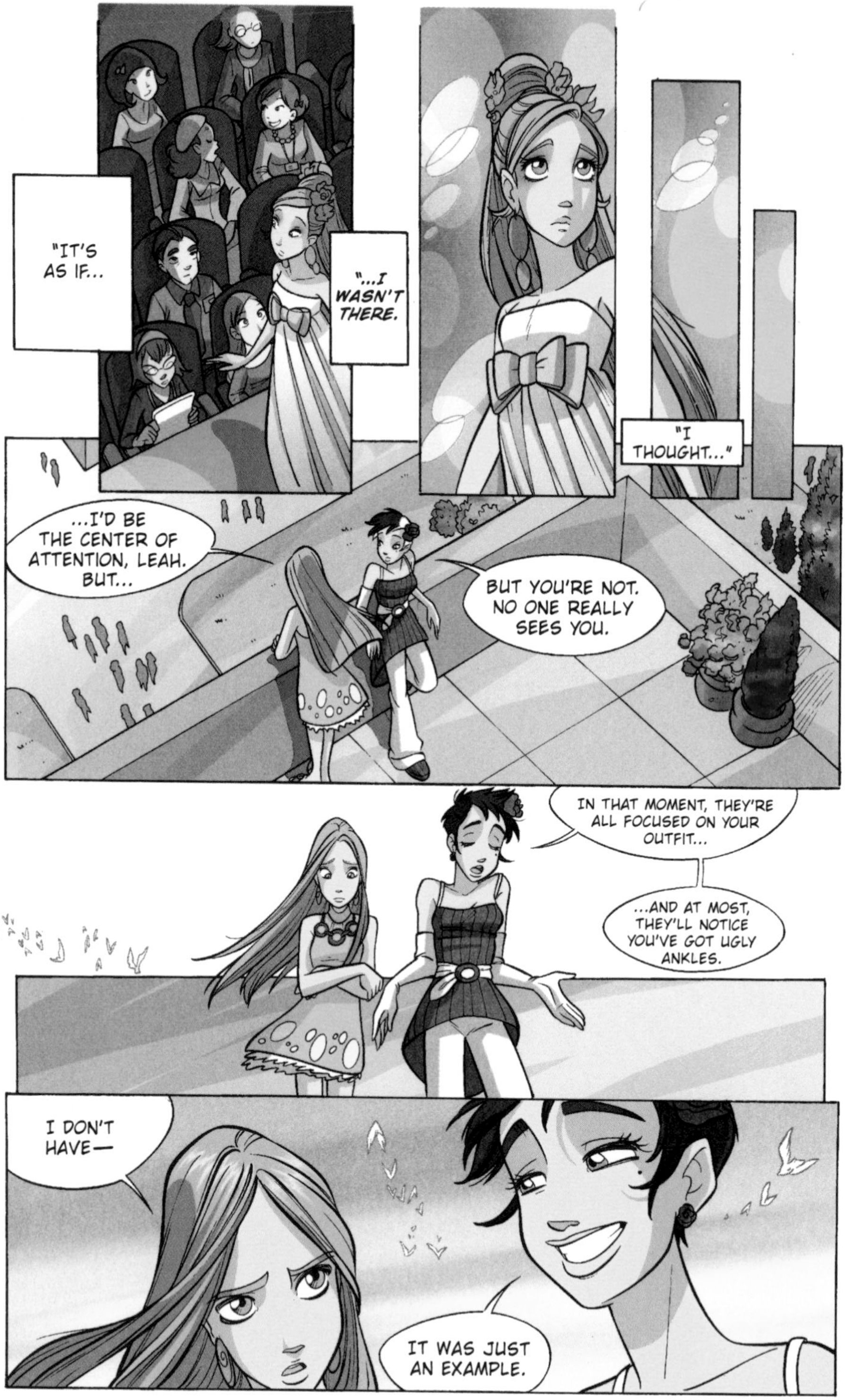
"IT'S AS IF...
"...I WASN'T THERE.
"I THOUGHT..."
...I'D BE THE CENTER OF ATTENTION, LEAH. BUT...
BUT YOU'RE NOT. NO ONE REALLY SEES YOU.
IN THAT MOMENT, THEY'RE ALL FOCUSED ON YOUR OUTFIT...
...AND AT MOST, THEY'LL NOTICE YOU'VE GOT UGLY ANKLES.
I DON'T HAVE—
IT WAS JUST AN EXAMPLE.

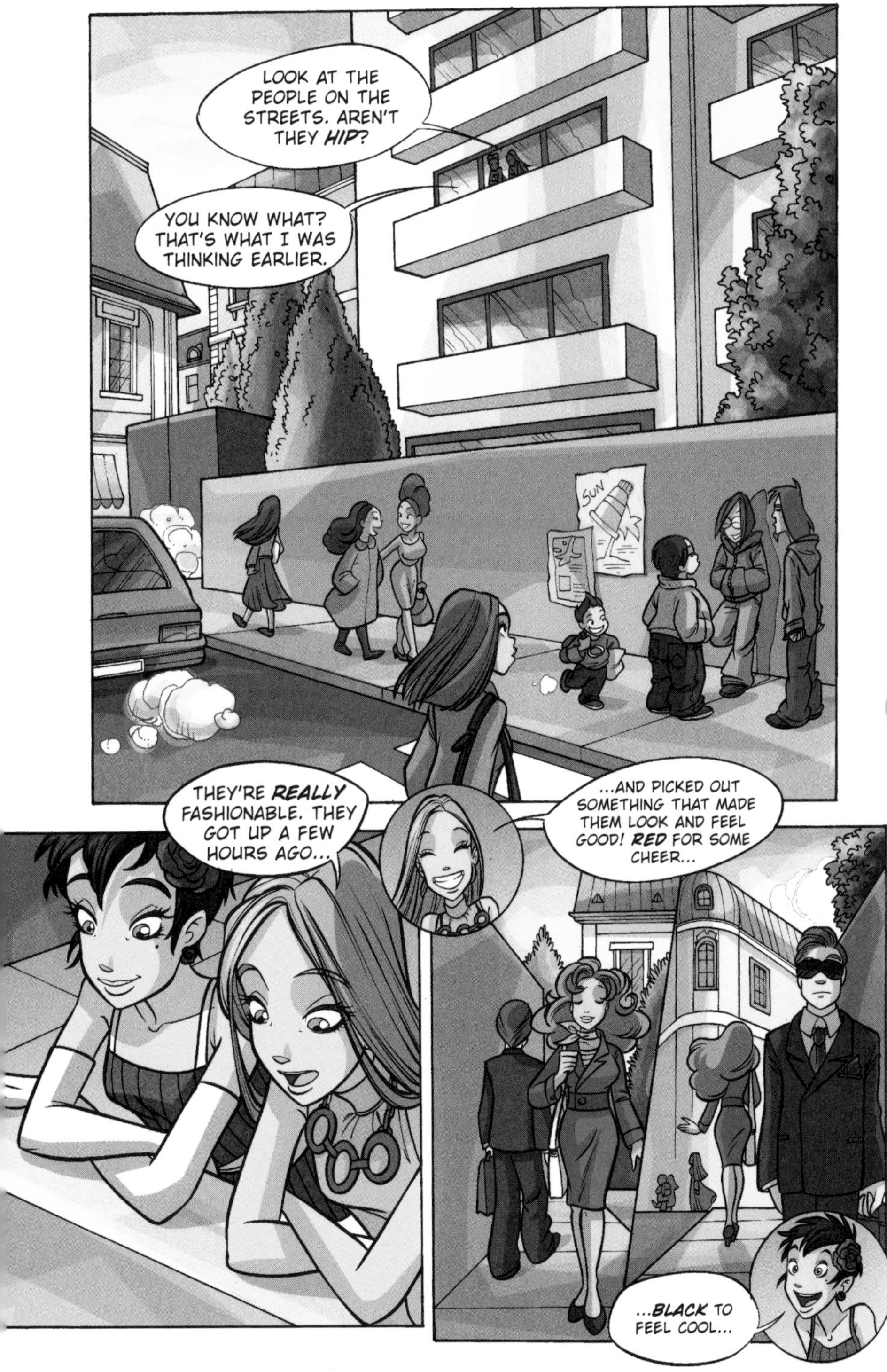
LOOK AT THE PEOPLE ON THE STREETS. AREN'T THEY *HIP*?
YOU KNOW WHAT? THAT'S WHAT I WAS THINKING EARLIER.
SUN
THEY'RE ***REALLY*** FASHIONABLE. THEY GOT UP A FEW HOURS AGO...
...AND PICKED OUT SOMETHING THAT MADE THEM LOOK AND FEEL GOOD! ***RED*** FOR SOME CHEER...
...***BLACK*** TO FEEL COOL...

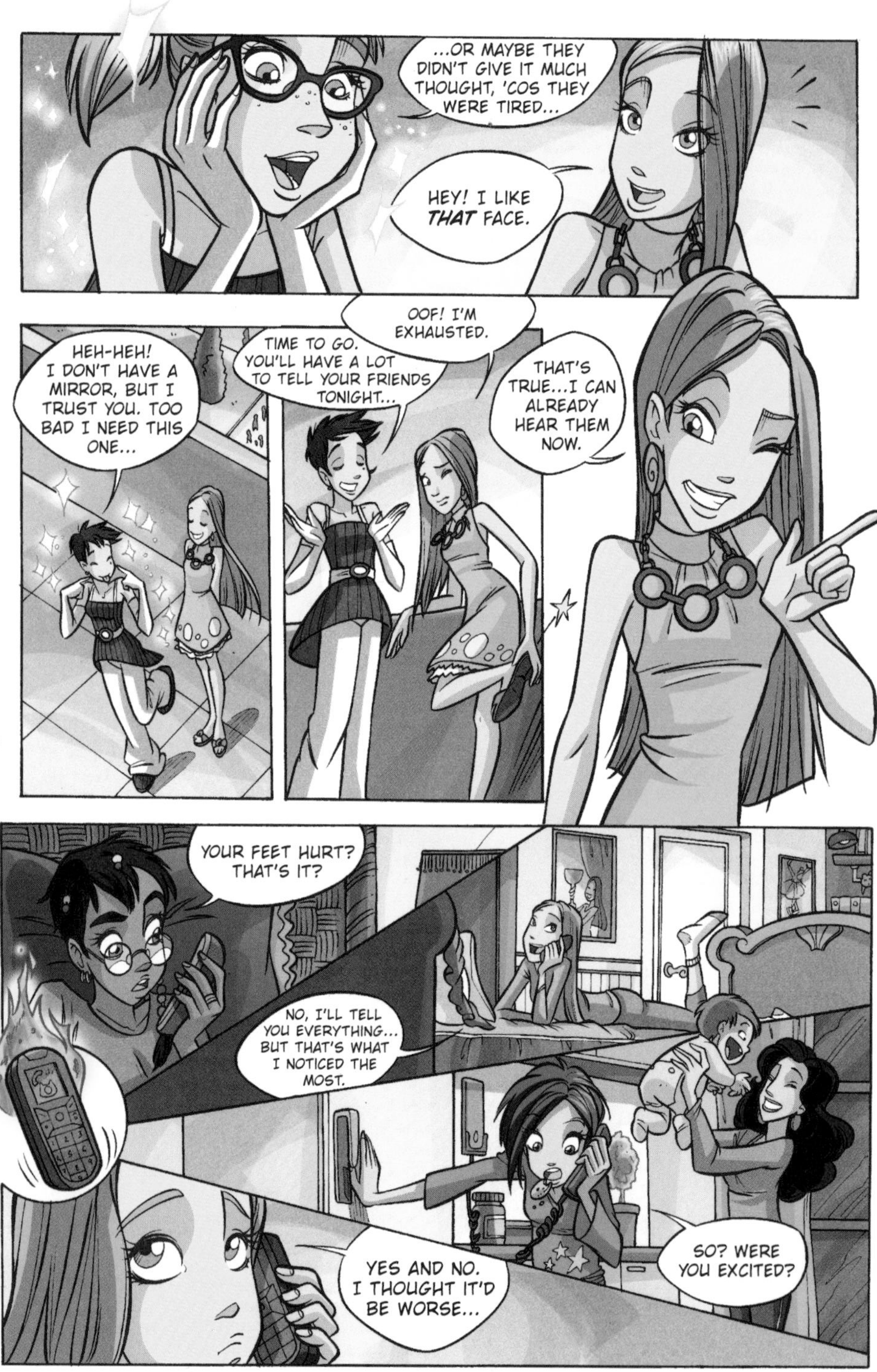
...OR MAYBE THEY DIDN'T GIVE IT MUCH THOUGHT, 'COS THEY WERE TIRED...
HEY! I LIKE *THAT* FACE.
HEH-HEH! I DON'T HAVE A MIRROR, BUT I TRUST YOU. TOO BAD I NEED THIS ONE...
TIME TO GO. YOU'LL HAVE A LOT TO TELL YOUR FRIENDS TONIGHT...
OOF! I'M EXHAUSTED.
THAT'S TRUE...I CAN ALREADY HEAR THEM NOW.
YOUR FEET HURT? THAT'S IT?
NO, I'LL TELL YOU EVERYTHING... BUT THAT'S WHAT I NOTICED THE MOST.
SO? WERE YOU EXCITED?
YES AND NO. I THOUGHT IT'D BE WORSE...

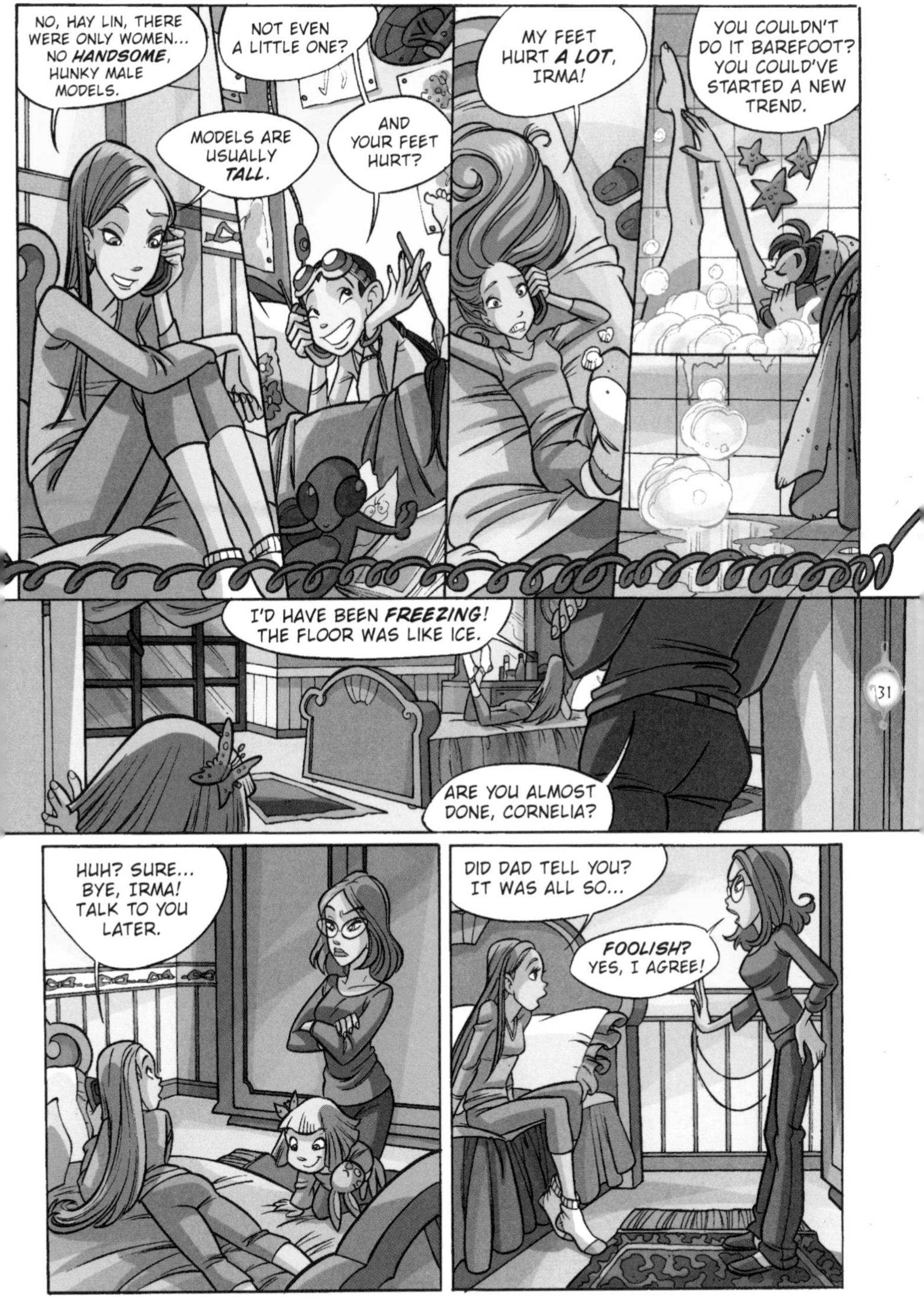

NO, HAY LIN, THERE WERE ONLY WOMEN... NO HANDSOME, HUNKY MALE MODELS.
NOT EVEN A LITTLE ONE?
MODELS ARE USUALLY TALL.
AND YOUR FEET HURT?
MY FEET HURT A LOT, IRMA!
YOU COULDN'T DO IT BAREFOOT? YOU COULD'VE STARTED A NEW TREND.
I'D HAVE BEEN FREEZING! THE FLOOR WAS LIKE ICE.
ARE YOU ALMOST DONE, CORNELIA?
31
HUH? SURE... BYE, IRMA! TALK TO YOU LATER.
DID DAD TELL YOU? IT WAS ALL SO...
FOOLISH? YES, I AGREE!

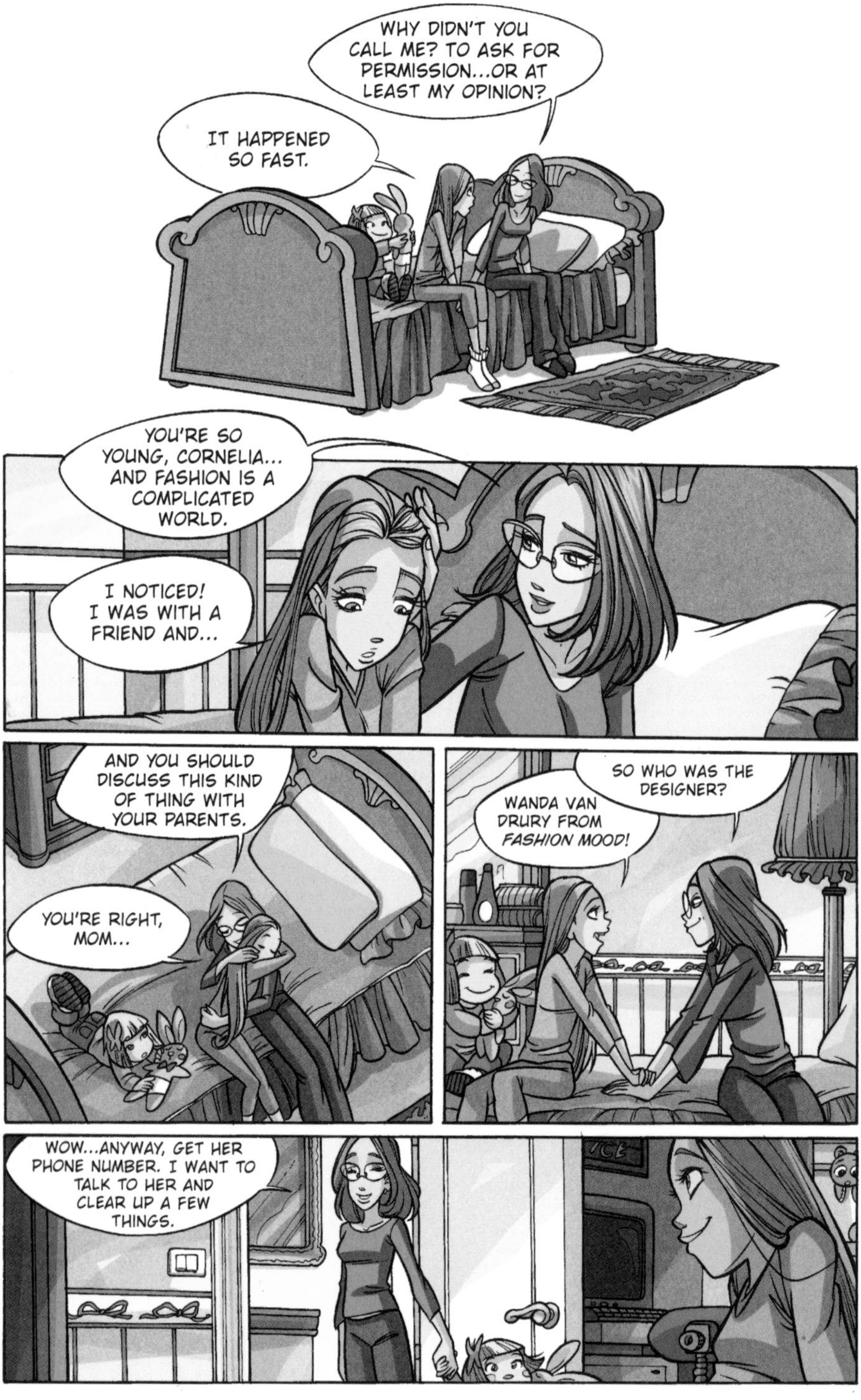
WHY DIDN'T YOU CALL ME? TO ASK FOR PERMISSION...OR AT LEAST MY OPINION?
IT HAPPENED SO FAST.
YOU'RE SO YOUNG, CORNELIA... AND FASHION IS A COMPLICATED WORLD.
I NOTICED! I WAS WITH A FRIEND AND...
AND YOU SHOULD DISCUSS THIS KIND OF THING WITH YOUR PARENTS.
YOU'RE RIGHT, MOM...
SO WHO WAS THE DESIGNER?
WANDA VAN DRURY FROM *FASHION MOOD!*
WOW...ANYWAY, GET HER PHONE NUMBER. I WANT TO TALK TO HER AND CLEAR UP A FEW THINGS.

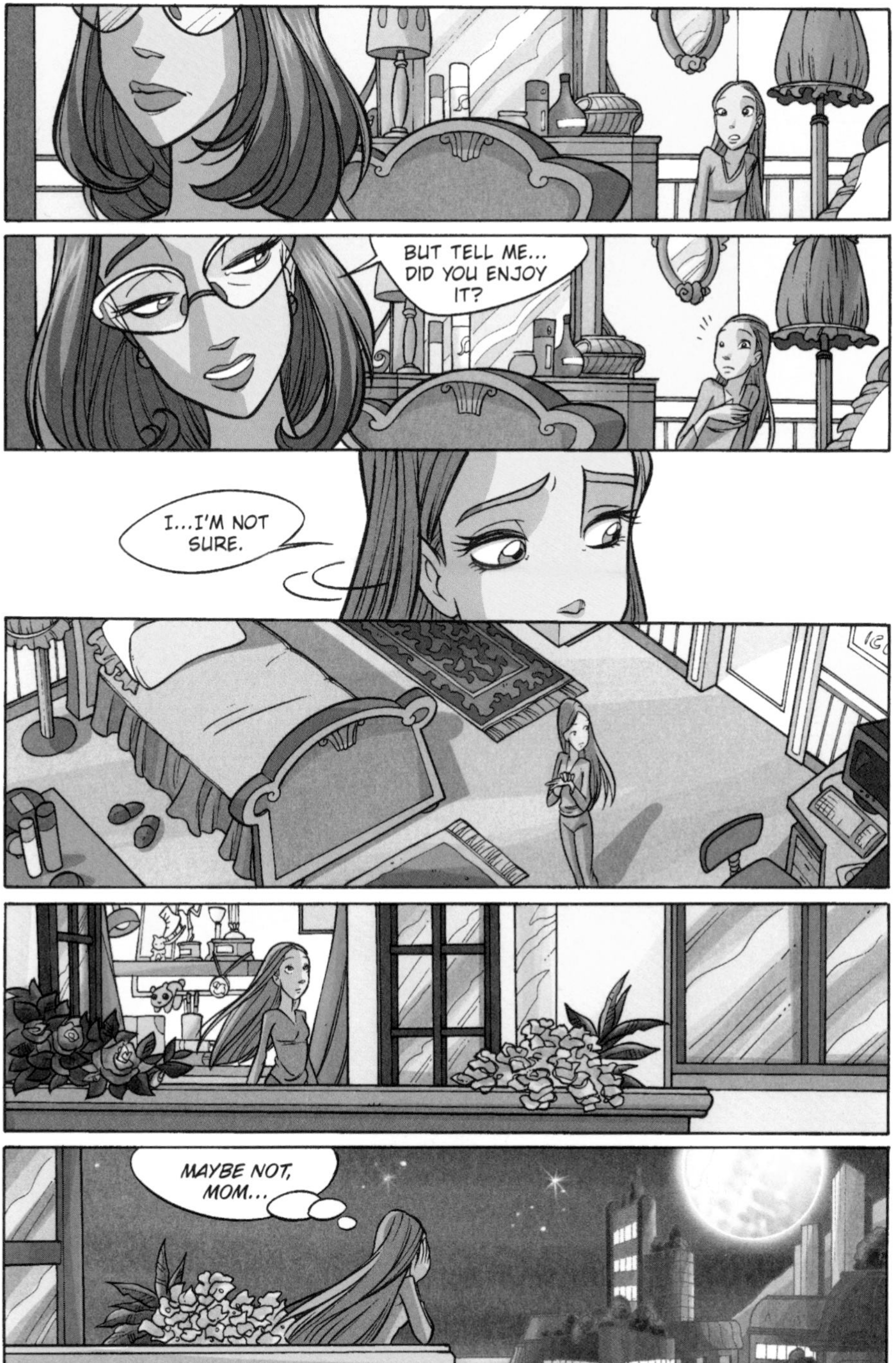
BUT TELL ME...
DID YOU ENJOY
IT?
I...I'M NOT
SURE.
MAYBE NOT,
MOM...

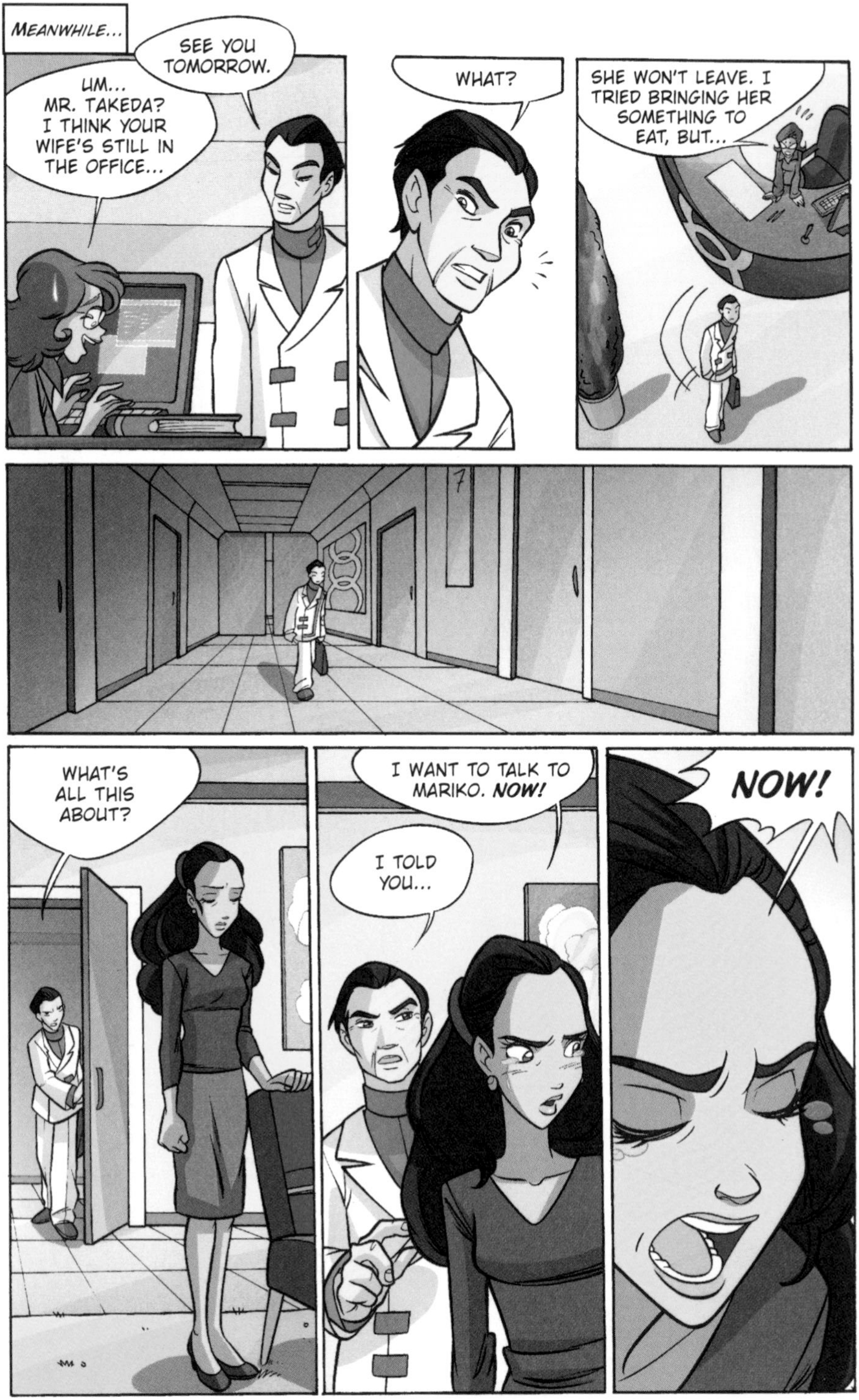
MEANWHILE...
UM... MR. TAKEDA? I THINK YOUR WIFE'S STILL IN THE OFFICE...
SEE YOU TOMORROW.
WHAT?
SHE WON'T LEAVE. I TRIED BRINGING HER SOMETHING TO EAT, BUT...
7
WHAT'S ALL THIS ABOUT?
I WANT TO TALK TO MARIKO. NOW!
I TOLD YOU...
NOW!

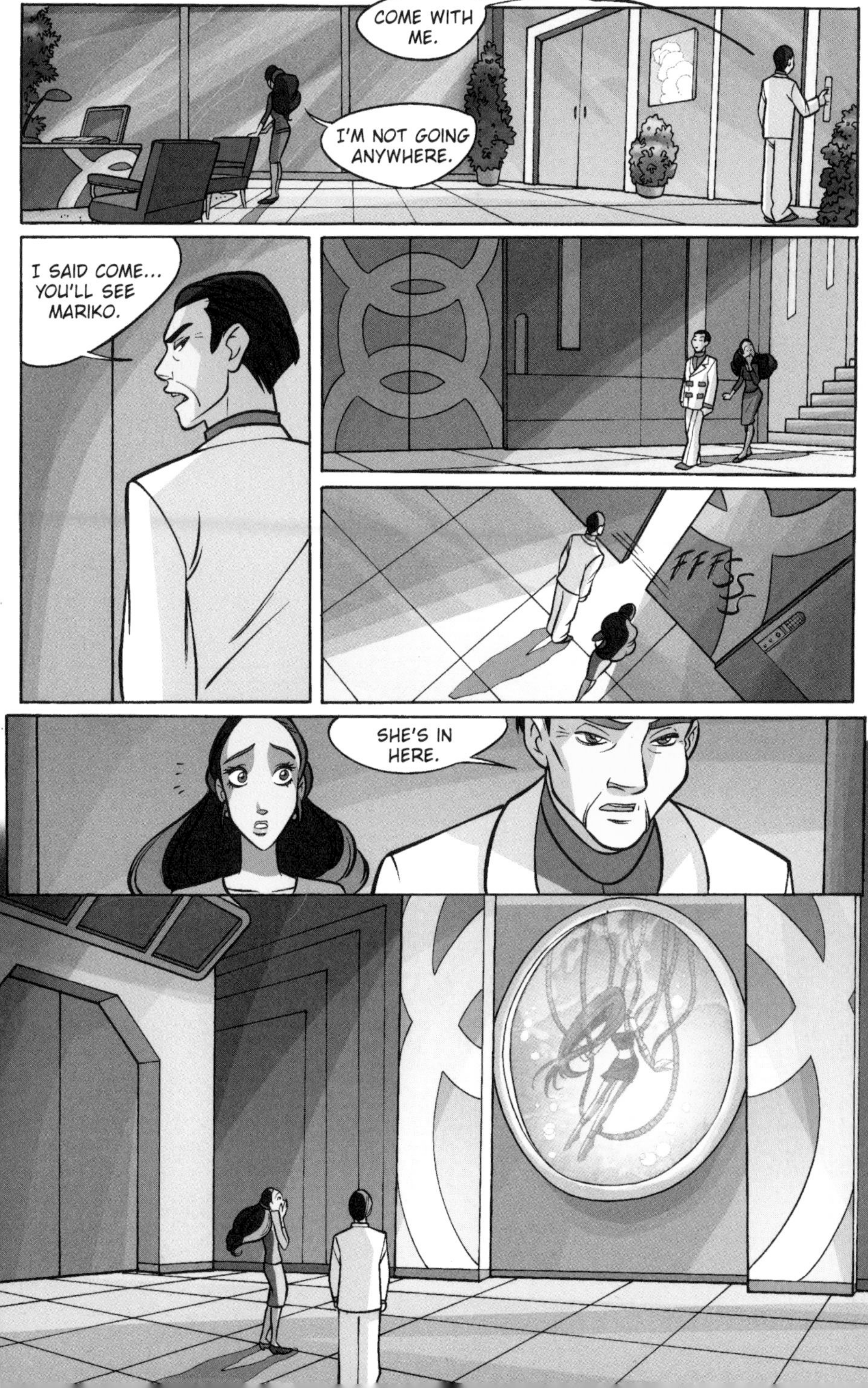
COME WITH ME.
I'M NOT GOING ANYWHERE.
I SAID COME... YOU'LL SEE MARIKO.
FFFSSS
SHE'S IN HERE.

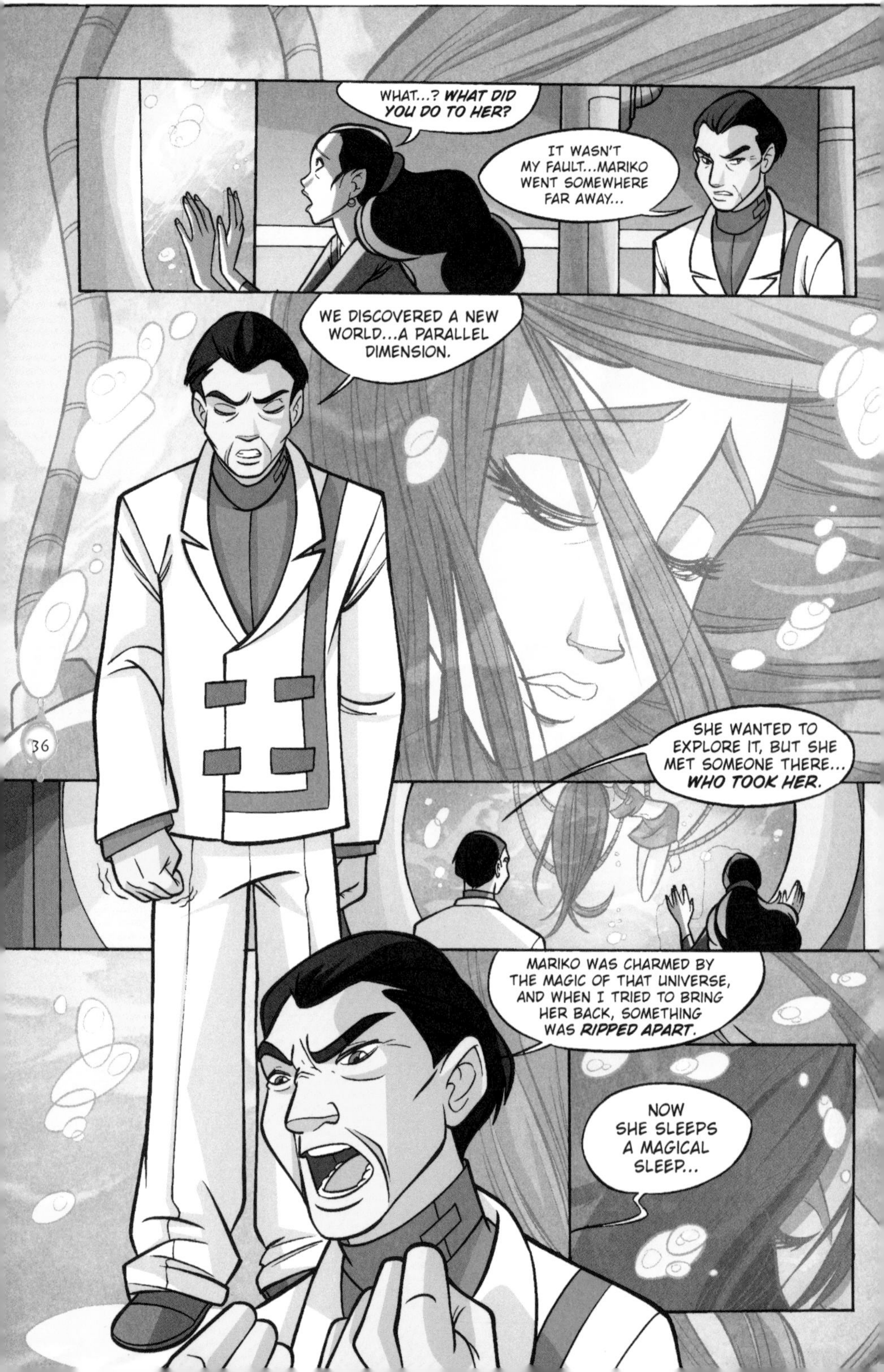
WHAT...? ***WHAT DID YOU DO TO HER?***
IT WASN'T MY FAULT...MARIKO WENT SOMEWHERE FAR AWAY...
WE DISCOVERED A NEW WORLD...A PARALLEL DIMENSION.
SHE WANTED TO EXPLORE IT, BUT SHE MET SOMEONE THERE... ***WHO TOOK HER.***
MARIKO WAS CHARMED BY THE MAGIC OF THAT UNIVERSE, AND WHEN I TRIED TO BRING HER BACK, SOMETHING WAS ***RIPPED APART.***
NOW SHE SLEEPS A MAGICAL SLEEP...

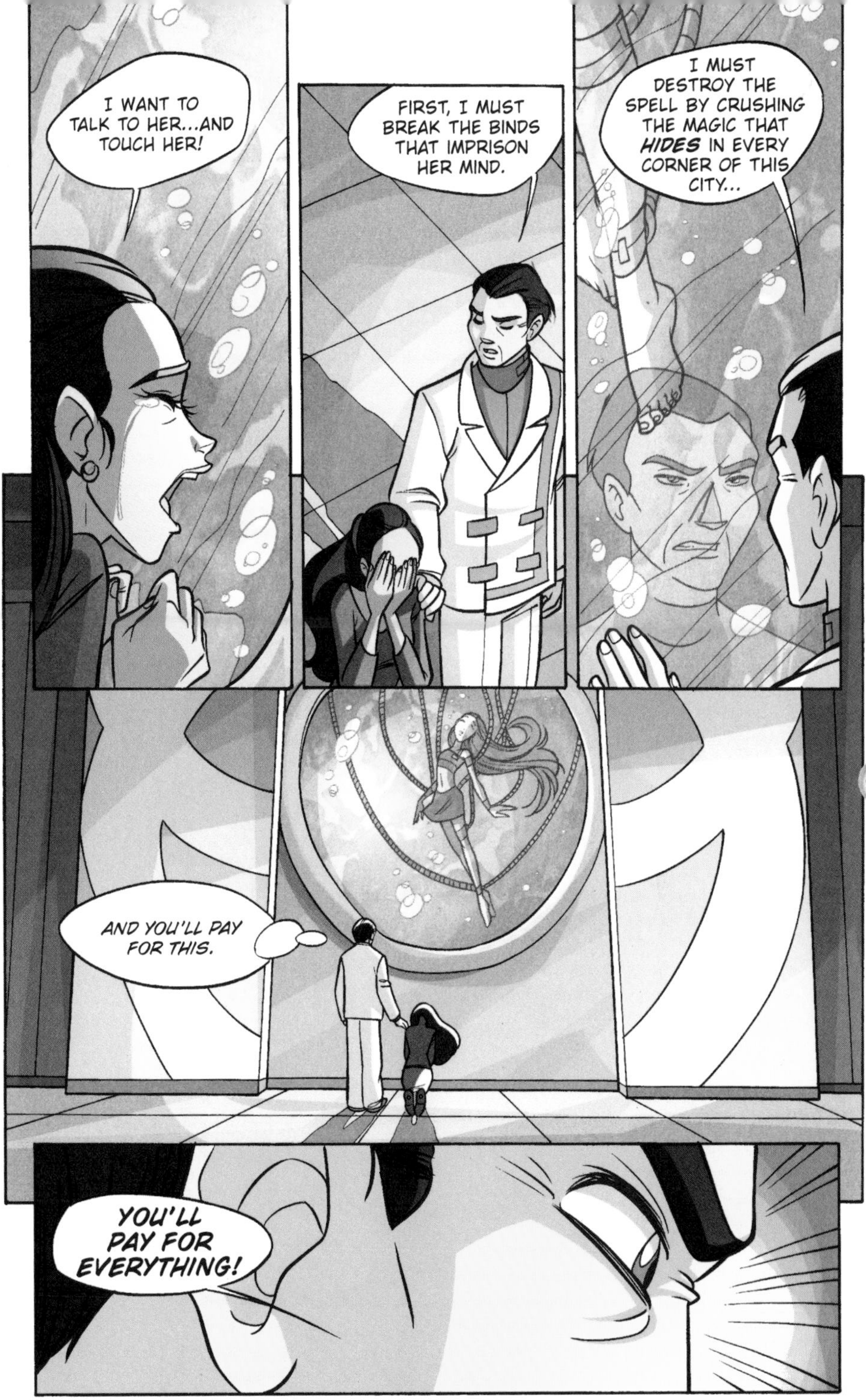
I WANT TO TALK TO HER...AND TOUCH HER!
FIRST, I MUST BREAK THE BINDS THAT IMPRISON HER MIND.
I MUST DESTROY THE SPELL BY CRUSHING THE MAGIC THAT *HIDES* IN EVERY CORNER OF THIS CITY...
AND YOU'LL PAY FOR THIS.
YOU'LL PAY FOR EVERYTHING!

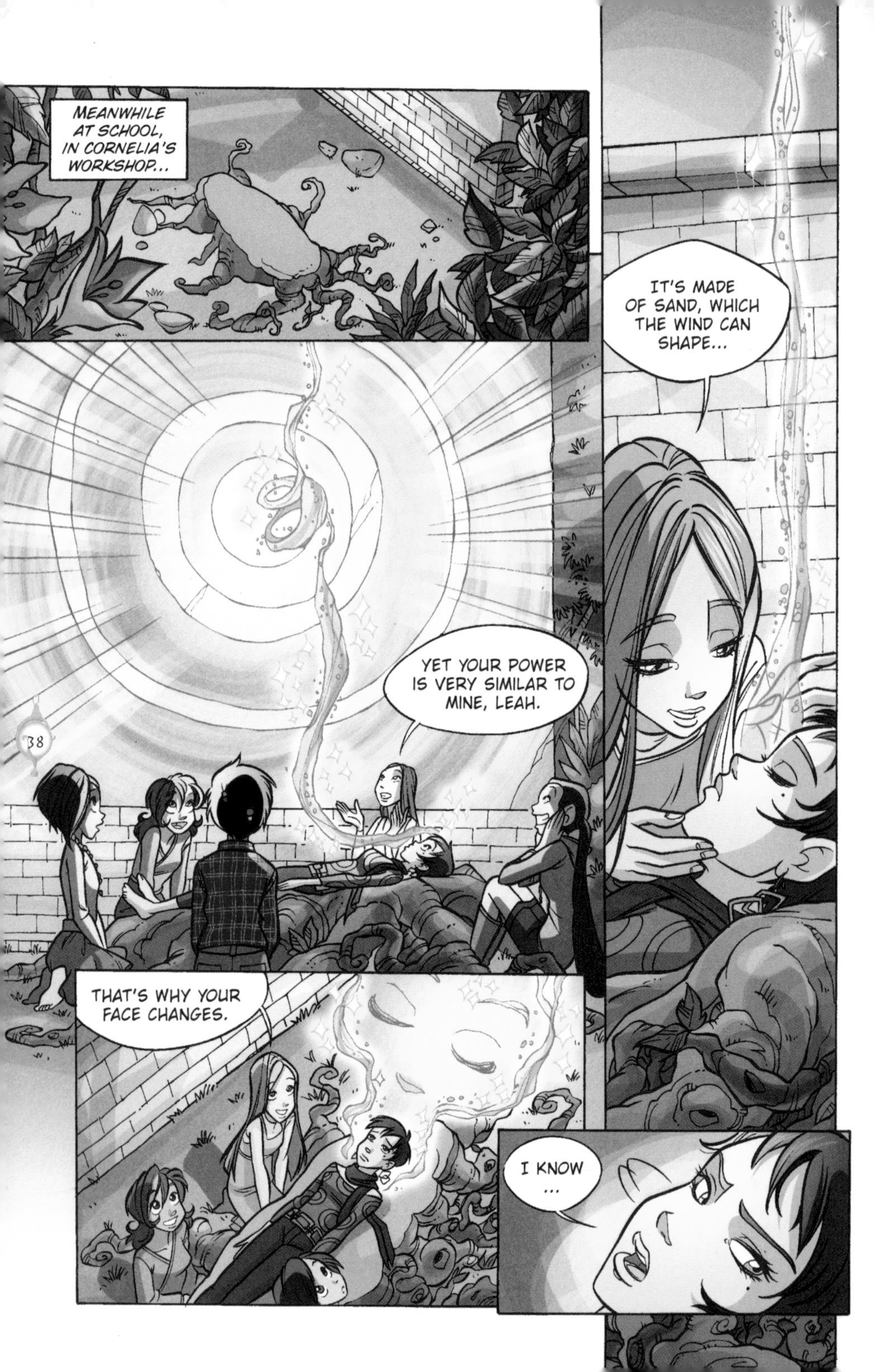
MEANWHILE AT SCHOOL, IN CORNELIA'S WORKSHOP...
YET YOUR POWER IS VERY SIMILAR TO MINE, LEAH.
IT'S MADE OF SAND, WHICH THE WIND CAN SHAPE...
THAT'S WHY YOUR FACE CHANGES.
I KNOW ...

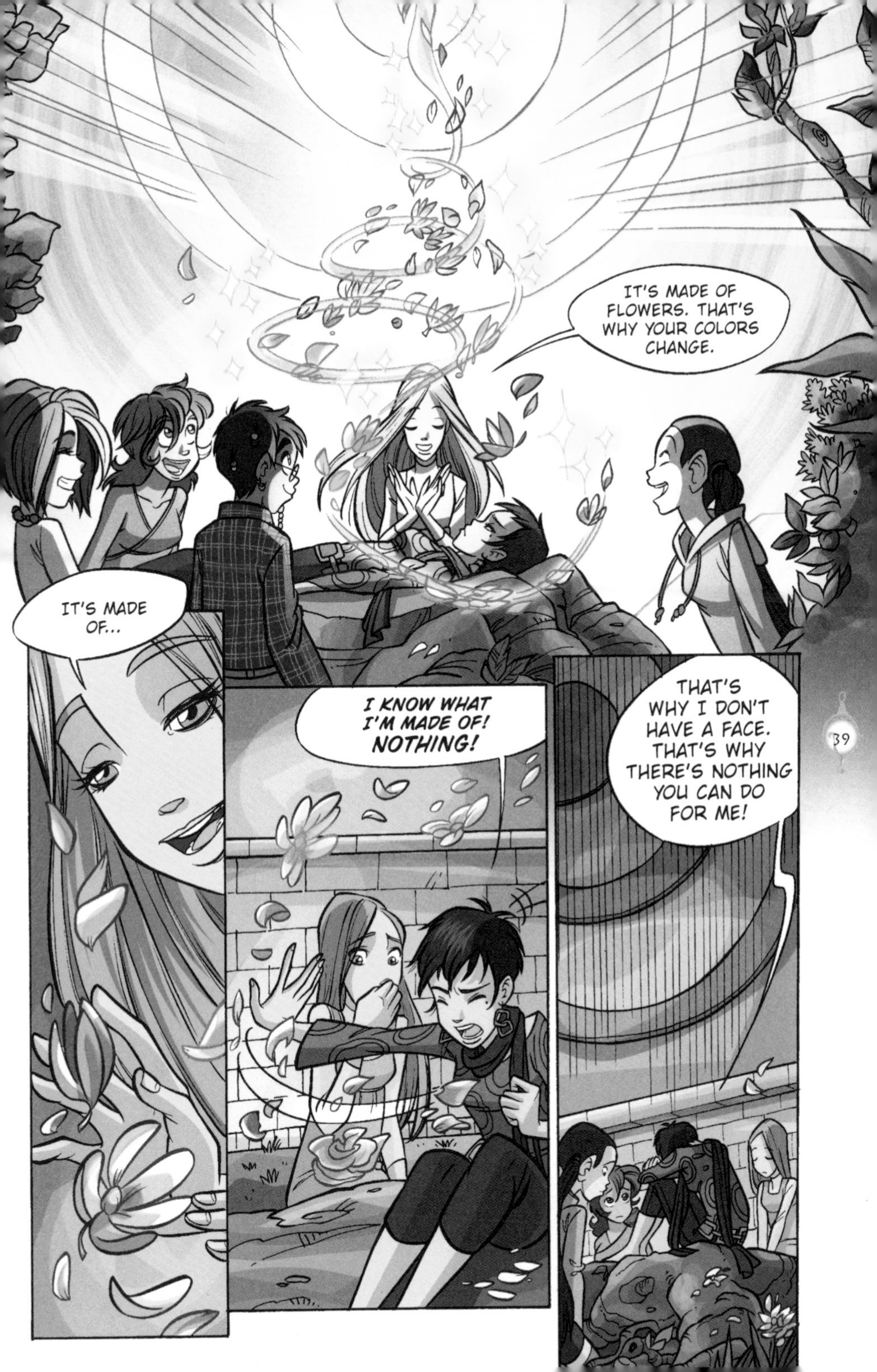
IT'S MADE OF FLOWERS. THAT'S WHY YOUR COLORS CHANGE.
IT'S MADE OF...
I KNOW WHAT I'M MADE OF! NOTHING!
THAT'S WHY I DON'T HAVE A FACE. THAT'S WHY THERE'S NOTHING YOU CAN DO FOR ME!

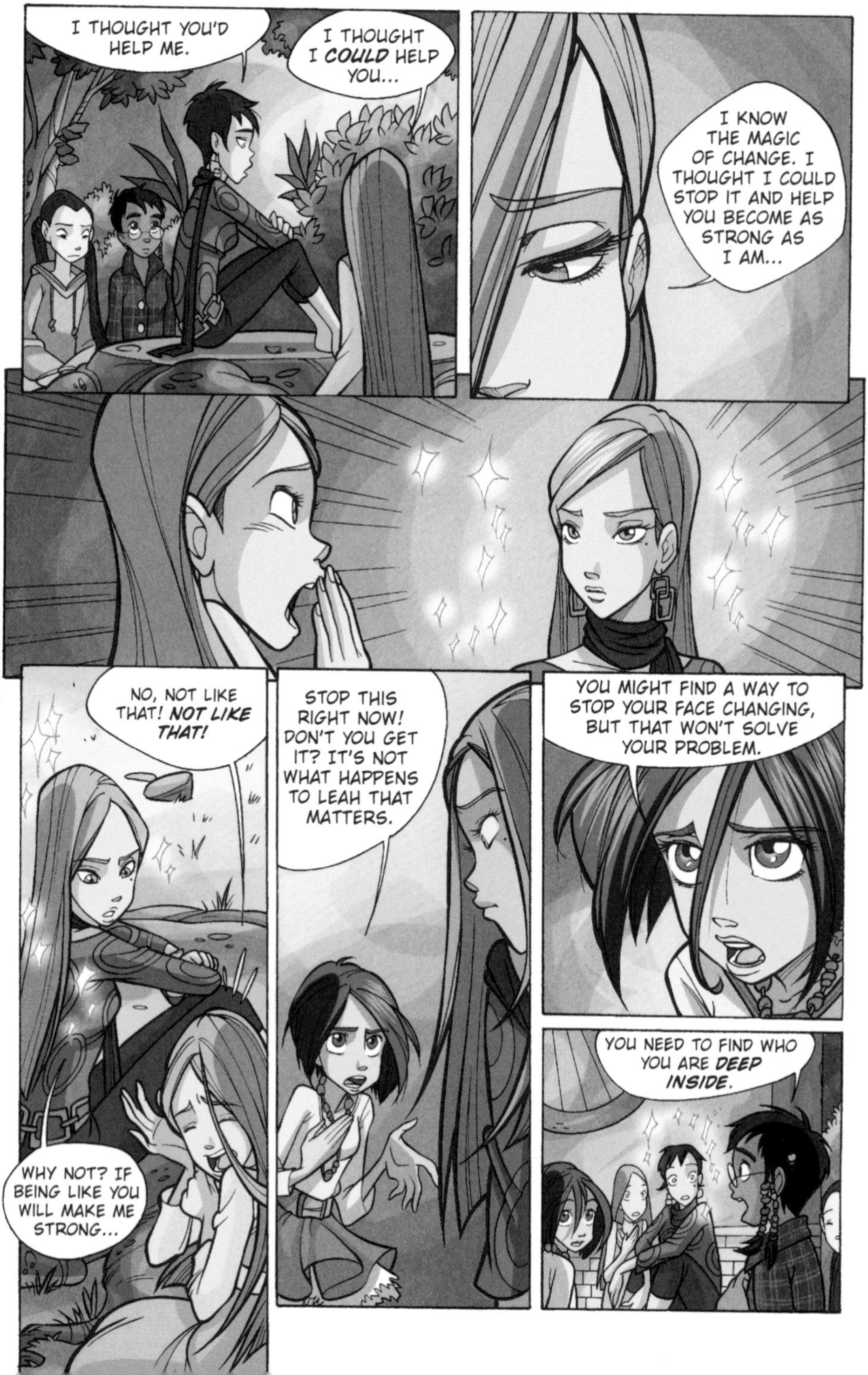
I THOUGHT YOU'D HELP ME.
I THOUGHT I COULD HELP YOU...
I KNOW THE MAGIC OF CHANGE. I THOUGHT I COULD STOP IT AND HELP YOU BECOME AS STRONG AS I AM...
NO, NOT LIKE THAT! NOT LIKE THAT!
WHY NOT? IF BEING LIKE YOU WILL MAKE ME STRONG...
STOP THIS RIGHT NOW! DON'T YOU GET IT? IT'S NOT WHAT HAPPENS TO LEAH THAT MATTERS.
YOU MIGHT FIND A WAY TO STOP YOUR FACE CHANGING, BUT THAT WON'T SOLVE YOUR PROBLEM.
YOU NEED TO FIND WHO YOU ARE DEEP INSIDE.

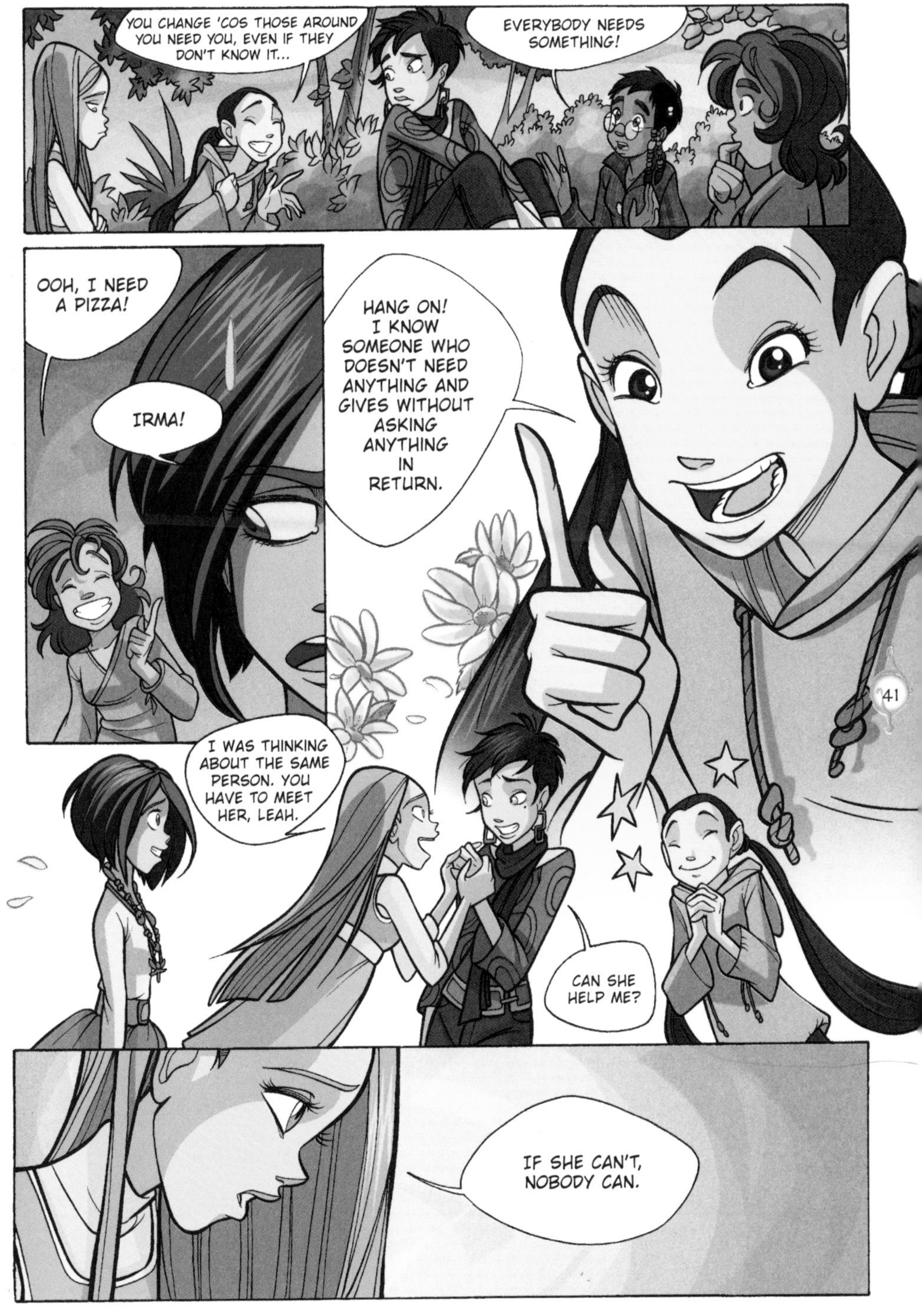

YOU CHANGE 'COS THOSE AROUND YOU NEED YOU, EVEN IF THEY DON'T KNOW IT...
EVERYBODY NEEDS SOMETHING!
OOH, I NEED A PIZZA!
IRMA!
HANG ON! I KNOW SOMEONE WHO DOESN'T NEED ANYTHING AND GIVES WITHOUT ASKING ANYTHING IN RETURN.
I WAS THINKING ABOUT THE SAME PERSON. YOU HAVE TO MEET HER, LEAH.
CAN SHE HELP ME?
IF SHE CAN'T, NOBODY CAN.

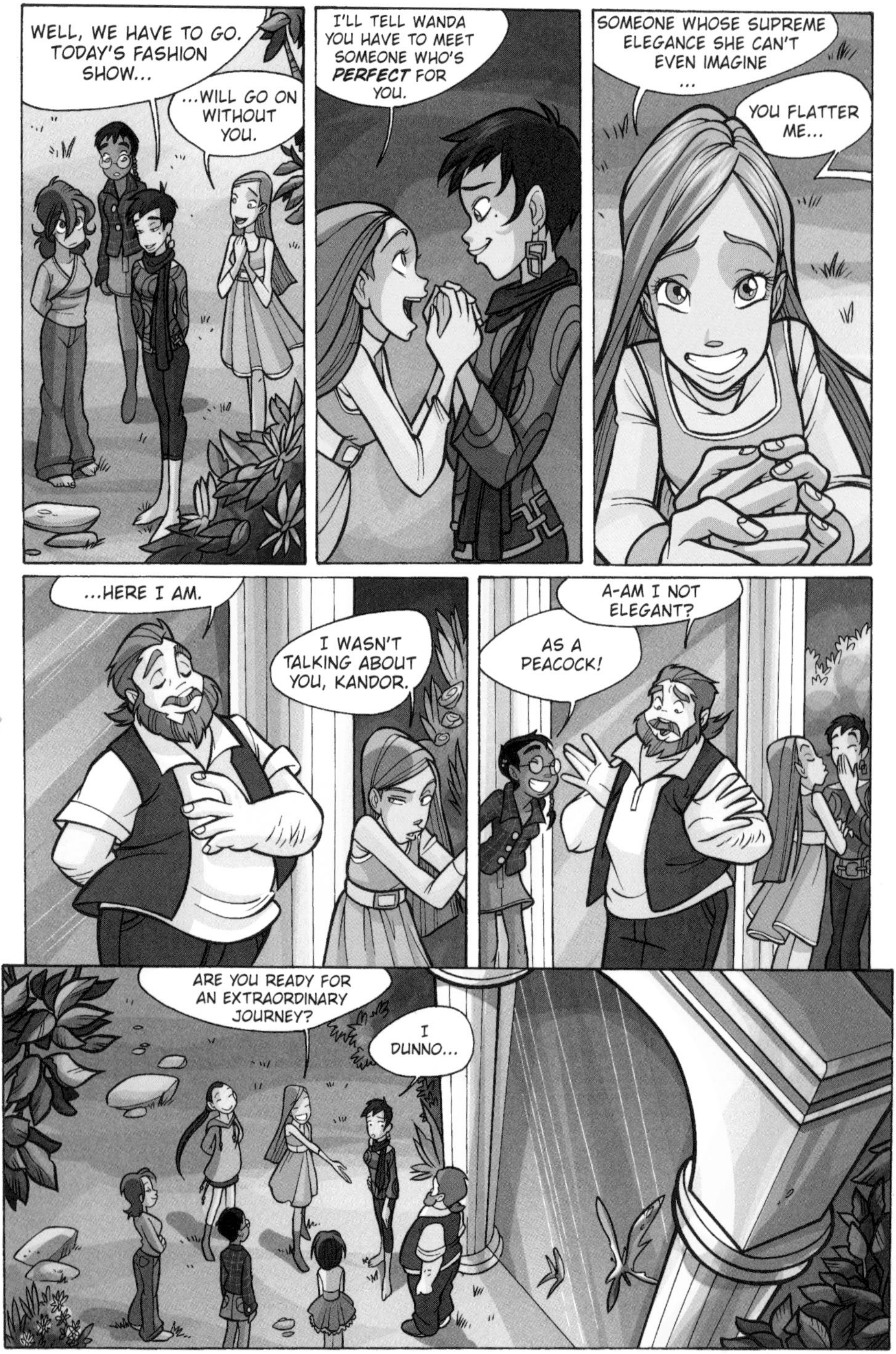
WELL, WE HAVE TO GO. TODAY'S FASHION SHOW...
...WILL GO ON WITHOUT YOU.
I'LL TELL WANDA YOU HAVE TO MEET SOMEONE WHO'S *PERFECT* FOR YOU.
SOMEONE WHOSE SUPREME ELEGANCE SHE CAN'T EVEN IMAGINE ...
YOU FLATTER ME...
...HERE I AM.
I WASN'T TALKING ABOUT YOU, KANDOR.
A-AM I NOT ELEGANT?
AS A PEACOCK!
ARE YOU READY FOR AN EXTRAORDINARY JOURNEY?
I DUNNO...

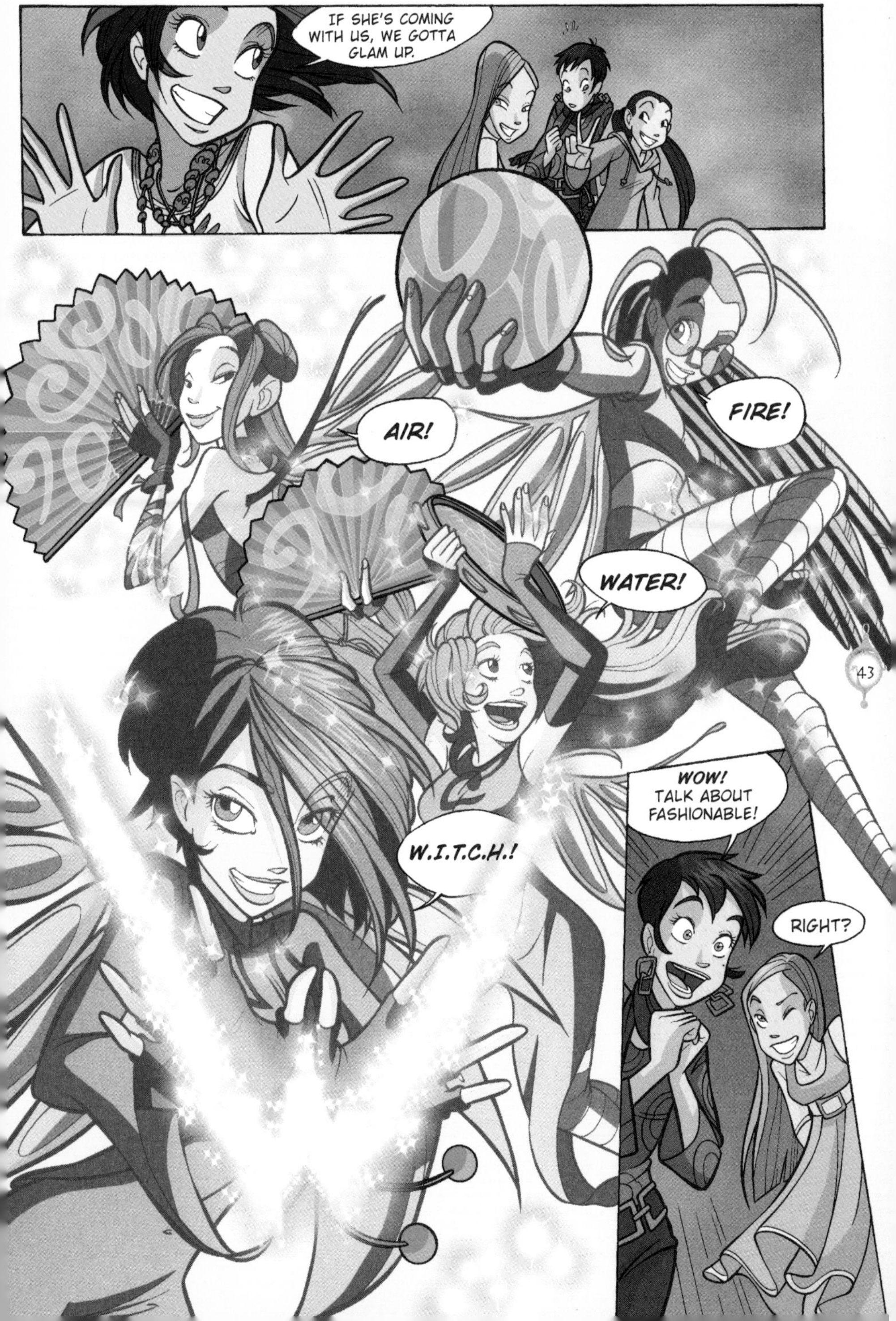
IF SHE'S COMING WITH US, WE GOTTA GLAM UP.
AIR!
FIRE!
WATER!
W.I.T.C.H.!
WOW! TALK ABOUT FASHIONABLE!
RIGHT?

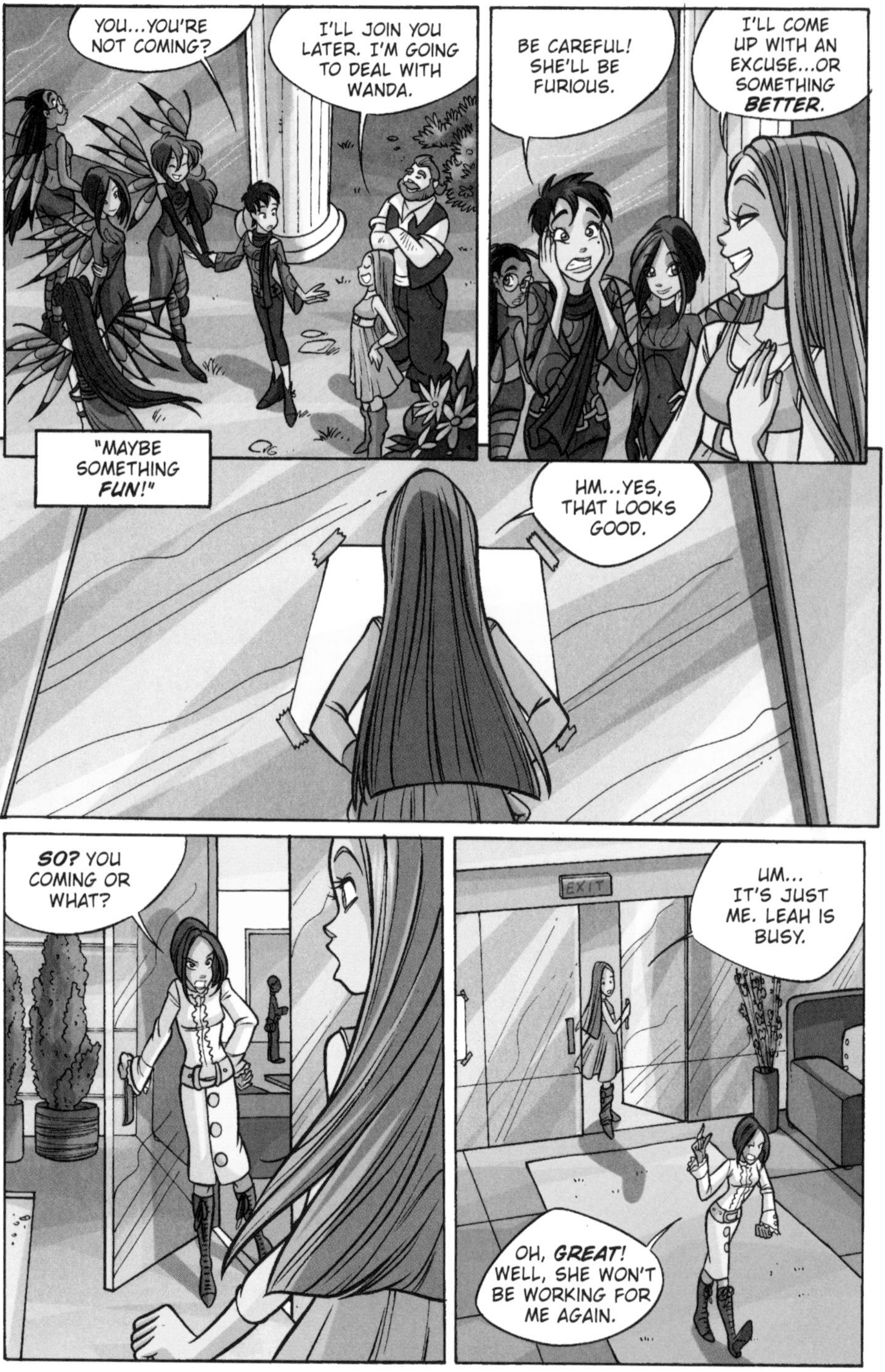
YOU...YOU'RE NOT COMING?
I'LL JOIN YOU LATER. I'M GOING TO DEAL WITH WANDA.
BE CAREFUL! SHE'LL BE FURIOUS.
I'LL COME UP WITH AN EXCUSE...OR SOMETHING **BETTER**.
"MAYBE SOMETHING **FUN**!"
HM...YES, THAT LOOKS GOOD.
SO? YOU COMING OR WHAT?
EXIT
UM... IT'S JUST ME. LEAH IS BUSY.
OH, **GREAT**! WELL, SHE WON'T BE WORKING FOR ME AGAIN.

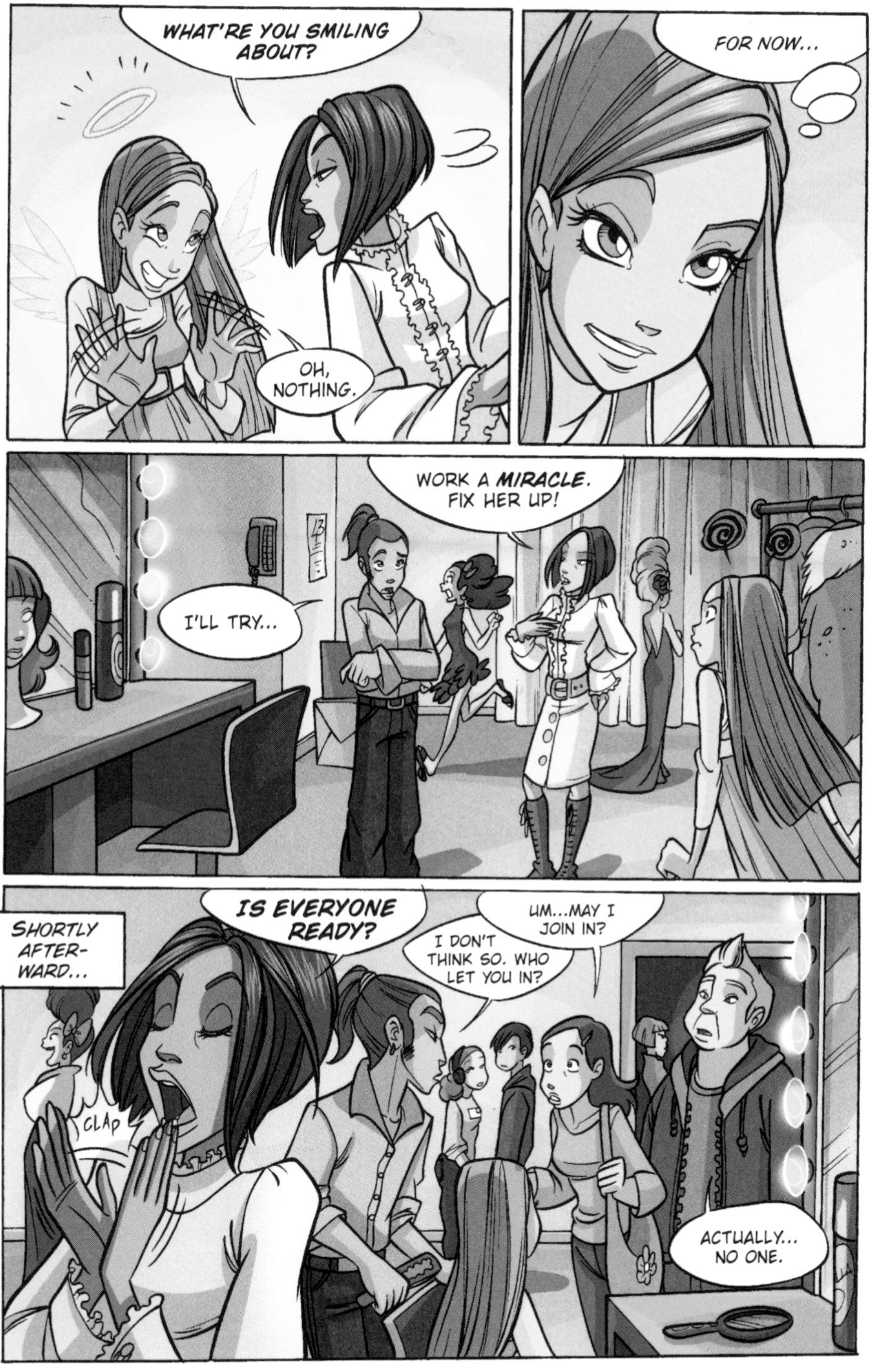
WHAT'RE YOU SMILING ABOUT?
OH, NOTHING.
FOR NOW...
WORK A MIRACLE. FIX HER UP!
I'LL TRY...
SHORTLY AFTER-WARD...
IS EVERYONE READY?
CLAP
I DON'T THINK SO. WHO LET YOU IN?
UM...MAY I JOIN IN?
ACTUALLY... NO ONE.

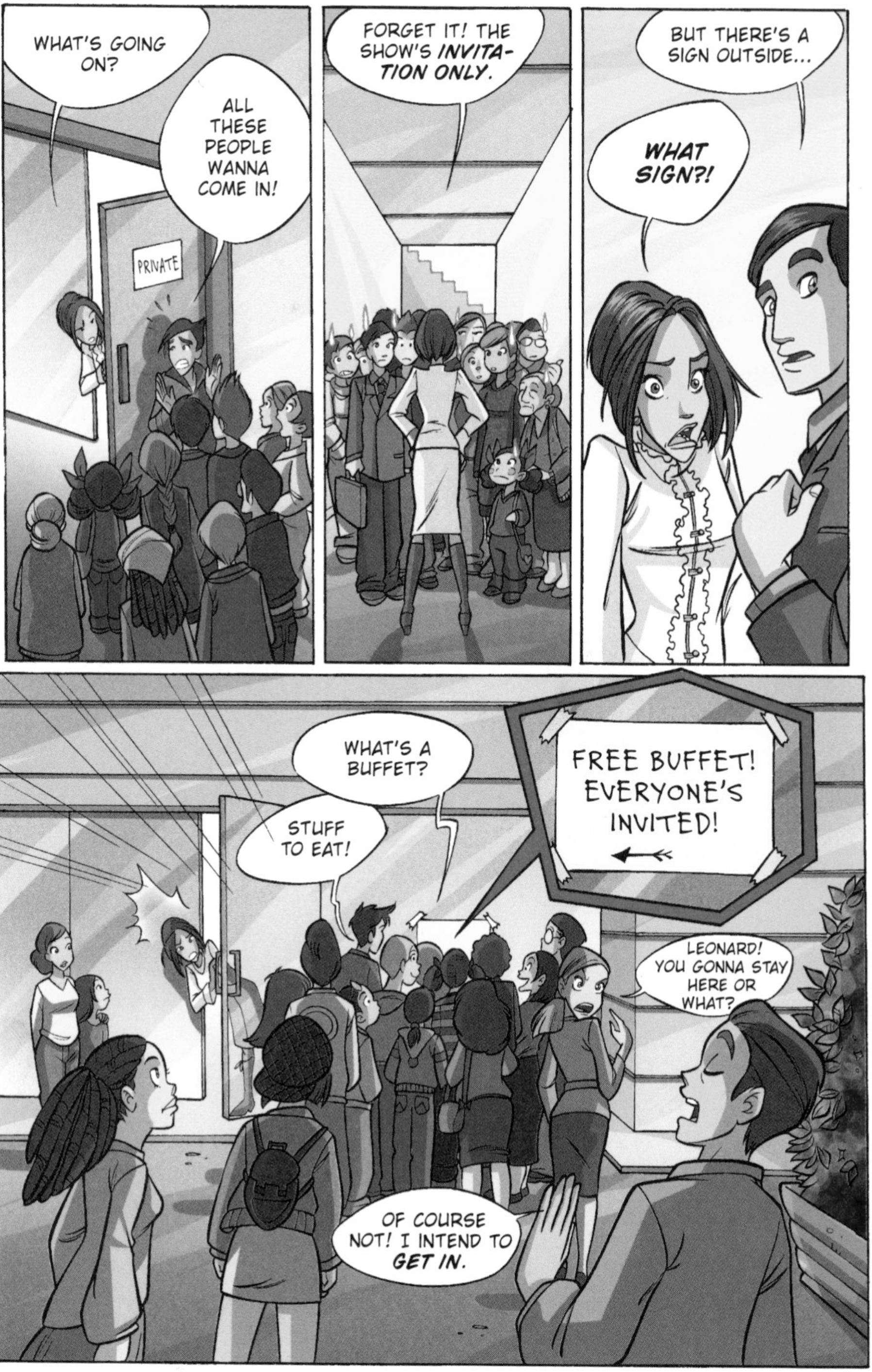
WHAT'S GOING ON?
ALL THESE PEOPLE WANNA COME IN!
PRIVATE
FORGET IT! THE SHOW'S INVITATION ONLY.
BUT THERE'S A SIGN OUTSIDE...
WHAT SIGN?!
WHAT'S A BUFFET?
STUFF TO EAT!
FREE BUFFET! EVERYONE'S INVITED!
LEONARD! YOU GONNA STAY HERE OR WHAT?
OF COURSE NOT! I INTEND TO GET IN.

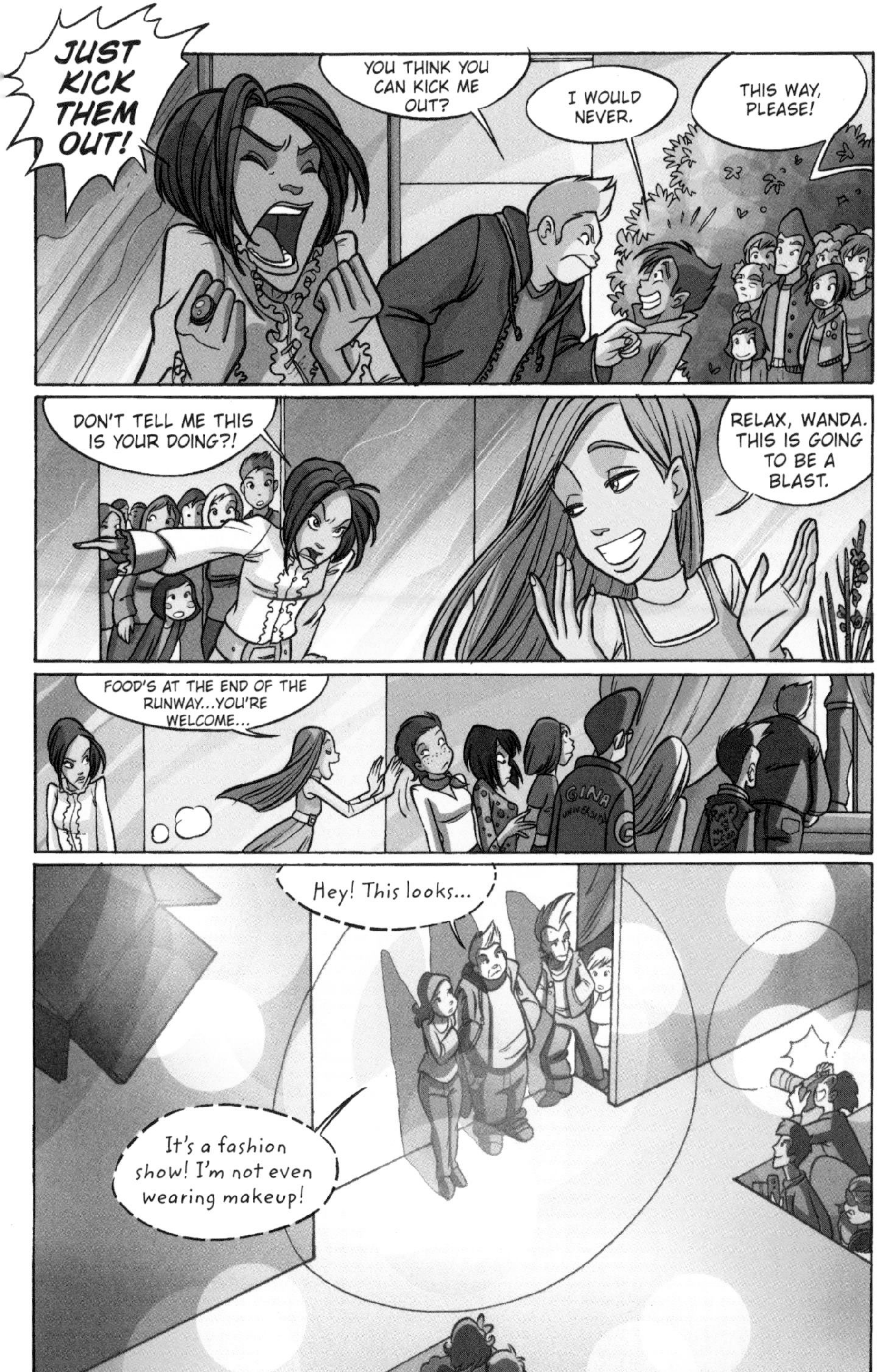
JUST KICK THEM OUT!
YOU THINK YOU CAN KICK ME OUT?
I WOULD NEVER.
THIS WAY, PLEASE!
DON'T TELL ME THIS IS YOUR DOING?!
RELAX, WANDA. THIS IS GOING TO BE A BLAST.
FOOD'S AT THE END OF THE RUNWAY...YOU'RE WELCOME...
GINA UNIVERSITY
Hey! This looks...
It's a fashion show! I'm not even wearing makeup!

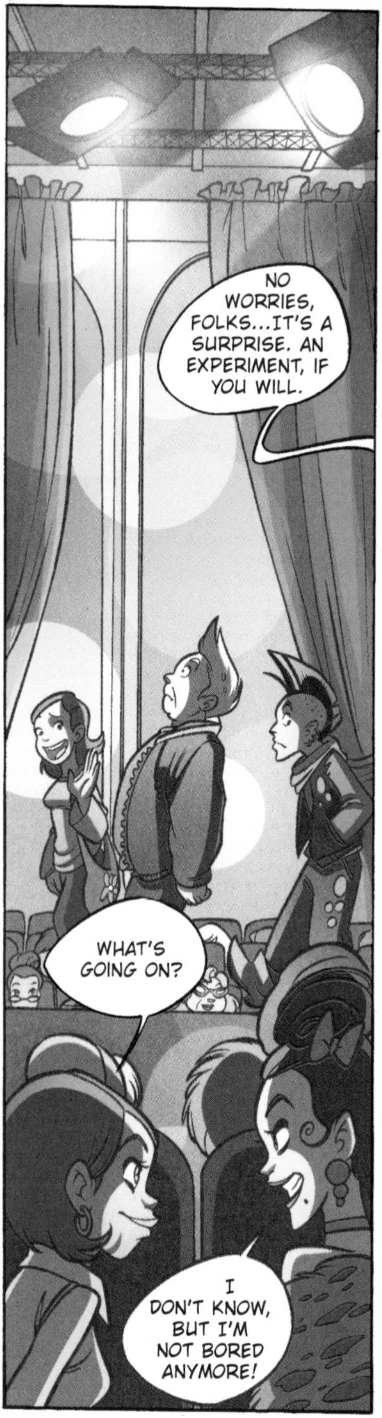
NO WORRIES, FOLKS...IT'S A SURPRISE. AN EXPERIMENT, IF YOU WILL.
WHAT'S GOING ON?
I DON'T KNOW, BUT I'M NOT BORED ANYMORE!

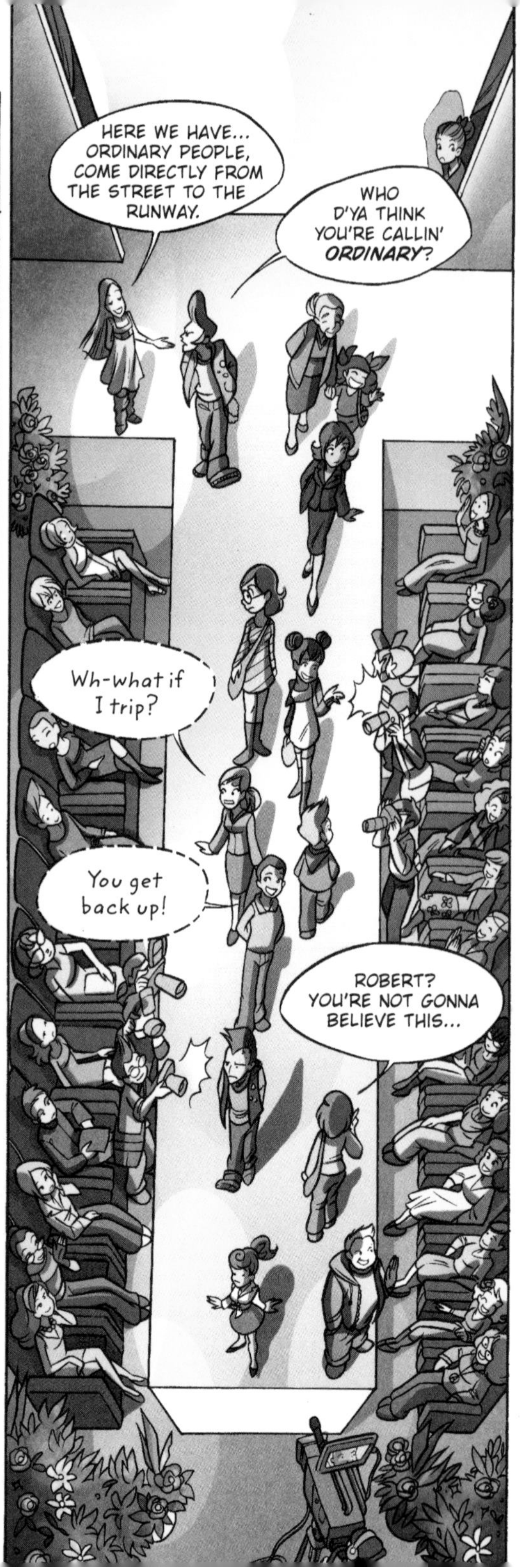
HERE WE HAVE... ORDINARY PEOPLE, COME DIRECTLY FROM THE STREET TO THE RUNWAY.
WHO D'YA THINK YOU'RE CALLIN' *ORDINARY*?
Wh-what if I trip?
You get back up!
ROBERT? YOU'RE NOT GONNA BELIEVE THIS...

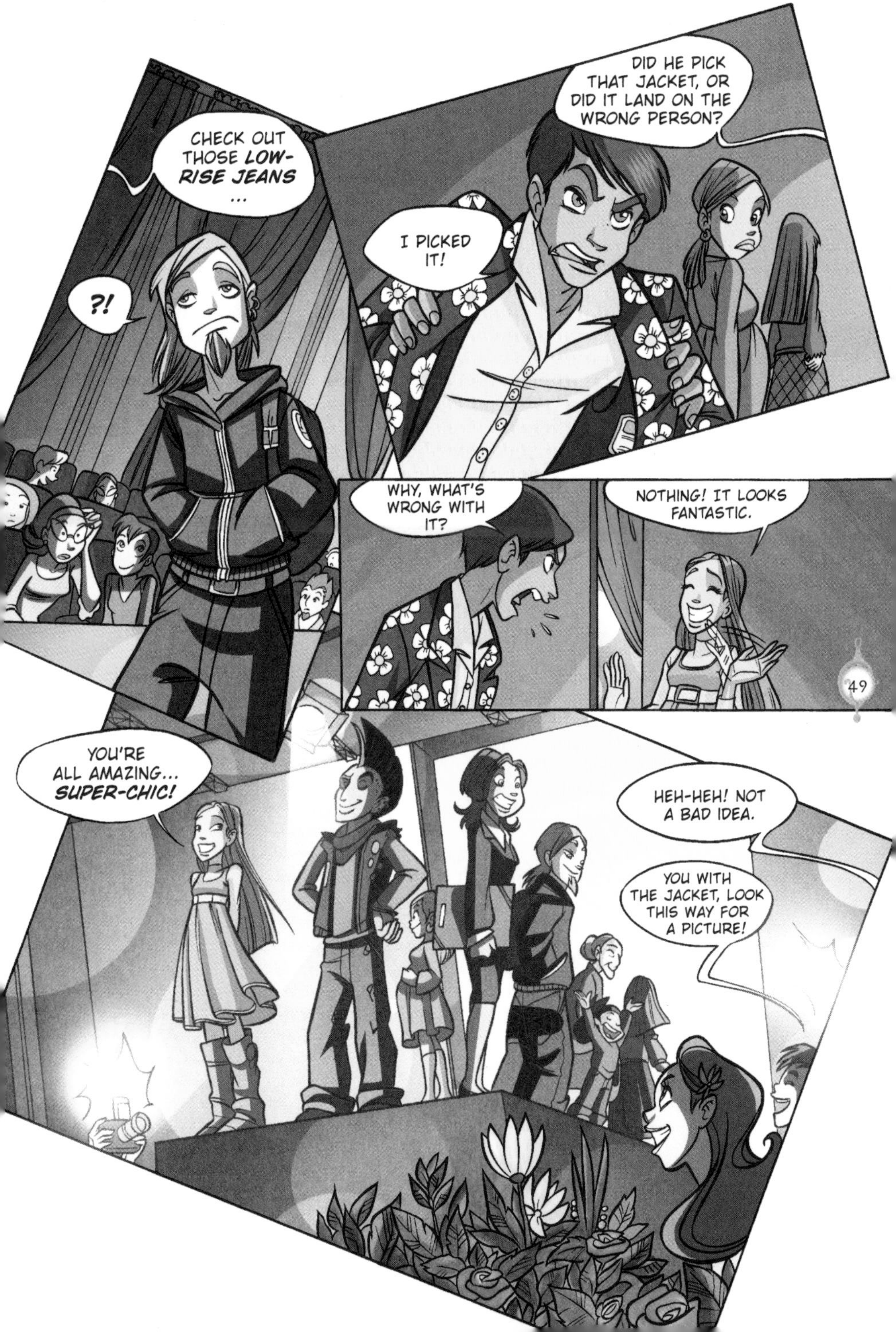
CHECK OUT THOSE LOW-RISE JEANS ...
?!
DID HE PICK THAT JACKET, OR DID IT LAND ON THE WRONG PERSON?
I PICKED IT!
WHY, WHAT'S WRONG WITH IT?
NOTHING! IT LOOKS FANTASTIC.
YOU'RE ALL AMAZING... SUPER-CHIC!
HEH-HEH! NOT A BAD IDEA.
YOU WITH THE JACKET, LOOK THIS WAY FOR A PICTURE!

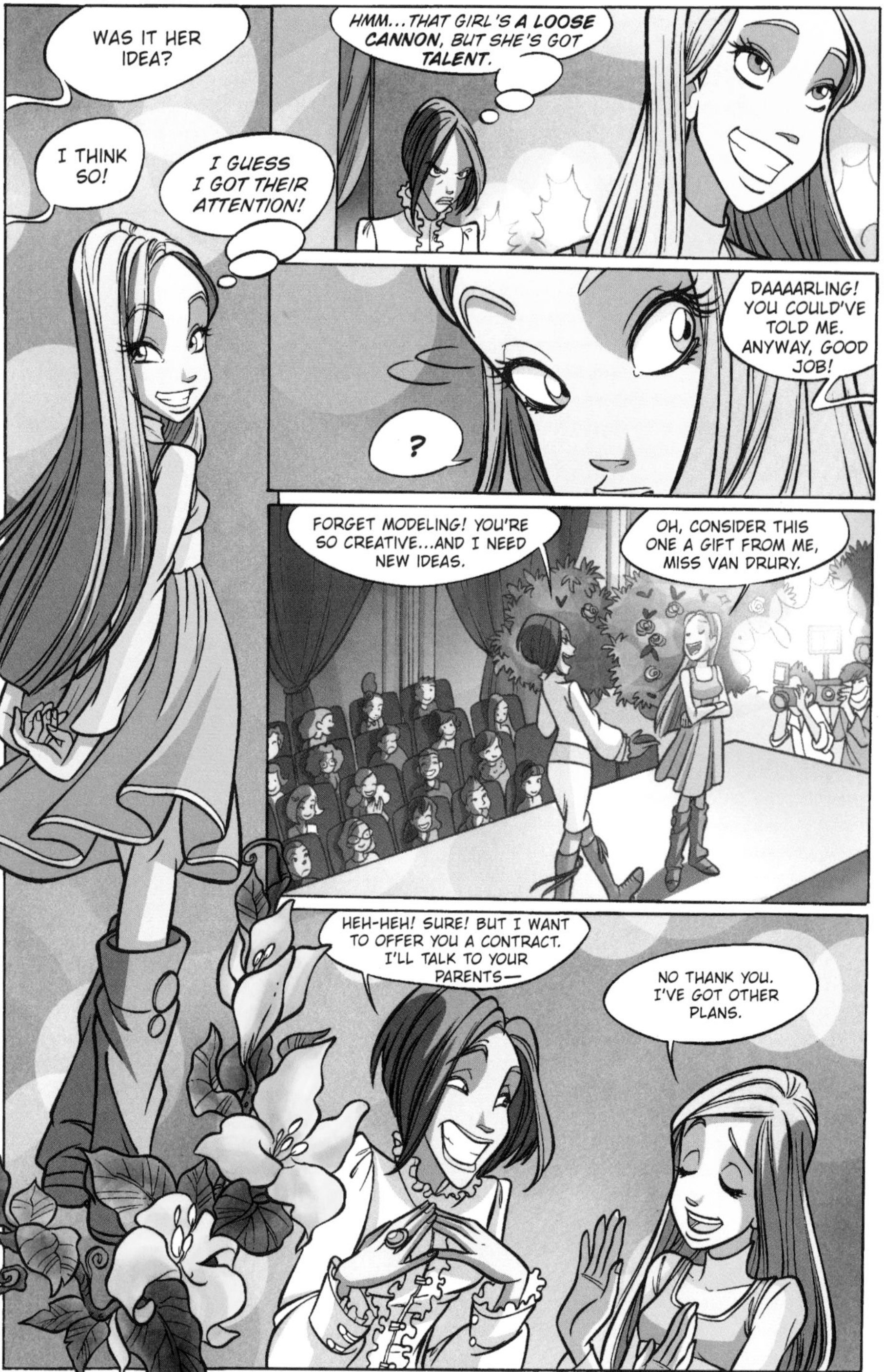
WAS IT HER IDEA?
I THINK SO!
I GUESS I GOT THEIR ATTENTION!
HMM...THAT GIRL'S A LOOSE CANNON, BUT SHE'S GOT TALENT.
DAAAARLING! YOU COULD'VE TOLD ME. ANYWAY, GOOD JOB!
?
FORGET MODELING! YOU'RE SO CREATIVE...AND I NEED NEW IDEAS.
OH, CONSIDER THIS ONE A GIFT FROM ME, MISS VAN DRURY.
HEH-HEH! SURE! BUT I WANT TO OFFER YOU A CONTRACT. I'LL TALK TO YOUR PARENTS—
NO THANK YOU. I'VE GOT OTHER PLANS.

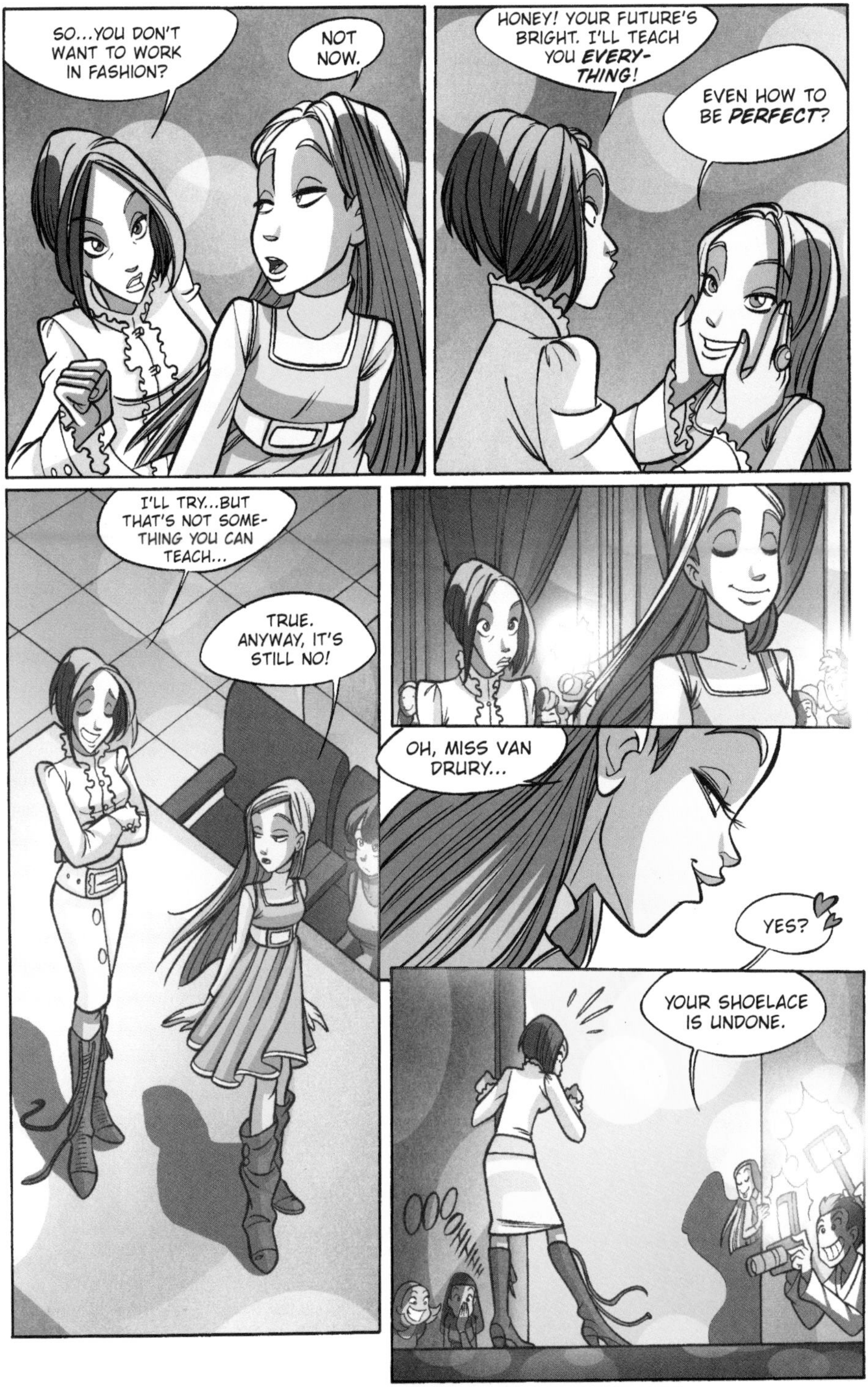
SO...YOU DON'T WANT TO WORK IN FASHION?
NOT NOW.
HONEY! YOUR FUTURE'S BRIGHT. I'LL TEACH YOU EVERYTHING!
EVEN HOW TO BE PERFECT?
I'LL TRY...BUT THAT'S NOT SOMETHING YOU CAN TEACH...
TRUE. ANYWAY, IT'S STILL NO!
OH, MISS VAN DRURY...
YES?
YOUR SHOELACE IS UNDONE.
OOOOHHHH

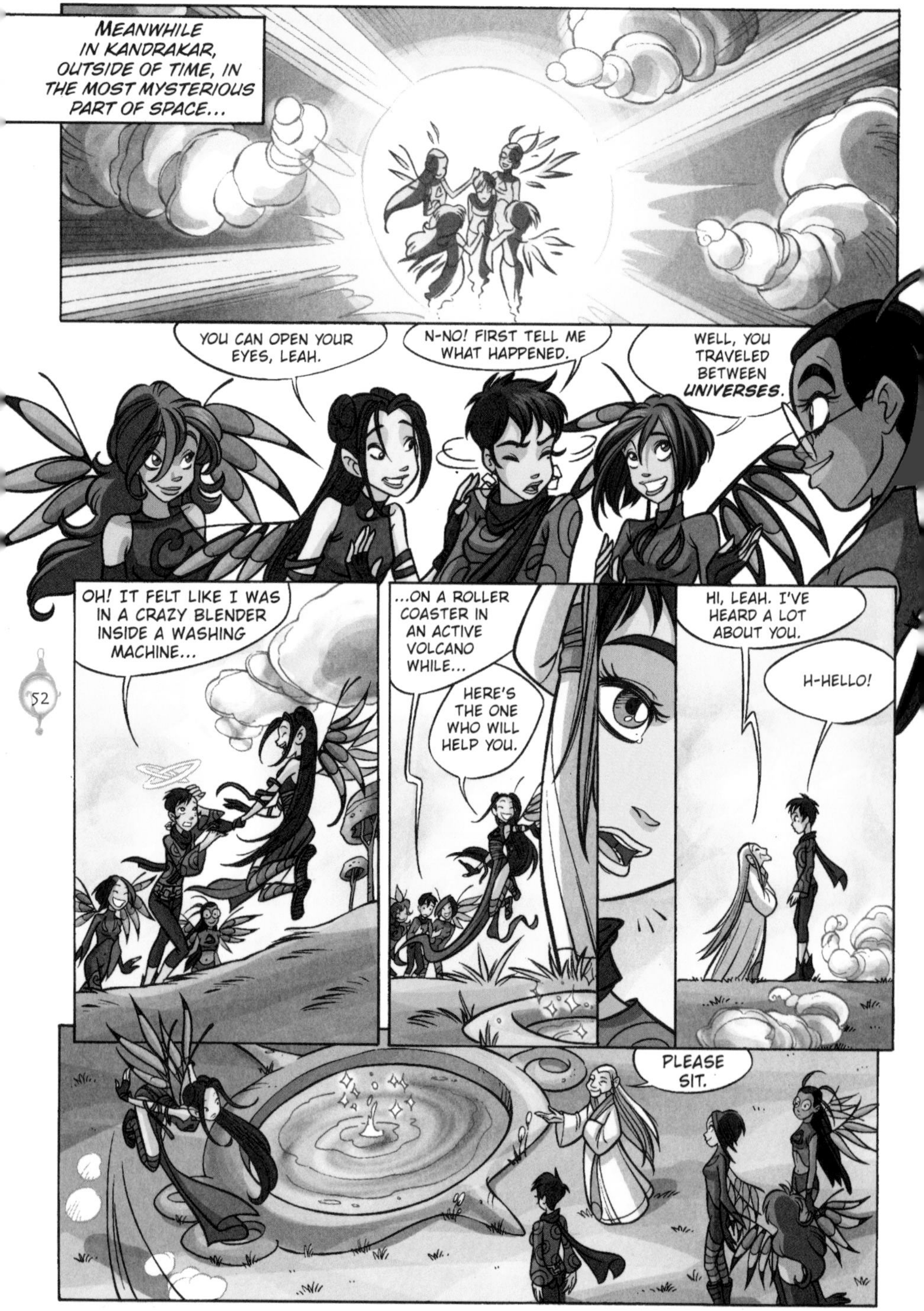
MEANWHILE IN KANDRAKAR, OUTSIDE OF TIME, IN THE MOST MYSTERIOUS PART OF SPACE...
YOU CAN OPEN YOUR EYES, LEAH.
N-NO! FIRST TELL ME WHAT HAPPENED.
WELL, YOU TRAVELED BETWEEN UNIVERSES.
OH! IT FELT LIKE I WAS IN A CRAZY BLENDER INSIDE A WASHING MACHINE...
...ON A ROLLER COASTER IN AN ACTIVE VOLCANO WHILE...
HERE'S THE ONE WHO WILL HELP YOU.
HI, LEAH. I'VE HEARD A LOT ABOUT YOU.
H-HELLO!
PLEASE SIT.

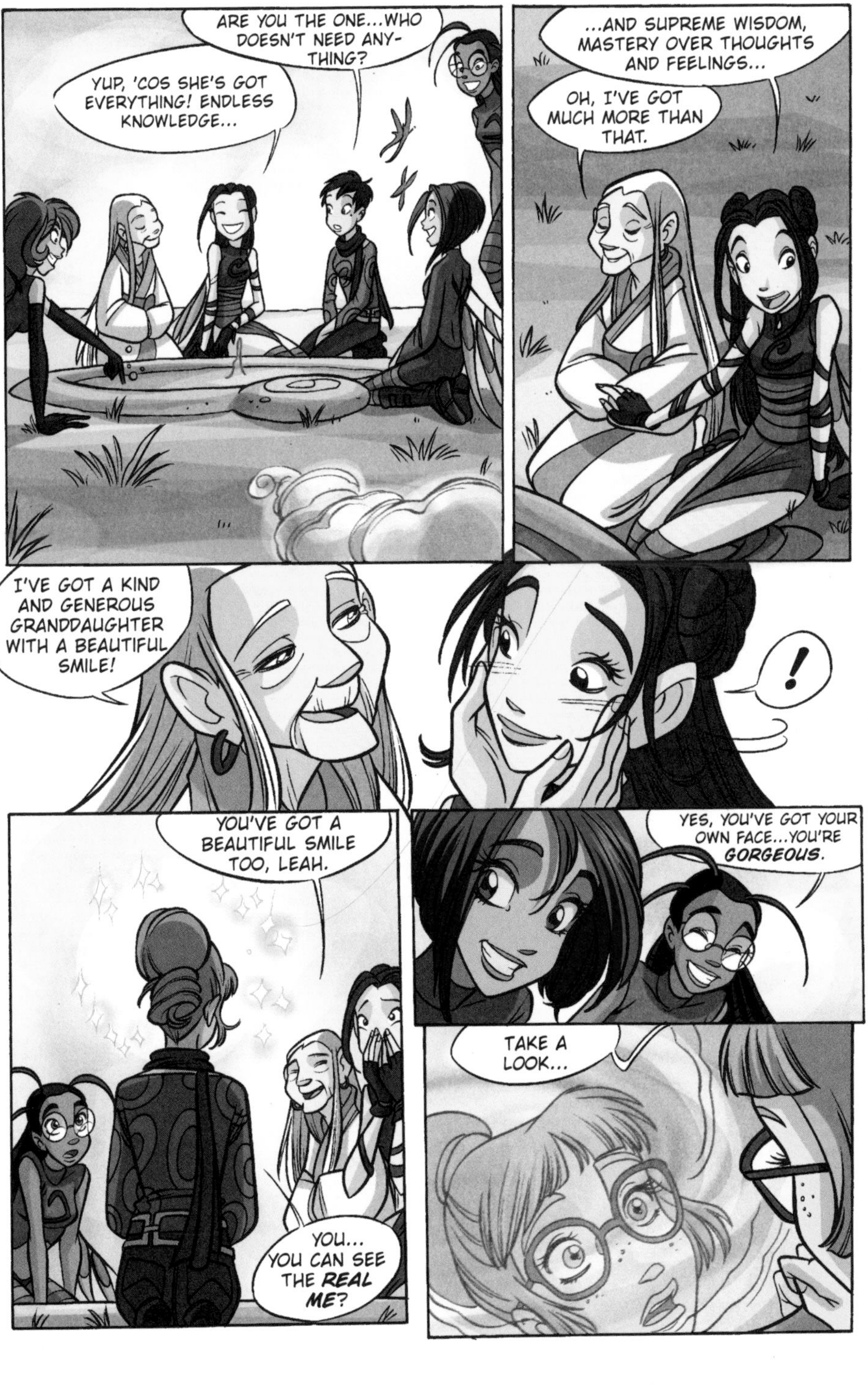
ARE YOU THE ONE...WHO DOESN'T NEED ANYTHING?
YUP, 'COS SHE'S GOT EVERYTHING! ENDLESS KNOWLEDGE...
...AND SUPREME WISDOM, MASTERY OVER THOUGHTS AND FEELINGS...
OH, I'VE GOT MUCH MORE THAN THAT.
I'VE GOT A KIND AND GENEROUS GRANDDAUGHTER WITH A BEAUTIFUL SMILE!
!
YOU'VE GOT A BEAUTIFUL SMILE TOO, LEAH.
YOU... YOU CAN SEE THE REAL ME?
YES, YOU'VE GOT YOUR OWN FACE...YOU'RE GORGEOUS.
TAKE A LOOK...

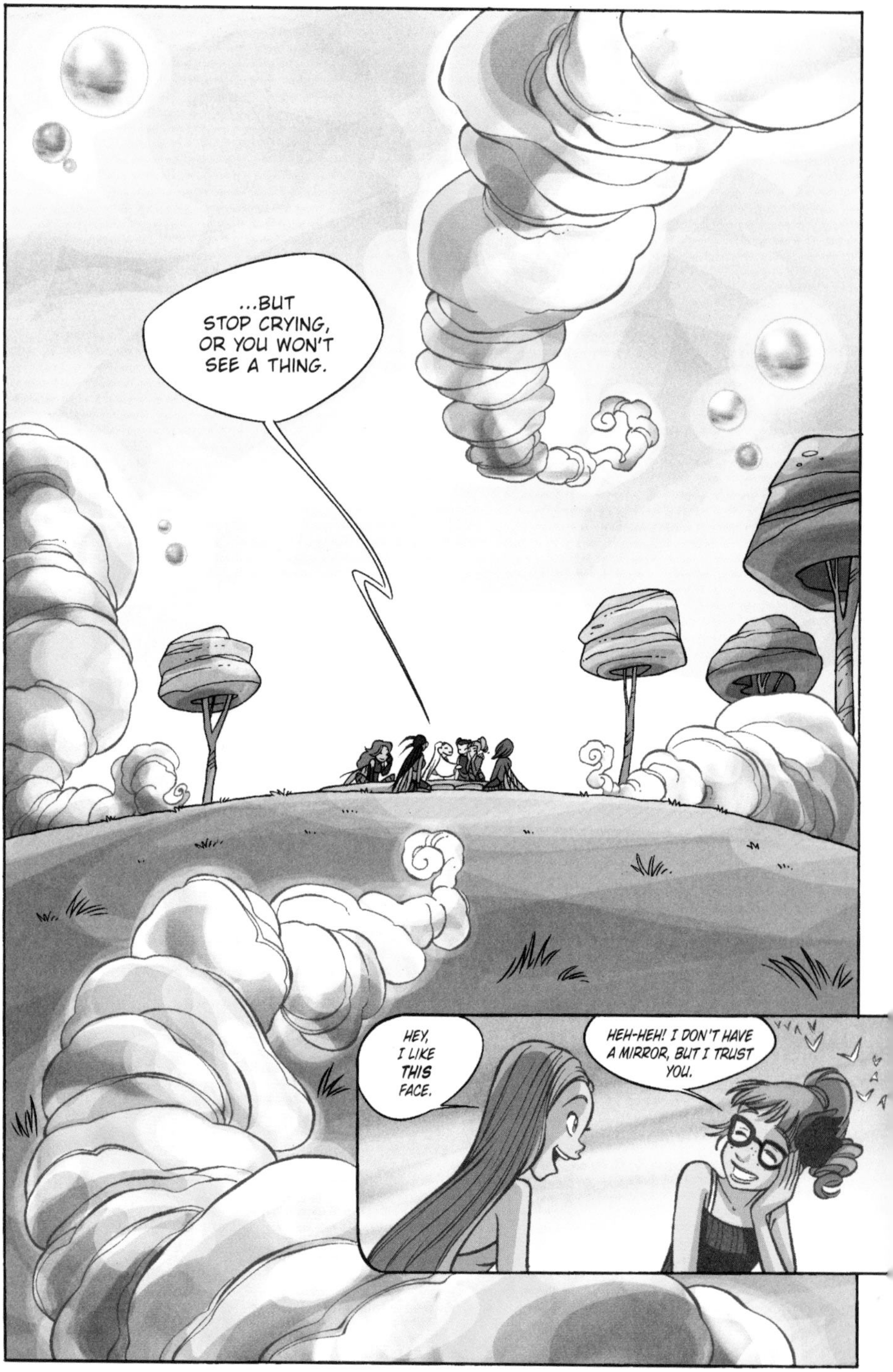
...BUT STOP CRYING, OR YOU WON'T SEE A THING.
HEY, I LIKE THIS FACE.
HEH-HEH! I DON'T HAVE A MIRROR, BUT I TRUST YOU.

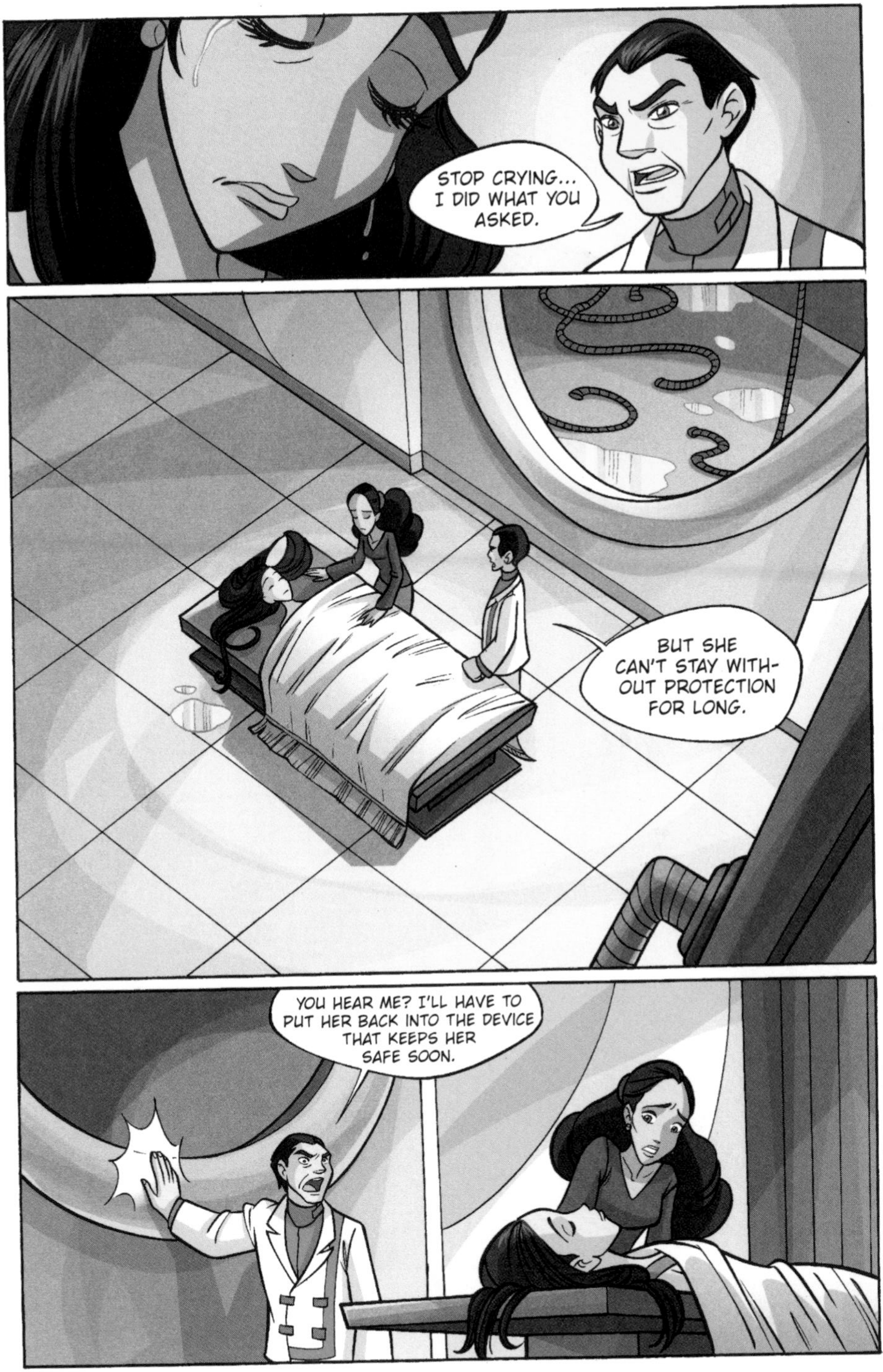
STOP CRYING... I DID WHAT YOU ASKED.
BUT SHE CAN'T STAY WITH-OUT PROTECTION FOR LONG.
YOU HEAR ME? I'LL HAVE TO PUT HER BACK INTO THE DEVICE THAT KEEPS HER SAFE SOON.

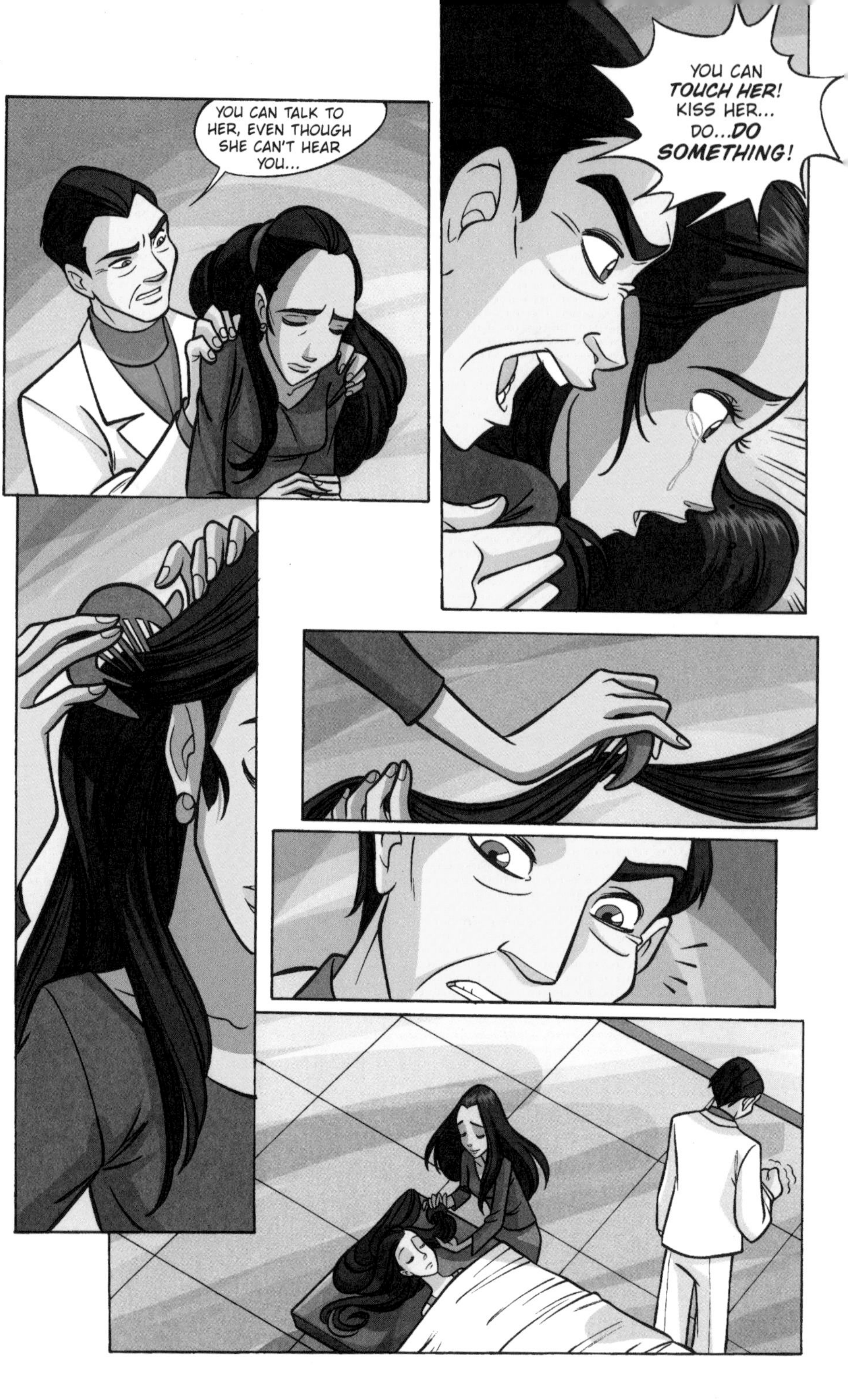
YOU CAN TALK TO HER, EVEN THOUGH SHE CAN'T HEAR YOU...
YOU CAN TOUCH HER! KISS HER... DO...DO SOMETHING!

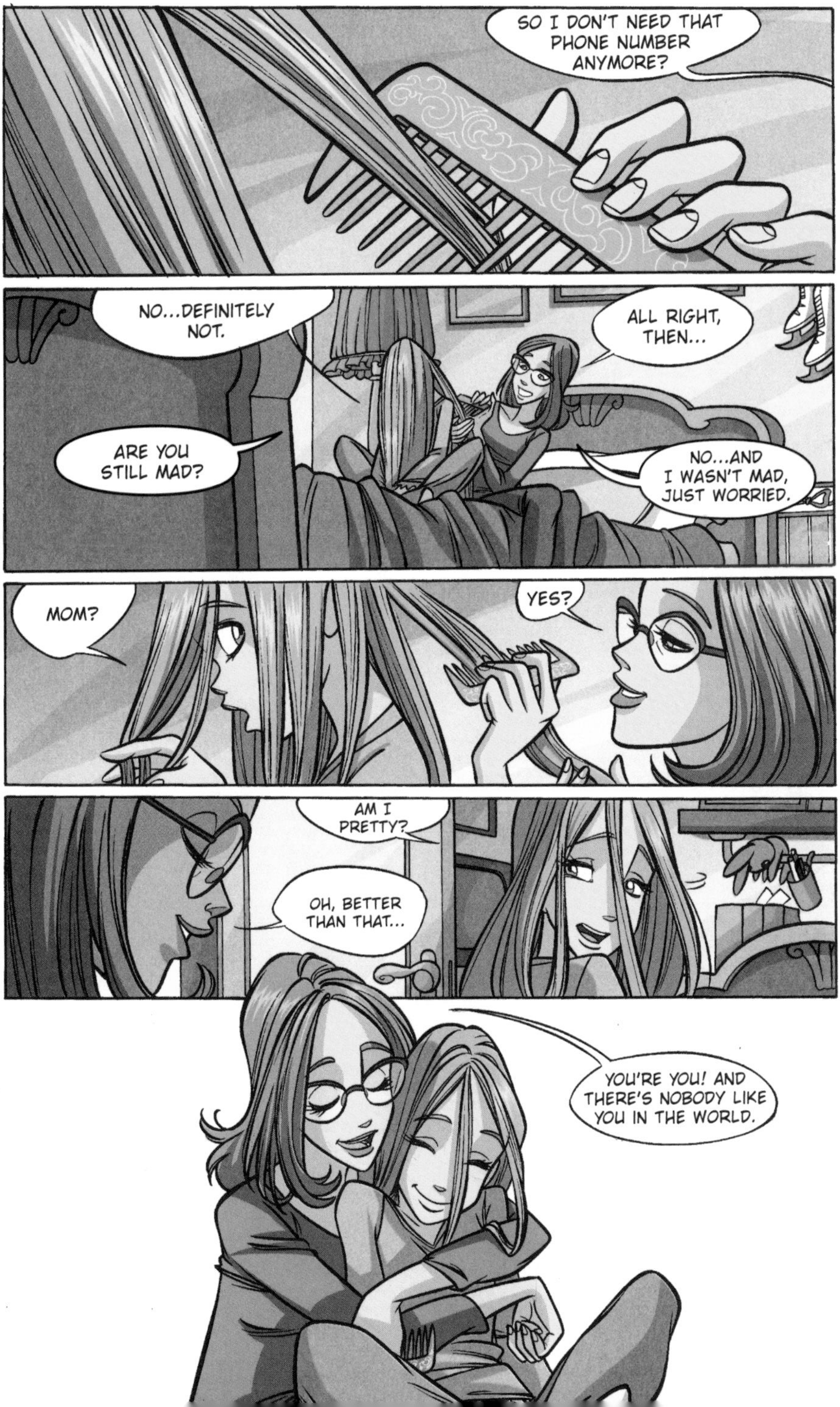
SO I DON'T NEED THAT PHONE NUMBER ANYMORE?
NO...DEFINITELY NOT.
ALL RIGHT, THEN...
ARE YOU STILL MAD?
NO...AND I WASN'T MAD, JUST WORRIED.
MOM?
YES?
AM I PRETTY?
OH, BETTER THAN THAT...
YOU'RE YOU! AND THERE'S NOBODY LIKE YOU IN THE WORLD.

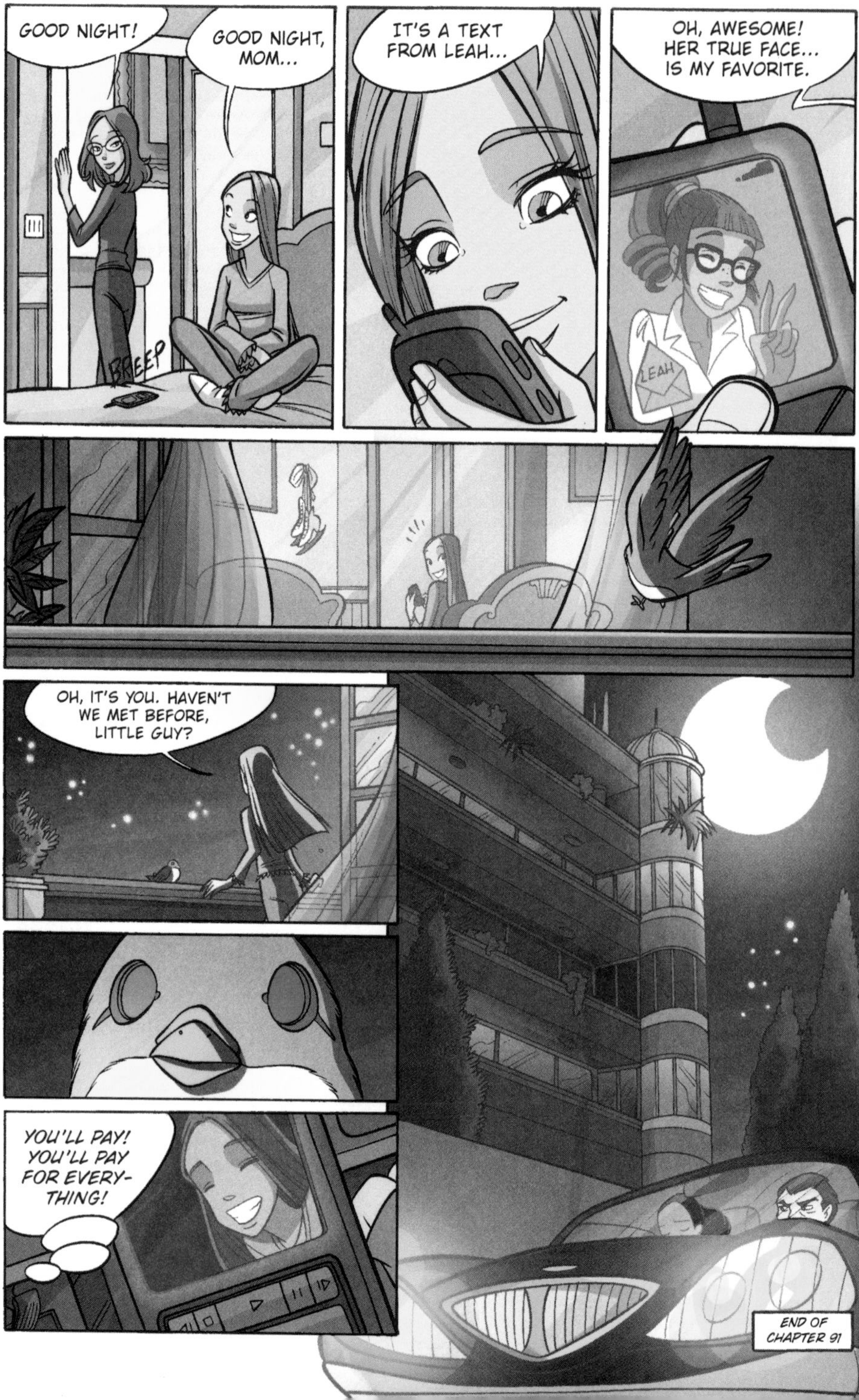
GOOD NIGHT!
GOOD NIGHT, MOM...
BREEP
IT'S A TEXT FROM LEAH...
OH, AWESOME! HER TRUE FACE... IS MY FAVORITE.
LEAH
OH, IT'S YOU. HAVEN'T WE MET BEFORE, LITTLE GUY?
YOU'LL PAY! YOU'LL PAY FOR EVERY-THING!
END OF CHAPTER 91

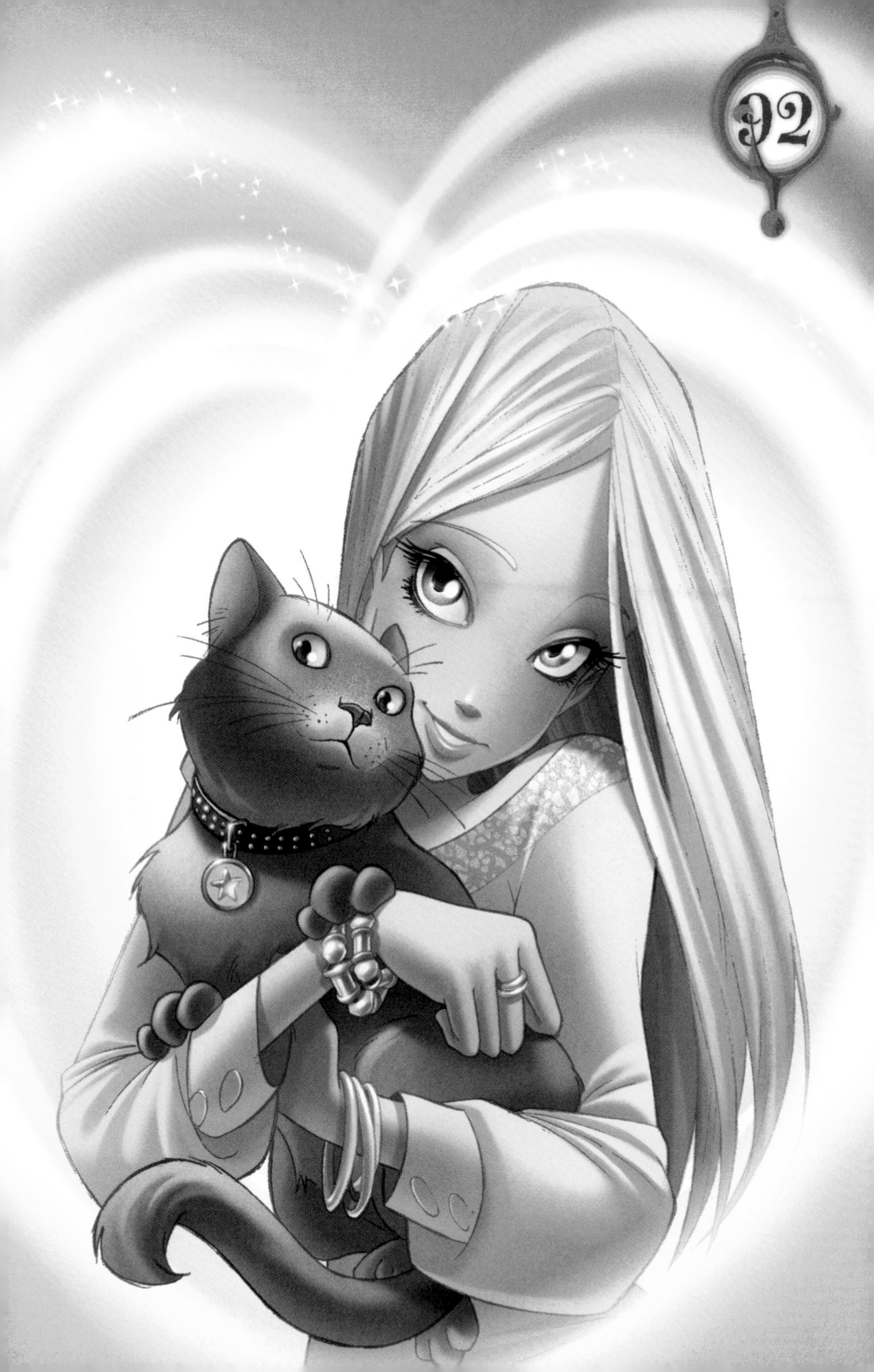
02

No Longer Alone

"Sometimes you feel lonely. But there are hundreds of hearts beating all around us!"

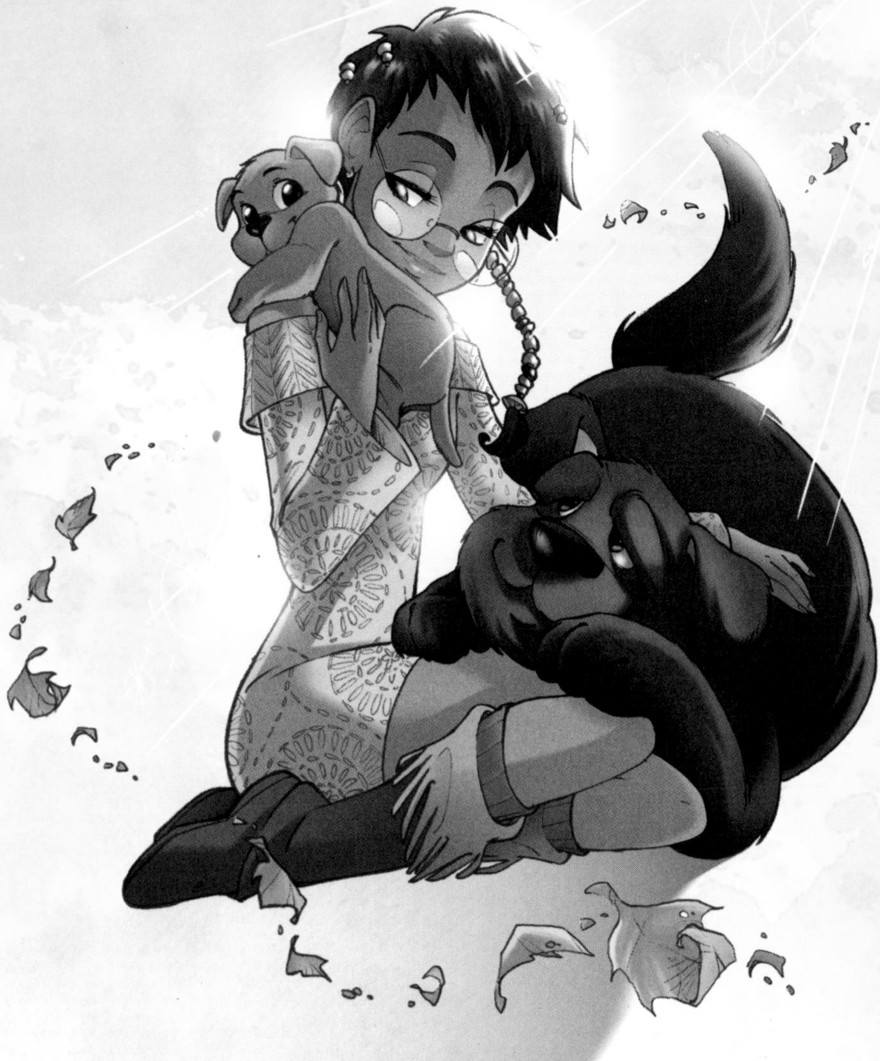

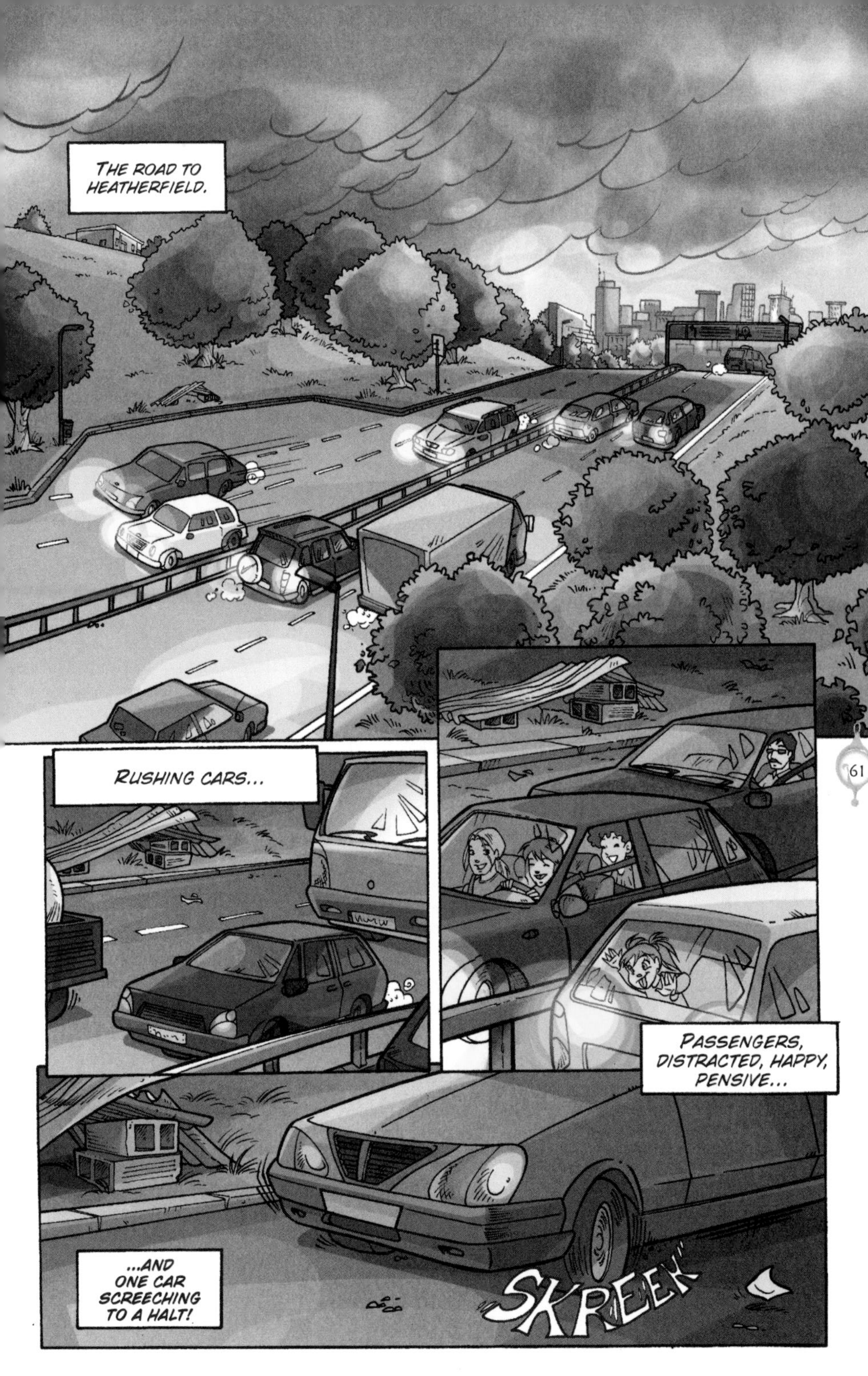

THE ROAD TO HEATHERFIELD.
RUSHING CARS...
PASSENGERS, DISTRACTED, HAPPY, PENSIVE...
...AND ONE CAR SCREECHING TO A HALT!
SKREEEK

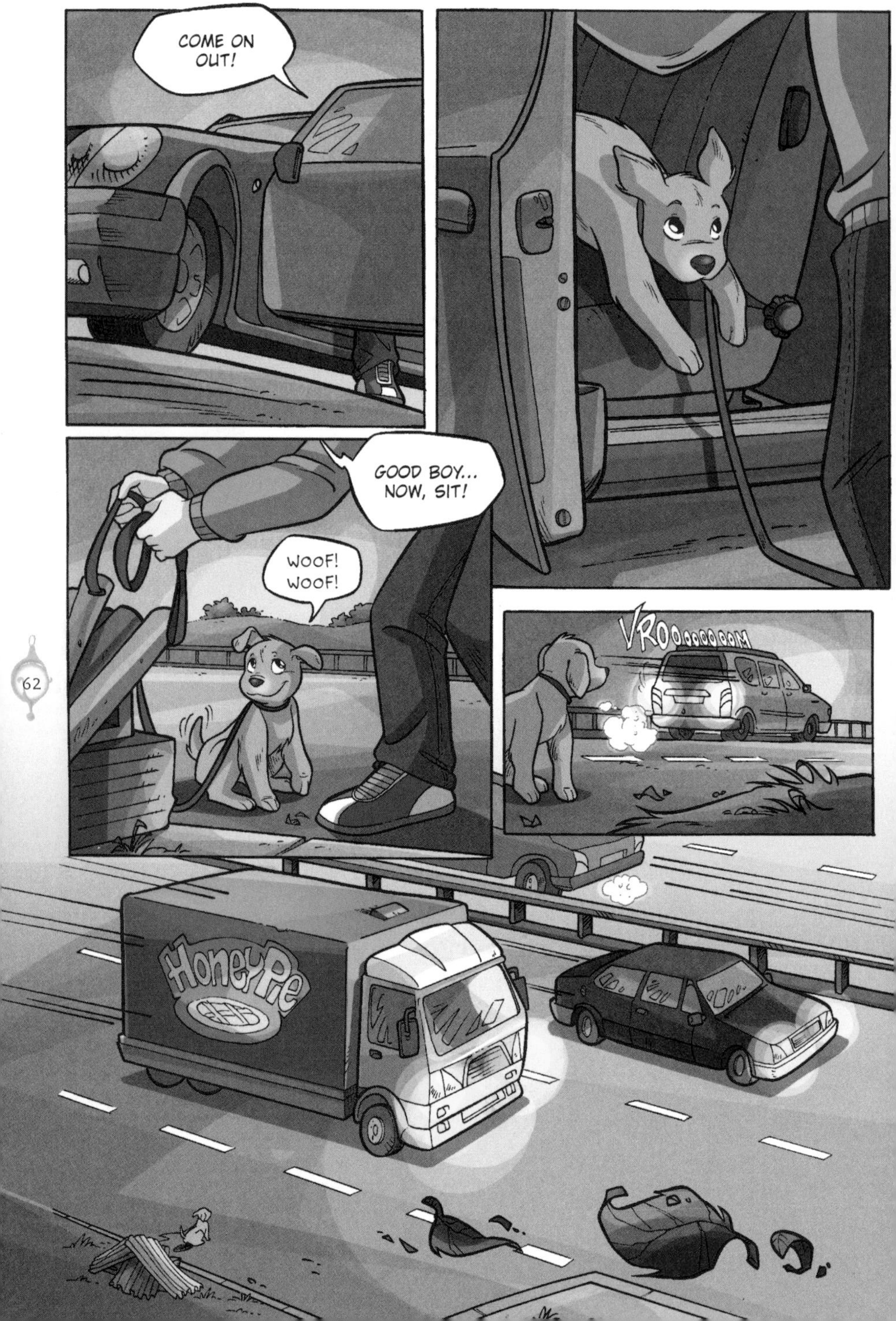
COME ON OUT!
GOOD BOY... NOW, SIT!
WOOF! WOOF!
VROOOOOOOOOM
HONEY PIE

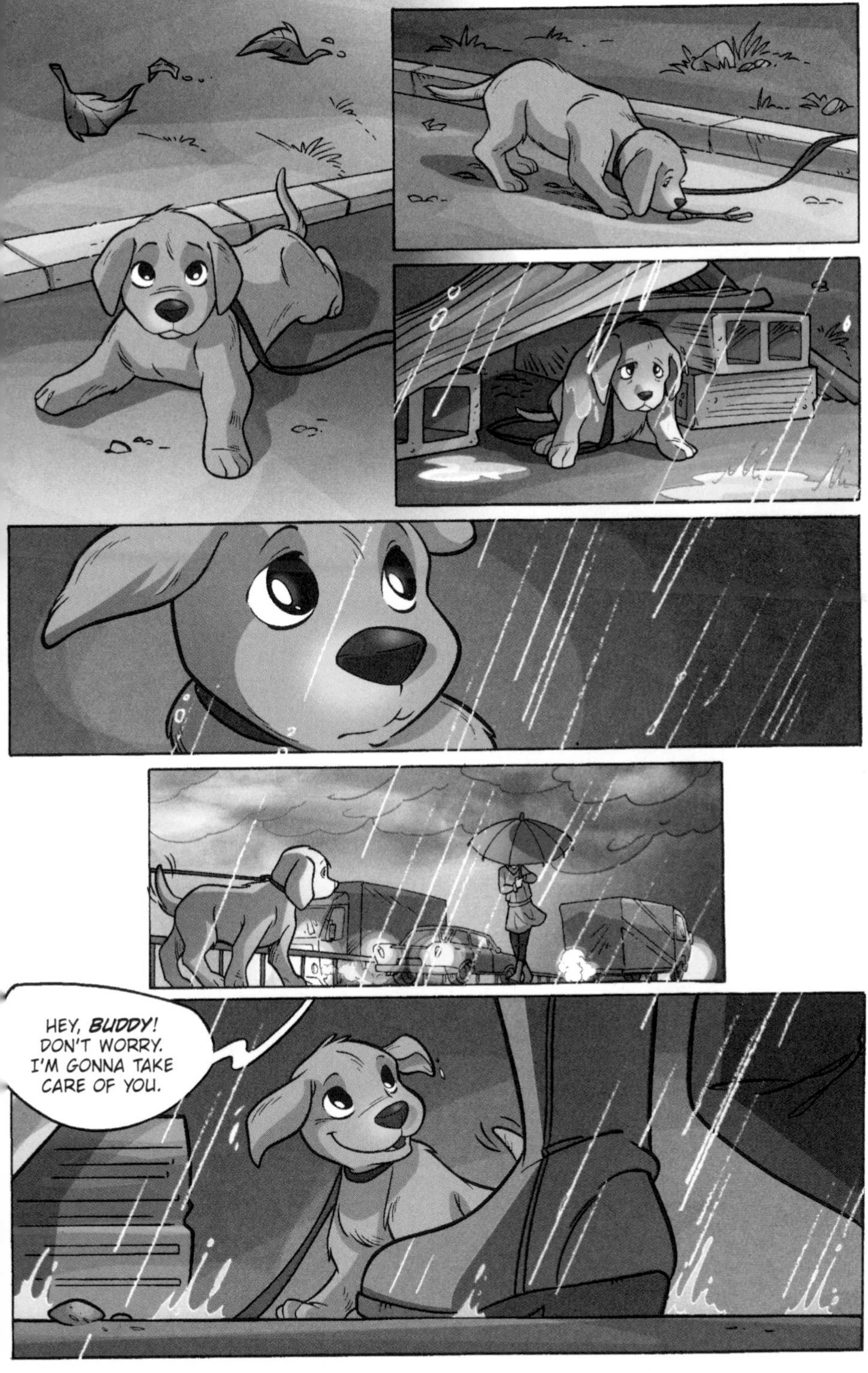
HEY, **BUDDY**! DON'T WORRY. I'M GONNA TAKE CARE OF YOU.

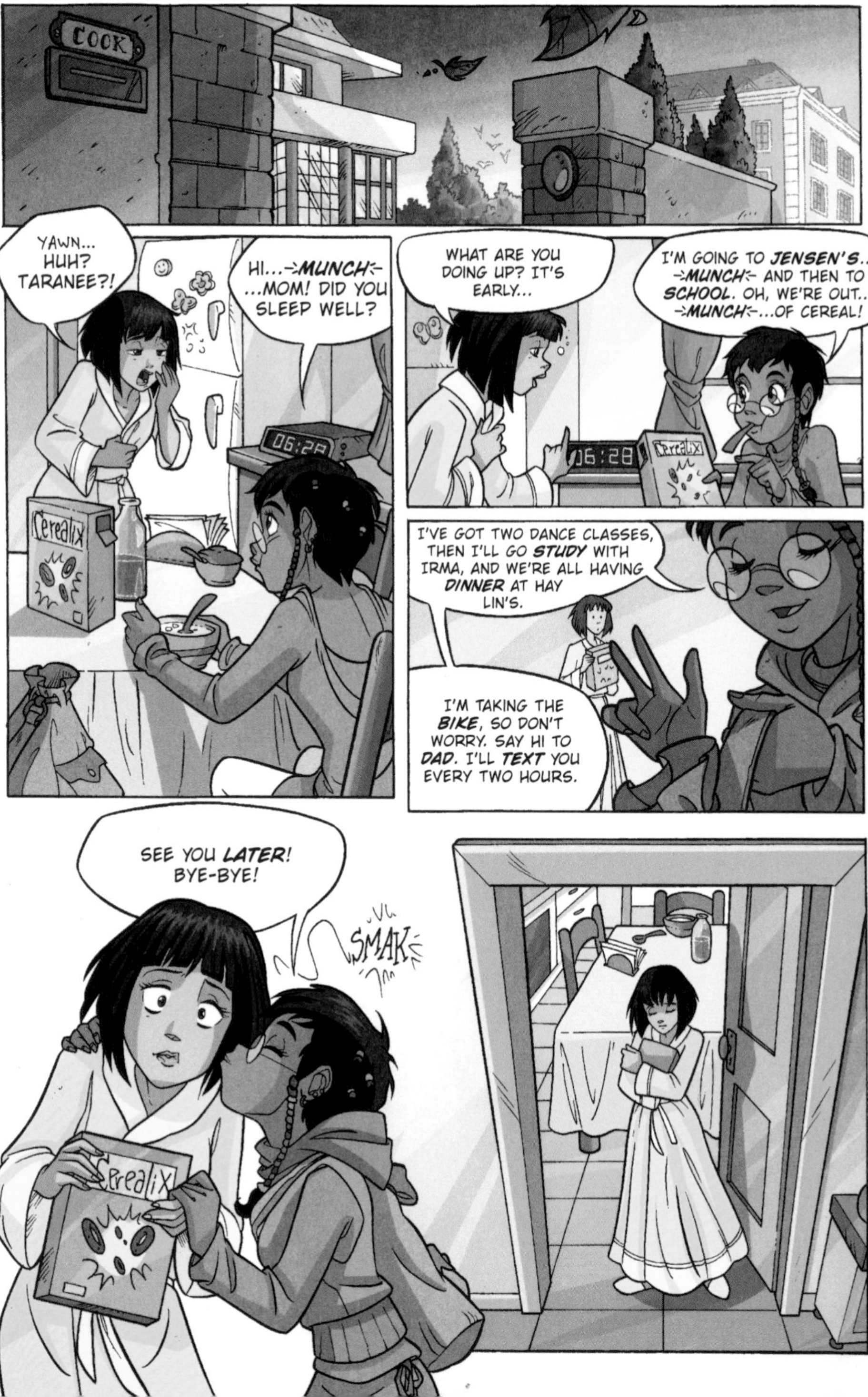
COOK
YAWN... HUH? TARANEE?!
HI... MUNCH ...MOM! DID YOU SLEEP WELL?
06:28
Cerealix
WHAT ARE YOU DOING UP? IT'S EARLY...
I'M GOING TO JENSEN'S.. MUNCH AND THEN TO SCHOOL. OH, WE'RE OUT... MUNCH ...OF CEREAL!
06:28
Cerealix
I'VE GOT TWO DANCE CLASSES, THEN I'LL GO STUDY WITH IRMA, AND WE'RE ALL HAVING DINNER AT HAY LIN'S.
I'M TAKING THE BIKE, SO DON'T WORRY. SAY HI TO DAD. I'LL TEXT YOU EVERY TWO HOURS.
SEE YOU LATER! BYE-BYE!
SMAK
Cerealix

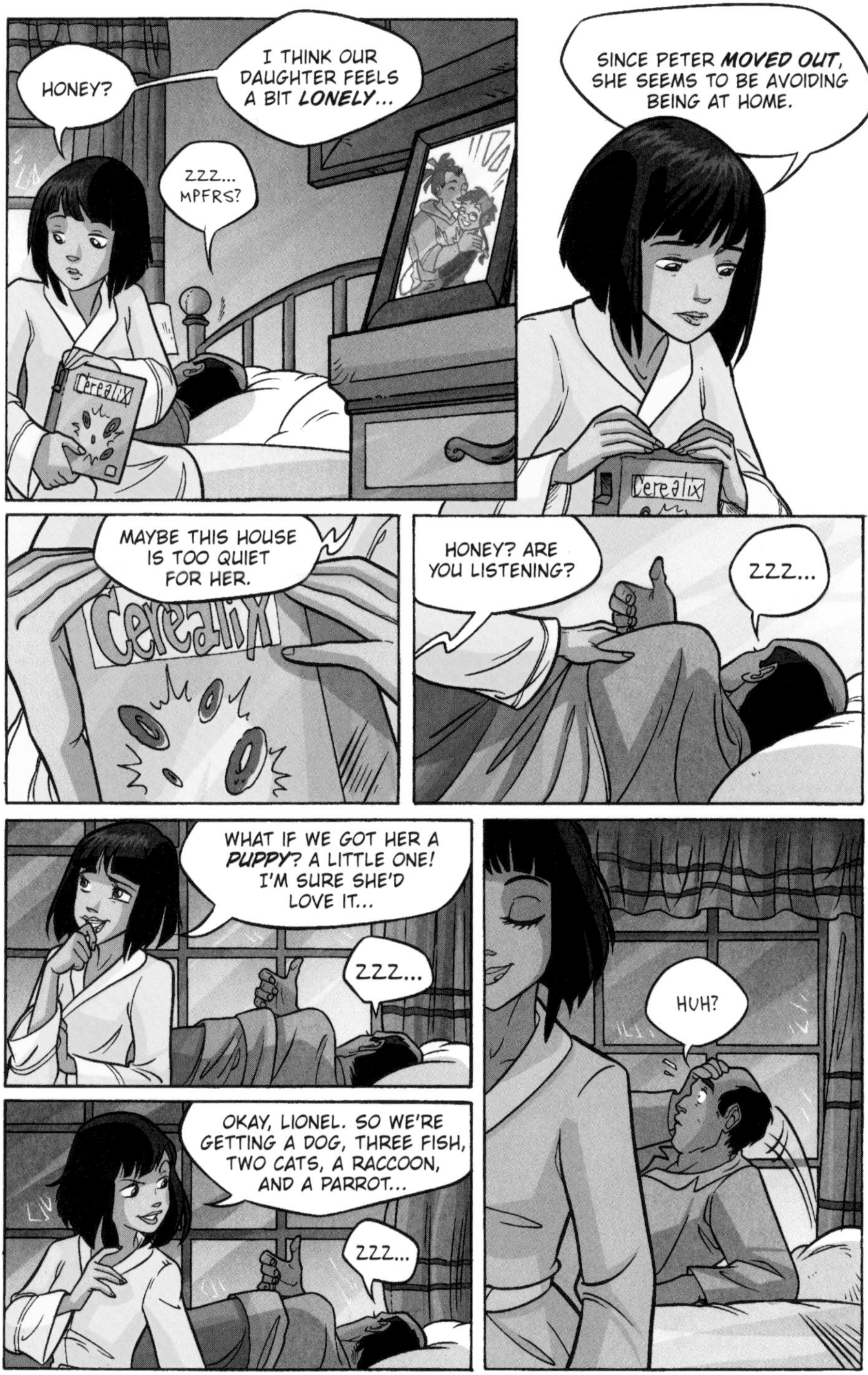
HONEY?
I THINK OUR DAUGHTER FEELS A BIT *LONELY*...
ZZZ... MPFRS?
SINCE PETER *MOVED OUT*, SHE SEEMS TO BE AVOIDING BEING AT HOME.
MAYBE THIS HOUSE IS TOO QUIET FOR HER.
HONEY? ARE YOU LISTENING?
ZZZ...
WHAT IF WE GOT HER A *PUPPY*? A LITTLE ONE! I'M SURE SHE'D LOVE IT...
ZZZ...
OKAY, LIONEL. SO WE'RE GETTING A DOG, THREE FISH, TWO CATS, A RACCOON, AND A PARROT...
ZZZ...
HUH?

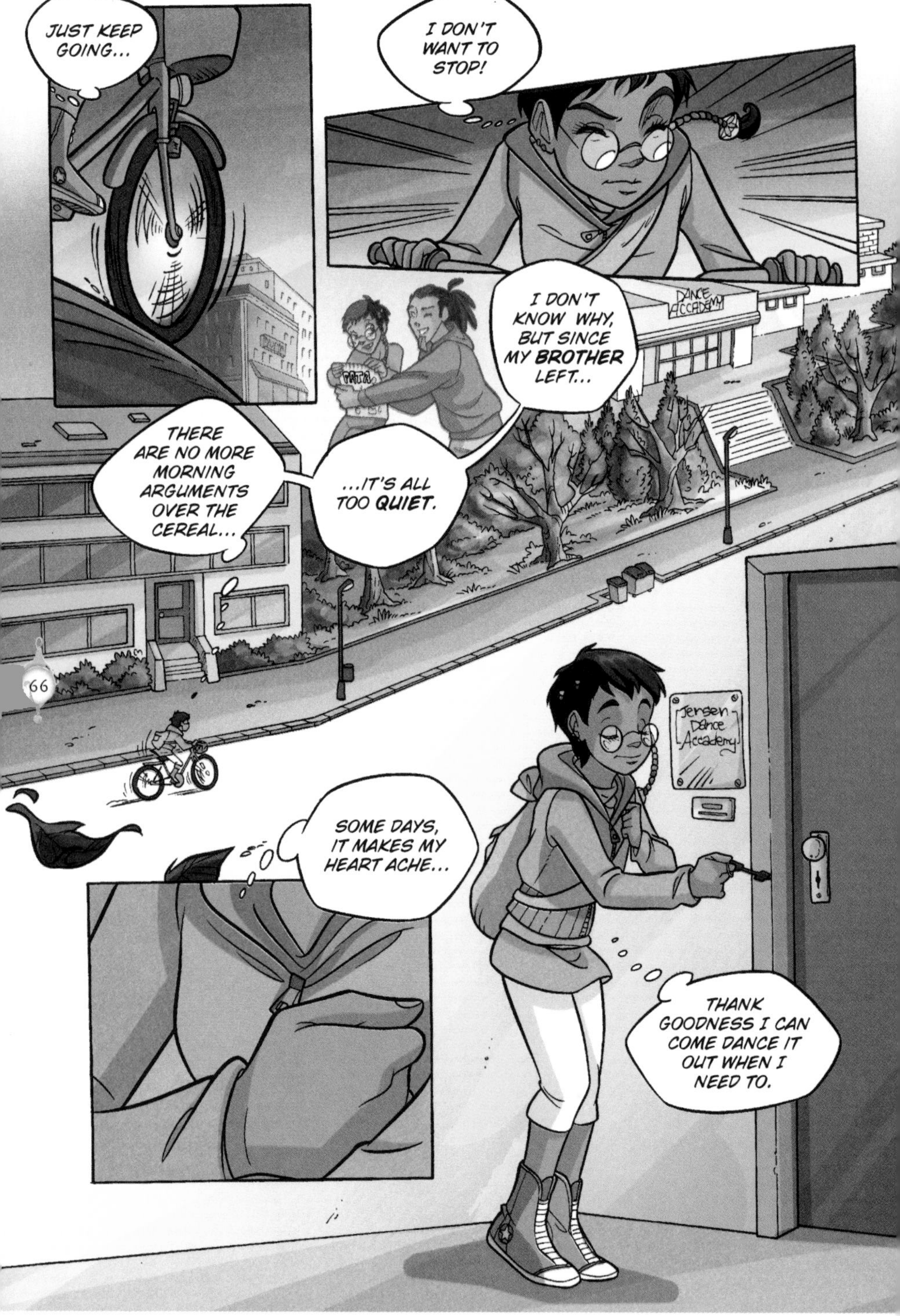
JUST KEEP GOING...
I DON'T WANT TO STOP!
I DON'T KNOW WHY, BUT SINCE MY BROTHER LEFT...
...IT'S ALL TOO QUIET.
THERE ARE NO MORE MORNING ARGUMENTS OVER THE CEREAL...
DANCE ACCADEMY
Jensen Dance Accademy
SOME DAYS, IT MAKES MY HEART ACHE...
THANK GOODNESS I CAN COME DANCE IT OUT WHEN I NEED TO.

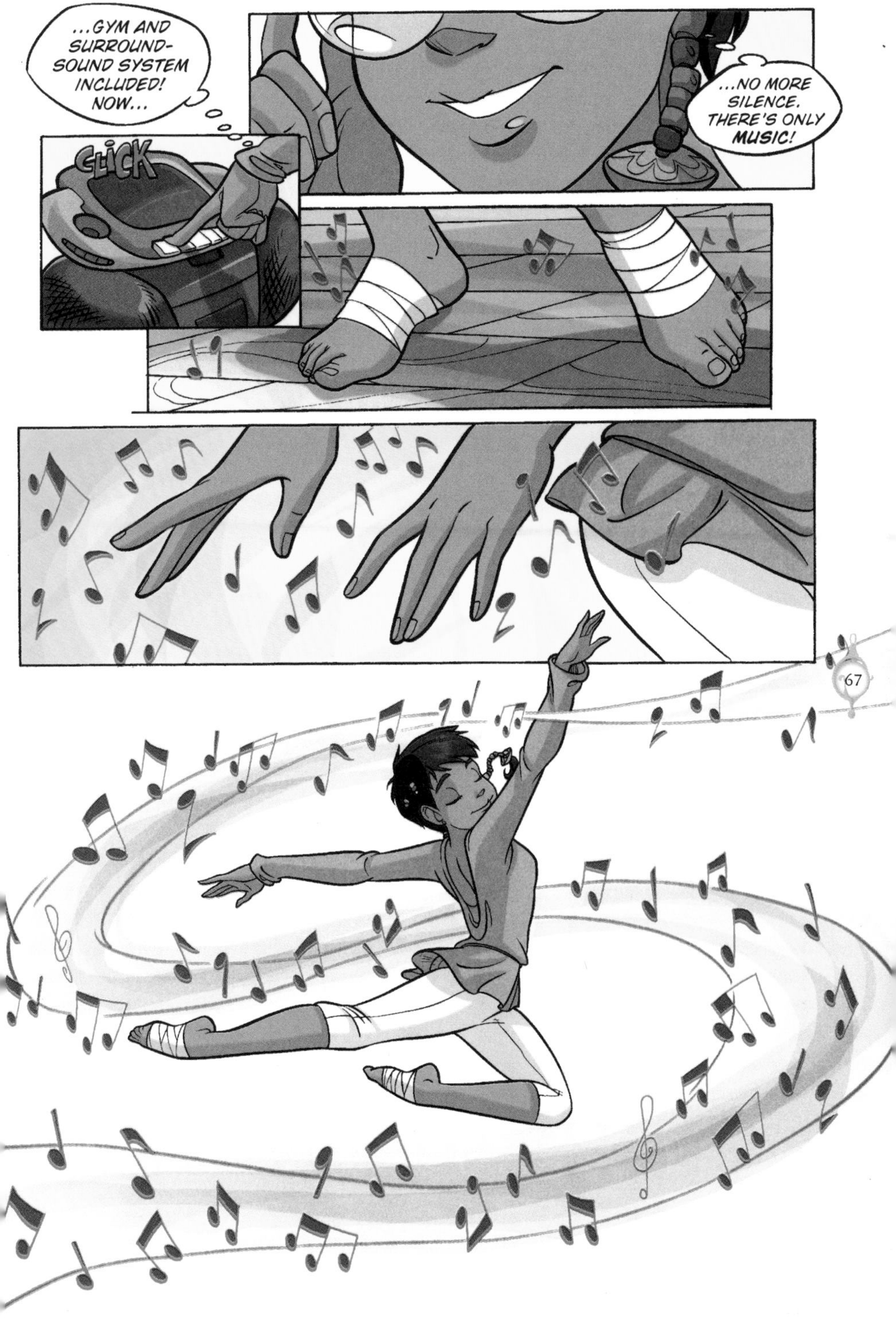
...GYM AND SURROUND-SOUND SYSTEM INCLUDED! NOW...
CLICK
...NO MORE SILENCE. THERE'S ONLY MUSIC!

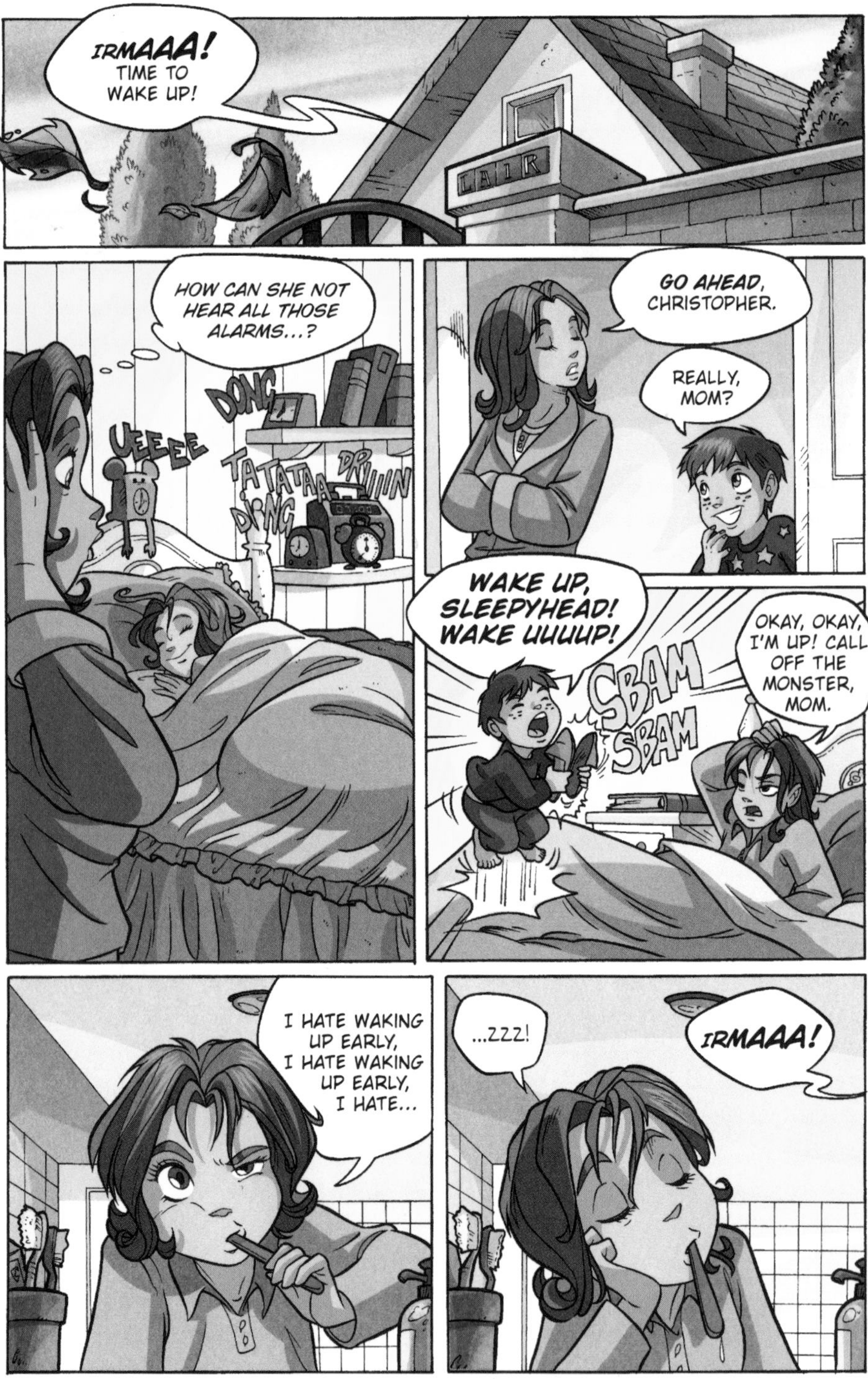
IRMAAA! TIME TO WAKE UP!
LAIR
HOW CAN SHE NOT HEAR ALL THOSE ALARMS...?
DONG
UEEEE
TATATAA
DRIIIIN
DING
GO AHEAD, CHRISTOPHER.
REALLY, MOM?
WAKE UP, SLEEPYHEAD! WAKE UUUUP!
SBAM
SBAM
OKAY, OKAY, I'M UP! CALL OFF THE MONSTER, MOM.
I HATE WAKING UP EARLY, I HATE WAKING UP EARLY, I HATE...
...ZZZ!
IRMAAA!

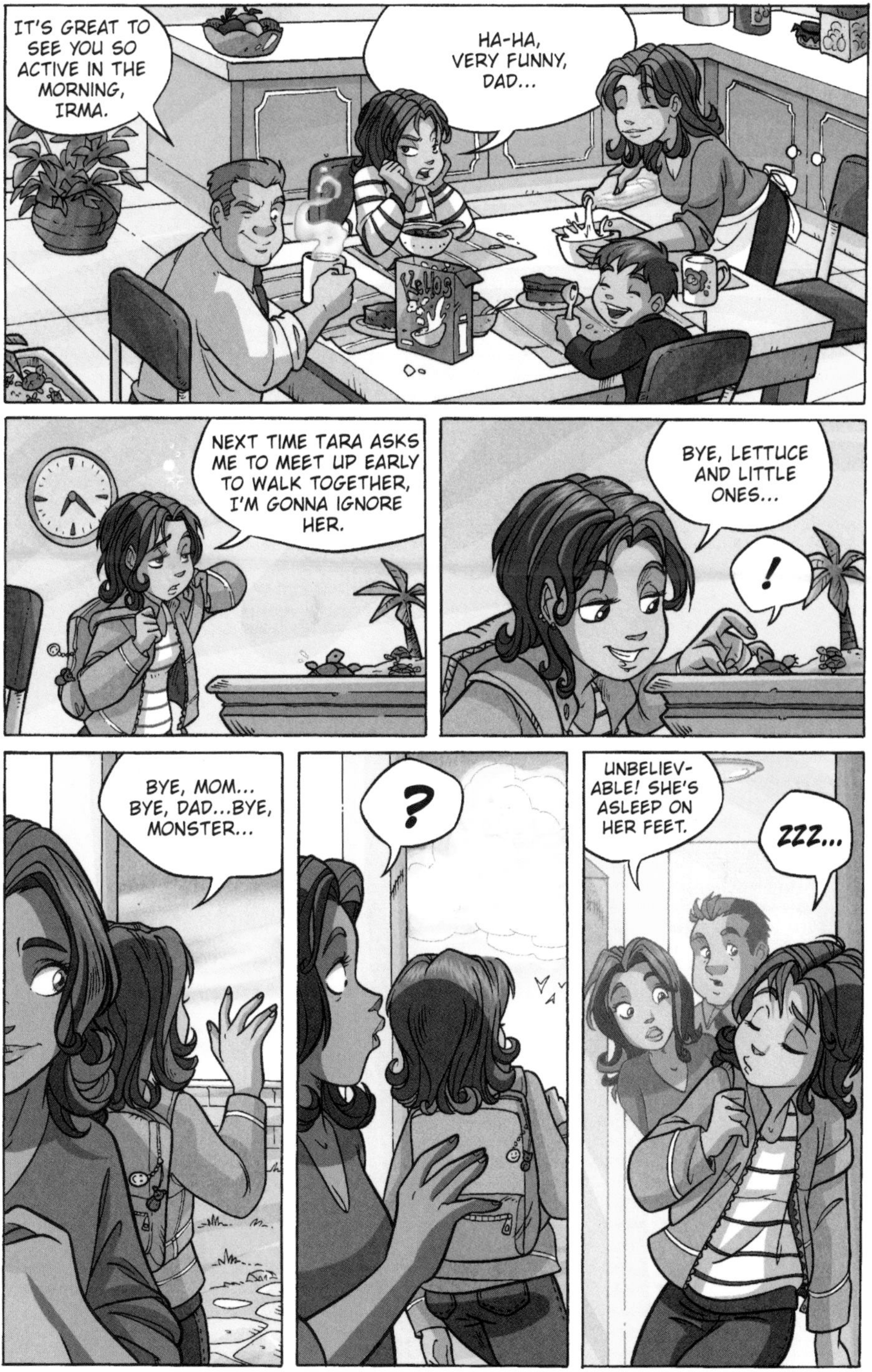
IT'S GREAT TO SEE YOU SO ACTIVE IN THE MORNING, IRMA.
HA-HA, VERY FUNNY, DAD...
NEXT TIME TARA ASKS ME TO MEET UP EARLY TO WALK TOGETHER, I'M GONNA IGNORE HER.
BYE, LETTUCE AND LITTLE ONES...
!
BYE, MOM... BYE, DAD...BYE, MONSTER...
?
UNBELIEV-ABLE! SHE'S ASLEEP ON HER FEET.
ZZZ...

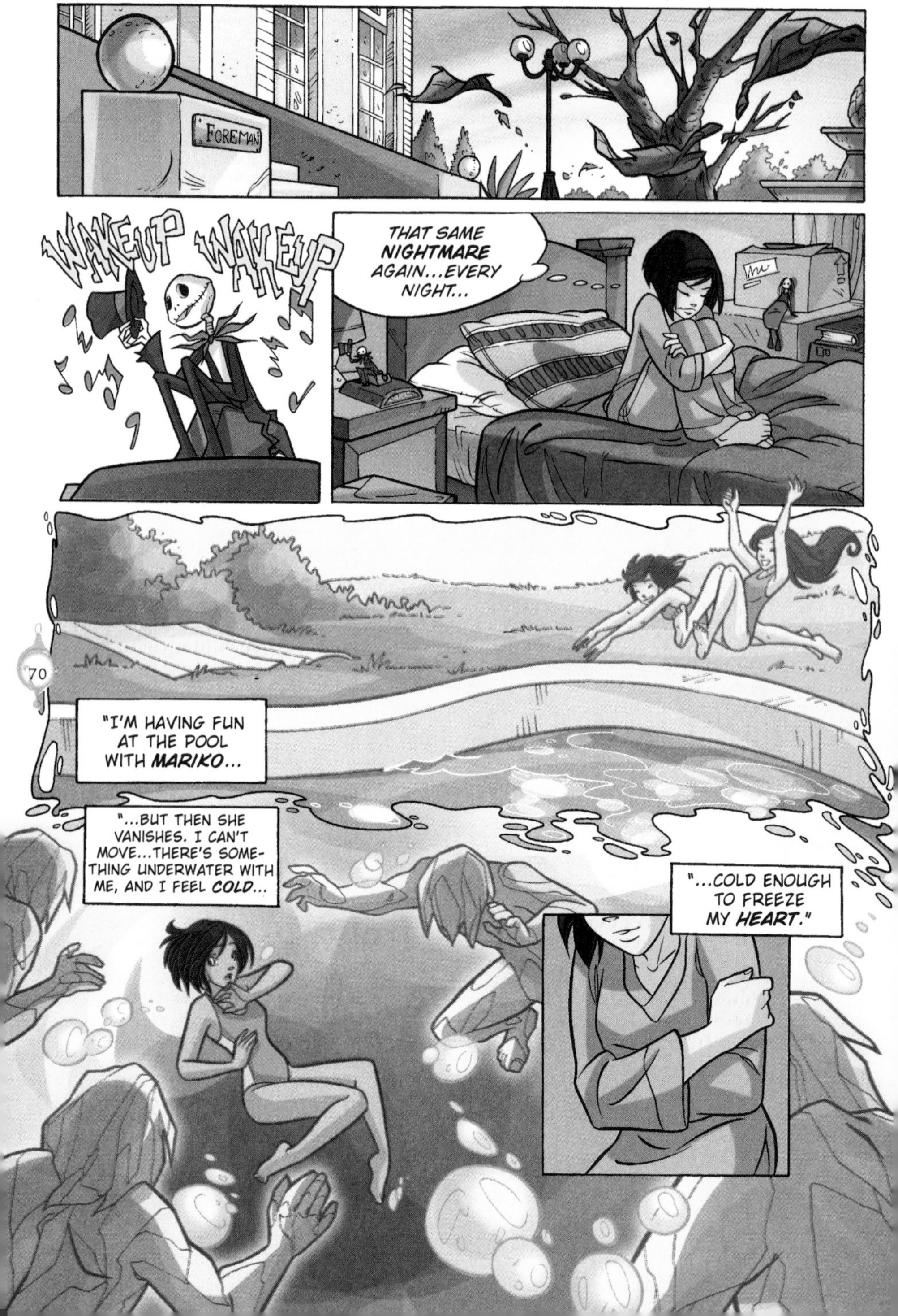
FOREMAN
WAKEUP WAKEUP
THAT SAME NIGHTMARE AGAIN...EVERY NIGHT...
"I'M HAVING FUN AT THE POOL WITH MARIKO...
"...BUT THEN SHE VANISHES. I CAN'T MOVE...THERE'S SOMETHING UNDERWATER WITH ME, AND I FEEL COLD...
"...COLD ENOUGH TO FREEZE MY HEART."

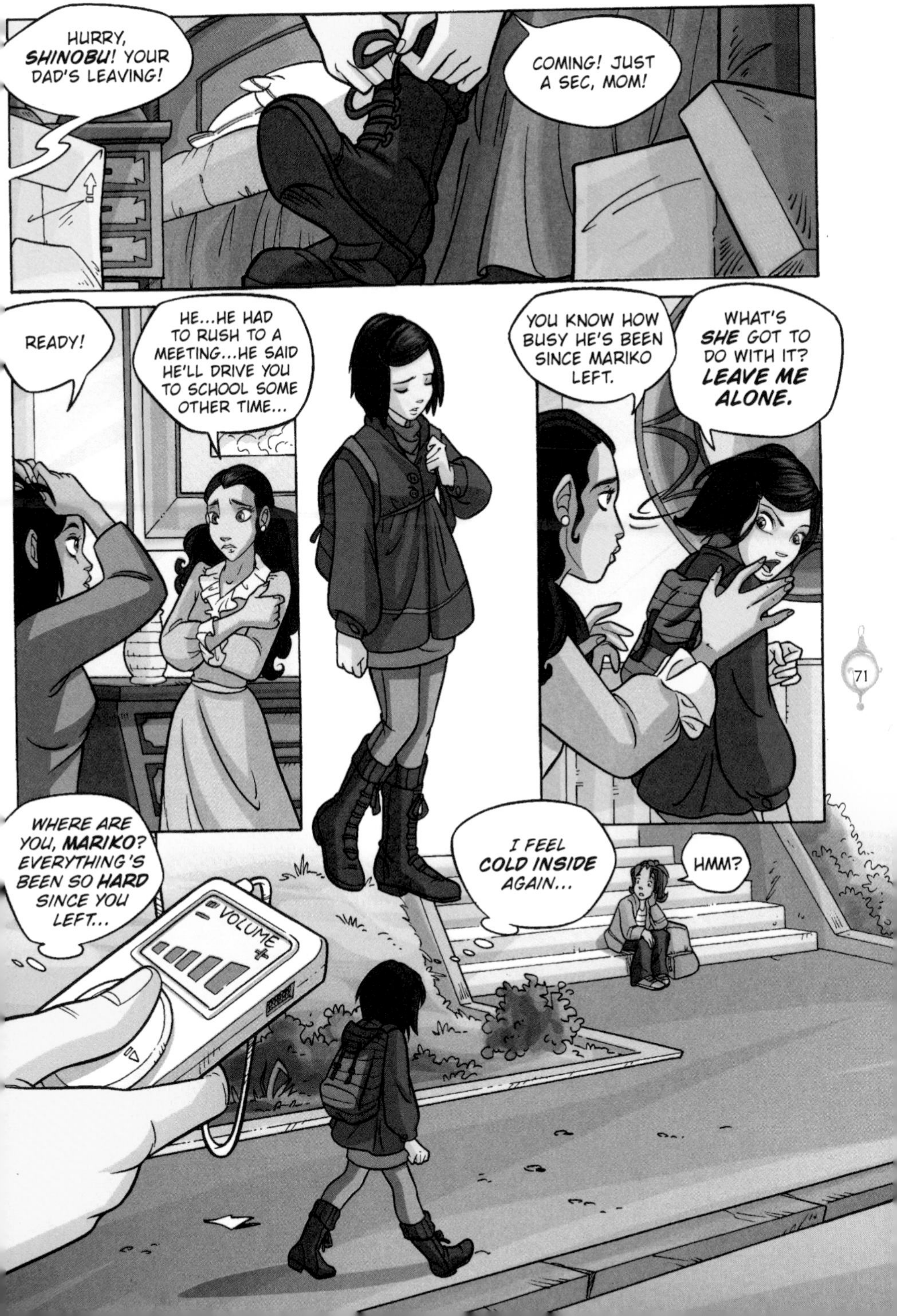
HURRY, SHINOBU! YOUR DAD'S LEAVING!
COMING! JUST A SEC, MOM!
READY!
HE...HE HAD TO RUSH TO A MEETING...HE SAID HE'LL DRIVE YOU TO SCHOOL SOME OTHER TIME...
YOU KNOW HOW BUSY HE'S BEEN SINCE MARIKO LEFT.
WHAT'S SHE GOT TO DO WITH IT? LEAVE ME ALONE.
WHERE ARE YOU, MARIKO? EVERYTHING'S BEEN SO HARD SINCE YOU LEFT...
VOLUME
I FEEL COLD INSIDE AGAIN...
HMM?

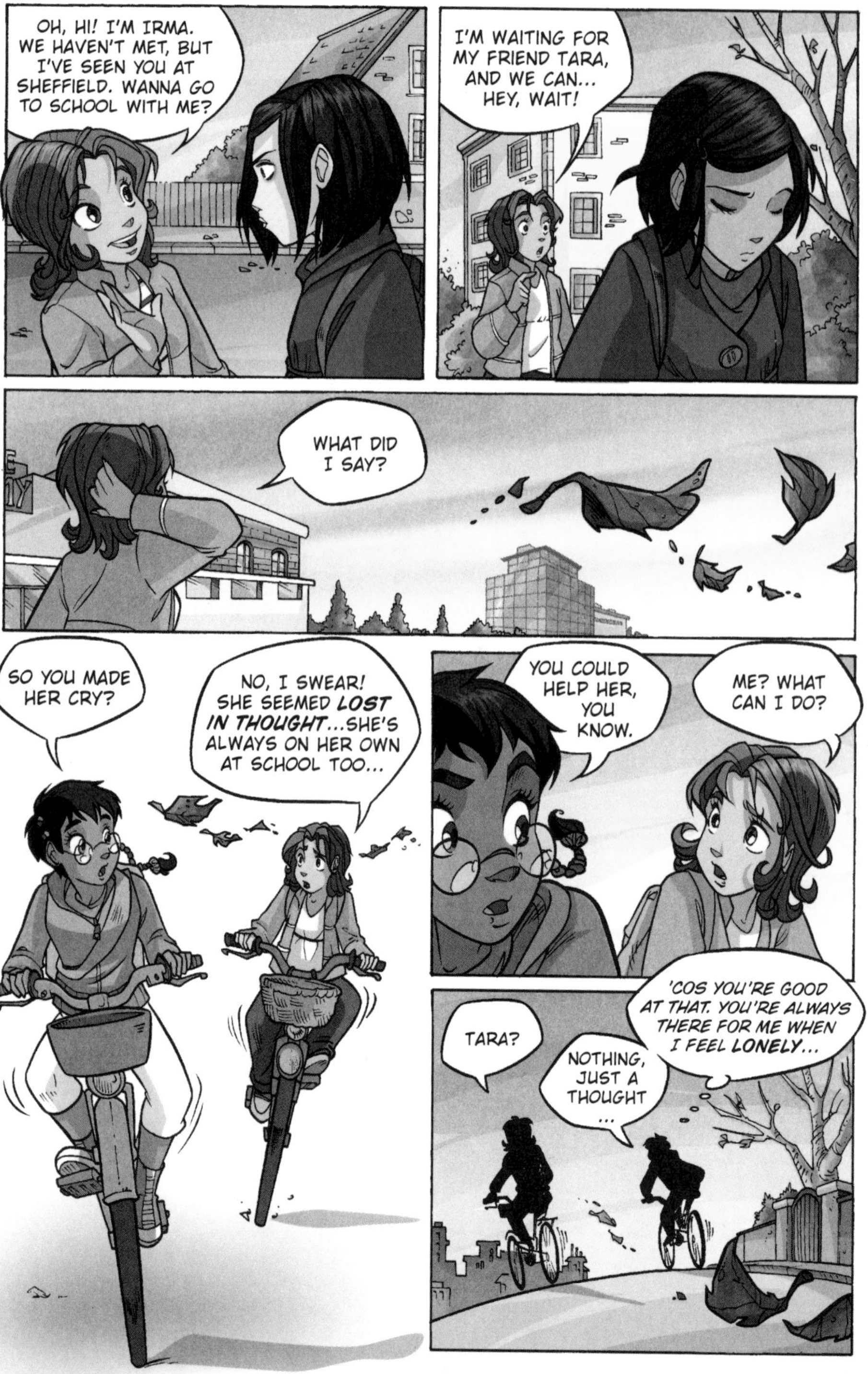
OH, HI! I'M IRMA. WE HAVEN'T MET, BUT I'VE SEEN YOU AT SHEFFIELD. WANNA GO TO SCHOOL WITH ME?
I'M WAITING FOR MY FRIEND TARA, AND WE CAN... HEY, WAIT!
WHAT DID I SAY?
SO YOU MADE HER CRY?
NO, I SWEAR! SHE SEEMED **LOST IN THOUGHT**...SHE'S ALWAYS ON HER OWN AT SCHOOL TOO...
YOU COULD HELP HER, YOU KNOW.
ME? WHAT CAN I DO?
'COS YOU'RE GOOD AT THAT. YOU'RE ALWAYS THERE FOR ME WHEN I FEEL **LONELY**...
TARA?
NOTHING, JUST A THOUGHT ...

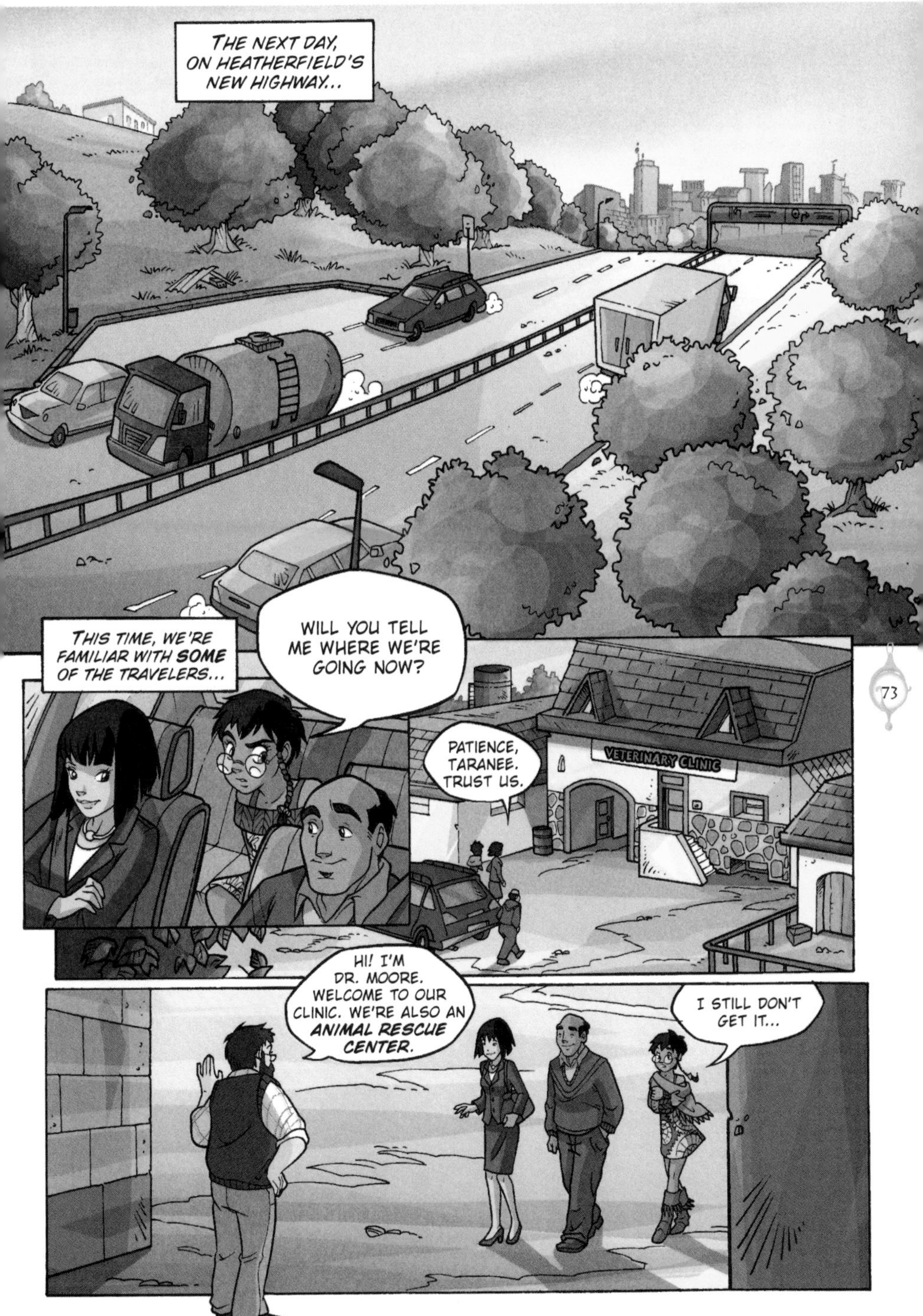

THE NEXT DAY, ON HEATHERFIELD'S NEW HIGHWAY...
THIS TIME, WE'RE FAMILIAR WITH SOME OF THE TRAVELERS...
WILL YOU TELL ME WHERE WE'RE GOING NOW?
PATIENCE, TARANEE. TRUST US.
VETERINARY CLINIC
HI! I'M DR. MOORE. WELCOME TO OUR CLINIC. WE'RE ALSO AN ANIMAL RESCUE CENTER.
I STILL DON'T GET IT...

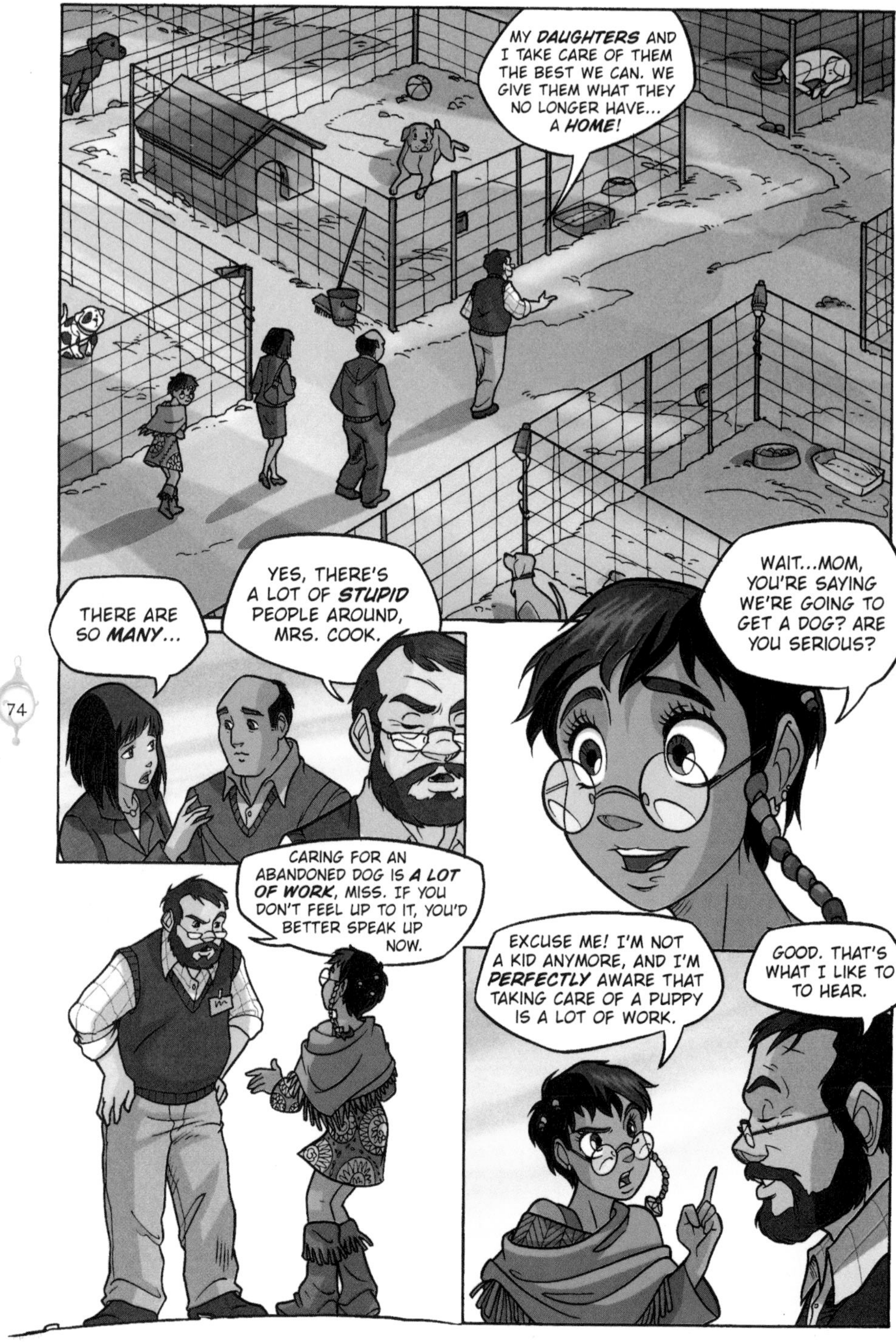

MY DAUGHTERS AND I TAKE CARE OF THEM THE BEST WE CAN. WE GIVE THEM WHAT THEY NO LONGER HAVE... A HOME!
THERE ARE SO MANY...
YES, THERE'S A LOT OF STUPID PEOPLE AROUND, MRS. COOK.
WAIT...MOM, YOU'RE SAYING WE'RE GOING TO GET A DOG? ARE YOU SERIOUS?
CARING FOR AN ABANDONED DOG IS A LOT OF WORK, MISS. IF YOU DON'T FEEL UP TO IT, YOU'D BETTER SPEAK UP NOW.
EXCUSE ME! I'M NOT A KID ANYMORE, AND I'M PERFECTLY AWARE THAT TAKING CARE OF A PUPPY IS A LOT OF WORK.
GOOD. THAT'S WHAT I LIKE TO TO HEAR.

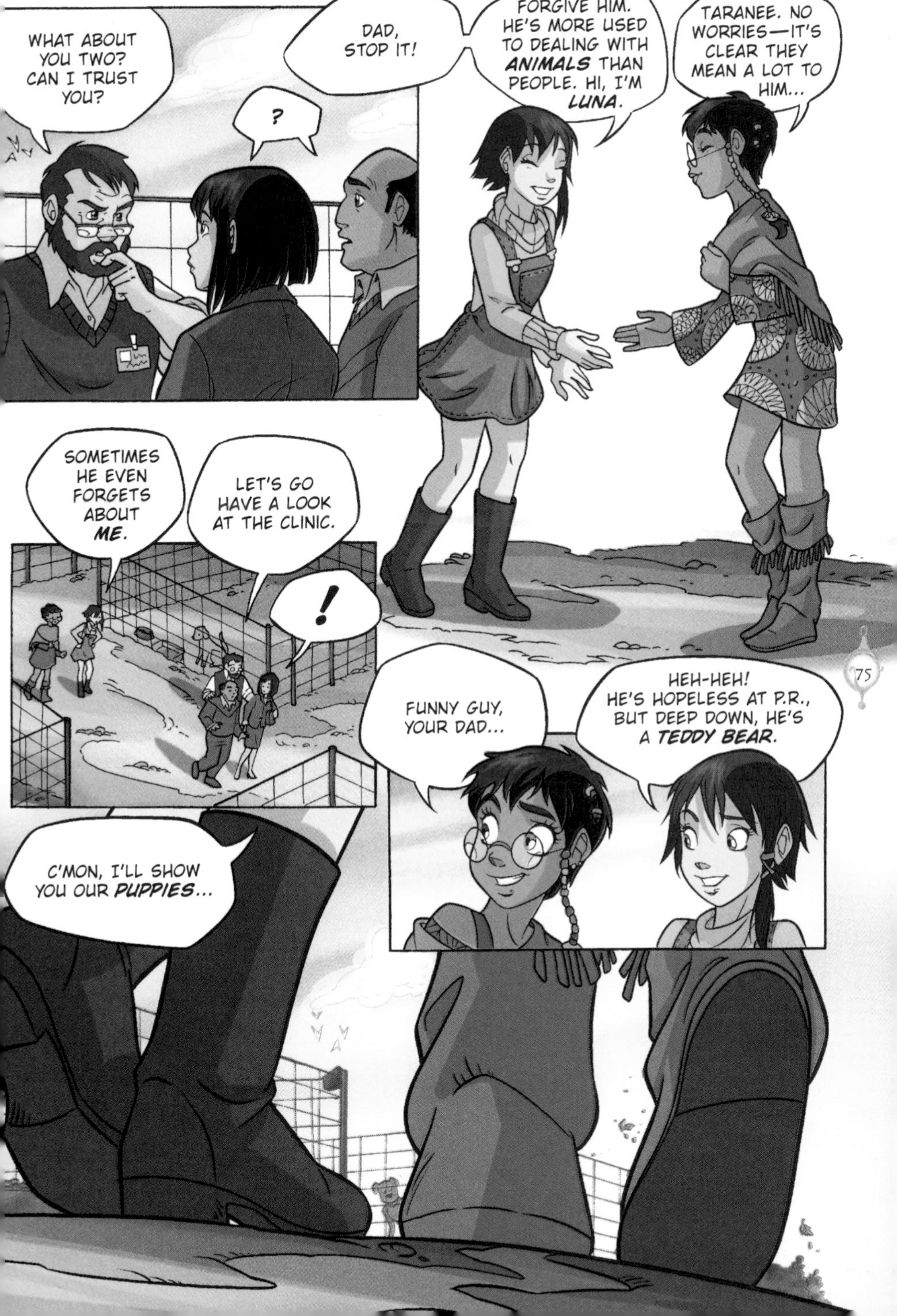
WHAT ABOUT YOU TWO? CAN I TRUST YOU?
?
DAD, STOP IT!
FORGIVE HIM. HE'S MORE USED TO DEALING WITH **ANIMALS** THAN PEOPLE. HI, I'M **LUNA**.
TARANEE. NO WORRIES—IT'S CLEAR THEY MEAN A LOT TO HIM...
SOMETIMES HE EVEN FORGETS ABOUT **ME**.
LET'S GO HAVE A LOOK AT THE CLINIC.
!
FUNNY GUY, YOUR DAD...
HEH-HEH! HE'S HOPELESS AT P.R., BUT DEEP DOWN, HE'S A **TEDDY BEAR**.
C'MON, I'LL SHOW YOU OUR **PUPPIES**...

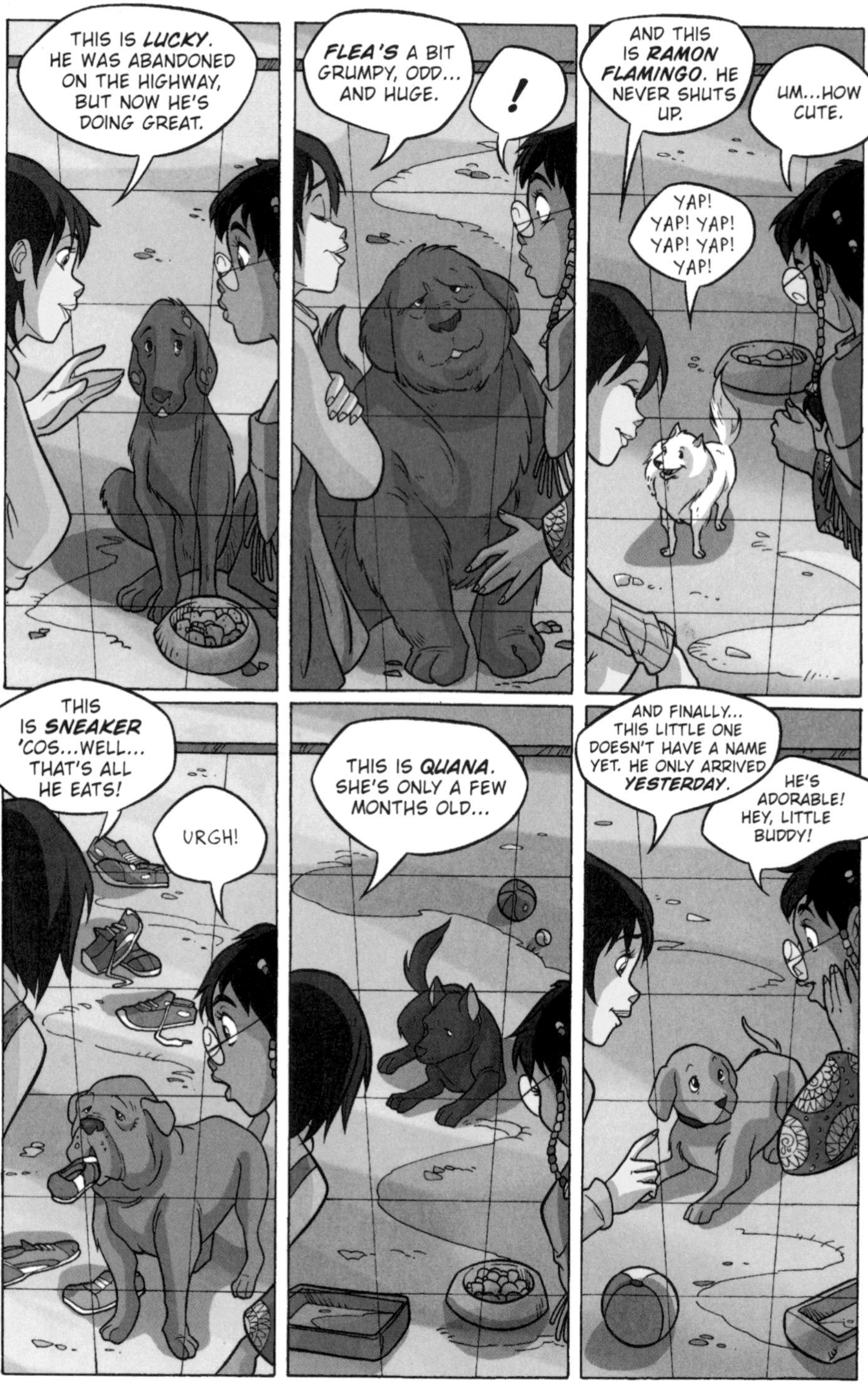
THIS IS LUCKY. HE WAS ABANDONED ON THE HIGHWAY, BUT NOW HE'S DOING GREAT.
FLEA'S A BIT GRUMPY, ODD... AND HUGE.
!
AND THIS IS RAMON FLAMINGO. HE NEVER SHUTS UP.
YAP! YAP! YAP! YAP! YAP! YAP!
UM...HOW CUTE.
THIS IS SNEAKER 'COS...WELL... THAT'S ALL HE EATS!
URGH!
THIS IS QUANA. SHE'S ONLY A FEW MONTHS OLD...
AND FINALLY... THIS LITTLE ONE DOESN'T HAVE A NAME YET. HE ONLY ARRIVED YESTERDAY.
HE'S ADORABLE! HEY, LITTLE BUDDY!

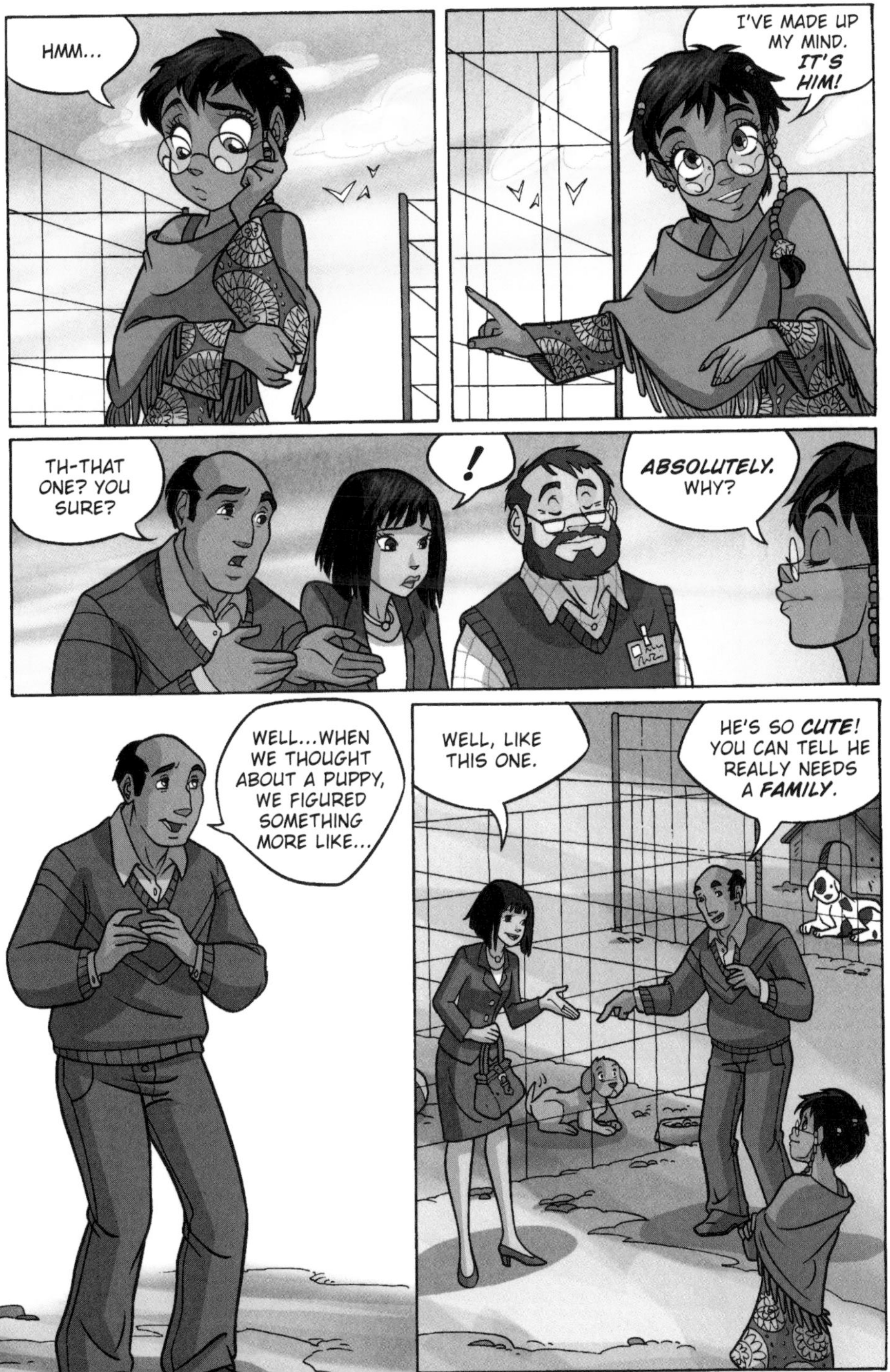
HMM...
I'VE MADE UP MY MIND. IT'S HIM!
TH-THAT ONE? YOU SURE?
!
ABSOLUTELY. WHY?
WELL...WHEN WE THOUGHT ABOUT A PUPPY, WE FIGURED SOMETHING MORE LIKE...
WELL, LIKE THIS ONE.
HE'S SO CUTE! YOU CAN TELL HE REALLY NEEDS A FAMILY.

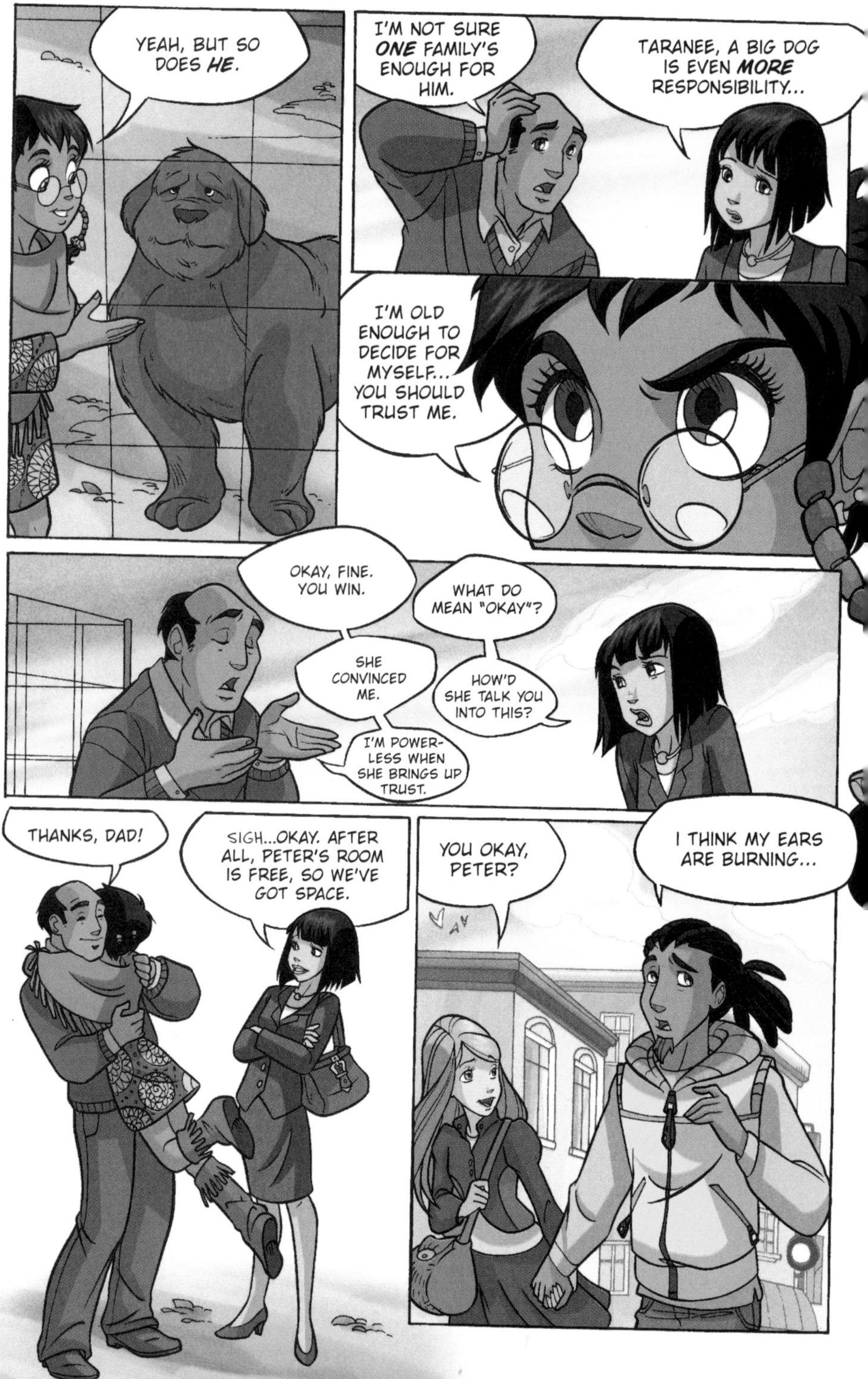

YEAH, BUT SO DOES *HE*.
I'M NOT SURE *ONE* FAMILY'S ENOUGH FOR HIM.
TARANEE, A BIG DOG IS EVEN *MORE* RESPONSIBILITY...
I'M OLD ENOUGH TO DECIDE FOR MYSELF... YOU SHOULD TRUST ME.
OKAY, FINE. YOU WIN.
WHAT DO MEAN "OKAY"?
SHE CONVINCED ME.
HOW'D SHE TALK YOU INTO THIS?
I'M POWERLESS WHEN SHE BRINGS UP TRUST.
THANKS, DAD!
SIGH...OKAY. AFTER ALL, PETER'S ROOM IS FREE, SO WE'VE GOT SPACE.
YOU OKAY, PETER?
I THINK MY EARS ARE BURNING...

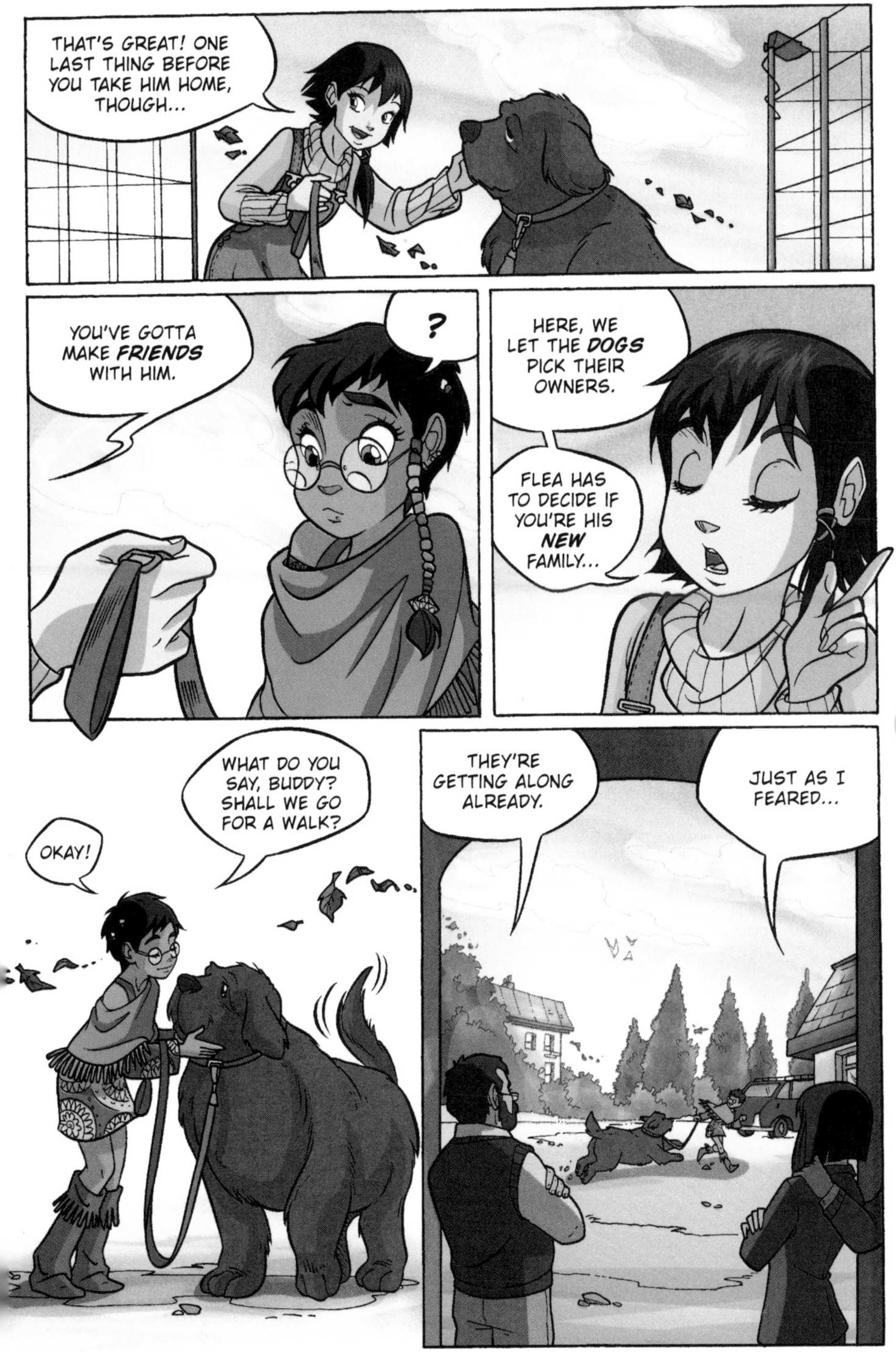
THAT'S GREAT! ONE LAST THING BEFORE YOU TAKE HIM HOME, THOUGH...
YOU'VE GOTTA MAKE **FRIENDS** WITH HIM.
?
HERE, WE LET THE **DOGS** PICK THEIR OWNERS.
FLEA HAS TO DECIDE IF YOU'RE HIS **NEW** FAMILY...
WHAT DO YOU SAY, BUDDY? SHALL WE GO FOR A WALK?
OKAY!
THEY'RE GETTING ALONG ALREADY.
JUST AS I FEARED...

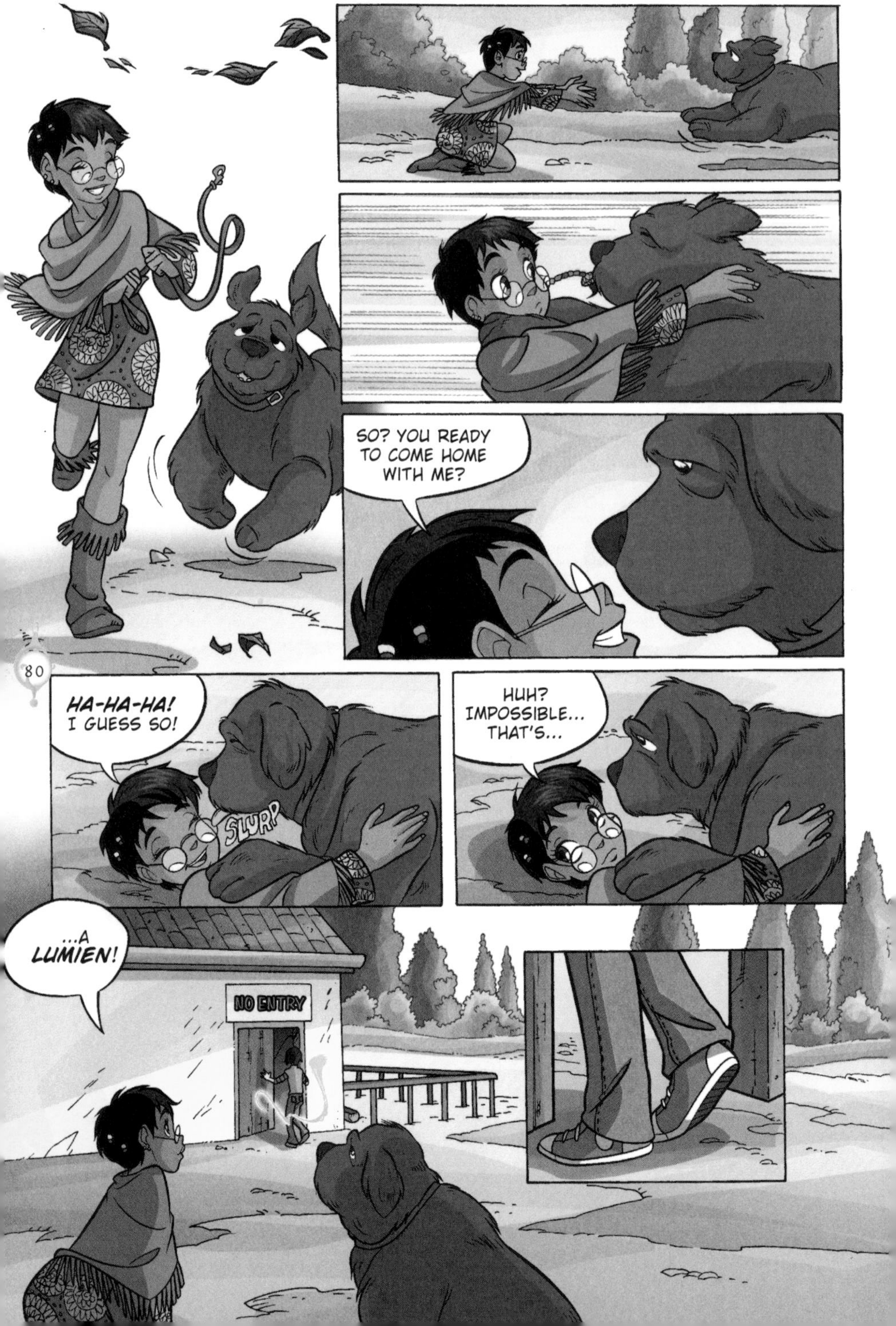
SO? YOU READY TO COME HOME WITH ME?
HA-HA-HA! I GUESS SO!
SLURP
HUH? IMPOSSIBLE... THAT'S...
...A LUMIEN!
NO ENTRY

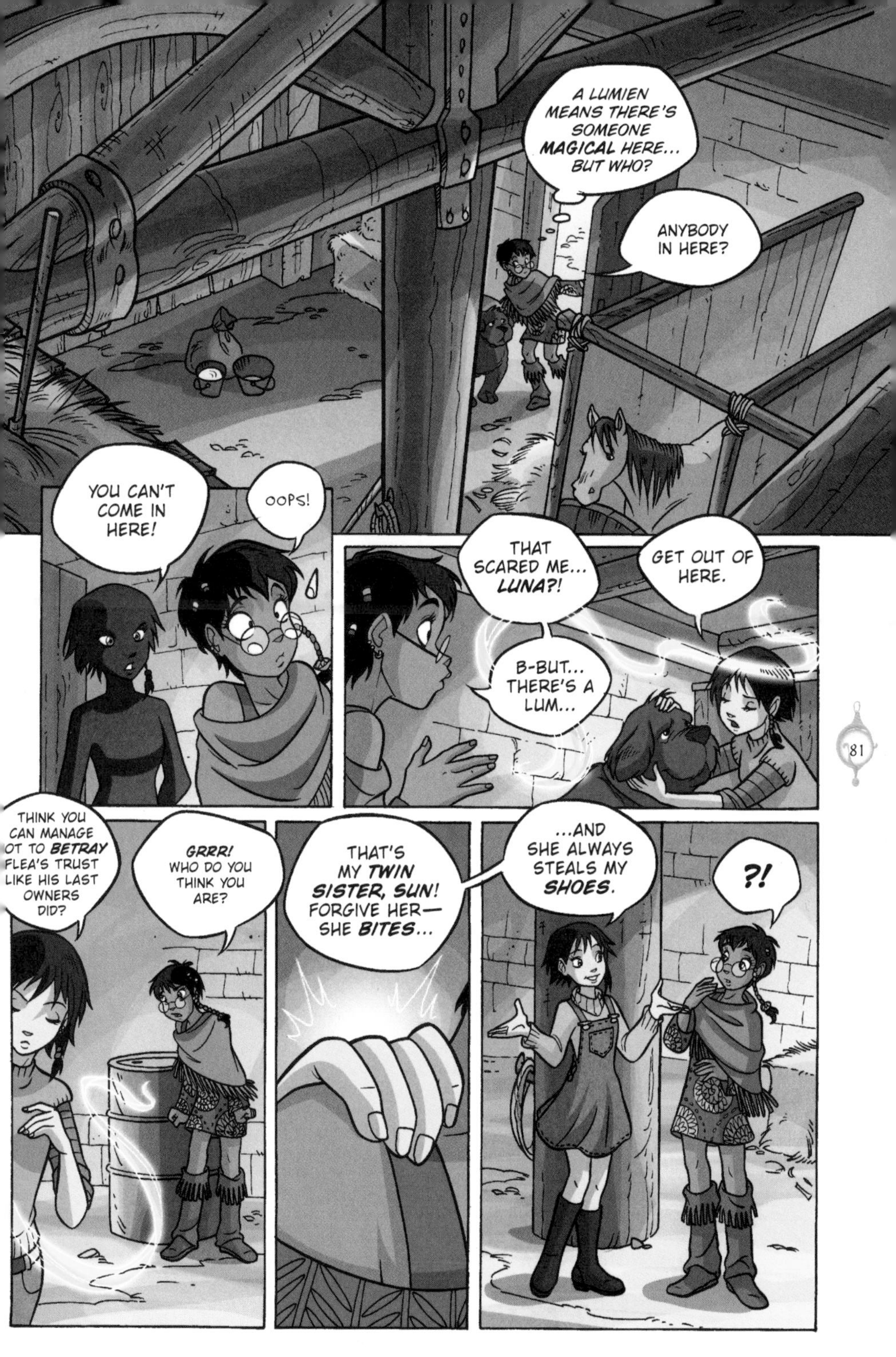
A LUMIEN MEANS THERE'S SOMEONE MAGICAL HERE... BUT WHO?
ANYBODY IN HERE?
YOU CAN'T COME IN HERE!
OOPS!
THAT SCARED ME... LUNA?!
GET OUT OF HERE.
B-BUT... THERE'S A LUM...
THINK YOU CAN MANAGE OT TO BETRAY FLEA'S TRUST LIKE HIS LAST OWNERS DID?
GRRR! WHO DO YOU THINK YOU ARE?
THAT'S MY TWIN SISTER, SUN! FORGIVE HER— SHE BITES...
...AND SHE ALWAYS STEALS MY SHOES.
?!

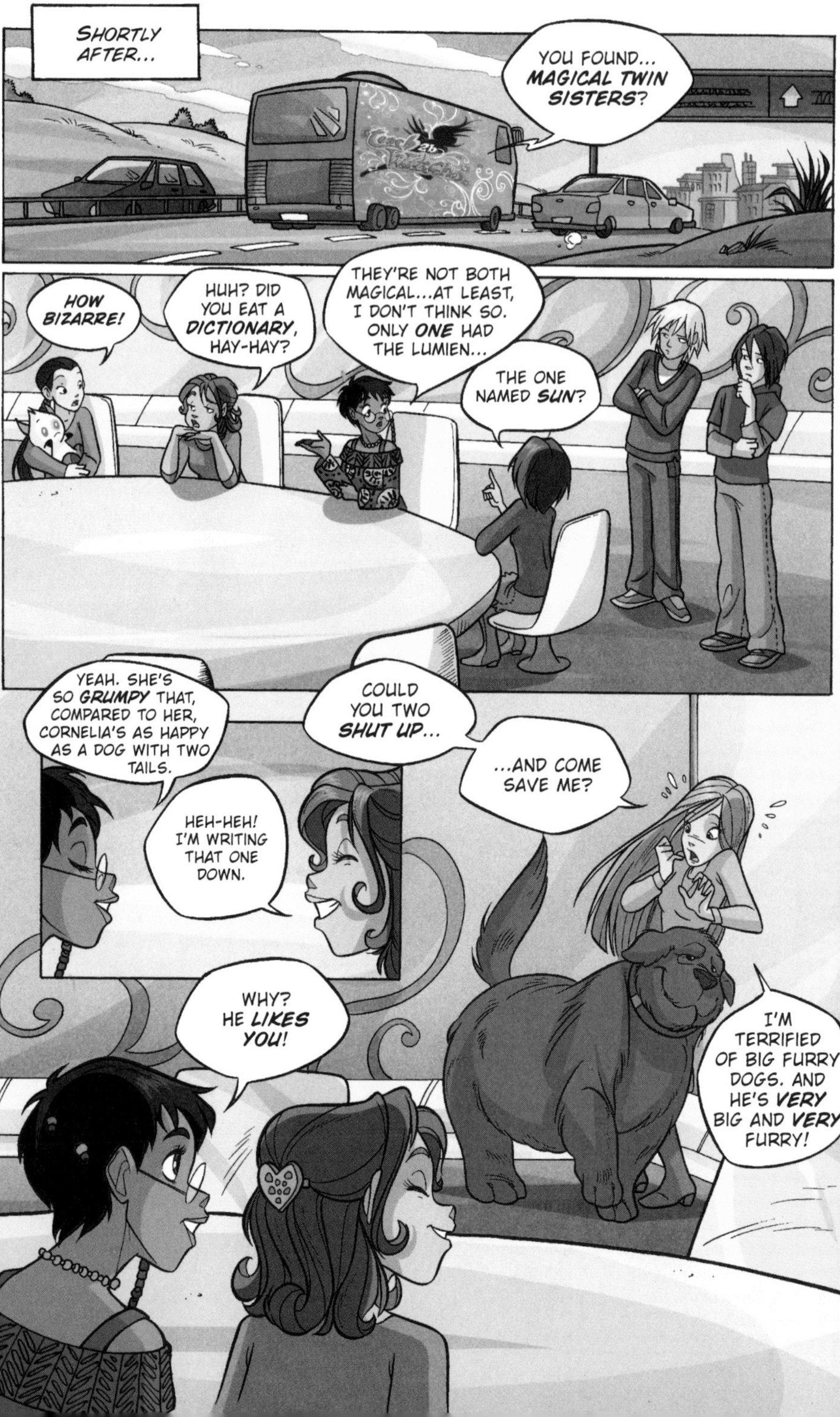
SHORTLY AFTER...
YOU FOUND... MAGICAL TWIN SISTERS?
HOW BIZARRE!
HUH? DID YOU EAT A DICTIONARY, HAY-HAY?
THEY'RE NOT BOTH MAGICAL...AT LEAST, I DON'T THINK SO. ONLY ONE HAD THE LUMIEN...
THE ONE NAMED SUN?
YEAH. SHE'S SO GRUMPY THAT, COMPARED TO HER, CORNELIA'S AS HAPPY AS A DOG WITH TWO TAILS.
HEH-HEH! I'M WRITING THAT ONE DOWN.
COULD YOU TWO SHUT UP...
...AND COME SAVE ME?
WHY? HE LIKES YOU!
I'M TERRIFIED OF BIG FURRY DOGS. AND HE'S VERY BIG AND VERY FURRY!

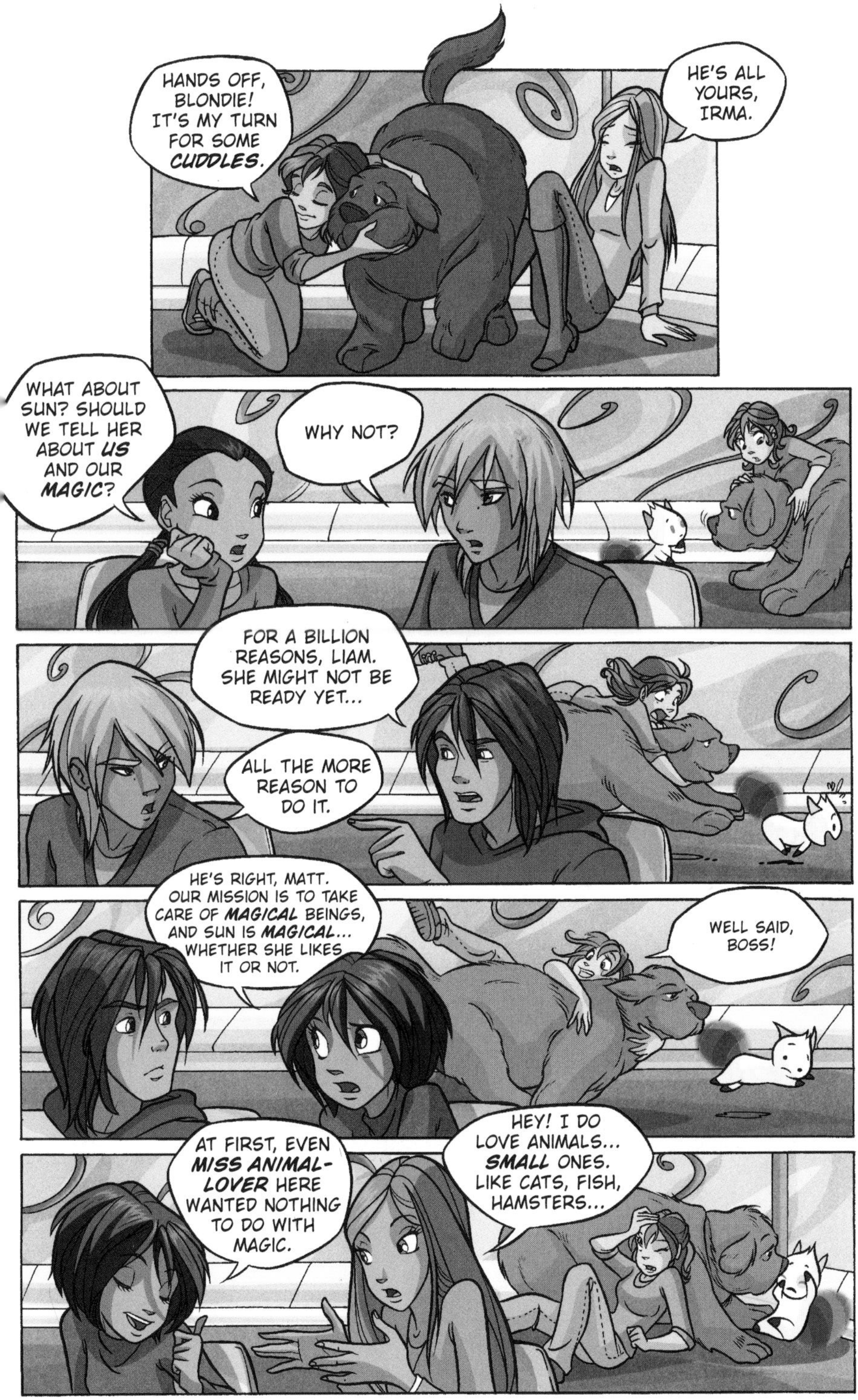
HANDS OFF, BLONDIE! IT'S MY TURN FOR SOME CUDDLES.
HE'S ALL YOURS, IRMA.
WHAT ABOUT SUN? SHOULD WE TELL HER ABOUT US AND OUR MAGIC?
WHY NOT?
FOR A BILLION REASONS, LIAM. SHE MIGHT NOT BE READY YET...
ALL THE MORE REASON TO DO IT.
HE'S RIGHT, MATT. OUR MISSION IS TO TAKE CARE OF MAGICAL BEINGS, AND SUN IS MAGICAL... WHETHER SHE LIKES IT OR NOT.
WELL SAID, BOSS!
AT FIRST, EVEN MISS ANIMAL-LOVER HERE WANTED NOTHING TO DO WITH MAGIC.
HEY! I DO LOVE ANIMALS... SMALL ONES. LIKE CATS, FISH, HAMSTERS...

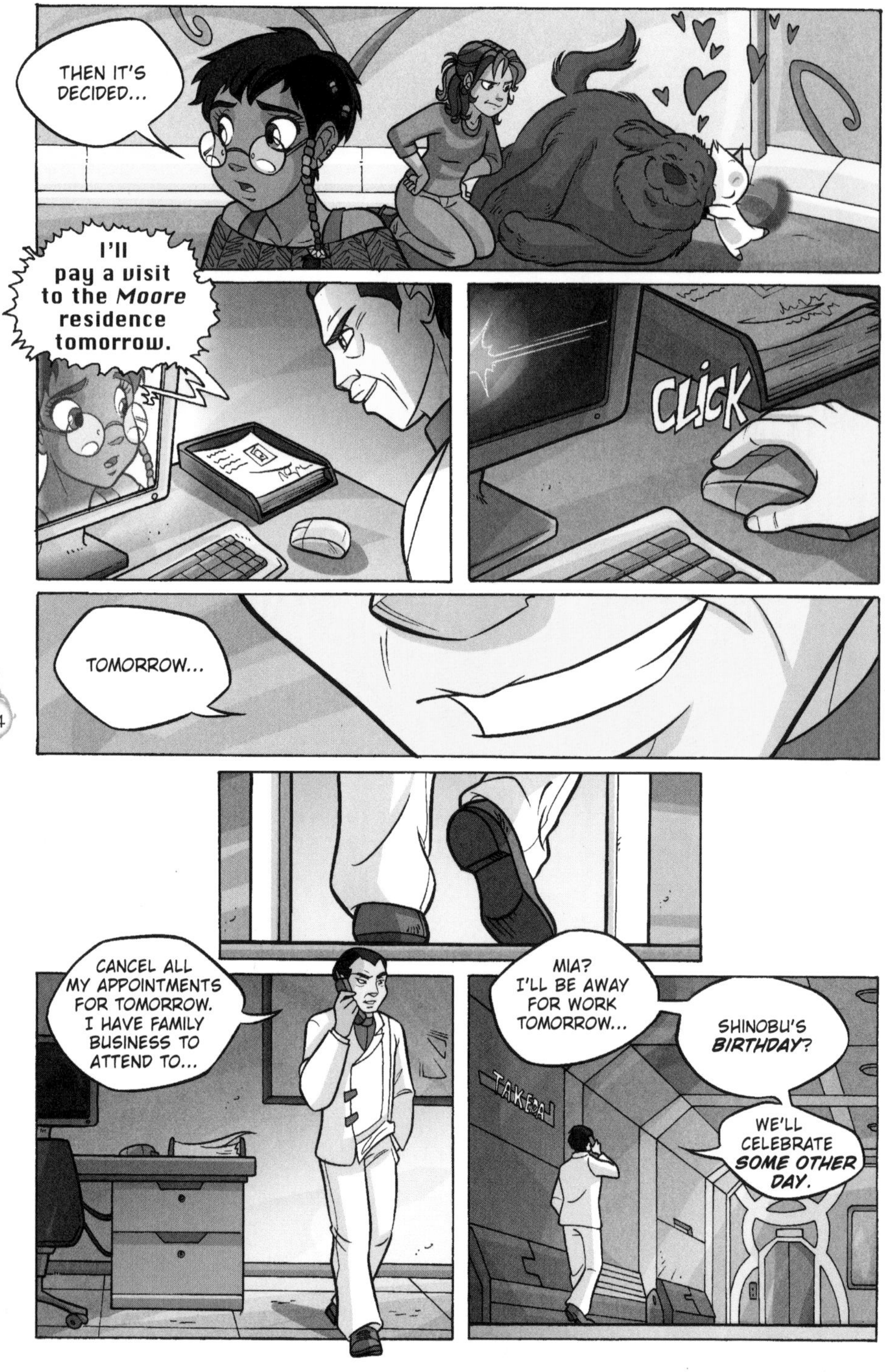
THEN IT'S DECIDED...
I'll pay a visit to the *Moore* residence tomorrow.
CLICK
TOMORROW...
CANCEL ALL MY APPOINTMENTS FOR TOMORROW. I HAVE FAMILY BUSINESS TO ATTEND TO...
MIA? I'LL BE AWAY FOR WORK TOMORROW...
SHINOBU'S *BIRTHDAY*?
WE'LL CELEBRATE *SOME OTHER DAY*.
TAKEDA

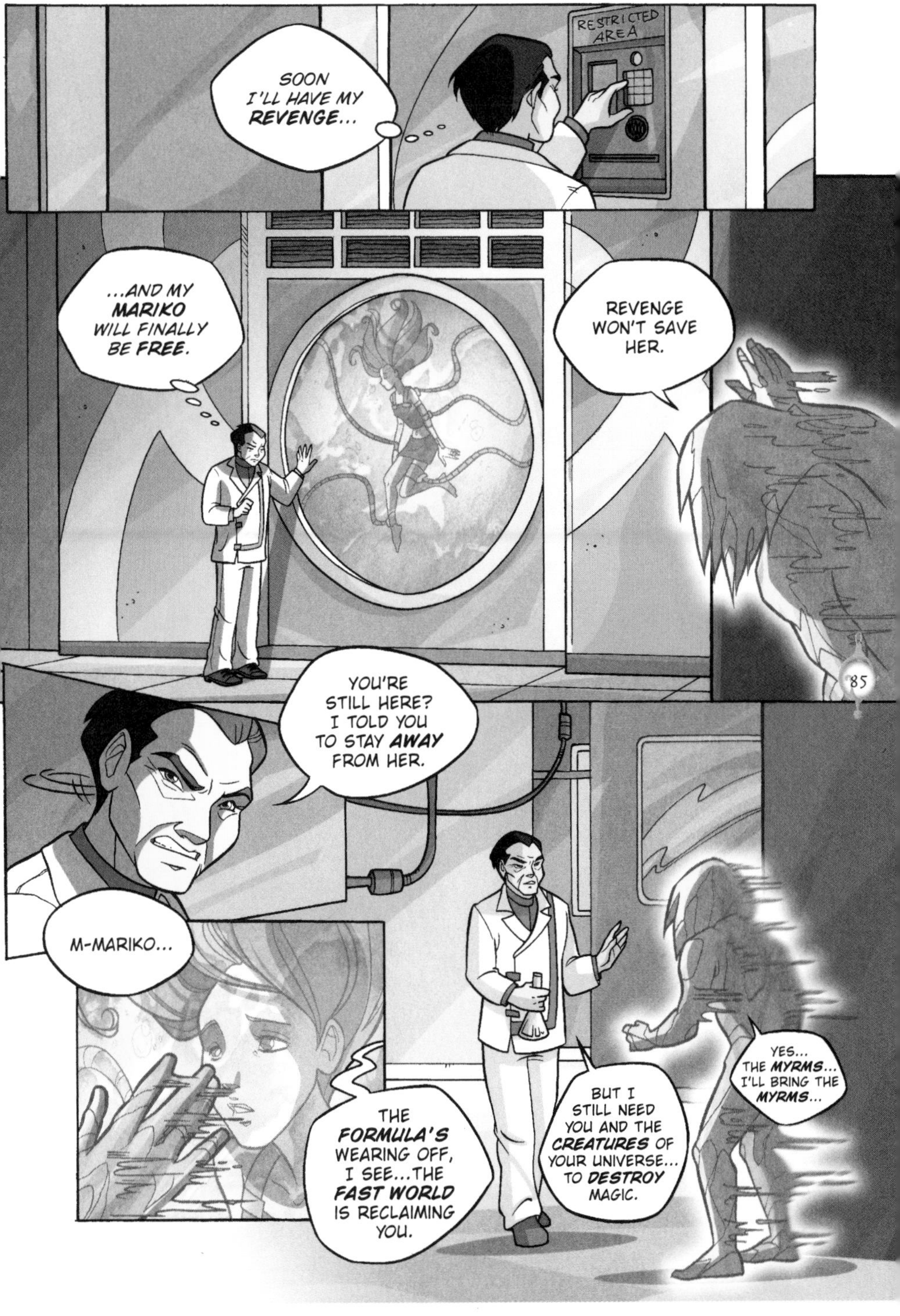
RESTRICTED AREA
SOON I'LL HAVE MY REVENGE...
...AND MY MARIKO WILL FINALLY BE FREE.
REVENGE WON'T SAVE HER.
YOU'RE STILL HERE? I TOLD YOU TO STAY AWAY FROM HER.
M-MARIKO...
THE FORMULA'S WEARING OFF, I SEE...THE FAST WORLD IS RECLAIMING YOU.
BUT I STILL NEED YOU AND THE CREATURES OF YOUR UNIVERSE... TO DESTROY MAGIC.
YES... THE MYRMS... I'LL BRING THE MYRMS...

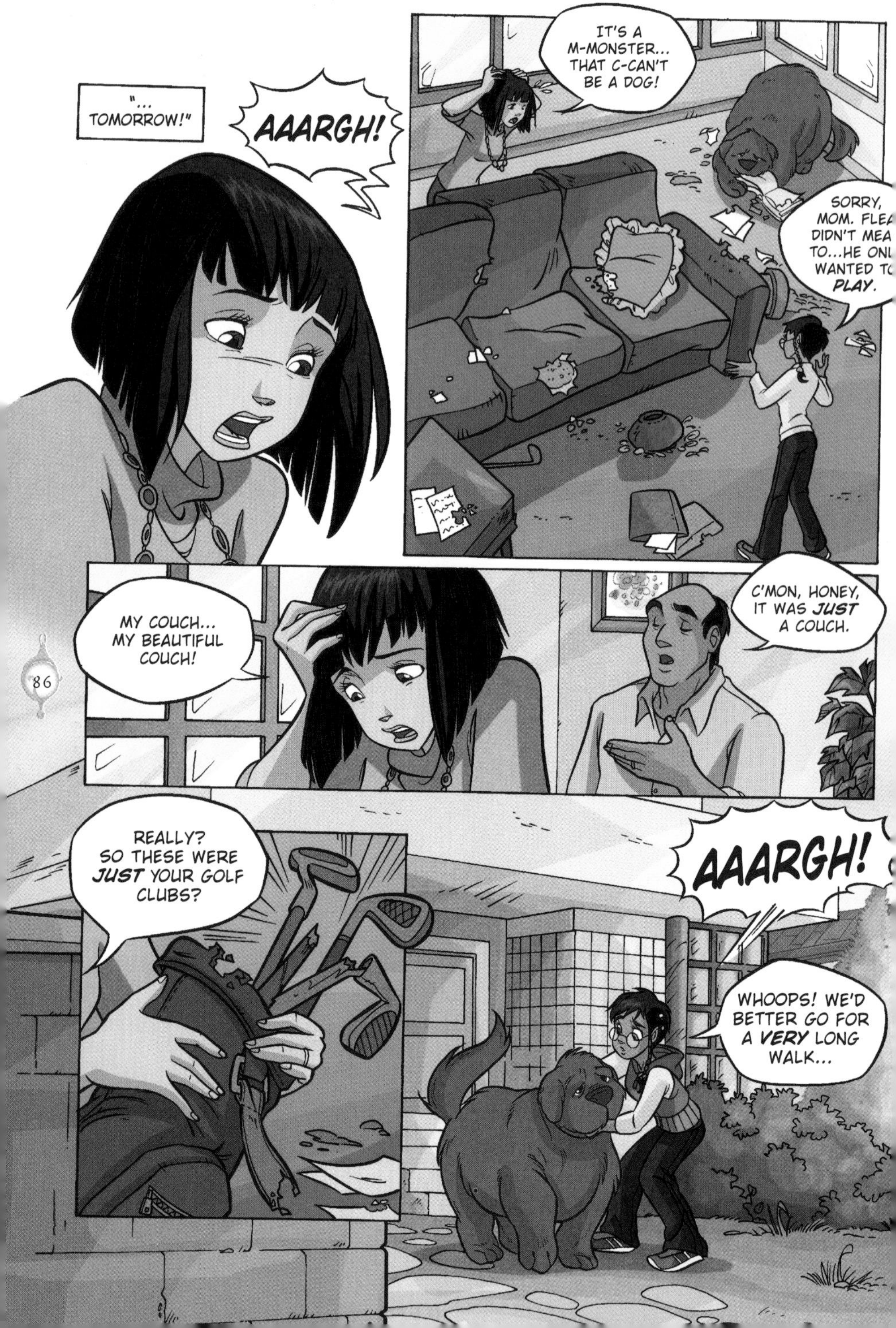
"...
TOMORROW!"
AAARGH!
IT'S A M-MONSTER... THAT C-CAN'T BE A DOG!
SORRY, MOM. FLEA DIDN'T MEA TO...HE ONL WANTED T PLAY.
MY COUCH... MY BEAUTIFUL COUCH!
C'MON, HONEY, IT WAS JUST A COUCH.
REALLY? SO THESE WERE JUST YOUR GOLF CLUBS?
AAARGH!
WHOOPS! WE'D BETTER GO FOR A VERY LONG WALK...

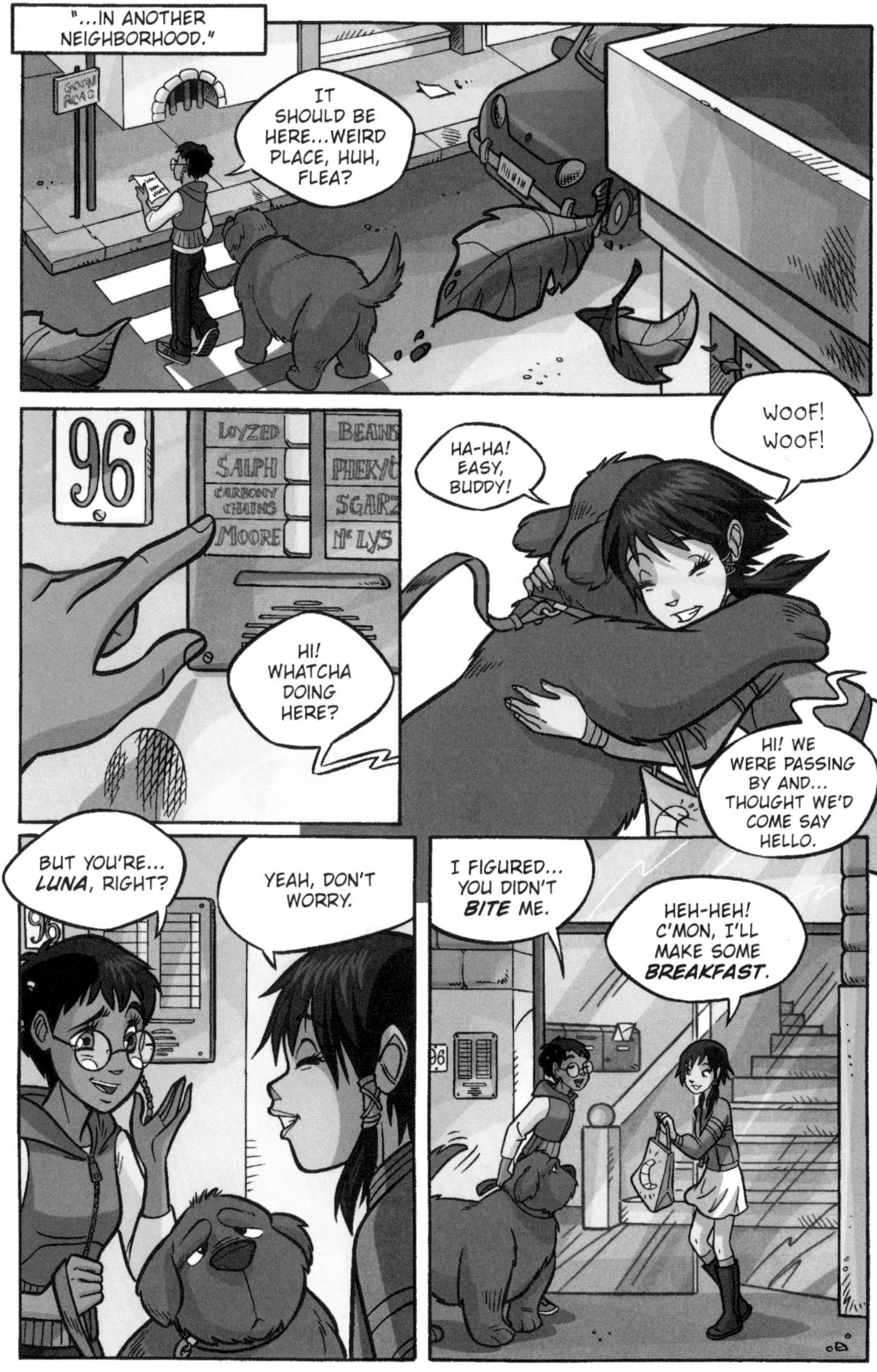
"...IN ANOTHER NEIGHBORHOOD."
IT SHOULD BE HERE...WEIRD PLACE, HUH, FLEA?
96
LOYZED
SALPH
CARBONY/ CHUINS
MOORE
BEANS
SGARZ
Mc LYS
HI! WHATCHA DOING HERE?
HA-HA! EASY, BUDDY!
WOOF! WOOF!
HI! WE WERE PASSING BY AND... THOUGHT WE'D COME SAY HELLO.
BUT YOU'RE... ***LUNA***, RIGHT?
YEAH, DON'T WORRY.
I FIGURED... YOU DIDN'T ***BITE*** ME.
HEH-HEH! C'MON, I'LL MAKE SOME ***BREAKFAST***.

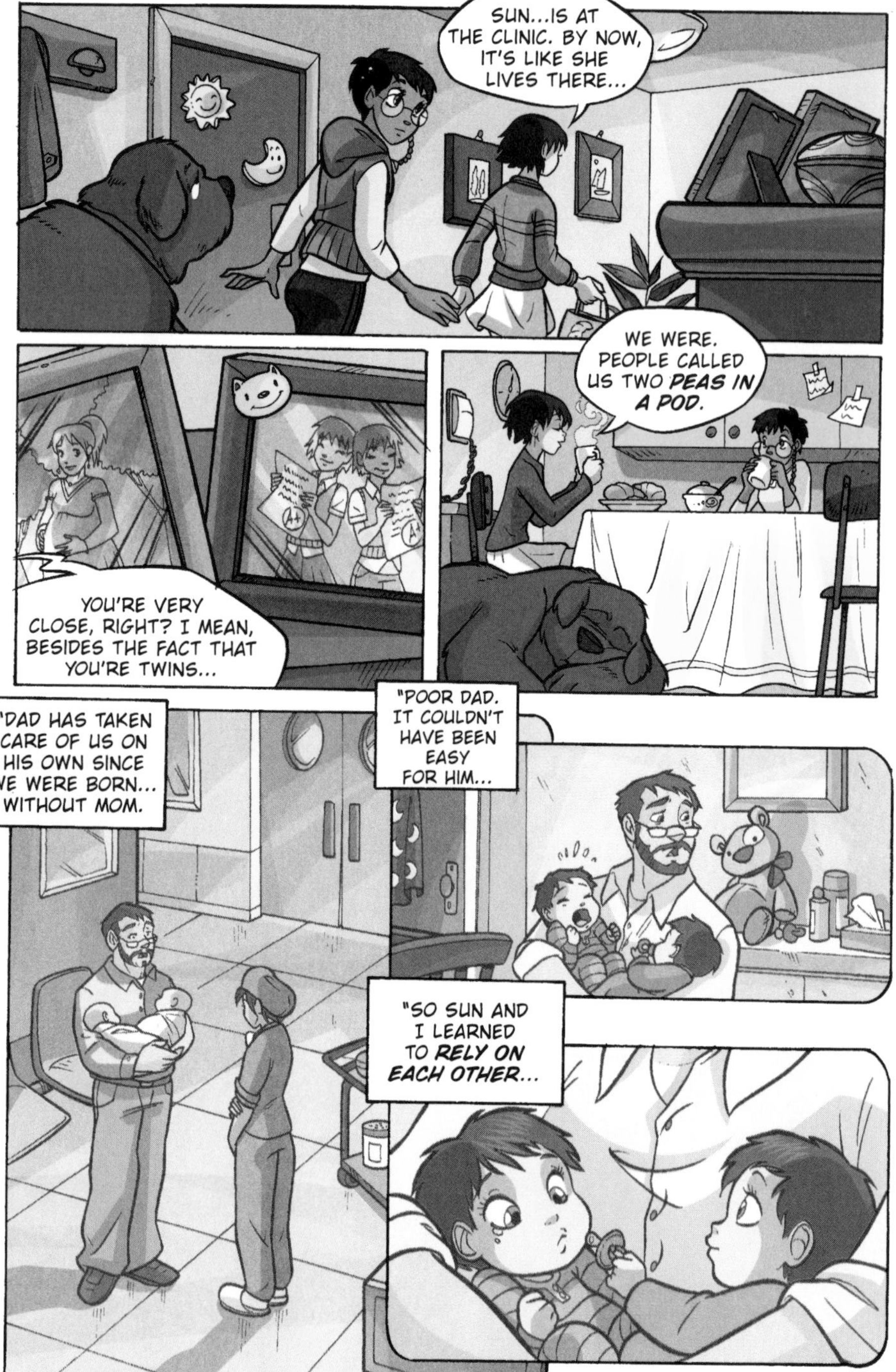

SUN...IS AT THE CLINIC. BY NOW, IT'S LIKE SHE LIVES THERE...
YOU'RE VERY CLOSE, RIGHT? I MEAN, BESIDES THE FACT THAT YOU'RE TWINS...
WE WERE. PEOPLE CALLED US TWO PEAS IN A POD.
"DAD HAS TAKEN CARE OF US ON HIS OWN SINCE WE WERE BORN... WITHOUT MOM.
"POOR DAD. IT COULDN'T HAVE BEEN EASY FOR HIM...
"SO SUN AND I LEARNED TO RELY ON EACH OTHER...

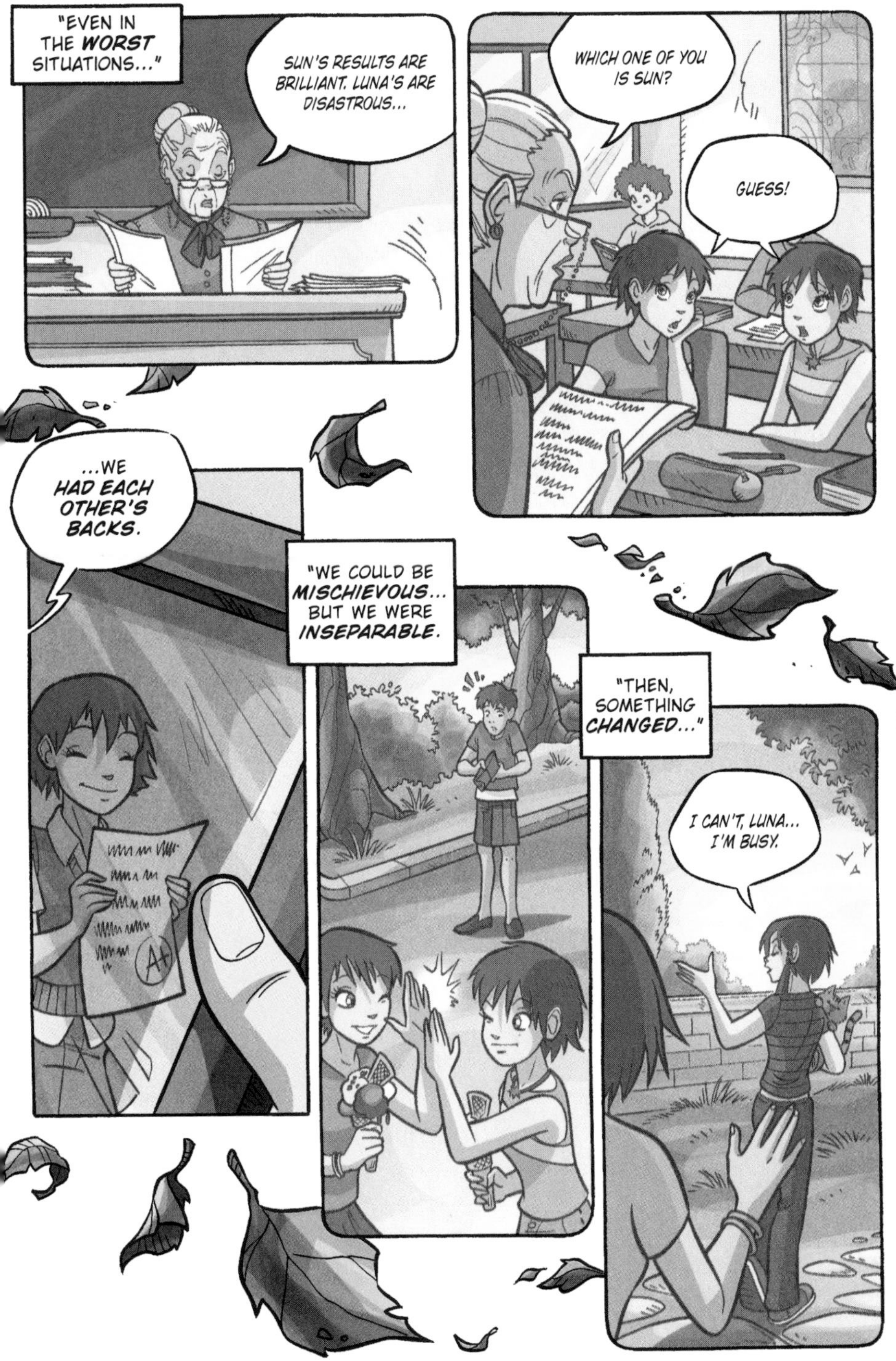
"EVEN IN THE WORST SITUATIONS..."
SUN'S RESULTS ARE BRILLIANT. LUNA'S ARE DISASTROUS...
WHICH ONE OF YOU IS SUN?
GUESS!
...WE HAD EACH OTHER'S BACKS.
A+
"WE COULD BE MISCHIEVOUS... BUT WE WERE INSEPARABLE.
"THEN, SOMETHING CHANGED..."
I CAN'T, LUNA... I'M BUSY.

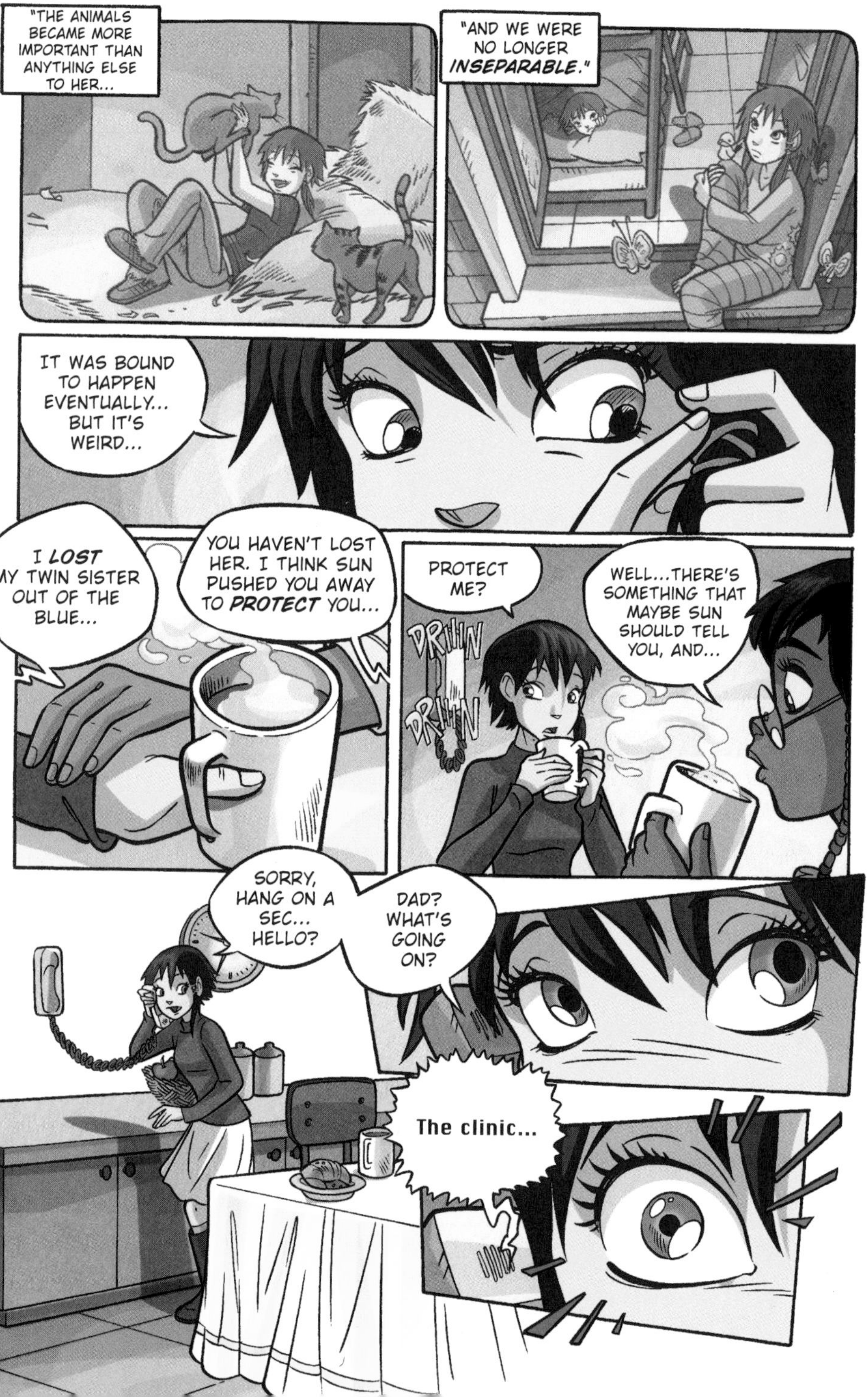
"THE ANIMALS BECAME MORE IMPORTANT THAN ANYTHING ELSE TO HER...
"AND WE WERE NO LONGER *INSEPARABLE*."
IT WAS BOUND TO HAPPEN EVENTUALLY... BUT IT'S WEIRD...
I *LOST* MY TWIN SISTER OUT OF THE BLUE...
YOU HAVEN'T LOST HER. I THINK SUN PUSHED YOU AWAY TO *PROTECT* YOU...
PROTECT ME?
WELL...THERE'S SOMETHING THAT MAYBE SUN SHOULD TELL YOU, AND...
DRIIIN
DRIIIN
SORRY, HANG ON A SEC... HELLO?
DAD? WHAT'S GOING ON?
The clinic...

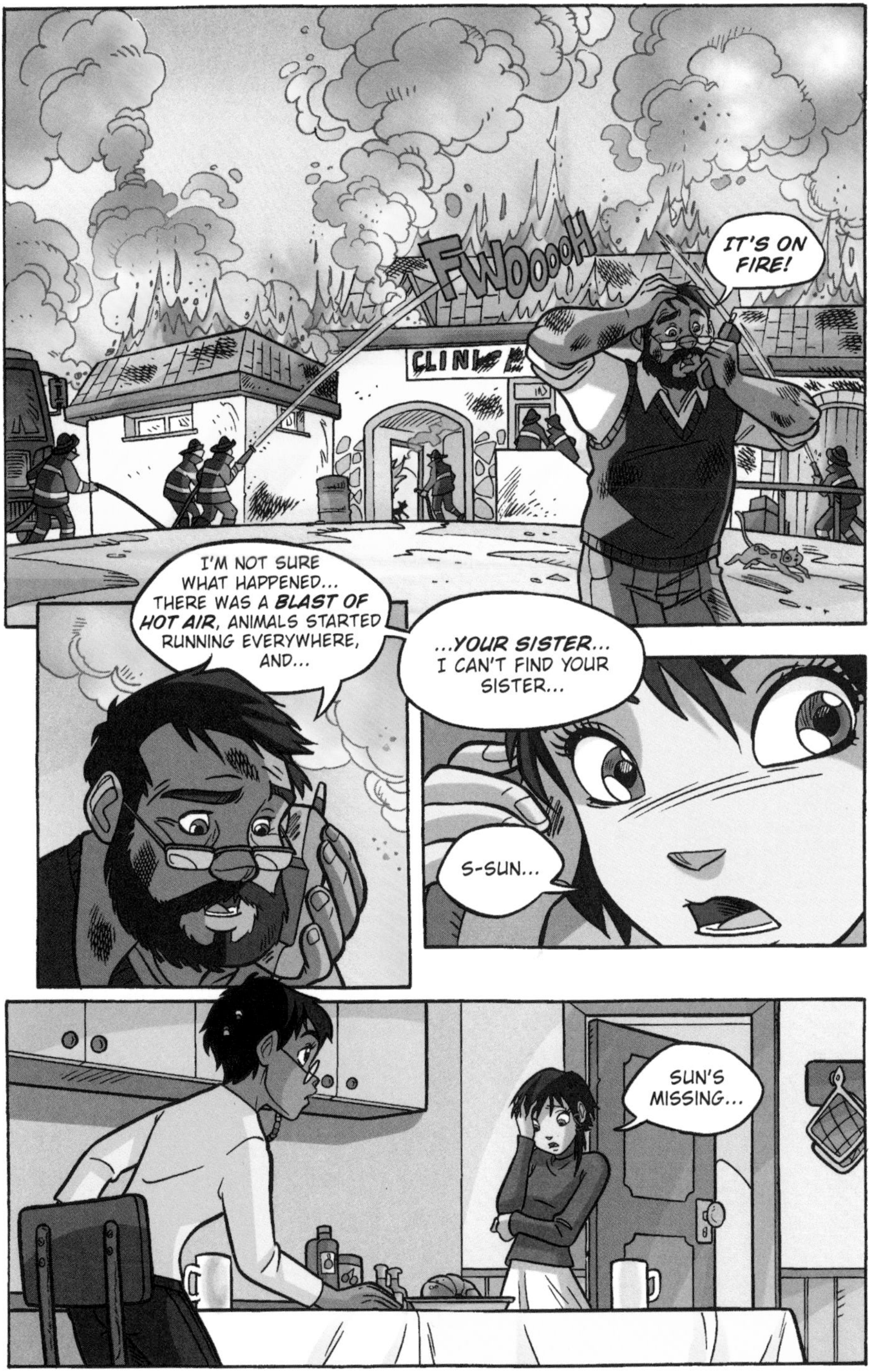
FWOOOOH
CLINI
IT'S ON FIRE!
I'M NOT SURE WHAT HAPPENED... THERE WAS A **BLAST OF HOT AIR**, ANIMALS STARTED RUNNING EVERYWHERE, AND...
...**YOUR SISTER**... I CAN'T FIND YOUR SISTER...
S-SUN...
SUN'S MISSING...

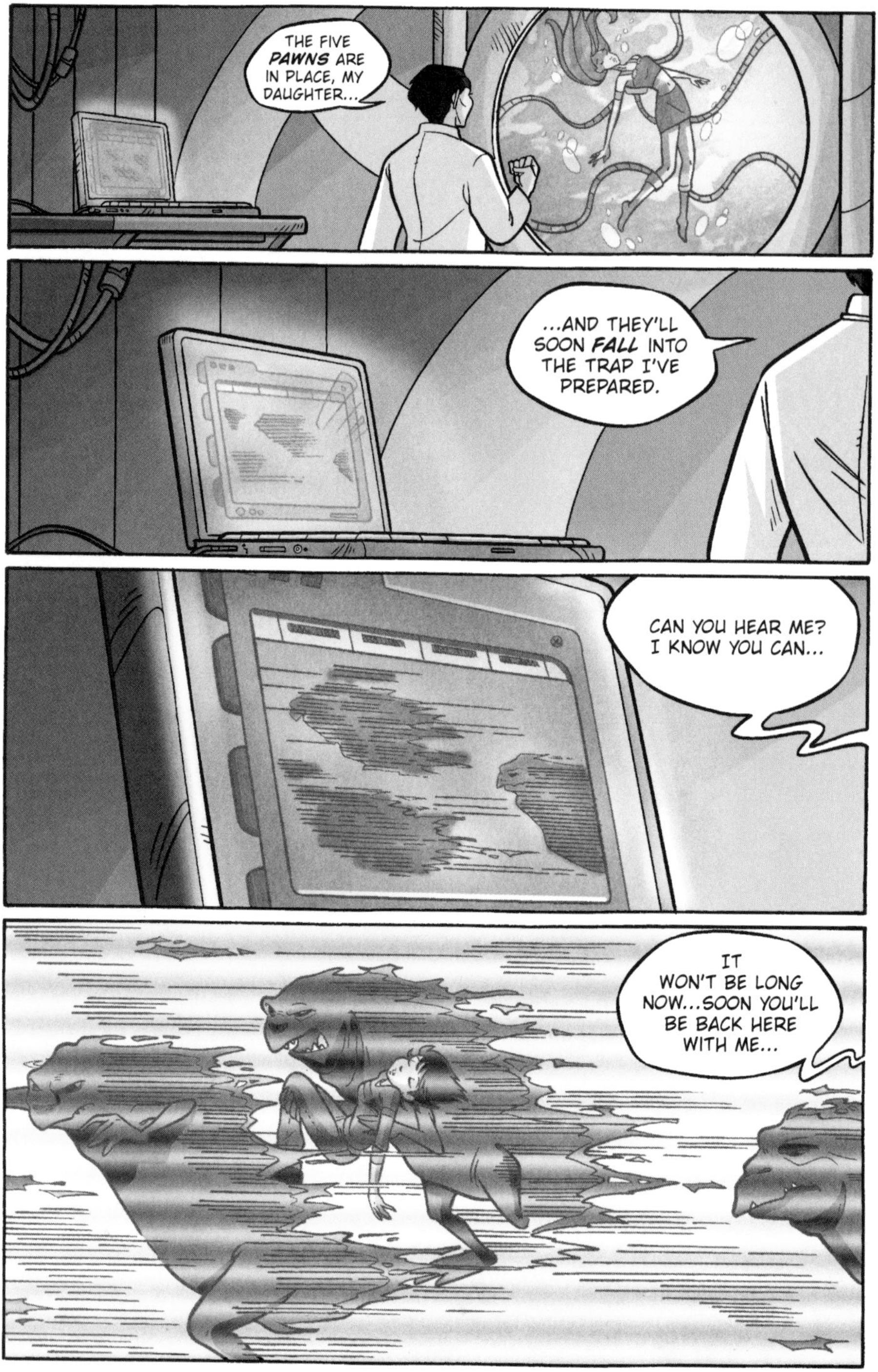
THE FIVE PAWNS ARE IN PLACE, MY DAUGHTER...
...AND THEY'LL SOON FALL INTO THE TRAP I'VE PREPARED.
CAN YOU HEAR ME? I KNOW YOU CAN...
IT WON'T BE LONG NOW...SOON YOU'LL BE BACK HERE WITH ME...

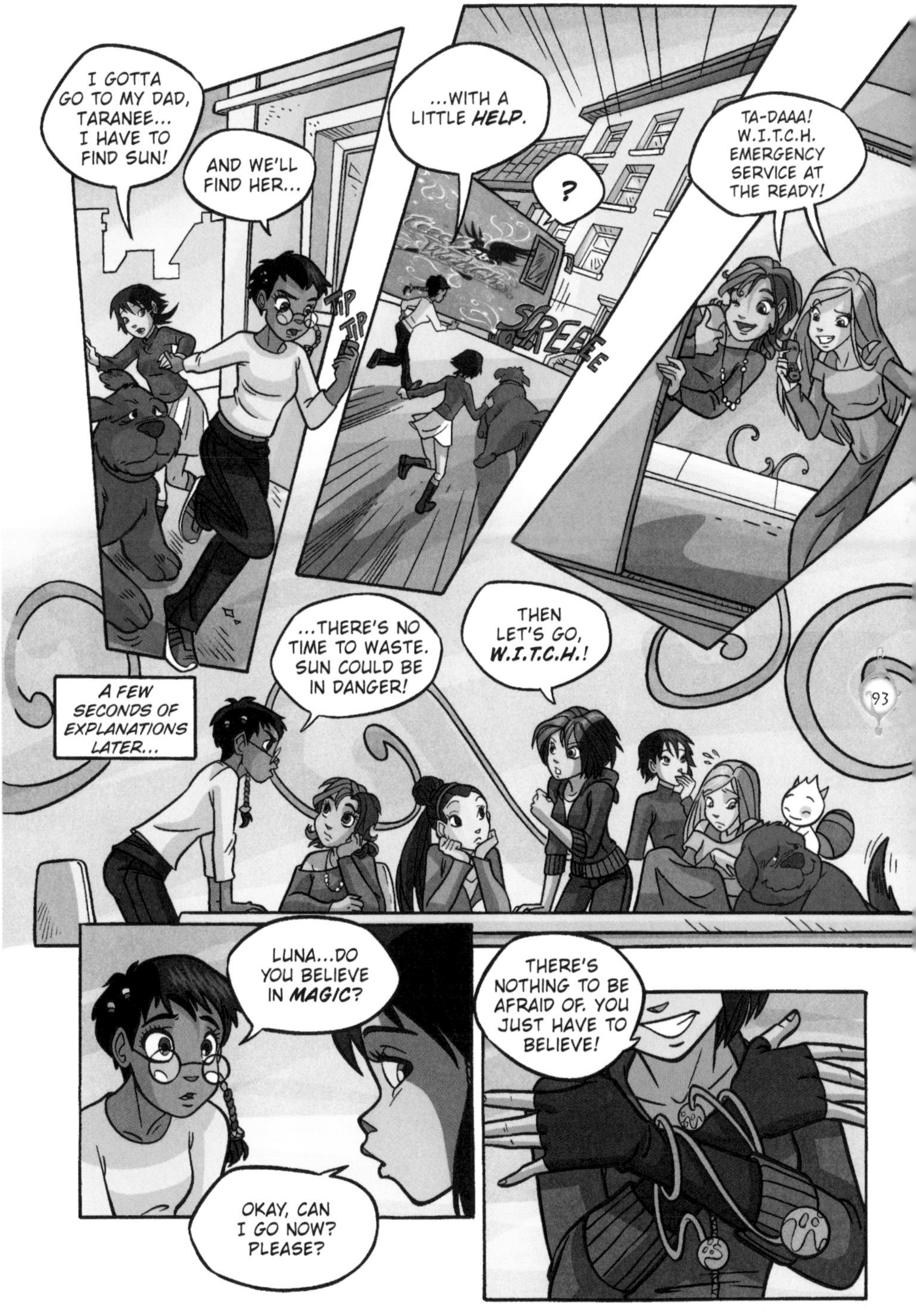
I GOTTA GO TO MY DAD, TARANEE... I HAVE TO FIND SUN!
AND WE'LL FIND HER...
TIP TIP
...WITH A LITTLE HELP.
?
SIREEEE
TA-DAAA! W.I.T.C.H. EMERGENCY SERVICE AT THE READY!
A FEW SECONDS OF EXPLANATIONS LATER...
...THERE'S NO TIME TO WASTE. SUN COULD BE IN DANGER!
THEN LET'S GO, W.I.T.C.H.!
LUNA...DO YOU BELIEVE IN MAGIC?
OKAY, CAN I GO NOW? PLEASE?
THERE'S NOTHING TO BE AFRAID OF. YOU JUST HAVE TO BELIEVE!

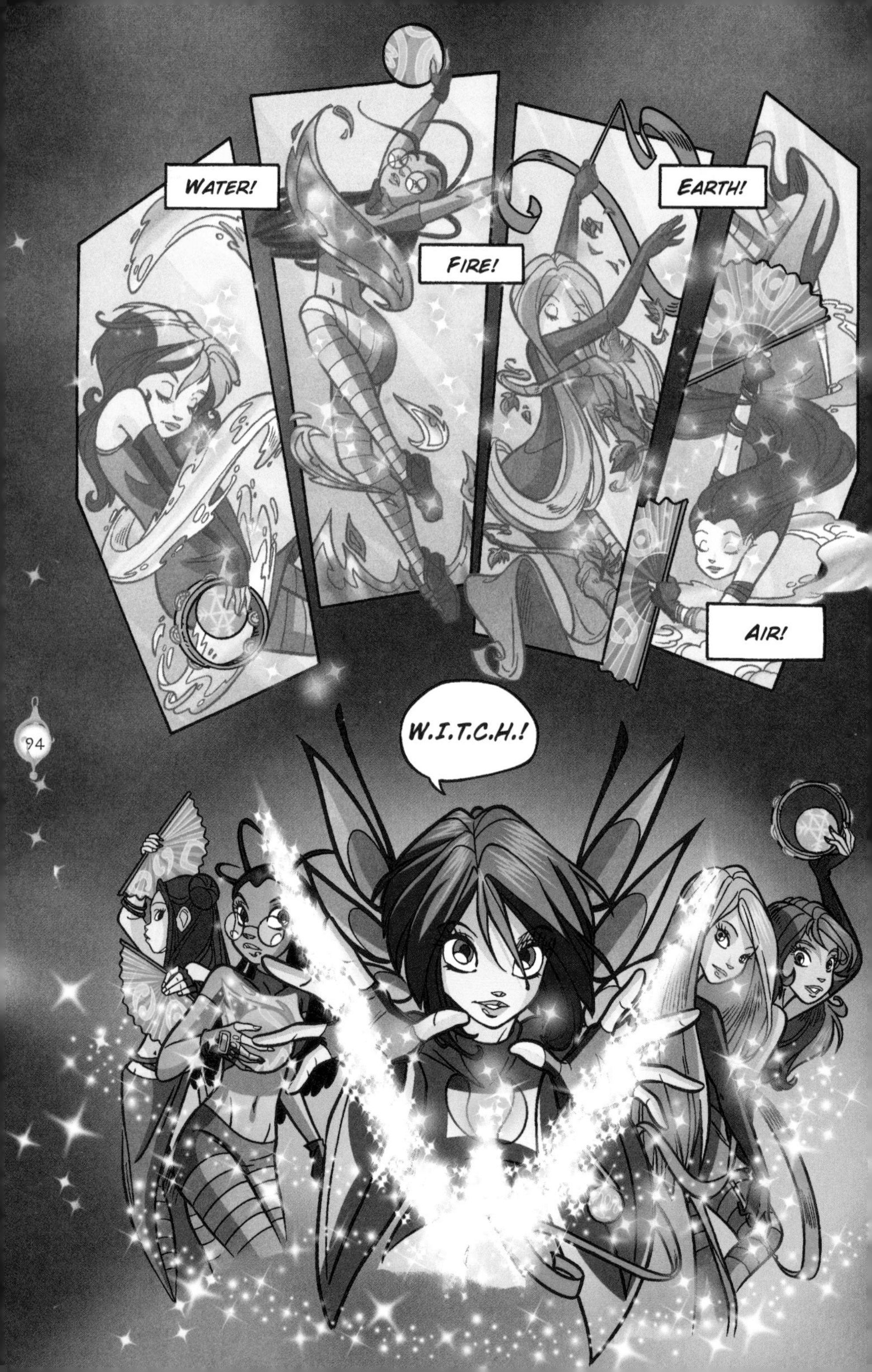
WATER!
FIRE!
EARTH!
AIR!
W.I.T.C.H.!

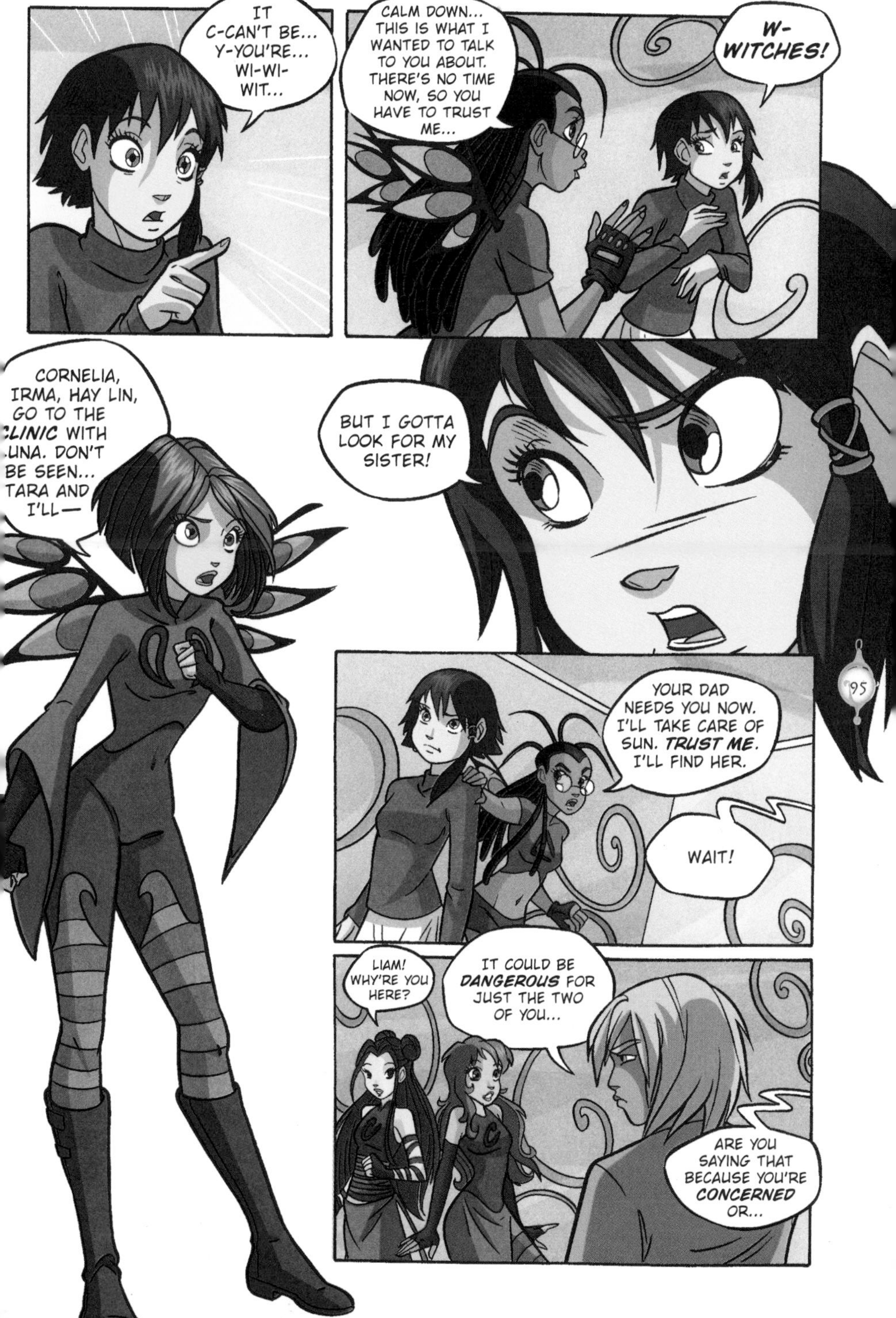

IT C-CAN'T BE... Y-YOU'RE... WI-WI-WIT...
CALM DOWN... THIS IS WHAT I WANTED TO TALK TO YOU ABOUT. THERE'S NO TIME NOW, SO YOU HAVE TO TRUST ME...
W-WITCHES!
CORNELIA, IRMA, HAY LIN, GO TO THE CLINIC WITH LUNA. DON'T BE SEEN... TARA AND I'LL—
BUT I GOTTA LOOK FOR MY SISTER!
YOUR DAD NEEDS YOU NOW. I'LL TAKE CARE OF SUN. TRUST ME. I'LL FIND HER.
WAIT!
LIAM! WHY'RE YOU HERE?
IT COULD BE DANGEROUS FOR JUST THE TWO OF YOU...
ARE YOU SAYING THAT BECAUSE YOU'RE CONCERNED OR...

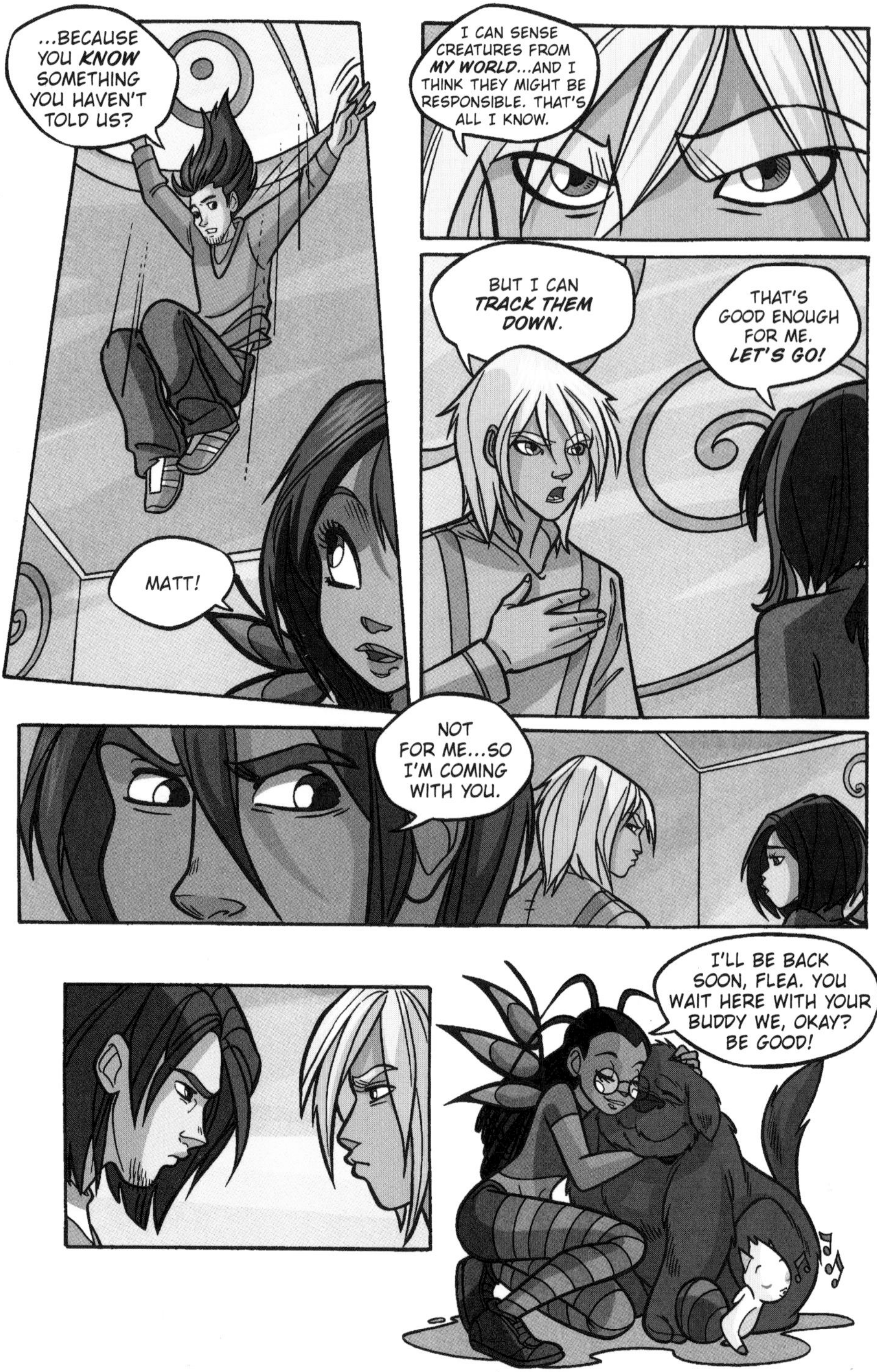
...BECAUSE YOU KNOW SOMETHING YOU HAVEN'T TOLD US?
MATT!
I CAN SENSE CREATURES FROM MY WORLD...AND I THINK THEY MIGHT BE RESPONSIBLE. THAT'S ALL I KNOW.
BUT I CAN TRACK THEM DOWN.
THAT'S GOOD ENOUGH FOR ME. LET'S GO!
NOT FOR ME...SO I'M COMING WITH YOU.
I'LL BE BACK SOON, FLEA. YOU WAIT HERE WITH YOUR BUDDY WE, OKAY? BE GOOD!

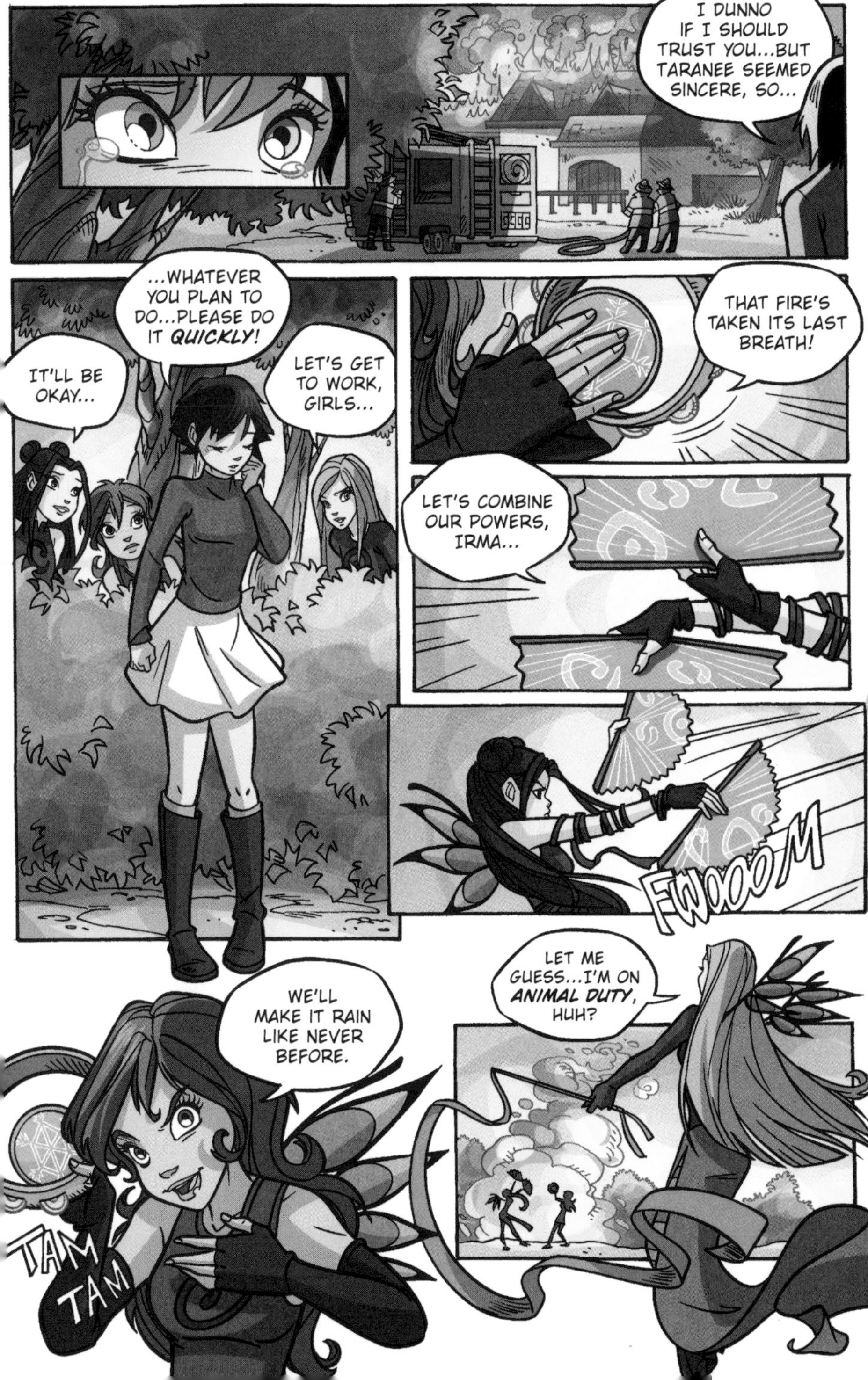
I DUNNO IF I SHOULD TRUST YOU...BUT TARANEE SEEMED SINCERE, SO...
...WHATEVER YOU PLAN TO DO...PLEASE DO IT *QUICKLY*!
IT'LL BE OKAY...
LET'S GET TO WORK, GIRLS...
THAT FIRE'S TAKEN ITS LAST BREATH!
LET'S COMBINE OUR POWERS, IRMA...
FWOOOM
WE'LL MAKE IT RAIN LIKE NEVER BEFORE.
TAM TAM
LET ME GUESS...I'M ON *ANIMAL DUTY*, HUH?

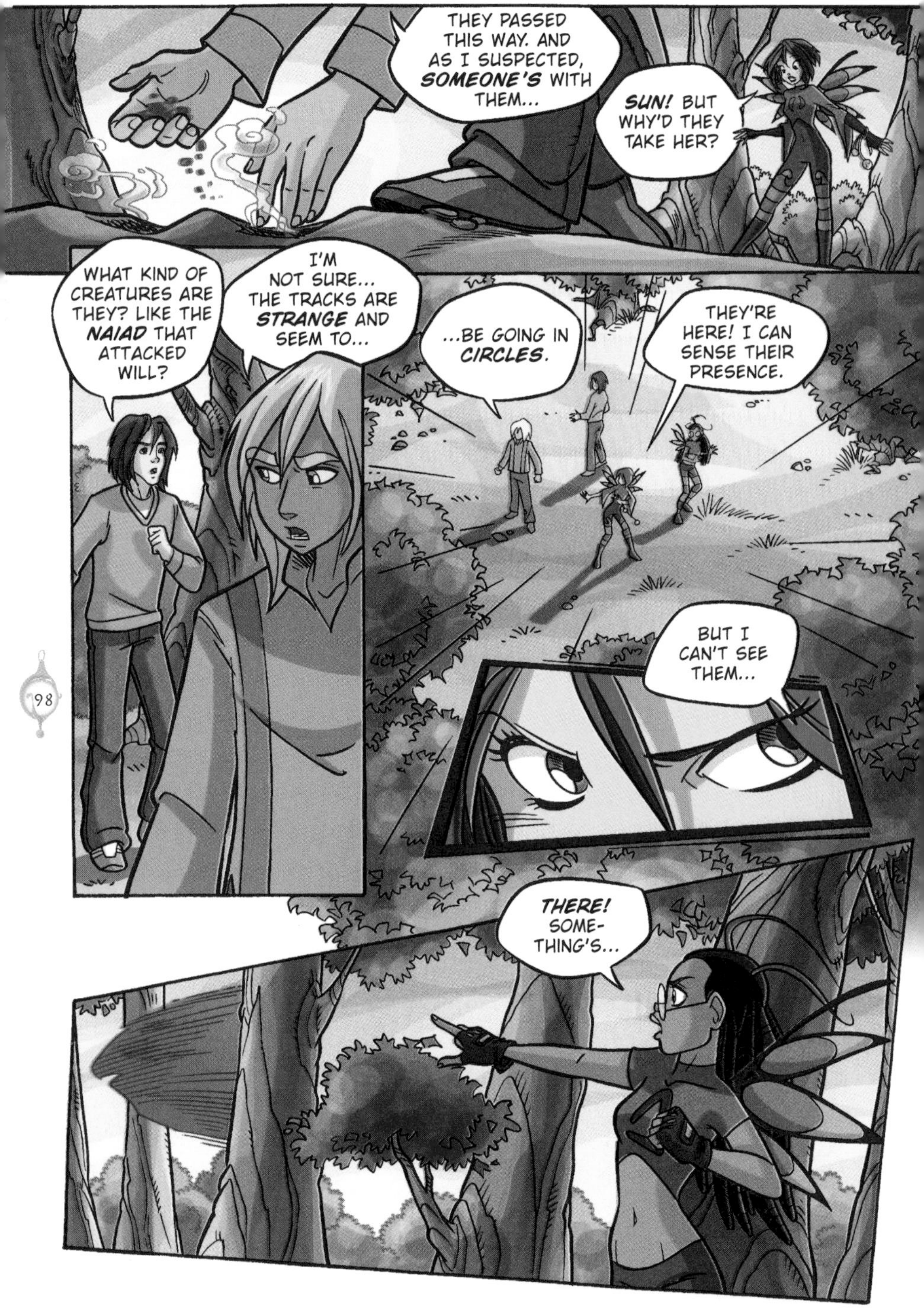
THEY PASSED THIS WAY. AND AS I SUSPECTED, **SOMEONE'S** WITH THEM...
SUN! BUT WHY'D THEY TAKE HER?
WHAT KIND OF CREATURES ARE THEY? LIKE THE **NAIAD** THAT ATTACKED WILL?
I'M NOT SURE... THE TRACKS ARE **STRANGE** AND SEEM TO...
...BE GOING IN **CIRCLES**.
THEY'RE HERE! I CAN SENSE THEIR PRESENCE.
BUT I CAN'T SEE THEM...
THERE! SOME-THING'S...

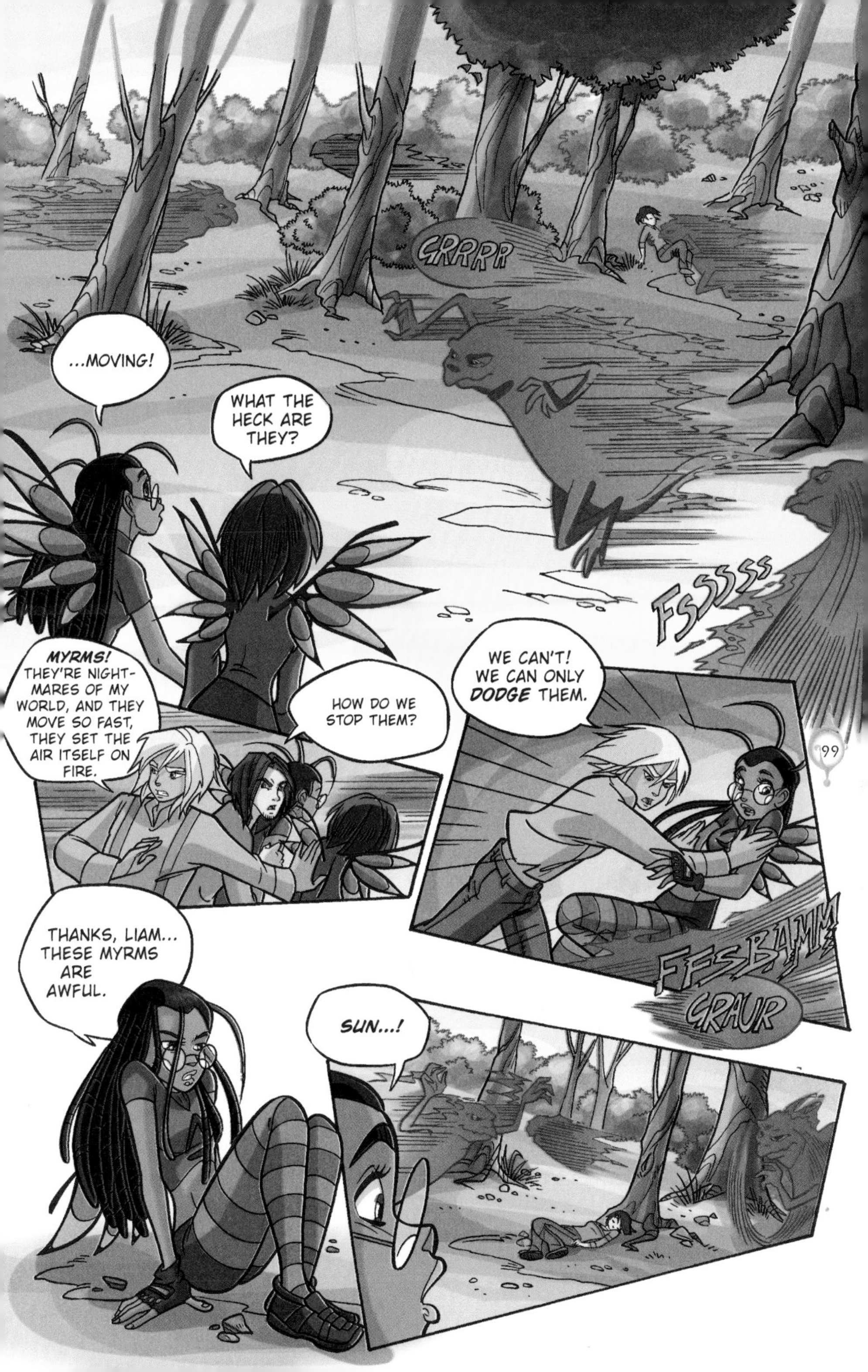
GRRRR
...MOVING!
WHAT THE HECK ARE THEY?
FSSSSS
MYRMS! THEY'RE NIGHTMARES OF MY WORLD, AND THEY MOVE SO FAST, THEY SET THE AIR ITSELF ON FIRE.
HOW DO WE STOP THEM?
WE CAN'T! WE CAN ONLY DODGE THEM.
FFSBAMM!
GRAUR
THANKS, LIAM... THESE MYRMS ARE AWFUL.
SUN...!

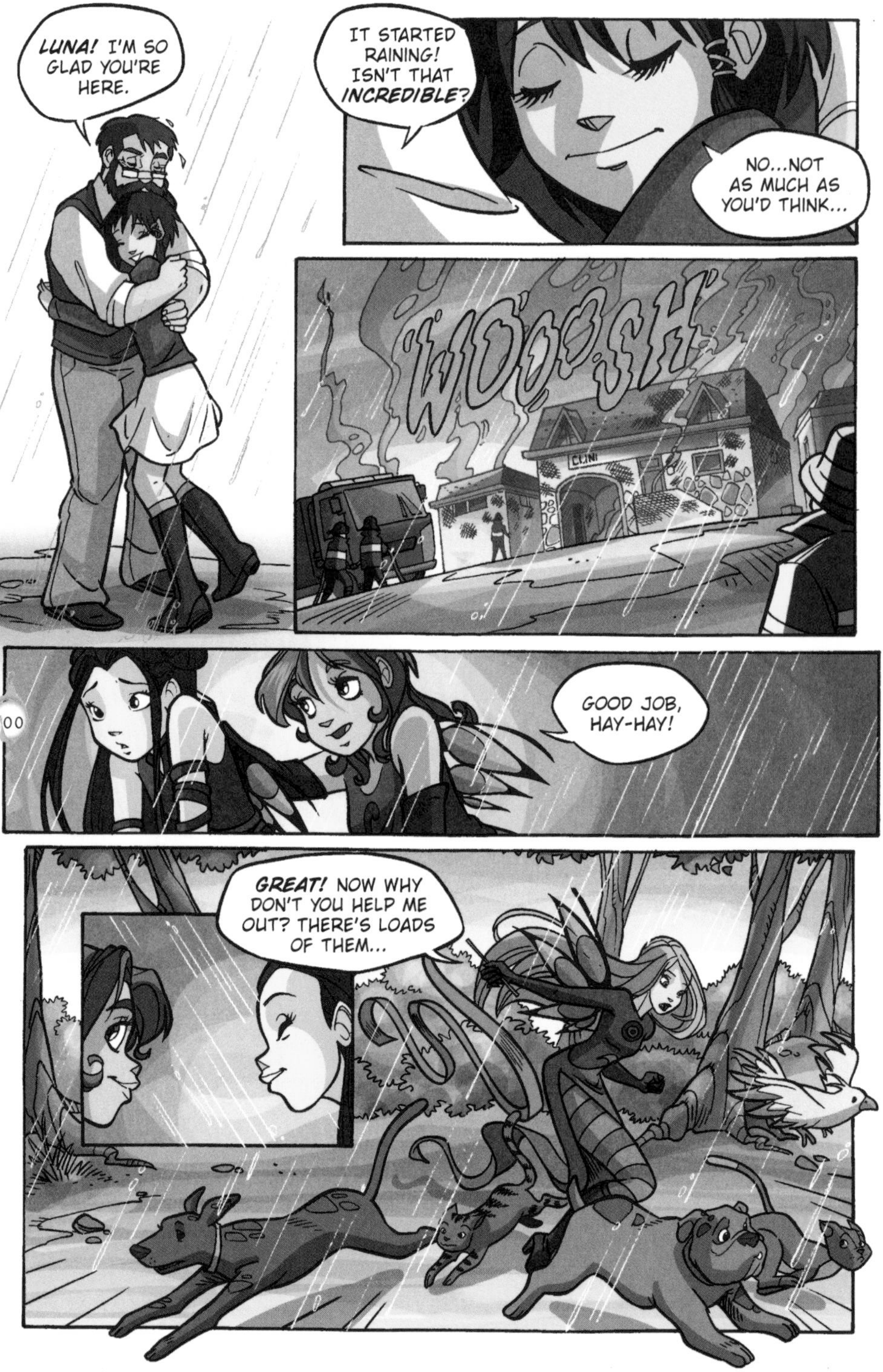
LUNA! I'M SO GLAD YOU'RE HERE.
IT STARTED RAINING! ISN'T THAT INCREDIBLE?
NO...NOT AS MUCH AS YOU'D THINK...
WOOOSH
GOOD JOB, HAY-HAY!
GREAT! NOW WHY DON'T YOU HELP ME OUT? THERE'S LOADS OF THEM...

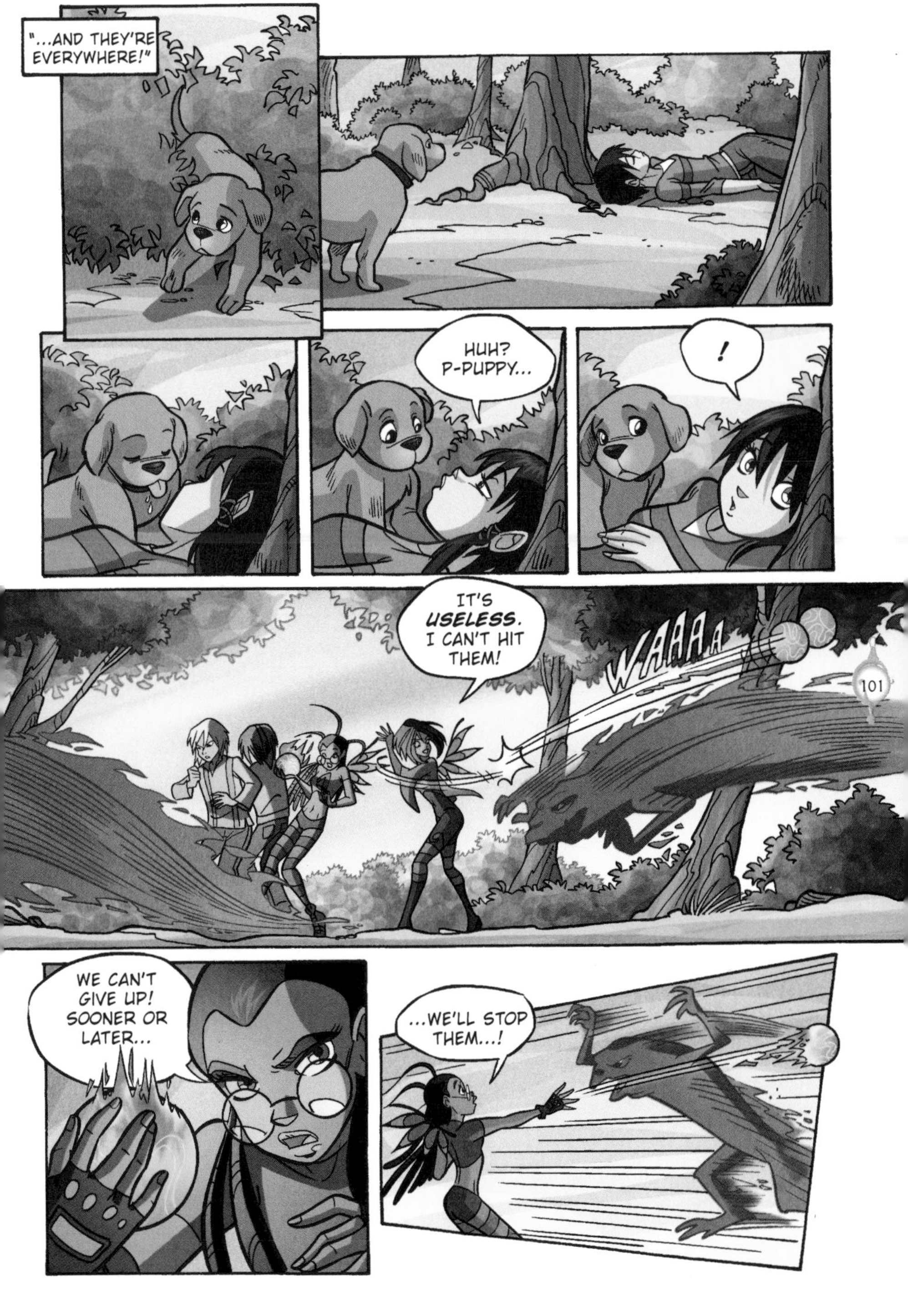
"...AND THEY'RE EVERYWHERE!"
HUH? P-PUPPY...
!
IT'S USELESS. I CAN'T HIT THEM!
WAAAA
WE CAN'T GIVE UP! SOONER OR LATER...
...WE'LL STOP THEM...!

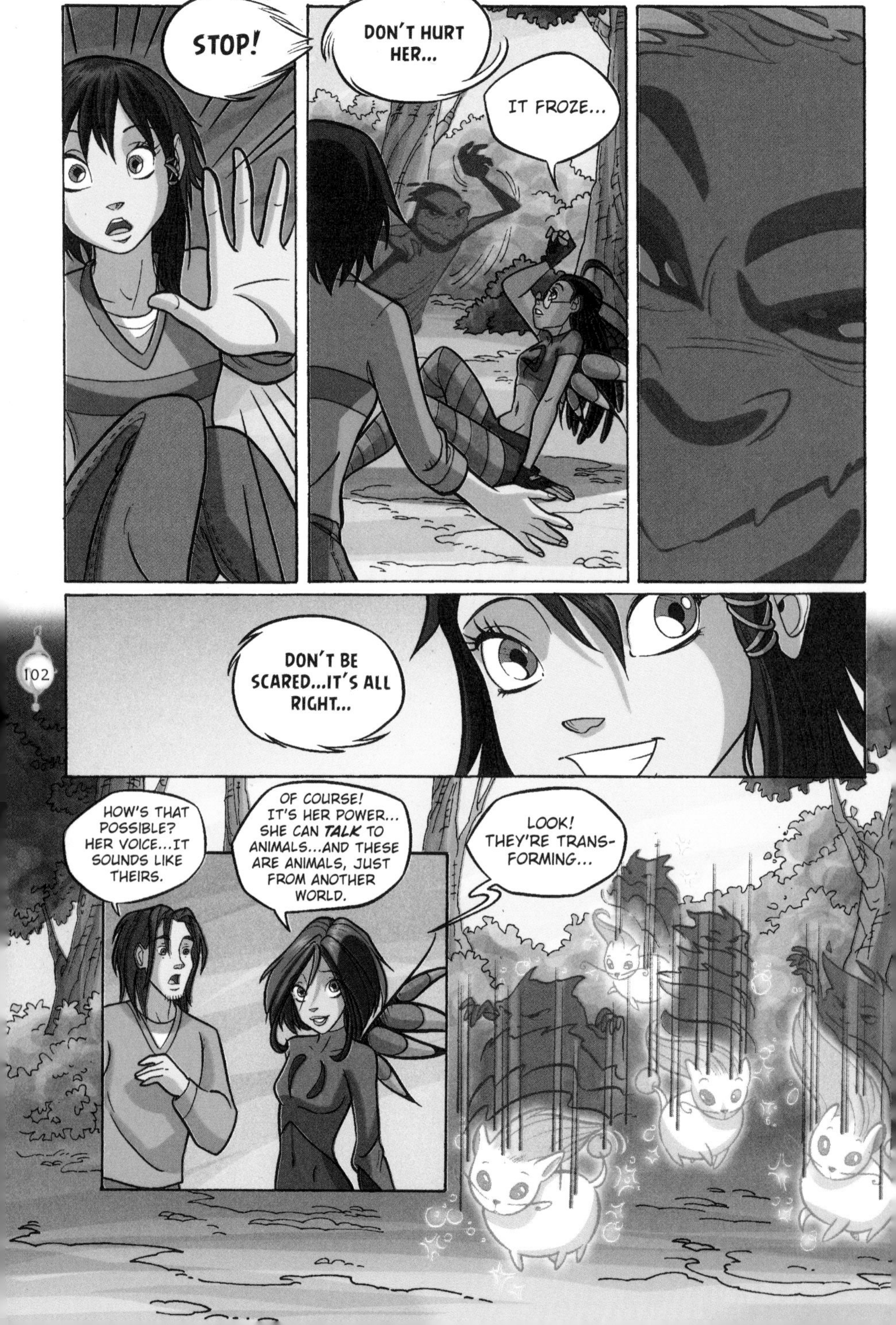
STOP!
DON'T HURT HER...
IT FROZE...
DON'T BE SCARED...IT'S ALL RIGHT...
HOW'S THAT POSSIBLE? HER VOICE...IT SOUNDS LIKE THEIRS.
OF COURSE! IT'S HER POWER... SHE CAN TALK TO ANIMALS...AND THESE ARE ANIMALS, JUST FROM ANOTHER WORLD.
LOOK! THEY'RE TRANS-FORMING...

102

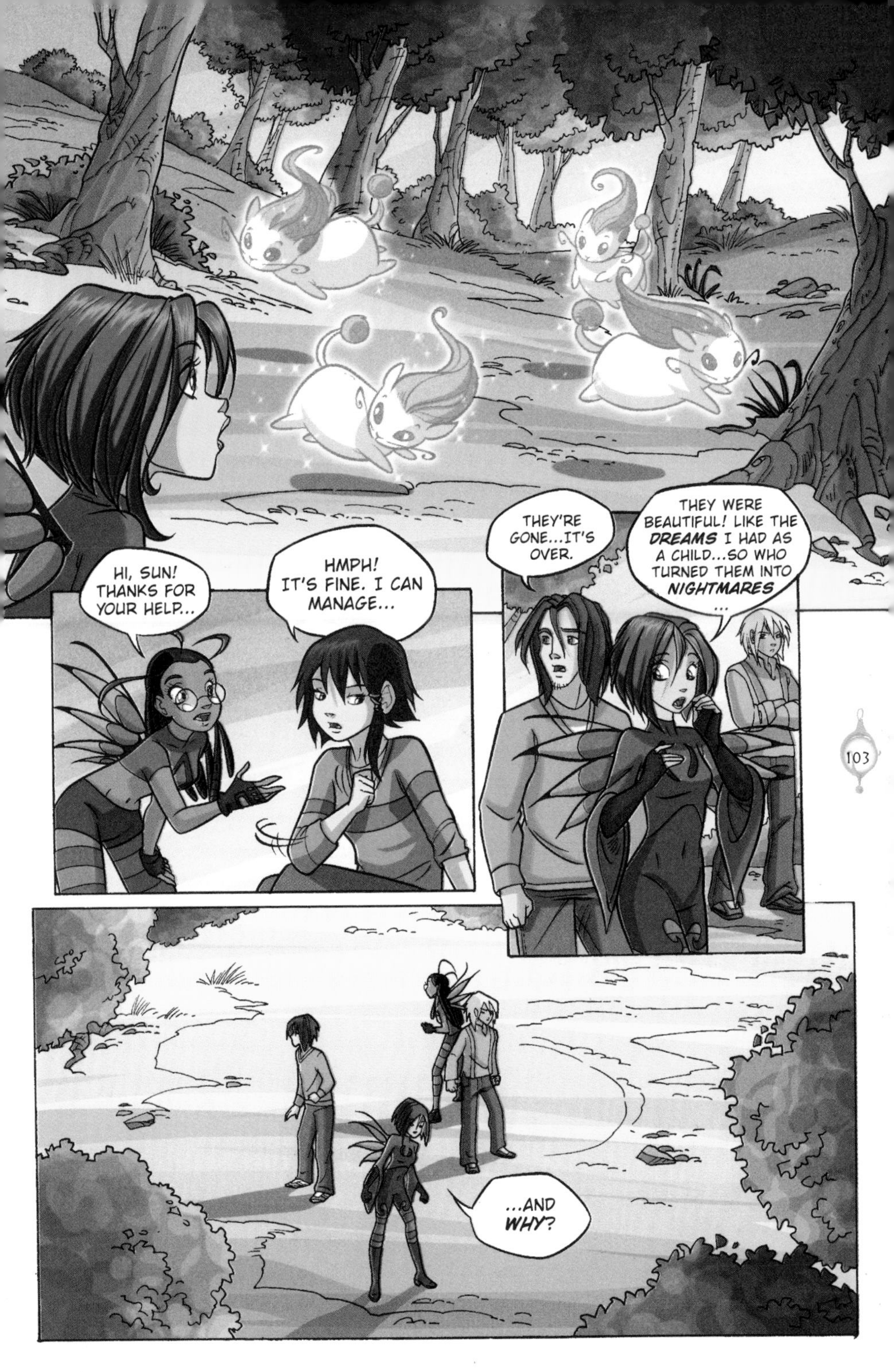
HI, SUN! THANKS FOR YOUR HELP...
HMPH! IT'S FINE. I CAN MANAGE...
THEY'RE GONE...IT'S OVER.
THEY WERE BEAUTIFUL! LIKE THE **DREAMS** I HAD AS A CHILD...SO WHO TURNED THEM INTO **NIGHTMARES**...
...AND **WHY**?

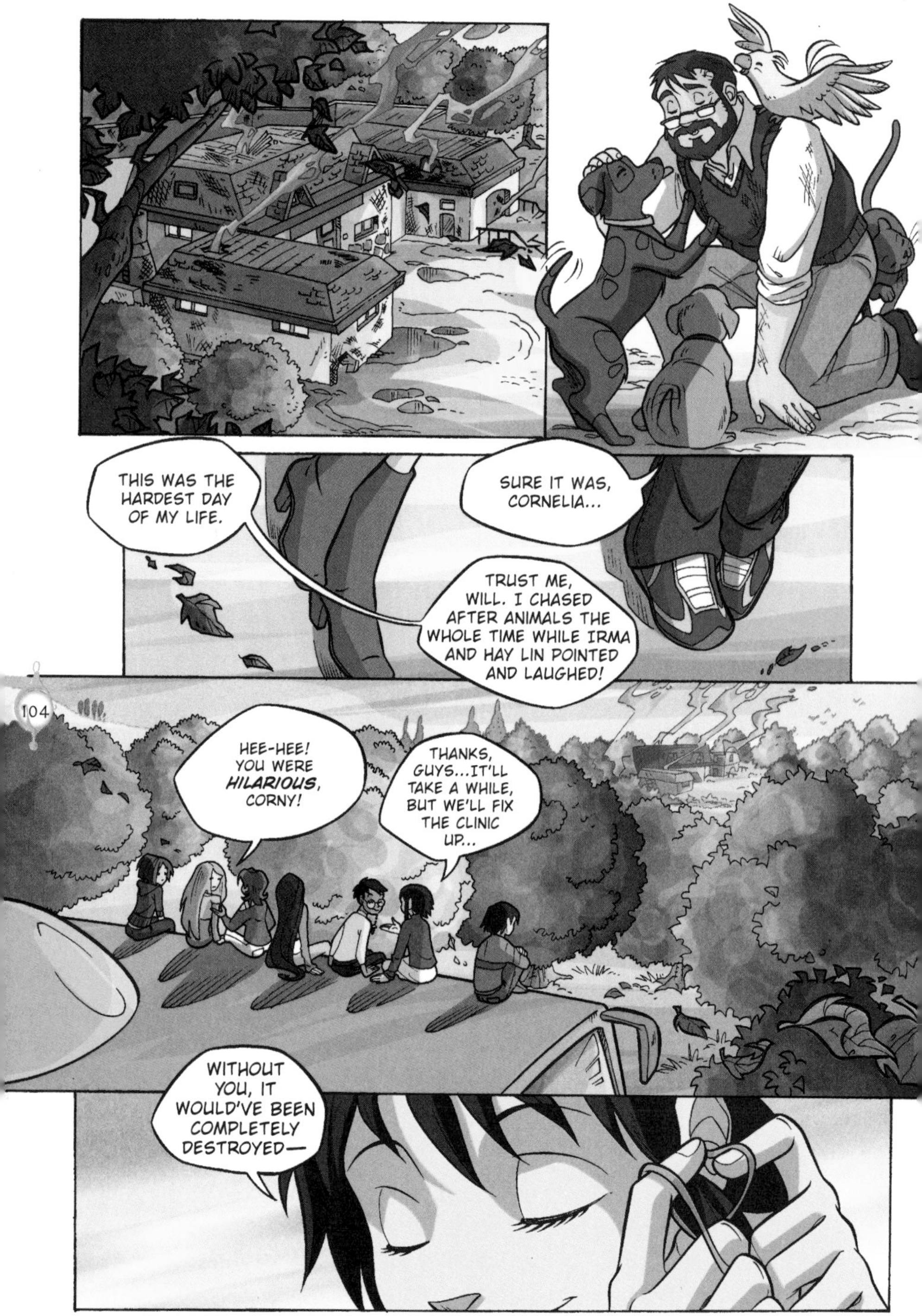

THIS WAS THE HARDEST DAY OF MY LIFE.
SURE IT WAS, CORNELIA...
TRUST ME, WILL. I CHASED AFTER ANIMALS THE WHOLE TIME WHILE IRMA AND HAY LIN POINTED AND LAUGHED!
HEE-HEE! YOU WERE *HILARIOUS*, CORNY!
THANKS, GUYS...IT'LL TAKE A WHILE, BUT WE'LL FIX THE CLINIC UP...
WITHOUT YOU, IT WOULD'VE BEEN COMPLETELY DESTROYED—

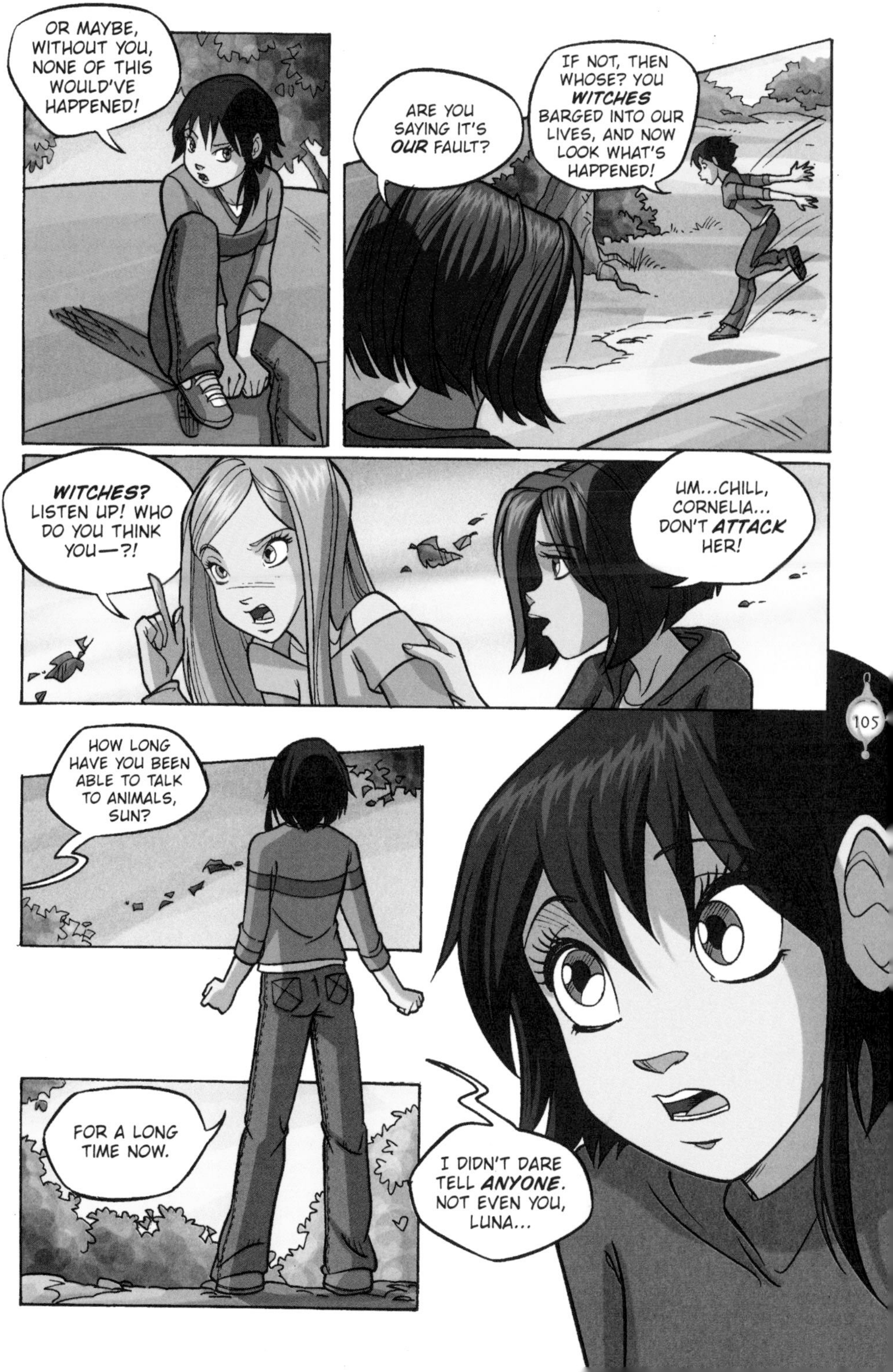
OR MAYBE, WITHOUT YOU, NONE OF THIS WOULD'VE HAPPENED!
ARE YOU SAYING IT'S *OUR* FAULT?
IF NOT, THEN WHOSE? YOU *WITCHES* BARGED INTO OUR LIVES, AND NOW LOOK WHAT'S HAPPENED!
WITCHES? LISTEN UP! WHO DO YOU THINK YOU—?!
UM...CHILL, CORNELIA... DON'T *ATTACK* HER!
HOW LONG HAVE YOU BEEN ABLE TO TALK TO ANIMALS, SUN?
FOR A LONG TIME NOW.
I DIDN'T DARE TELL *ANYONE*. NOT EVEN YOU, LUNA...

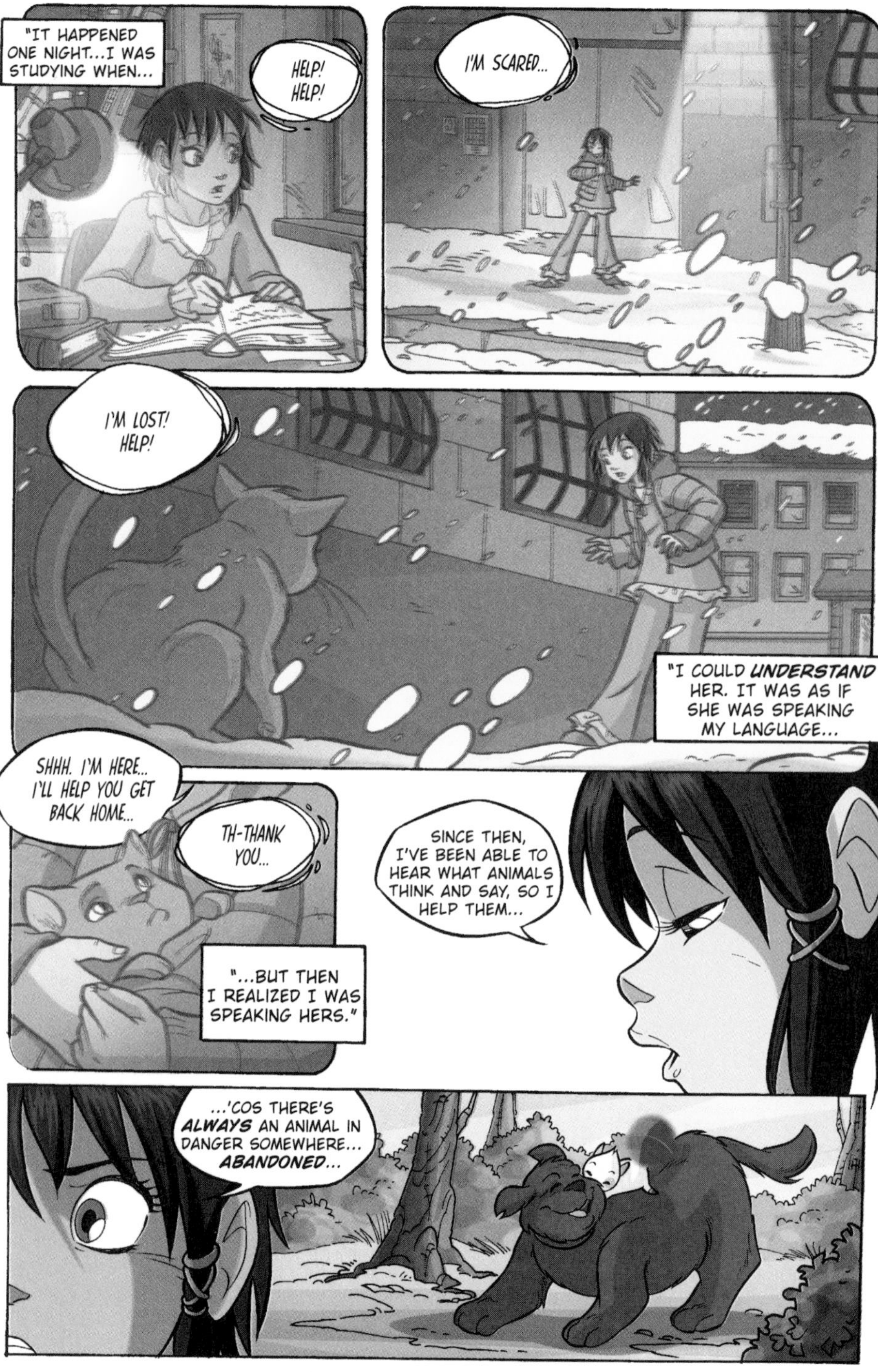
"IT HAPPENED ONE NIGHT...I WAS STUDYING WHEN...
HELP! HELP!
I'M SCARED...
I'M LOST! HELP!
"I COULD UNDERSTAND HER. IT WAS AS IF SHE WAS SPEAKING MY LANGUAGE...
SHHH. I'M HERE... I'LL HELP YOU GET BACK HOME...
TH-THANK YOU...
"...BUT THEN I REALIZED I WAS SPEAKING HERS."
SINCE THEN, I'VE BEEN ABLE TO HEAR WHAT ANIMALS THINK AND SAY, SO I HELP THEM...
...'COS THERE'S ALWAYS AN ANIMAL IN DANGER SOMEWHERE... ABANDONED...

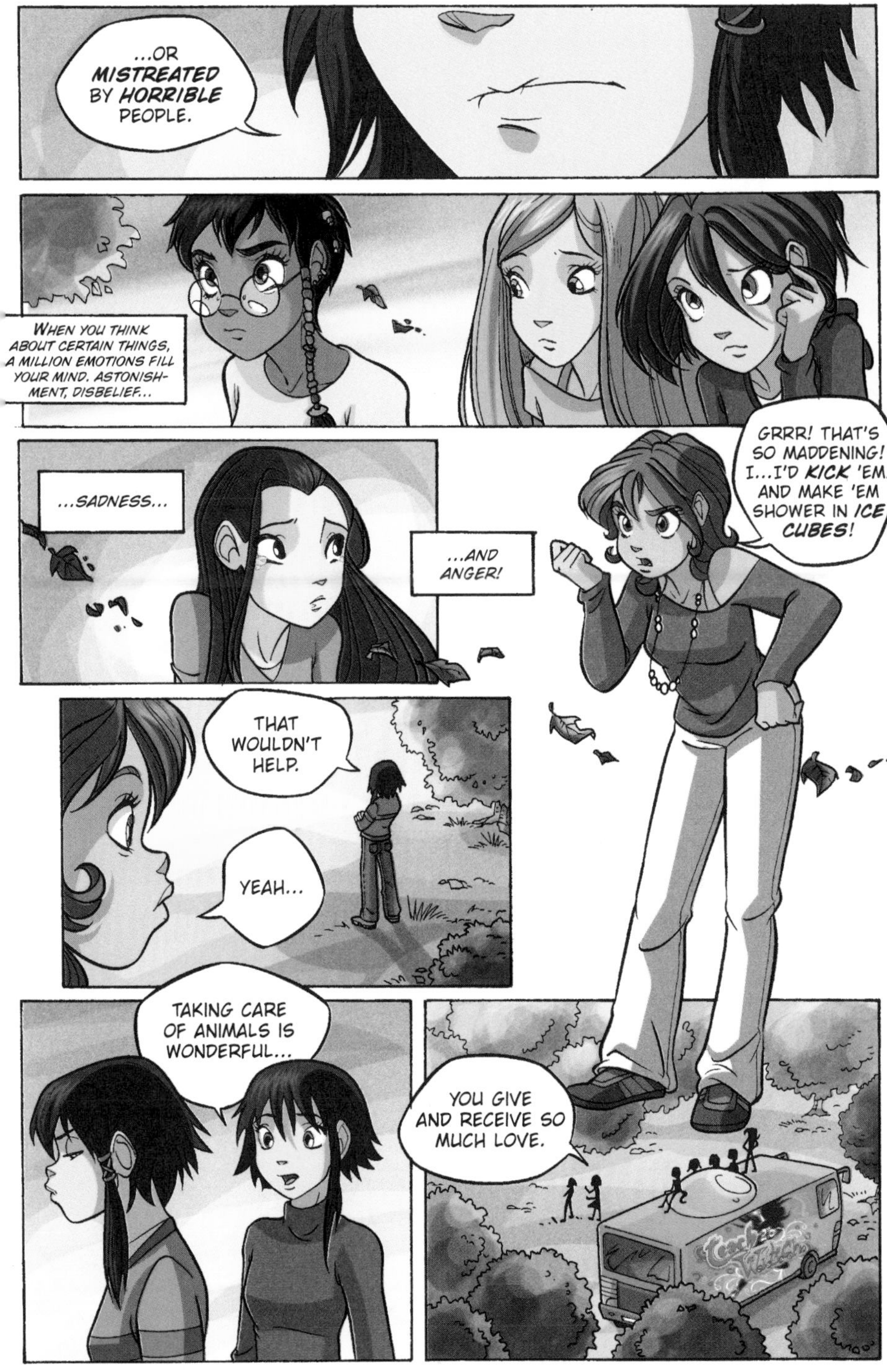

...OR MISTREATED BY HORRIBLE PEOPLE.
WHEN YOU THINK ABOUT CERTAIN THINGS, A MILLION EMOTIONS FILL YOUR MIND. ASTONISHMENT, DISBELIEF...
...SADNESS...
...AND ANGER!
GRRR! THAT'S SO MADDENING! I...I'D KICK 'EM! AND MAKE 'EM SHOWER IN ICE CUBES!
THAT WOULDN'T HELP.
YEAH...
TAKING CARE OF ANIMALS IS WONDERFUL...
YOU GIVE AND RECEIVE SO MUCH LOVE.

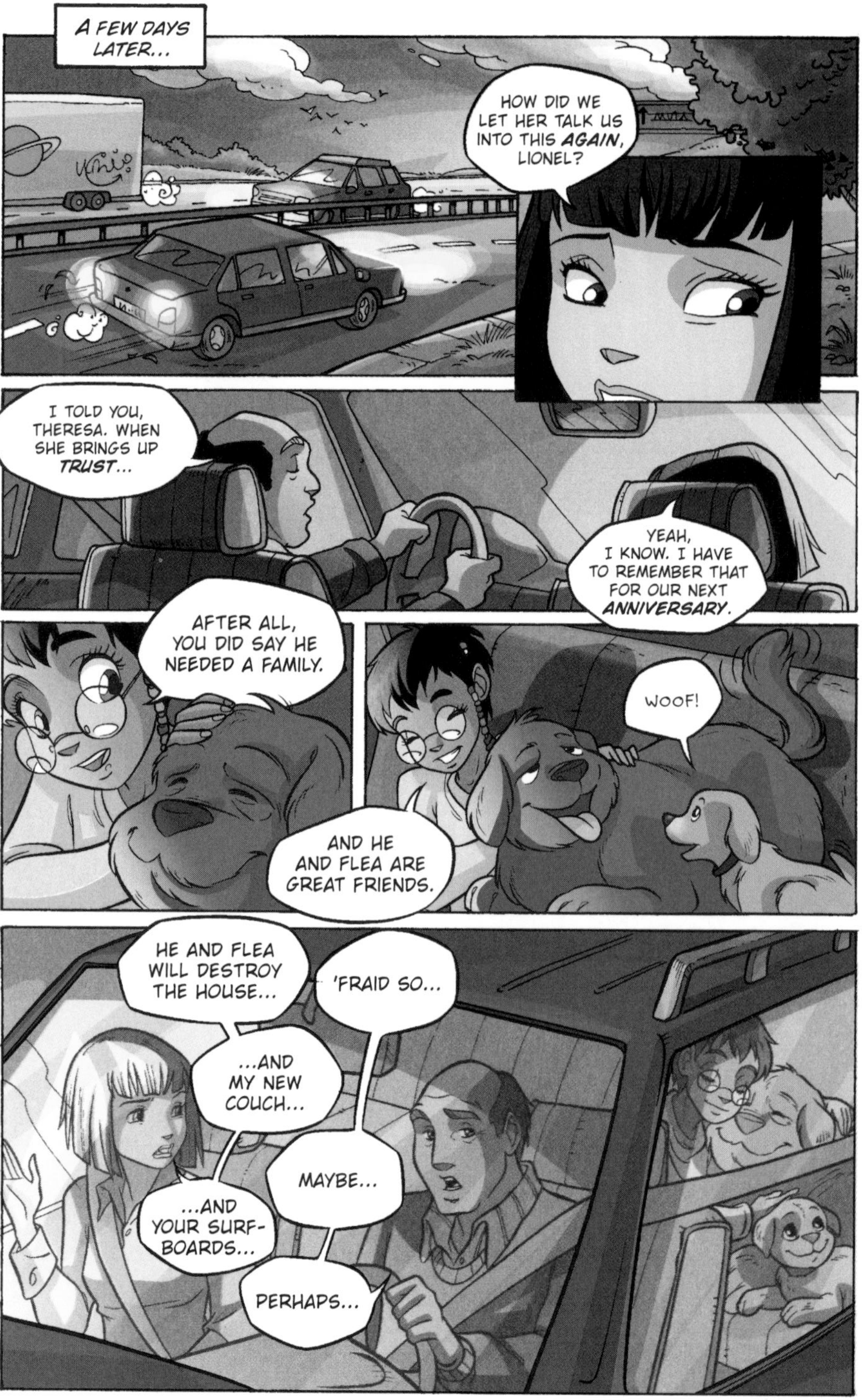
A FEW DAYS LATER...
HOW DID WE LET HER TALK US INTO THIS AGAIN, LIONEL?
I TOLD YOU, THERESA. WHEN SHE BRINGS UP TRUST...
YEAH, I KNOW. I HAVE TO REMEMBER THAT FOR OUR NEXT ANNIVERSARY.
AFTER ALL, YOU DID SAY HE NEEDED A FAMILY.
WOOF!
AND HE AND FLEA ARE GREAT FRIENDS.
HE AND FLEA WILL DESTROY THE HOUSE...
'FRAID SO...
...AND MY NEW COUCH...
MAYBE...
...AND YOUR SURF-BOARDS...
PERHAPS...

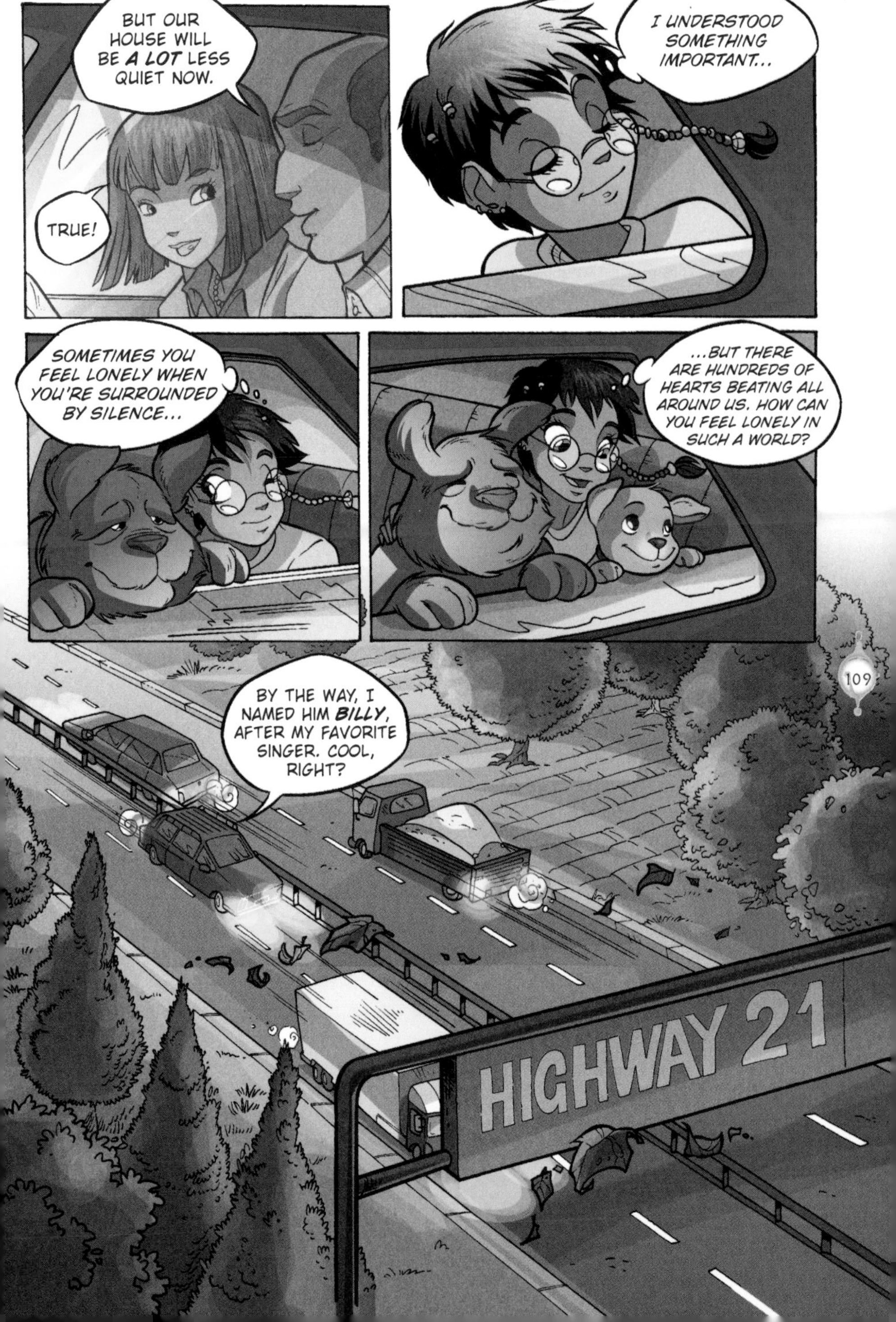

BUT OUR HOUSE WILL BE A LOT LESS QUIET NOW.
TRUE!
I UNDERSTOOD SOMETHING IMPORTANT...
SOMETIMES YOU FEEL LONELY WHEN YOU'RE SURROUNDED BY SILENCE...
...BUT THERE ARE HUNDREDS OF HEARTS BEATING ALL AROUND US. HOW CAN YOU FEEL LONELY IN SUCH A WORLD?
BY THE WAY, I NAMED HIM BILLY, AFTER MY FAVORITE SINGER. COOL, RIGHT?
HIGHWAY 21

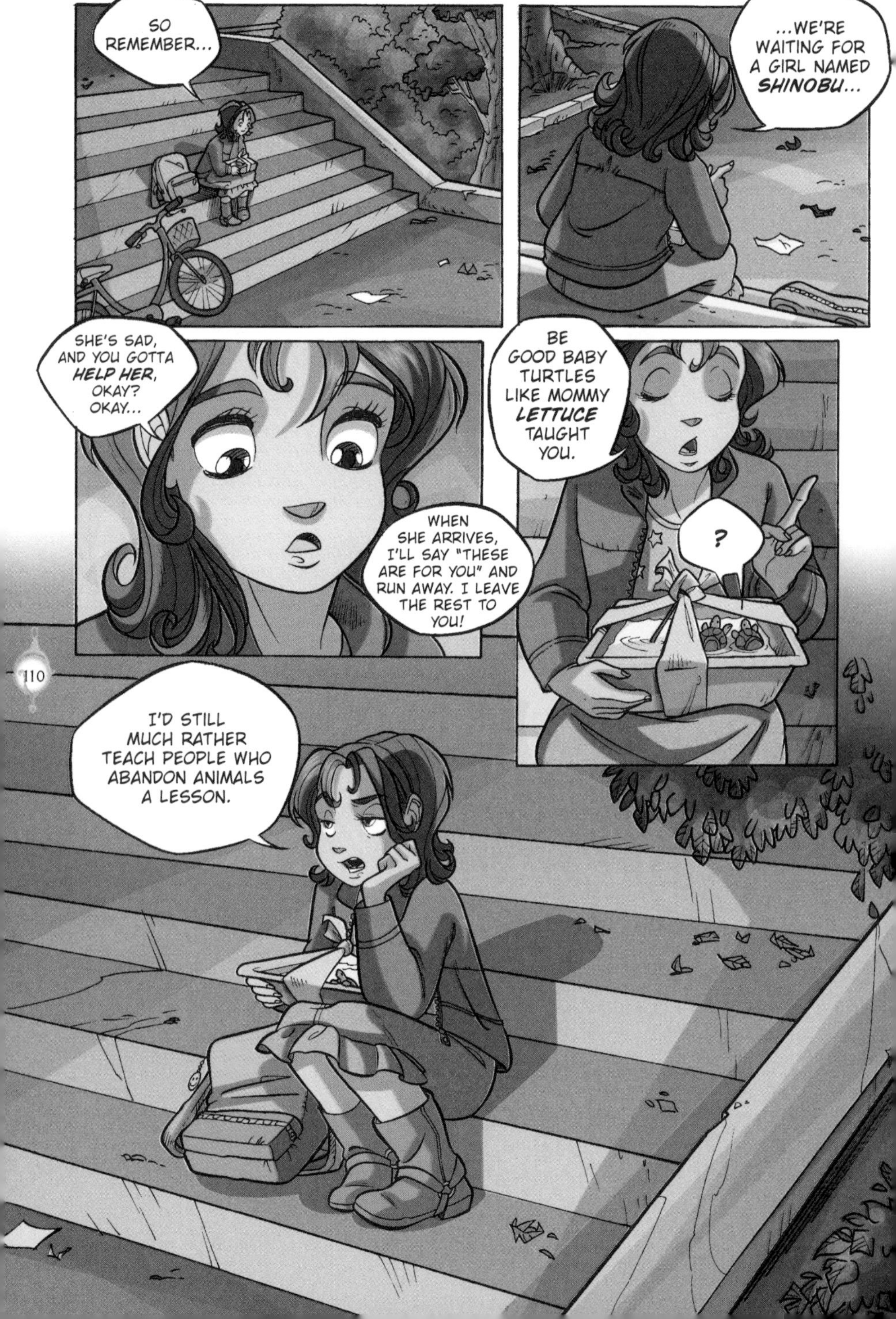
SO REMEMBER...
...WE'RE WAITING FOR A GIRL NAMED SHINOBU...
SHE'S SAD, AND YOU GOTTA HELP HER, OKAY? OKAY...
WHEN SHE ARRIVES, I'LL SAY "THESE ARE FOR YOU" AND RUN AWAY. I LEAVE THE REST TO YOU!
BE GOOD BABY TURTLES LIKE MOMMY LETTUCE TAUGHT YOU.
?
I'D STILL MUCH RATHER TEACH PEOPLE WHO ABANDON ANIMALS A LESSON.

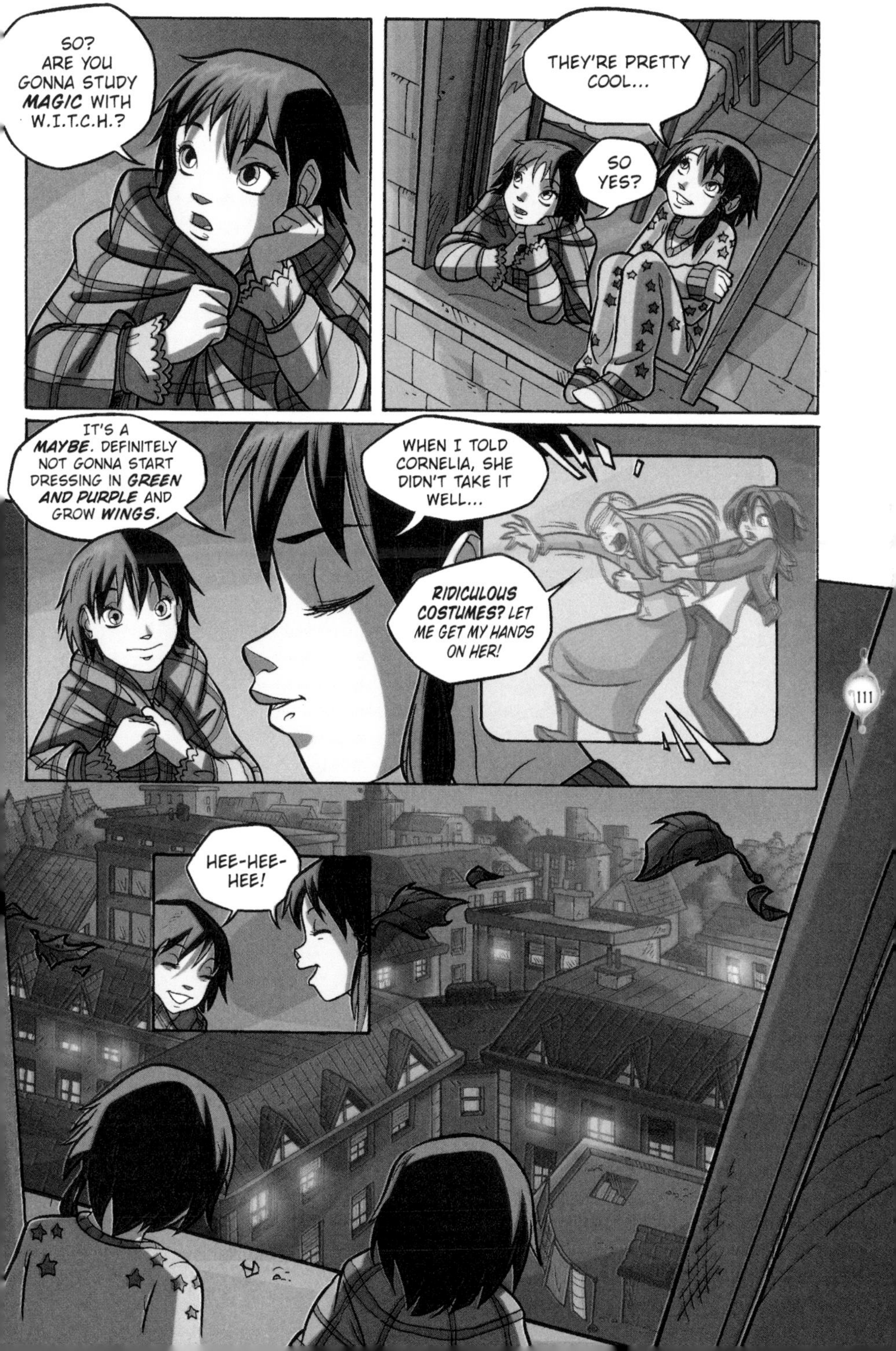
SO? ARE YOU GONNA STUDY MAGIC WITH W.I.T.C.H.?
THEY'RE PRETTY COOL...
SO YES?
IT'S A MAYBE. DEFINITELY NOT GONNA START DRESSING IN GREEN AND PURPLE AND GROW WINGS.
WHEN I TOLD CORNELIA, SHE DIDN'T TAKE IT WELL...
RIDICULOUS COSTUMES? LET ME GET MY HANDS ON HER!
HEE-HEE-HEE!

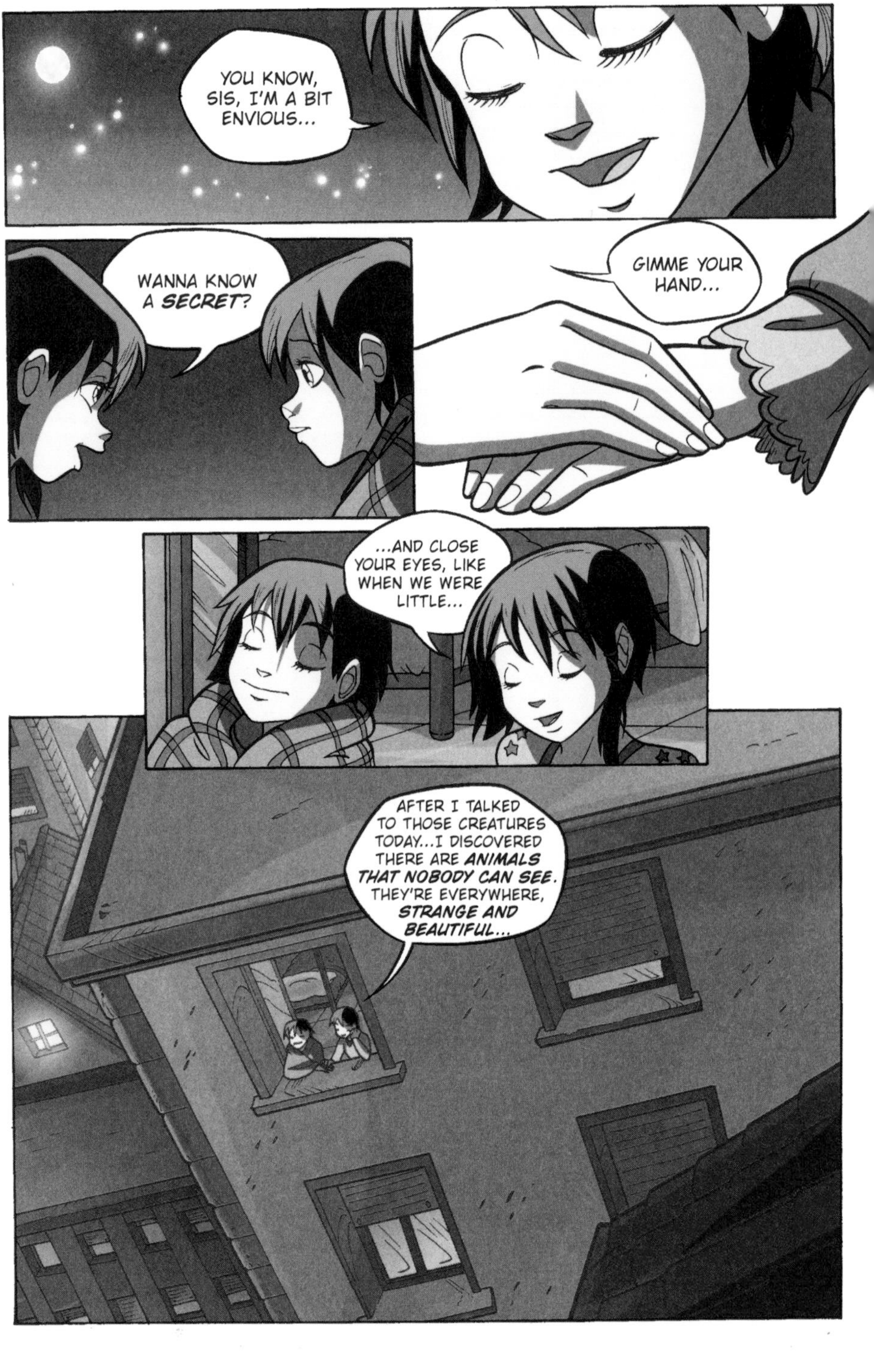
YOU KNOW, SIS, I'M A BIT ENVIOUS...
WANNA KNOW A SECRET?
GIMME YOUR HAND...
...AND CLOSE YOUR EYES, LIKE WHEN WE WERE LITTLE...
AFTER I TALKED TO THOSE CREATURES TODAY...I DISCOVERED THERE ARE ANIMALS THAT NOBODY CAN SEE. THEY'RE EVERYWHERE, STRANGE AND BEAUTIFUL...

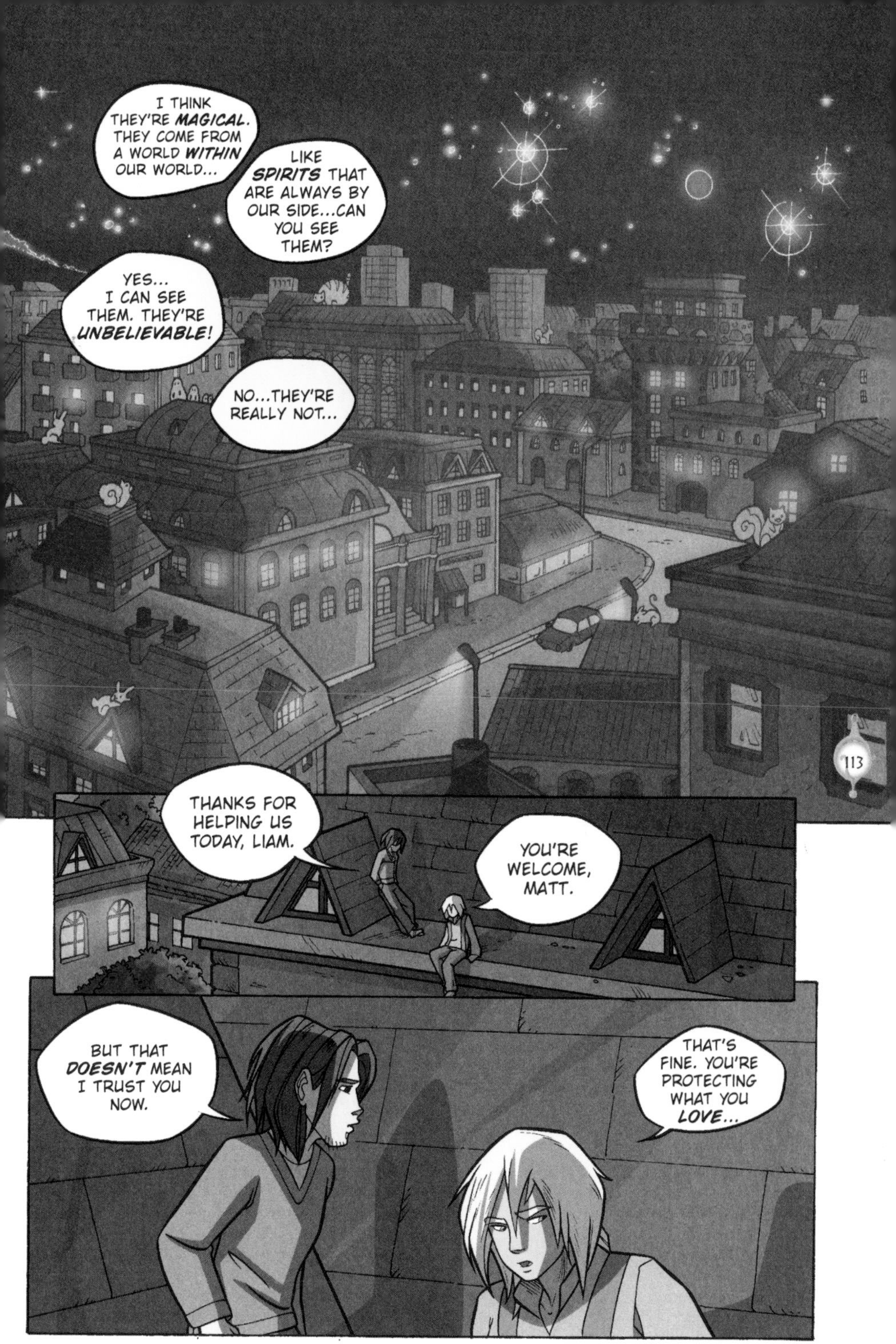
I THINK THEY'RE *MAGICAL*. THEY COME FROM A WORLD *WITHIN* OUR WORLD...
LIKE *SPIRITS* THAT ARE ALWAYS BY OUR SIDE...CAN YOU SEE THEM?
YES... I CAN SEE THEM. THEY'RE *UNBELIEVABLE*!
NO...THEY'RE REALLY NOT...
THANKS FOR HELPING US TODAY, LIAM.
YOU'RE WELCOME, MATT.
BUT THAT *DOESN'T* MEAN I TRUST YOU NOW.
THAT'S FINE. YOU'RE PROTECTING WHAT YOU *LOVE*...

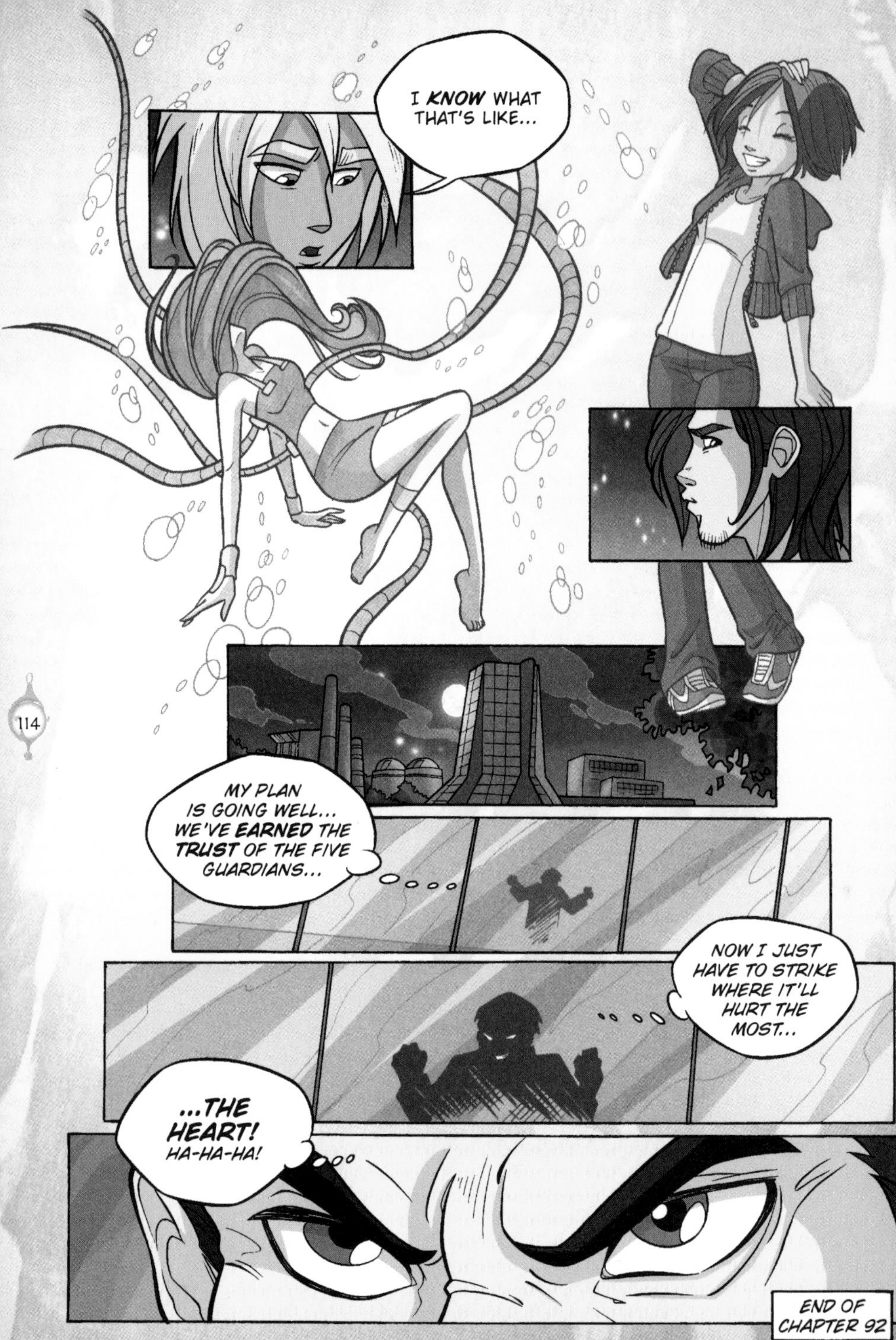
I KNOW WHAT THAT'S LIKE...
MY PLAN IS GOING WELL... WE'VE EARNED THE TRUST OF THE FIVE GUARDIANS...
NOW I JUST HAVE TO STRIKE WHERE IT'LL HURT THE MOST...
...THE HEART! HA-HA-HA!
END OF CHAPTER 92

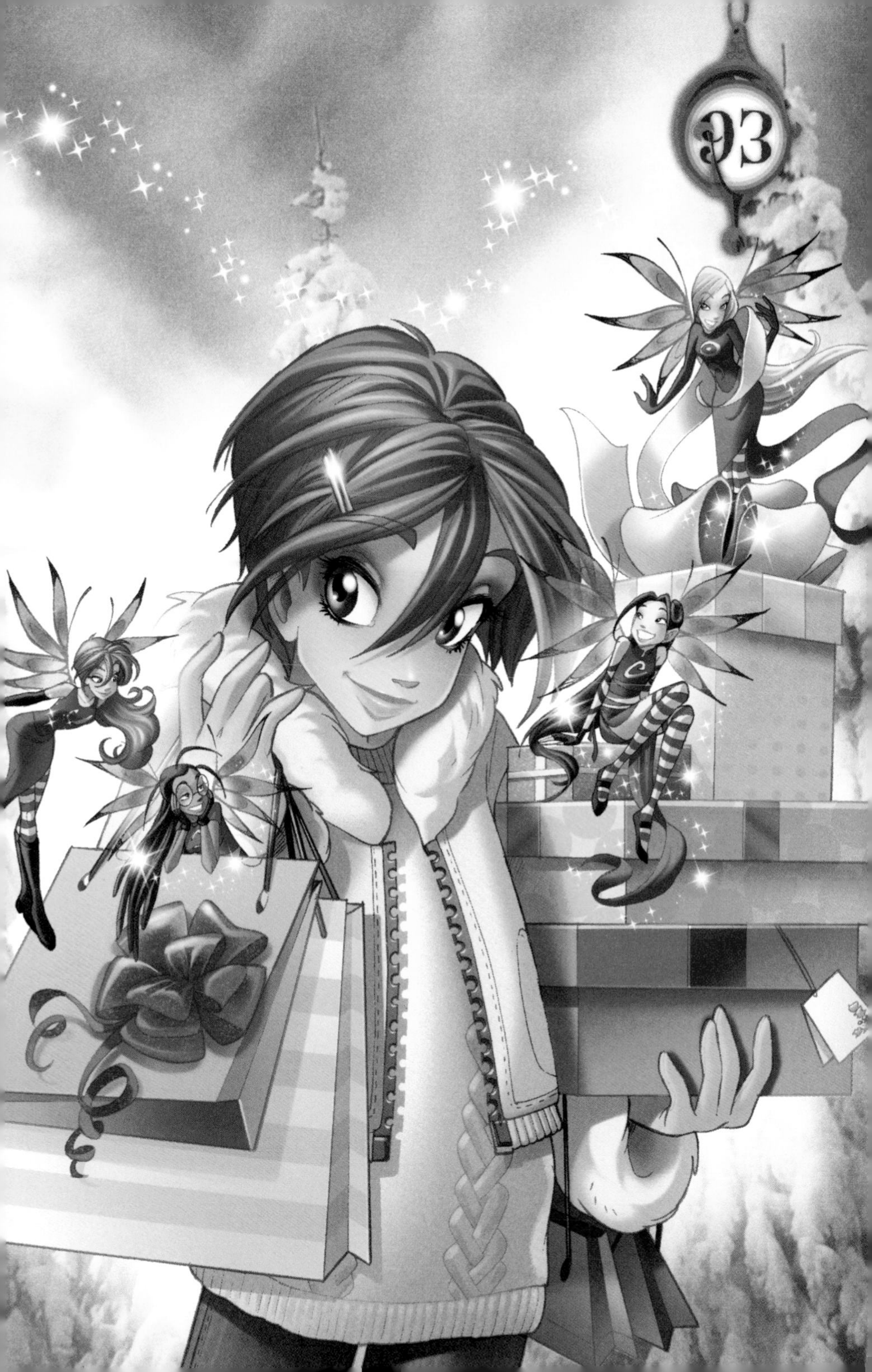
93

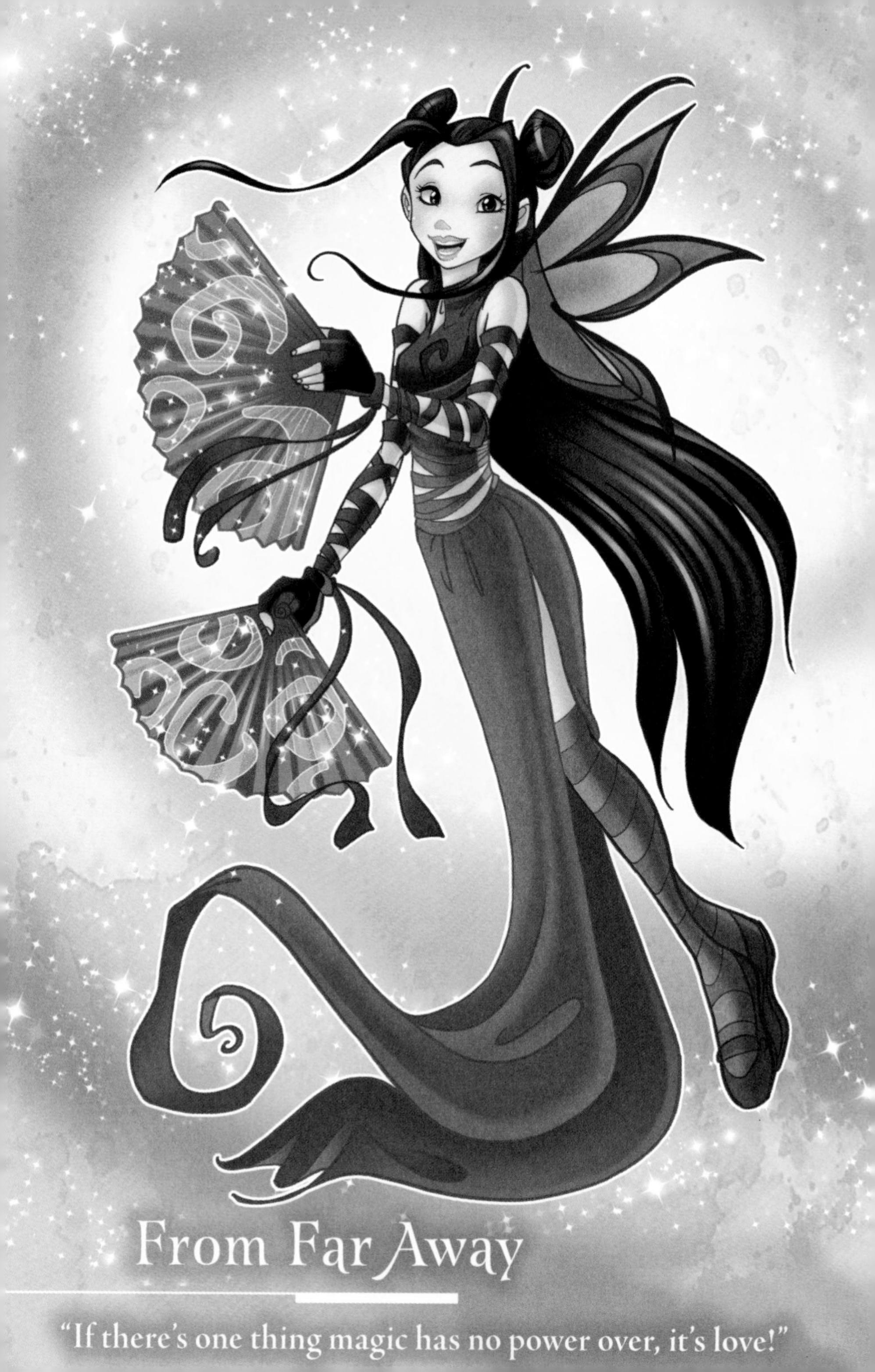

From Far Away

"If there's one thing magic has no power over, it's love!"

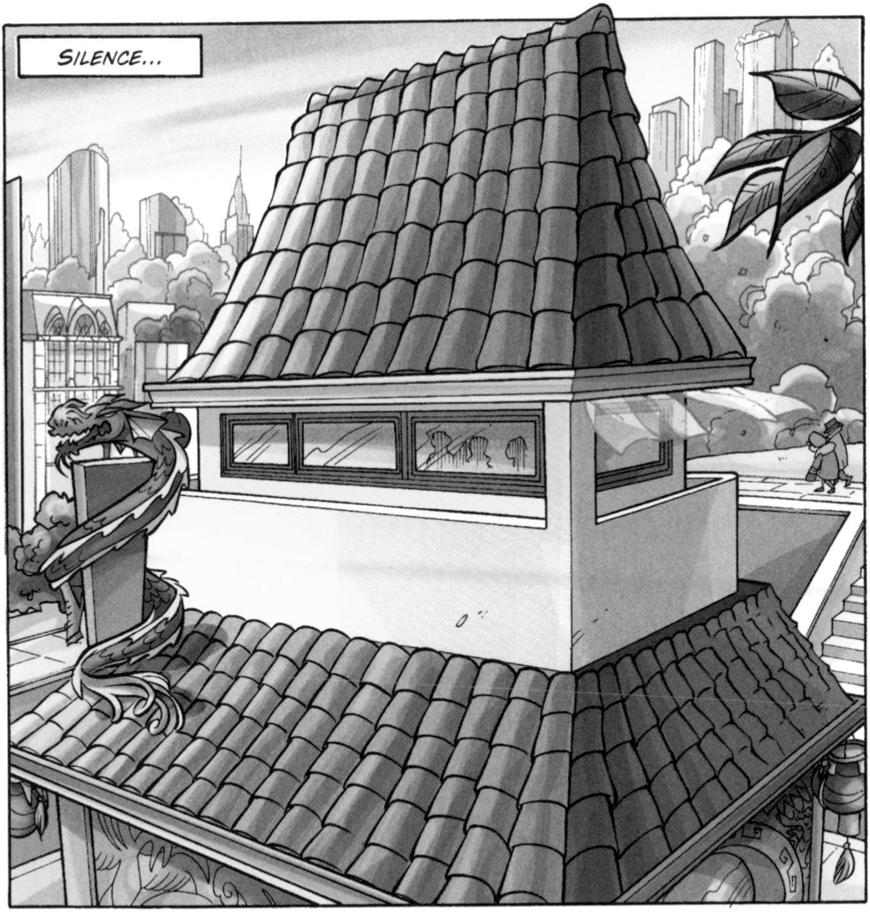
SILENCE...

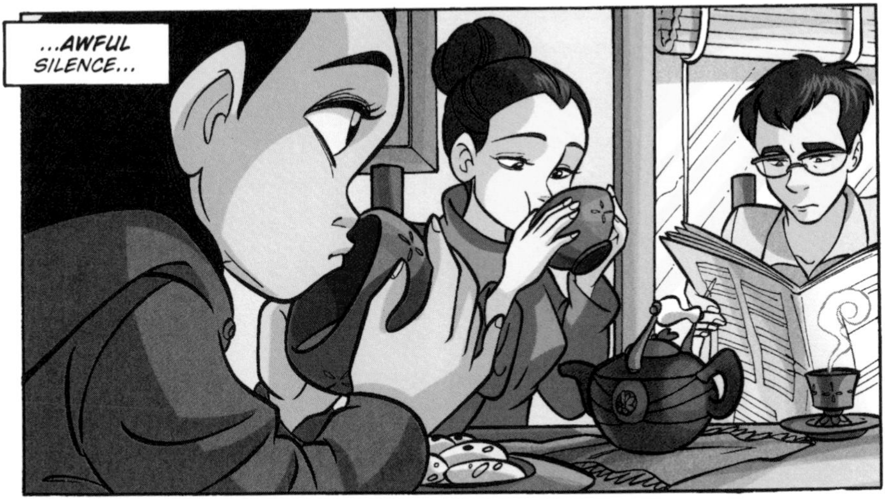
...AWFUL SILENCE...

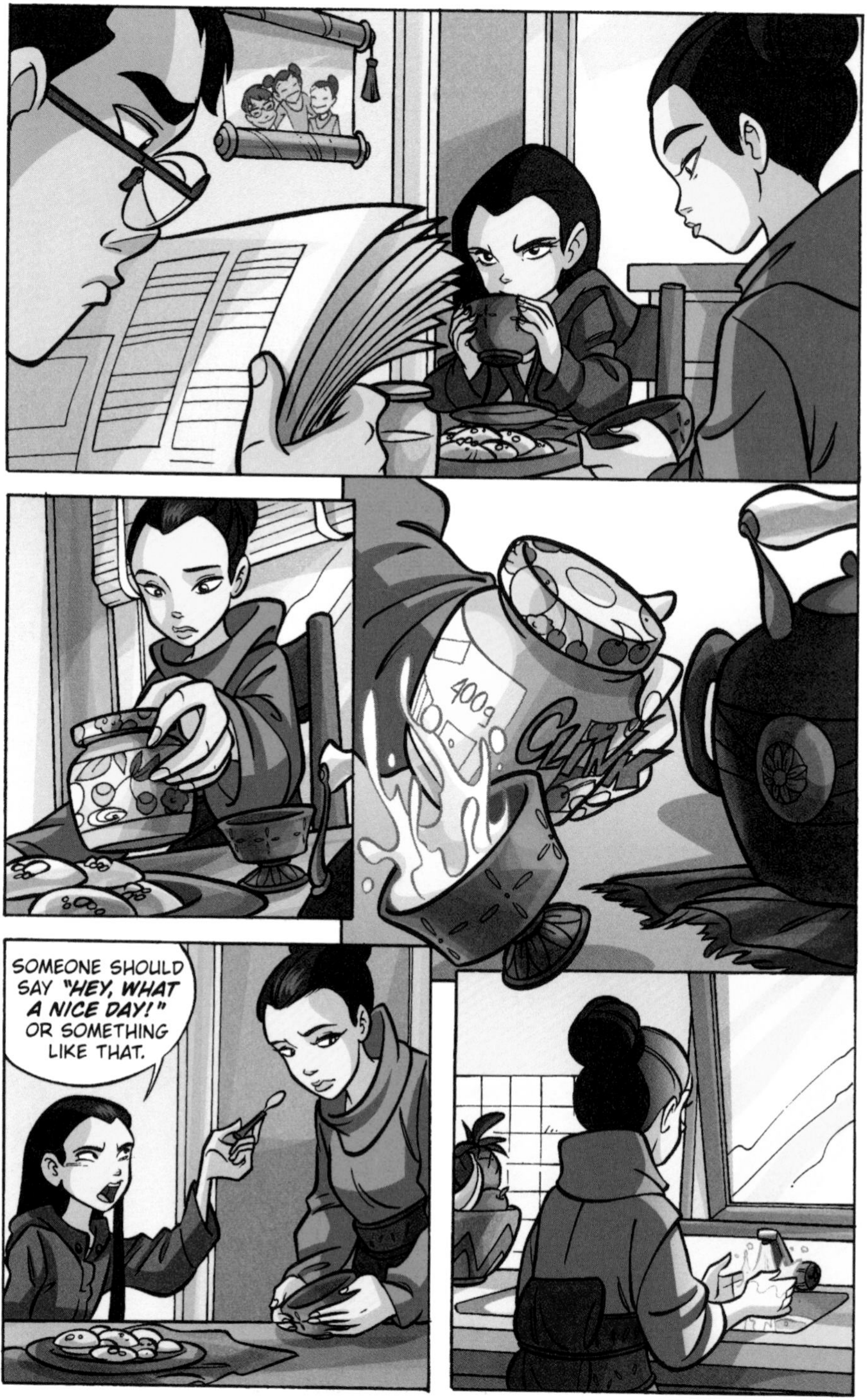
400g
CLINK
SOMEONE SHOULD SAY "HEY, WHAT A NICE DAY!" OR SOMETHING LIKE THAT.

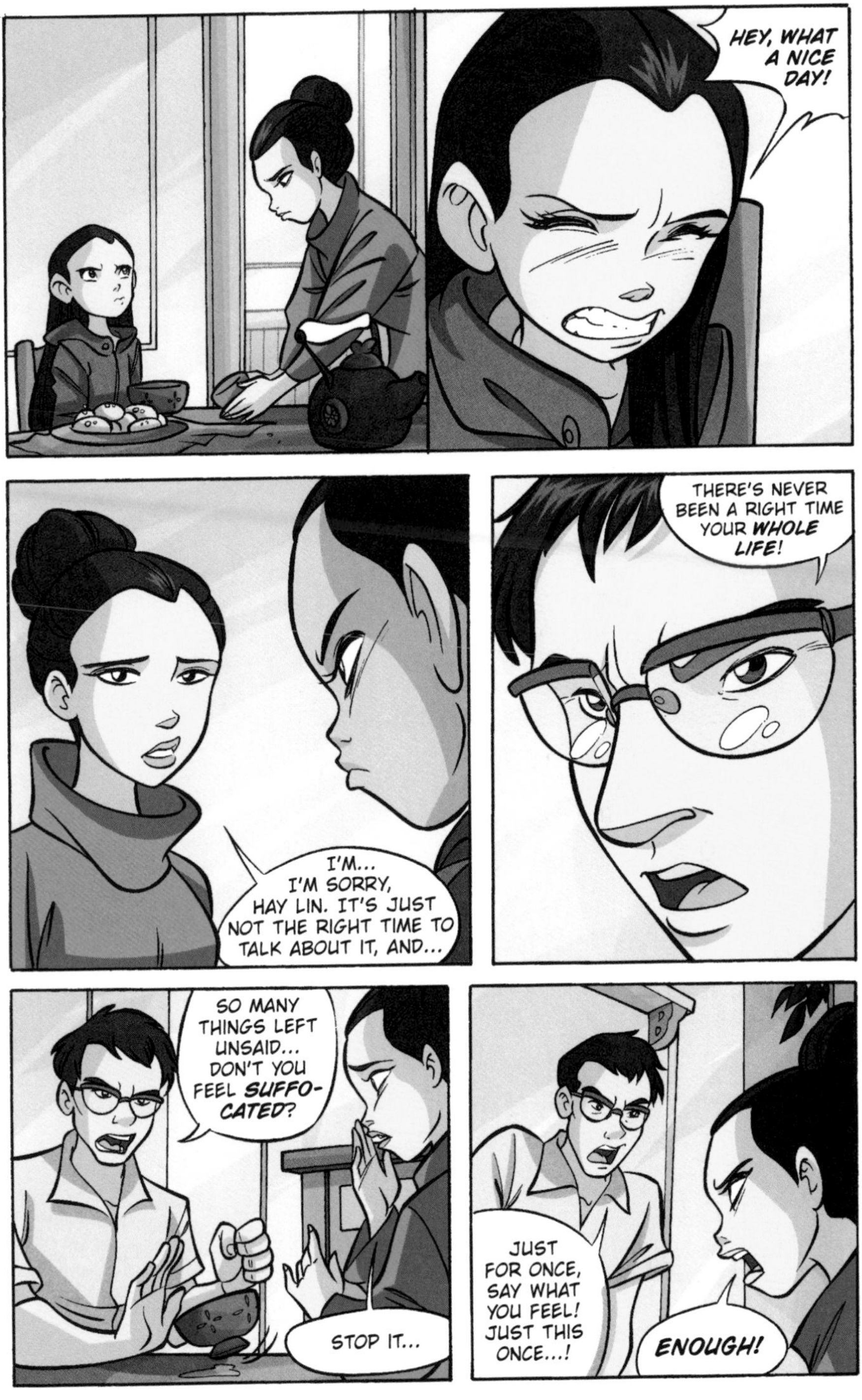
HEY, WHAT A NICE DAY!
I'M... I'M SORRY, HAY LIN. IT'S JUST NOT THE RIGHT TIME TO TALK ABOUT IT, AND...
THERE'S NEVER BEEN A RIGHT TIME YOUR WHOLE LIFE!
SO MANY THINGS LEFT UNSAID... DON'T YOU FEEL SUFFOCATED?
STOP IT...
JUST FOR ONCE, SAY WHAT YOU FEEL! JUST THIS ONCE...!
ENOUGH!

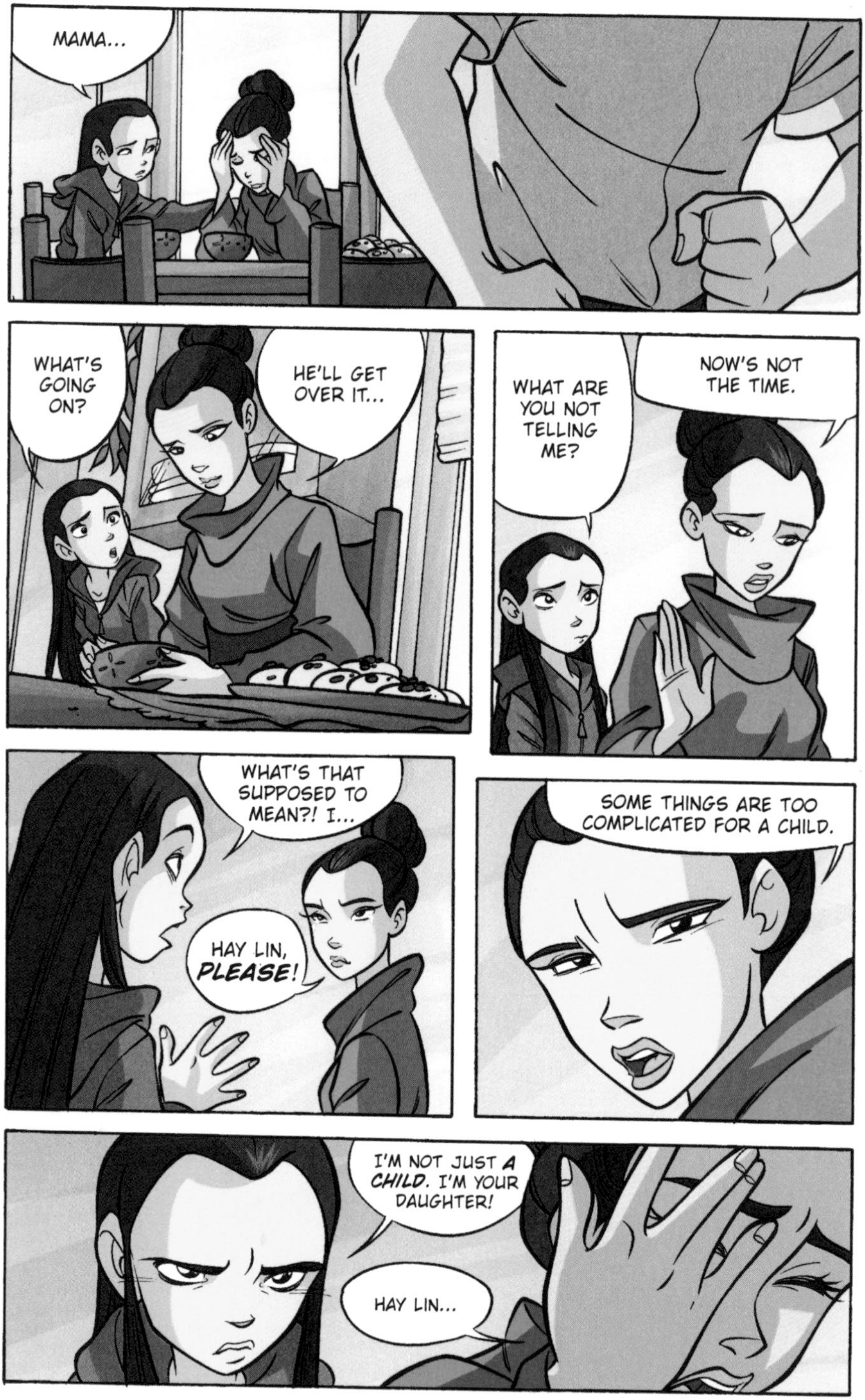
MAMA...
WHAT'S GOING ON?
HE'LL GET OVER IT...
WHAT ARE YOU NOT TELLING ME?
NOW'S NOT THE TIME.
WHAT'S THAT SUPPOSED TO MEAN?! I...
HAY LIN, PLEASE!
SOME THINGS ARE TOO COMPLICATED FOR A CHILD.
I'M NOT JUST A CHILD. I'M YOUR DAUGHTER!
HAY LIN...

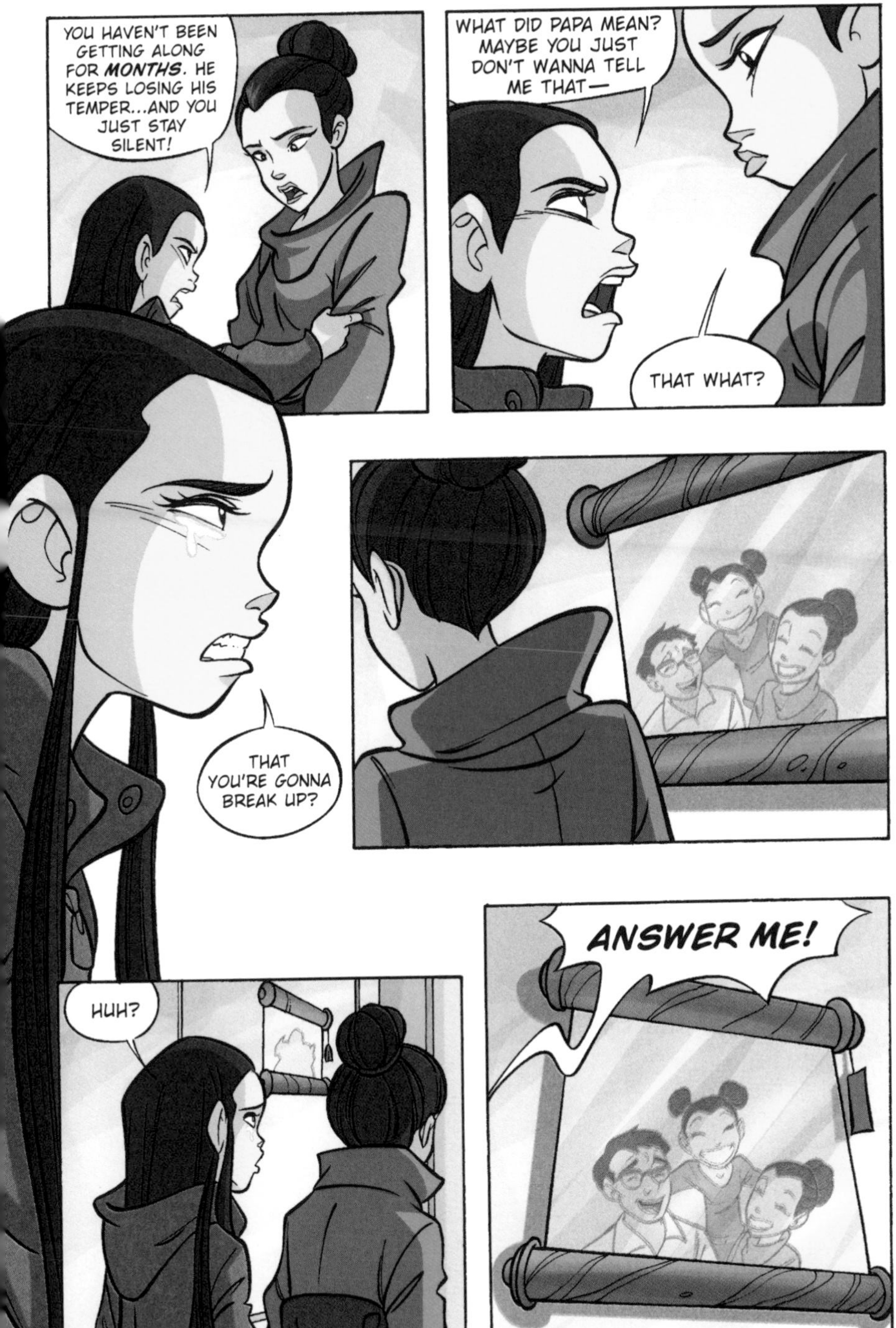
YOU HAVEN'T BEEN GETTING ALONG FOR MONTHS. HE KEEPS LOSING HIS TEMPER...AND YOU JUST STAY SILENT!
WHAT DID PAPA MEAN? MAYBE YOU JUST DON'T WANNA TELL ME THAT—
THAT WHAT?
THAT YOU'RE GONNA BREAK UP?
ANSWER ME!
HUH?

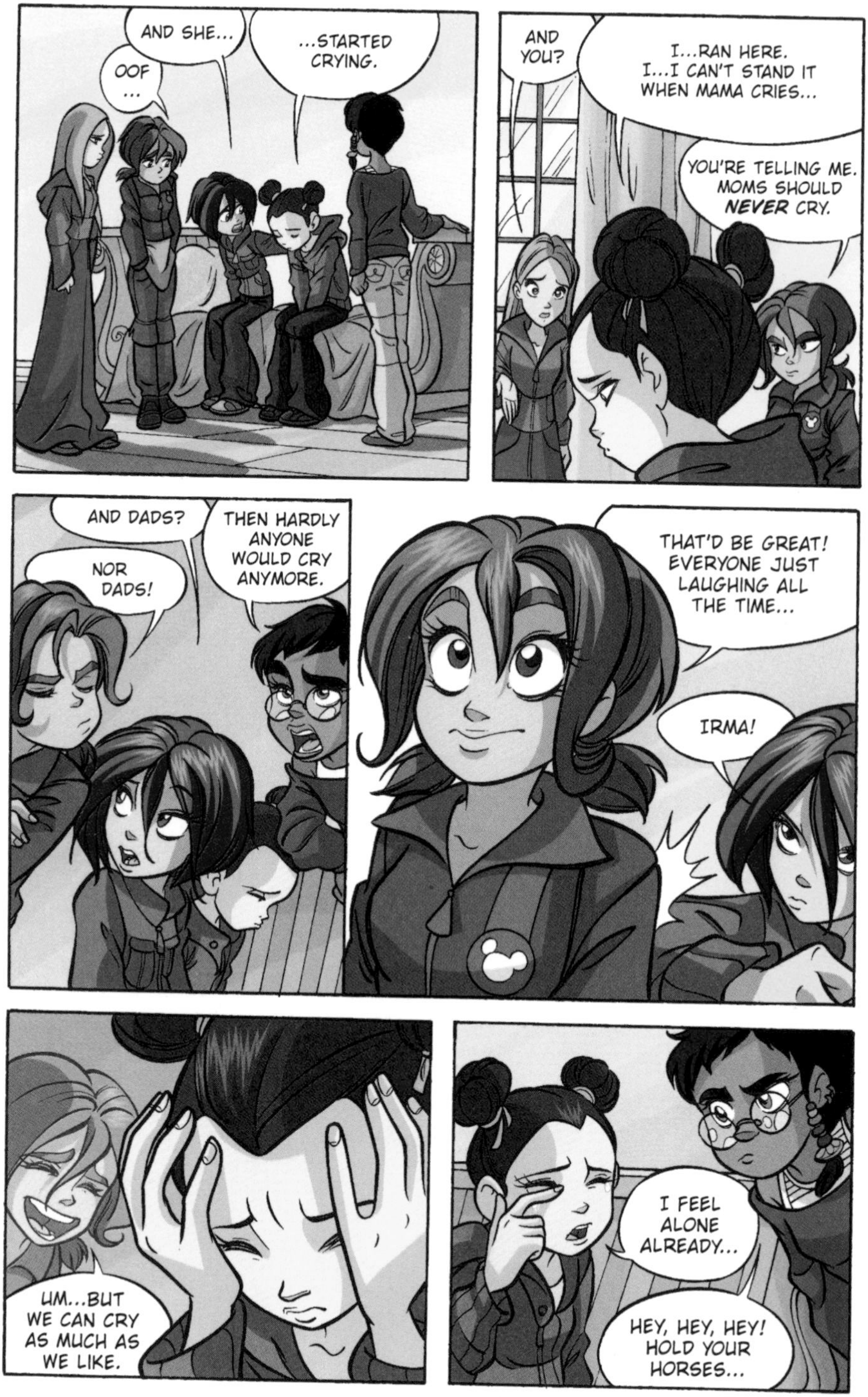
AND SHE...
OOF ...
...STARTED CRYING.
AND YOU?
I...RAN HERE. I...I CAN'T STAND IT WHEN MAMA CRIES...
YOU'RE TELLING ME. MOMS SHOULD NEVER CRY.
AND DADS?
NOR DADS!
THEN HARDLY ANYONE WOULD CRY ANYMORE.
THAT'D BE GREAT! EVERYONE JUST LAUGHING ALL THE TIME...
IRMA!
UM...BUT WE CAN CRY AS MUCH AS WE LIKE.
I FEEL ALONE ALREADY...
HEY, HEY, HEY! HOLD YOUR HORSES...

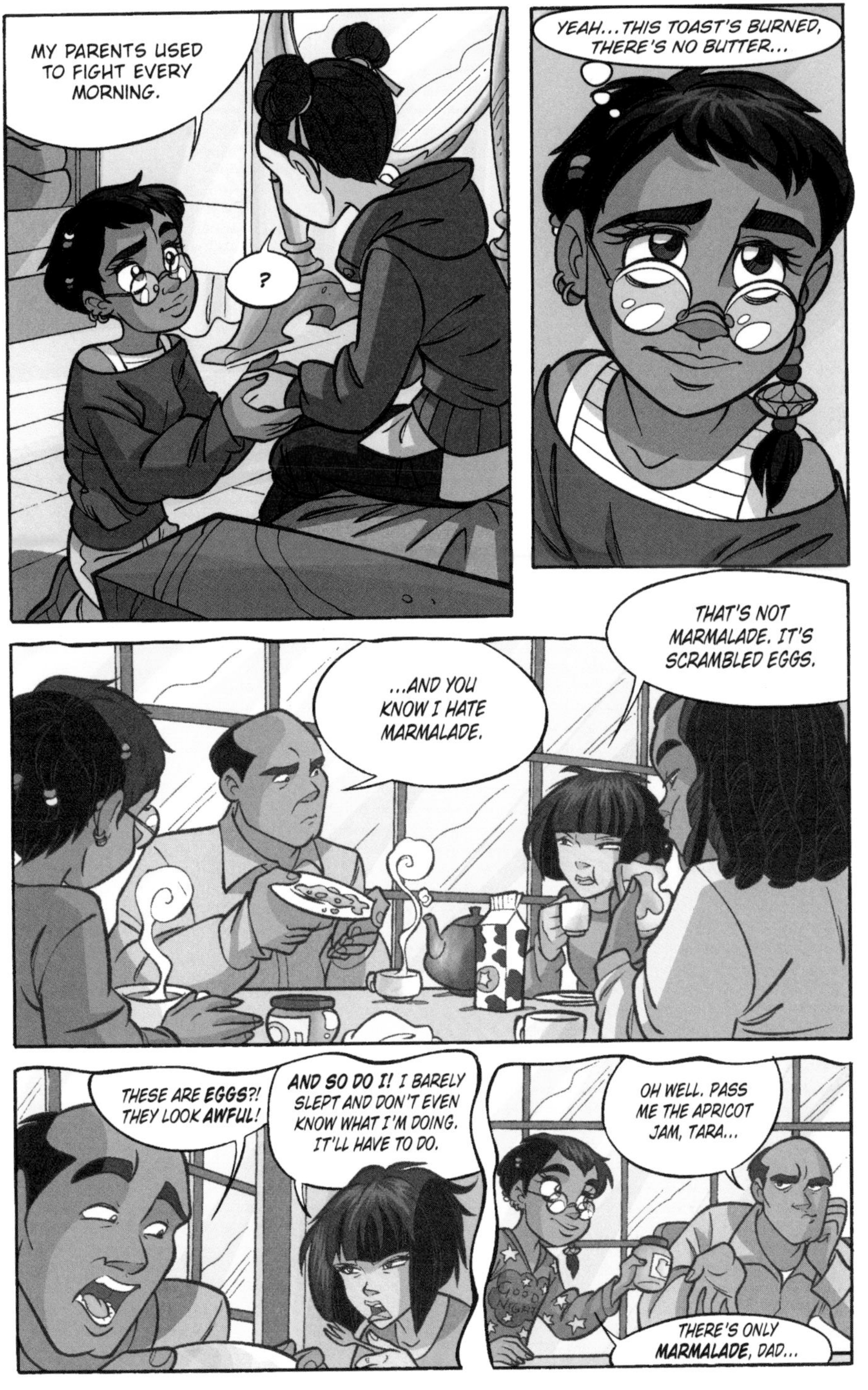

MY PARENTS USED TO FIGHT EVERY MORNING.
?
YEAH... THIS TOAST'S BURNED, THERE'S NO BUTTER...
...AND YOU KNOW I HATE MARMALADE.
THAT'S NOT MARMALADE. IT'S SCRAMBLED EGGS.
THESE ARE EGGS?! THEY LOOK AWFUL!
AND SO DO I! I BARELY SLEPT AND DON'T EVEN KNOW WHAT I'M DOING. IT'LL HAVE TO DO.
OH WELL. PASS ME THE APRICOT JAM, TARA...
THERE'S ONLY MARMALADE, DAD...

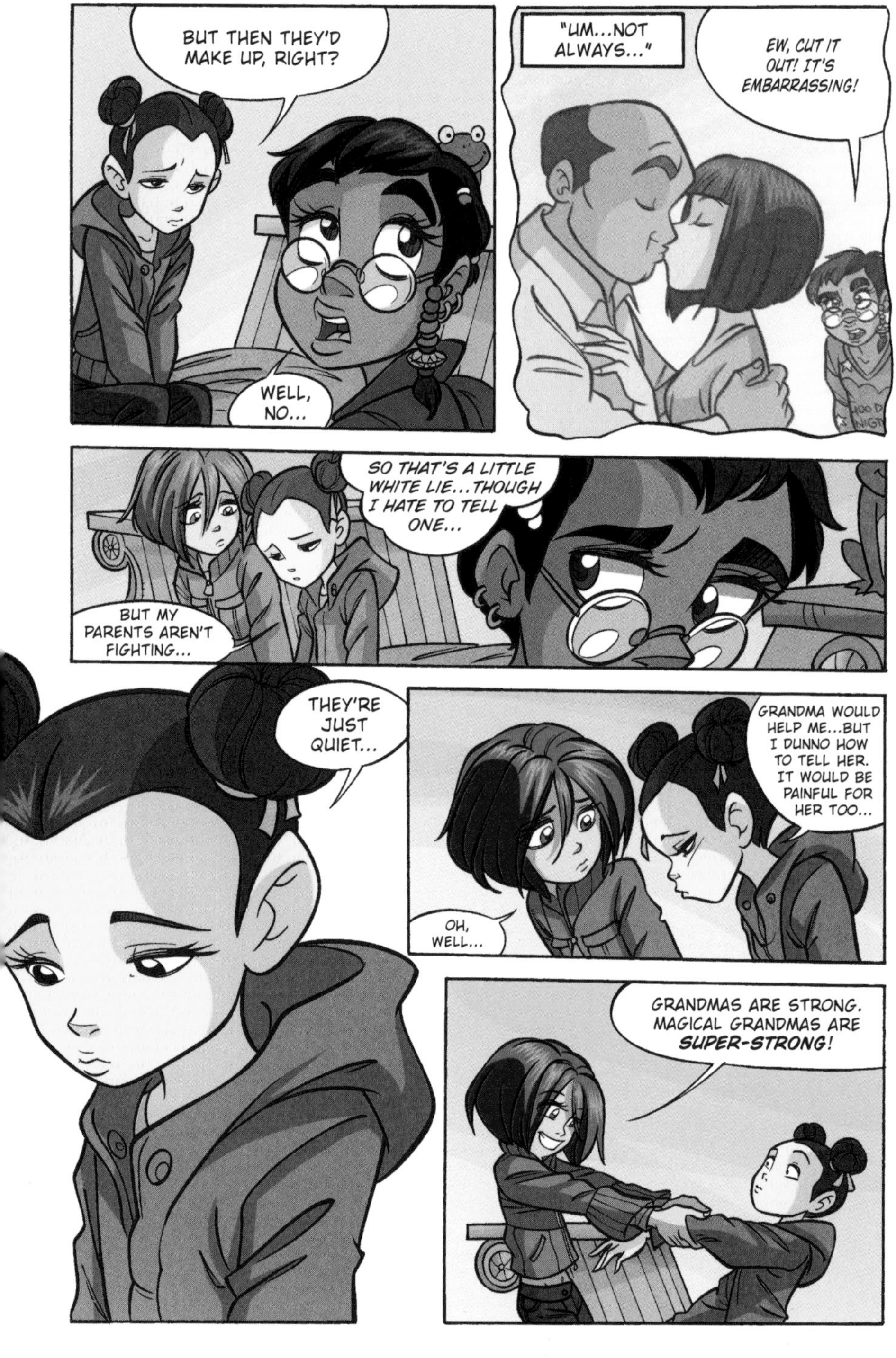
BUT THEN THEY'D MAKE UP, RIGHT?
WELL, NO...
"UM...NOT ALWAYS..."
EW, CUT IT OUT! IT'S EMBARRASSING!
SO THAT'S A LITTLE WHITE LIE...THOUGH I HATE TO TELL ONE...
BUT MY PARENTS AREN'T FIGHTING...
THEY'RE JUST QUIET...
GRANDMA WOULD HELP ME...BUT I DUNNO HOW TO TELL HER. IT WOULD BE PAINFUL FOR HER TOO...
OH, WELL...
GRANDMAS ARE STRONG. MAGICAL GRANDMAS ARE **SUPER-STRONG**!

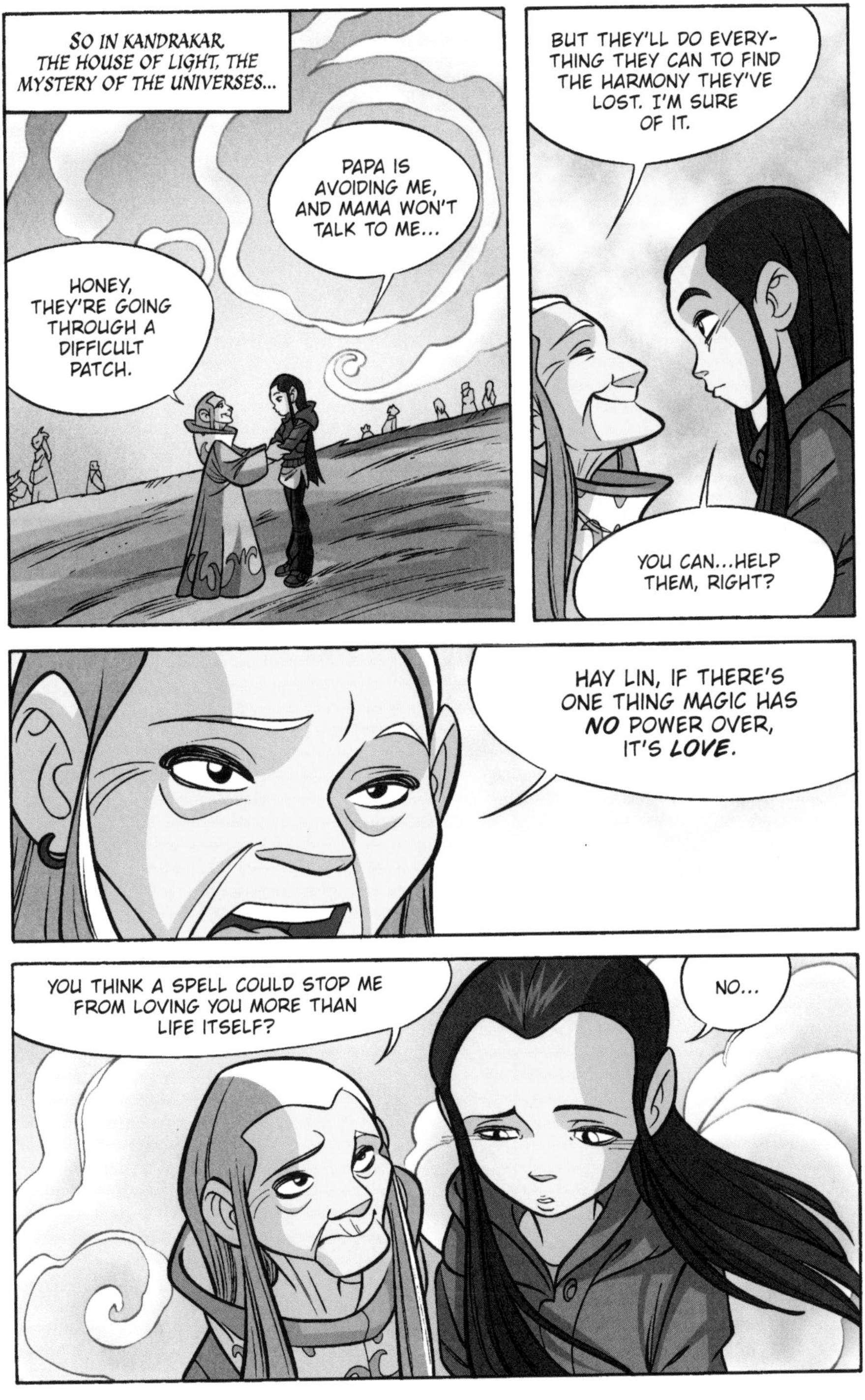
SO IN KANDRAKAR THE HOUSE OF LIGHT, THE MYSTERY OF THE UNIVERSES...
PAPA IS AVOIDING ME, AND MAMA WON'T TALK TO ME...
HONEY, THEY'RE GOING THROUGH A DIFFICULT PATCH.
BUT THEY'LL DO EVERY-THING THEY CAN TO FIND THE HARMONY THEY'VE LOST. I'M SURE OF IT.
YOU CAN...HELP THEM, RIGHT?
HAY LIN, IF THERE'S ONE THING MAGIC HAS NO POWER OVER, IT'S LOVE.
YOU THINK A SPELL COULD STOP ME FROM LOVING YOU MORE THAN LIFE ITSELF?
NO...

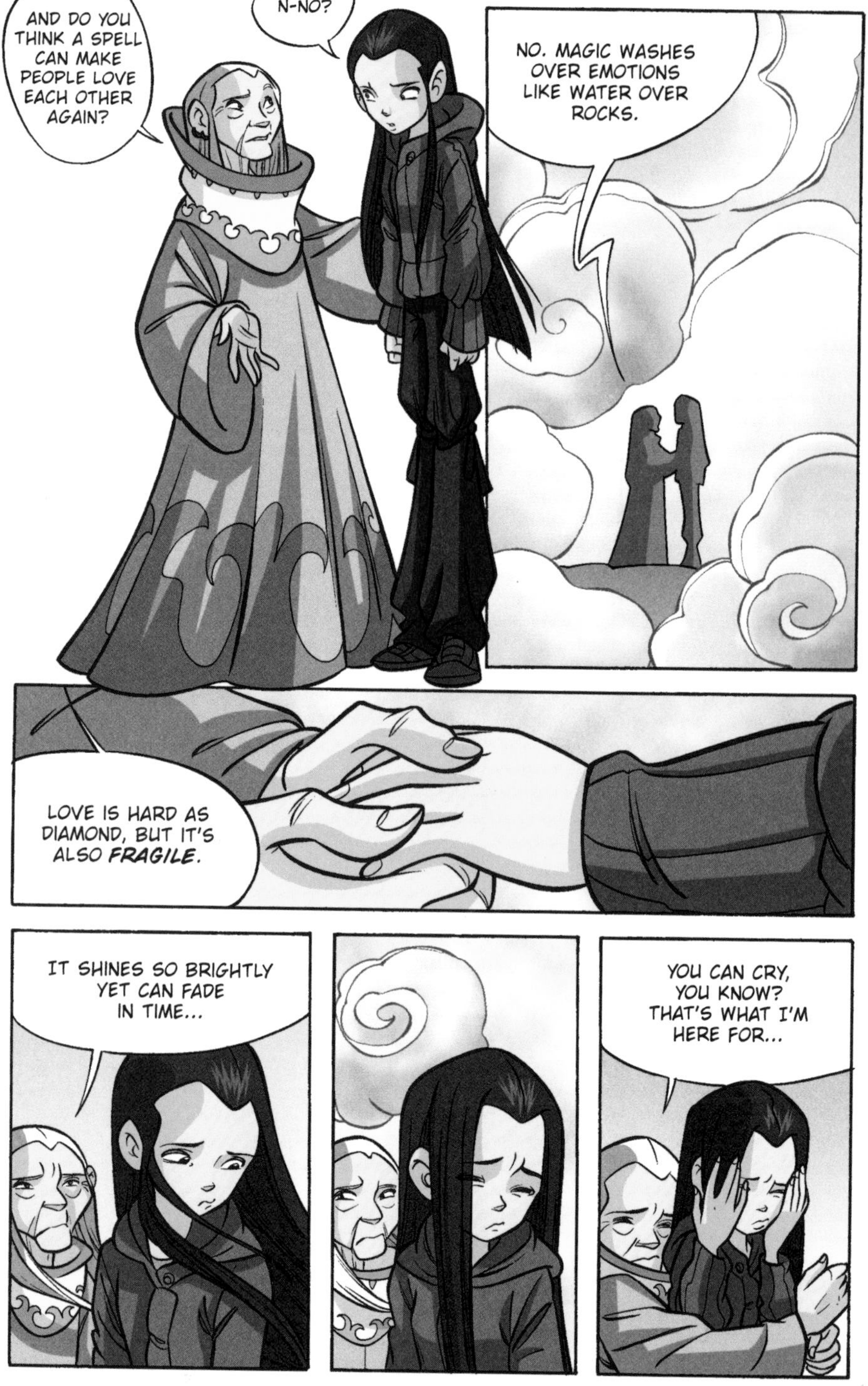
AND DO YOU THINK A SPELL CAN MAKE PEOPLE LOVE EACH OTHER AGAIN?
N-NO?
NO. MAGIC WASHES OVER EMOTIONS LIKE WATER OVER ROCKS.
LOVE IS HARD AS DIAMOND, BUT IT'S ALSO *FRAGILE*.
IT SHINES SO BRIGHTLY YET CAN FADE IN TIME...
YOU CAN CRY, YOU KNOW? THAT'S WHAT I'M HERE FOR...

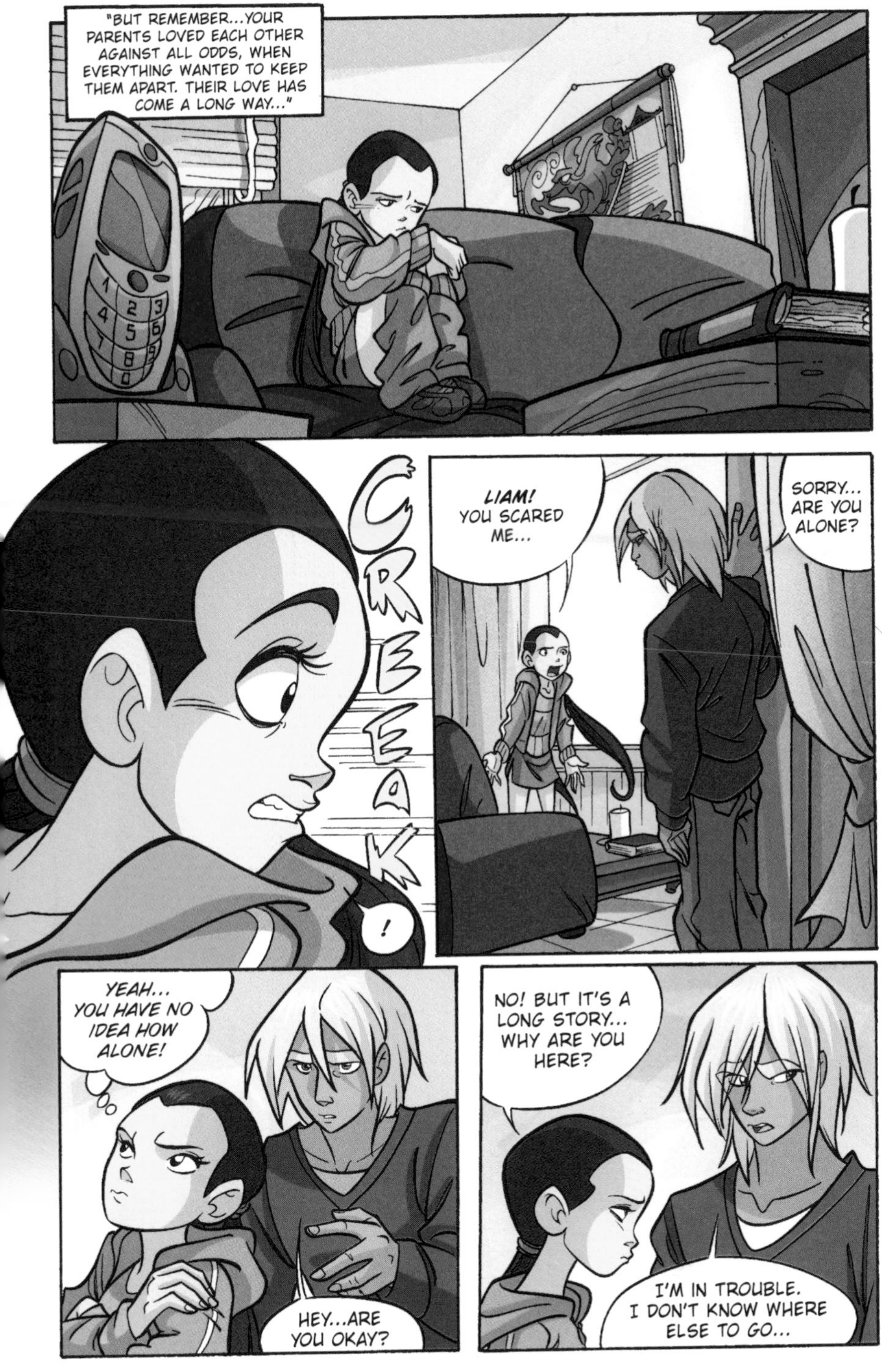
"BUT REMEMBER...YOUR PARENTS LOVED EACH OTHER AGAINST ALL ODDS, WHEN EVERYTHING WANTED TO KEEP THEM APART. THEIR LOVE HAS COME A LONG WAY..."
1 2 3 4 5 6 7 8 9 0
CREEAK
!
LIAM! YOU SCARED ME...
SORRY... ARE YOU ALONE?
YEAH... YOU HAVE NO IDEA HOW ALONE!
HEY...ARE YOU OKAY?
NO! BUT IT'S A LONG STORY... WHY ARE YOU HERE?
I'M IN TROUBLE. I DON'T KNOW WHERE ELSE TO GO...

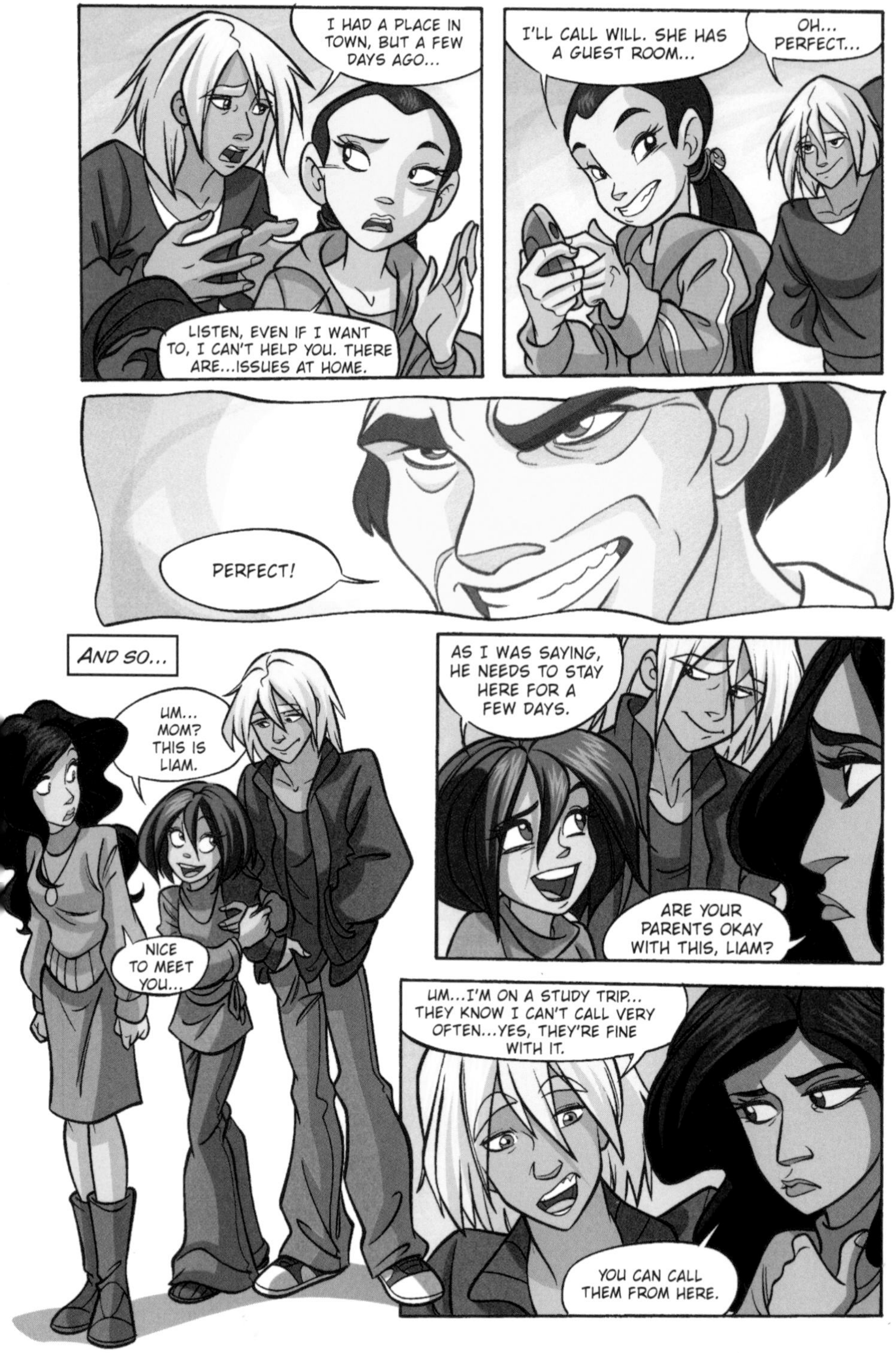
I HAD A PLACE IN TOWN, BUT A FEW DAYS AGO...
LISTEN, EVEN IF I WANT TO, I CAN'T HELP YOU. THERE ARE...ISSUES AT HOME.
I'LL CALL WILL. SHE HAS A GUEST ROOM...
OH... PERFECT...
PERFECT!
AND SO...
UM... MOM? THIS IS LIAM.
NICE TO MEET YOU...
AS I WAS SAYING, HE NEEDS TO STAY HERE FOR A FEW DAYS.
ARE YOUR PARENTS OKAY WITH THIS, LIAM?
UM...I'M ON A STUDY TRIP... THEY KNOW I CAN'T CALL VERY OFTEN...YES, THEY'RE FINE WITH IT.
YOU CAN CALL THEM FROM HERE.

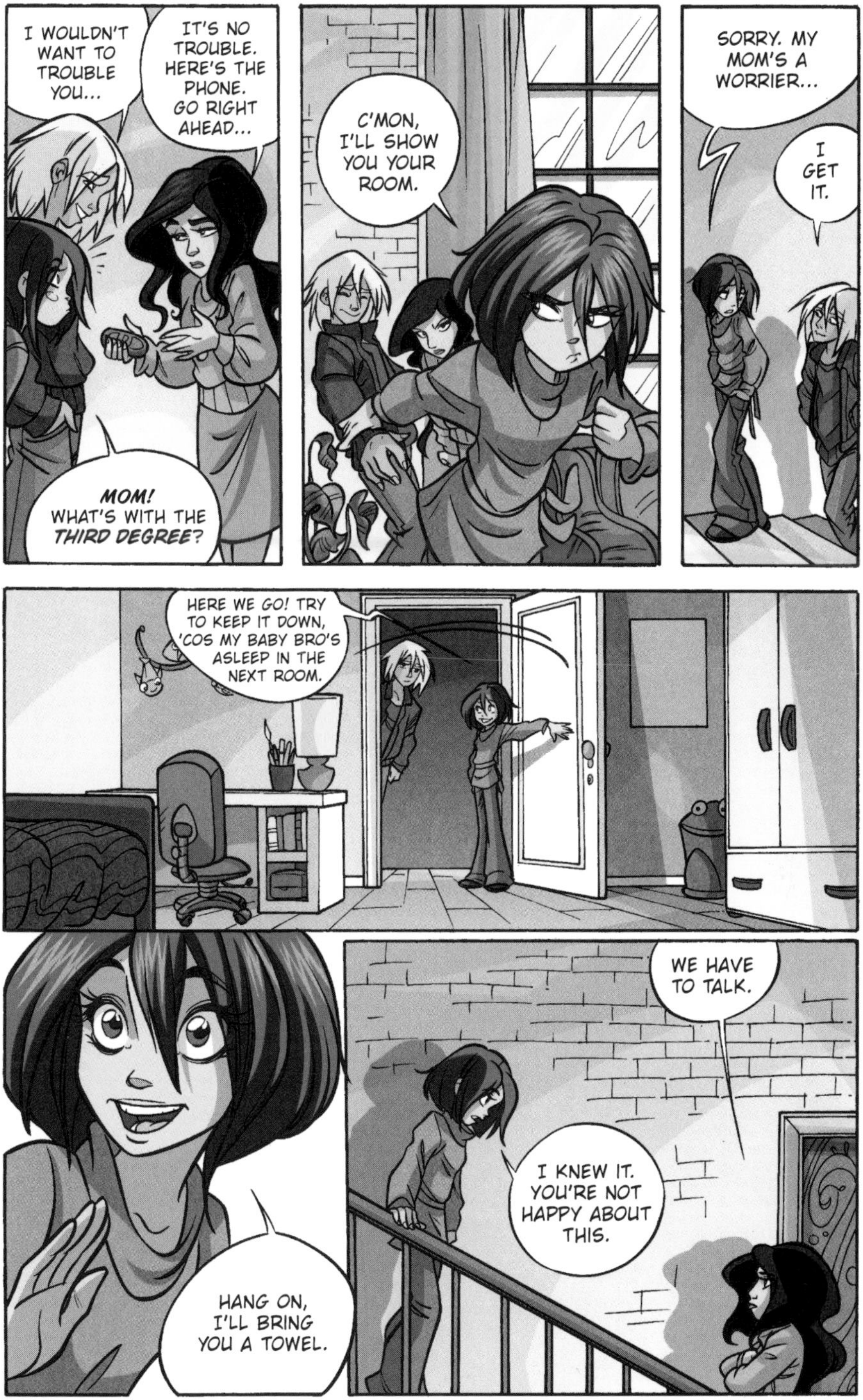
I WOULDN'T WANT TO TROUBLE YOU...
IT'S NO TROUBLE. HERE'S THE PHONE. GO RIGHT AHEAD...
MOM! WHAT'S WITH THE THIRD DEGREE?
C'MON, I'LL SHOW YOU YOUR ROOM.
SORRY. MY MOM'S A WORRIER...
I GET IT.
HERE WE GO! TRY TO KEEP IT DOWN, 'COS MY BABY BRO'S ASLEEP IN THE NEXT ROOM.
HANG ON, I'LL BRING YOU A TOWEL.
WE HAVE TO TALK.
I KNEW IT. YOU'RE NOT HAPPY ABOUT THIS.

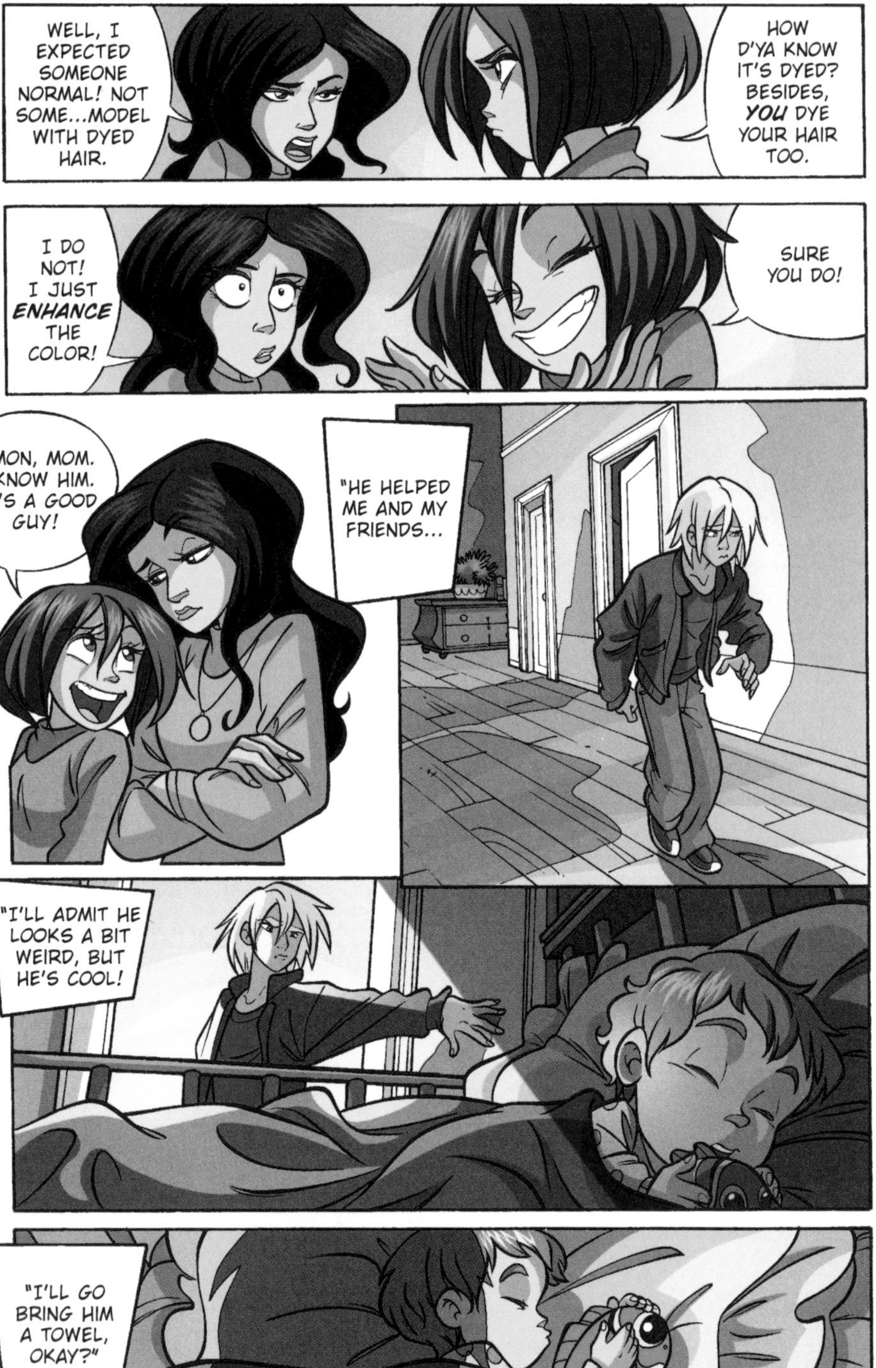
WELL, I EXPECTED SOMEONE NORMAL! NOT SOME...MODEL WITH DYED HAIR.
HOW D'YA KNOW IT'S DYED? BESIDES, YOU DYE YOUR HAIR TOO.
I DO NOT! I JUST ENHANCE THE COLOR!
SURE YOU DO!
C'MON, MOM. I KNOW HIM. HE'S A GOOD GUY!
"HE HELPED ME AND MY FRIENDS...
"I'LL ADMIT HE LOOKS A BIT WEIRD, BUT HE'S COOL!
"I'LL GO BRING HIM A TOWEL, OKAY?"

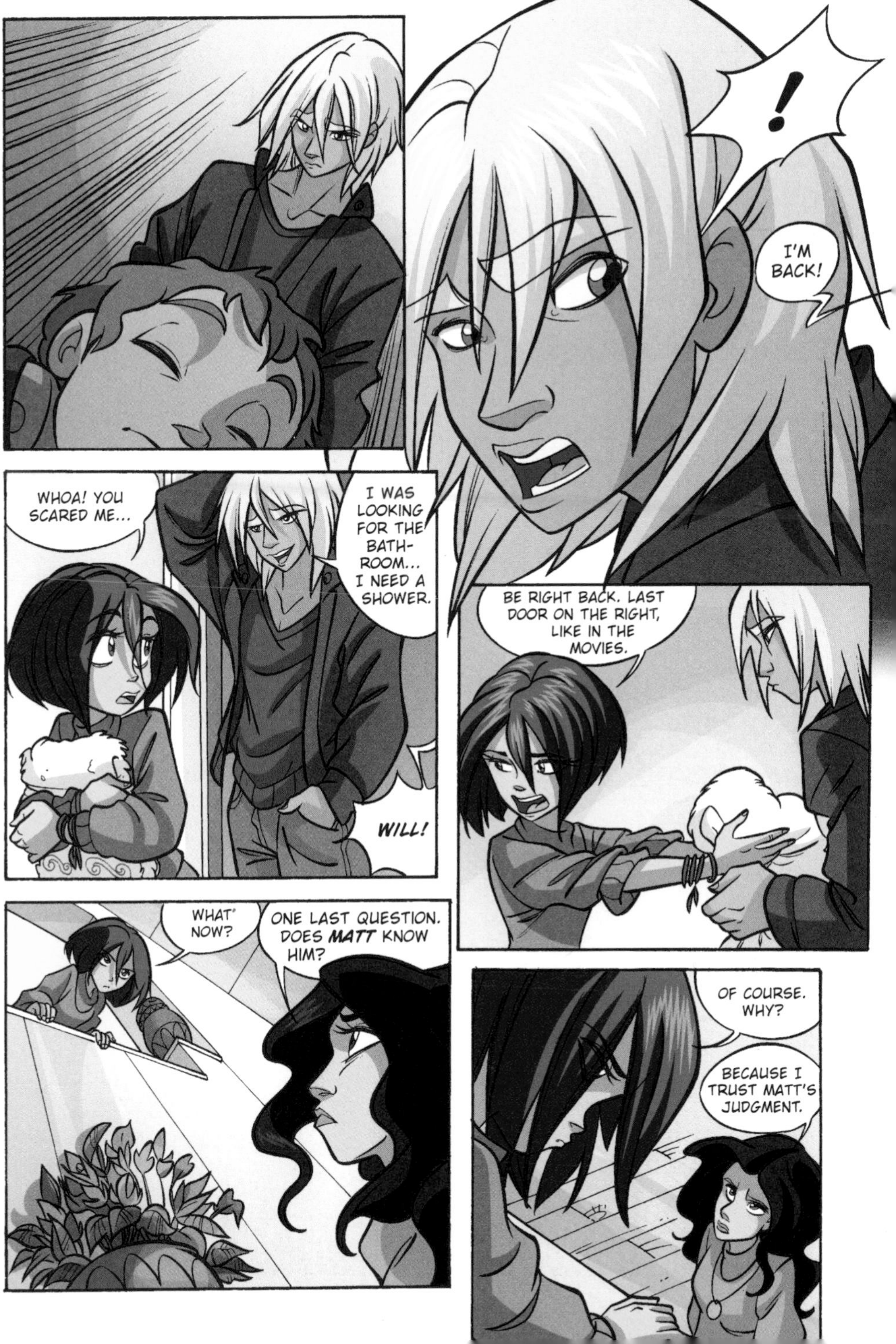
!
I'M BACK!
WHOA! YOU SCARED ME...
I WAS LOOKING FOR THE BATH-ROOM... I NEED A SHOWER.
WILL!
BE RIGHT BACK. LAST DOOR ON THE RIGHT, LIKE IN THE MOVIES.
WHAT NOW?
ONE LAST QUESTION. DOES MATT KNOW HIM?
OF COURSE. WHY?
BECAUSE I TRUST MATT'S JUDGMENT.

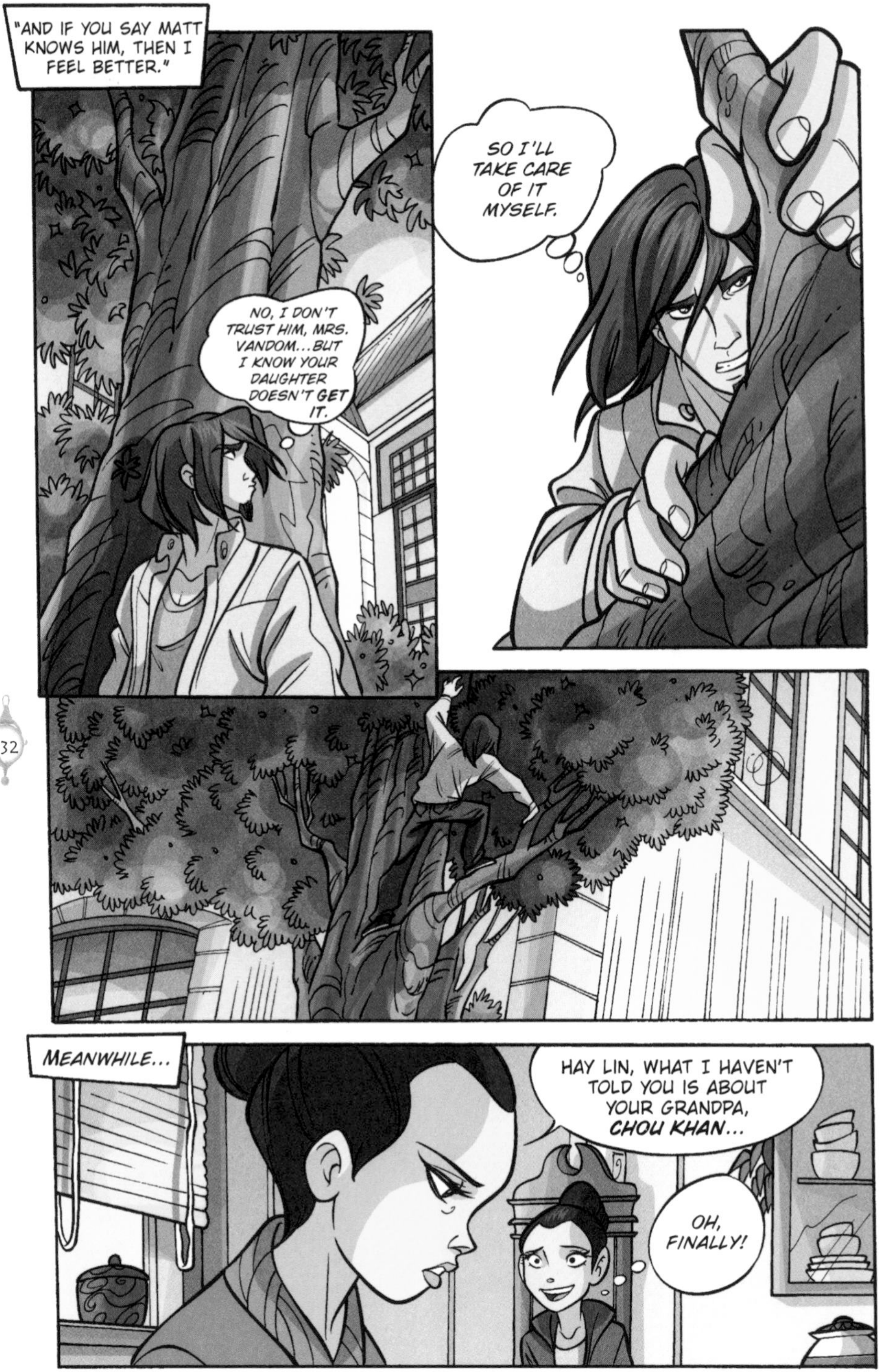
"AND IF YOU SAY MATT KNOWS HIM, THEN I FEEL BETTER."
NO, I DON'T TRUST HIM, MRS. VANDOM...BUT I KNOW YOUR DAUGHTER DOESN'T GET IT.
SO I'LL TAKE CARE OF IT MYSELF.
MEANWHILE...
HAY LIN, WHAT I HAVEN'T TOLD YOU IS ABOUT YOUR GRANDPA, CHOU KHAN...
OH, FINALLY!

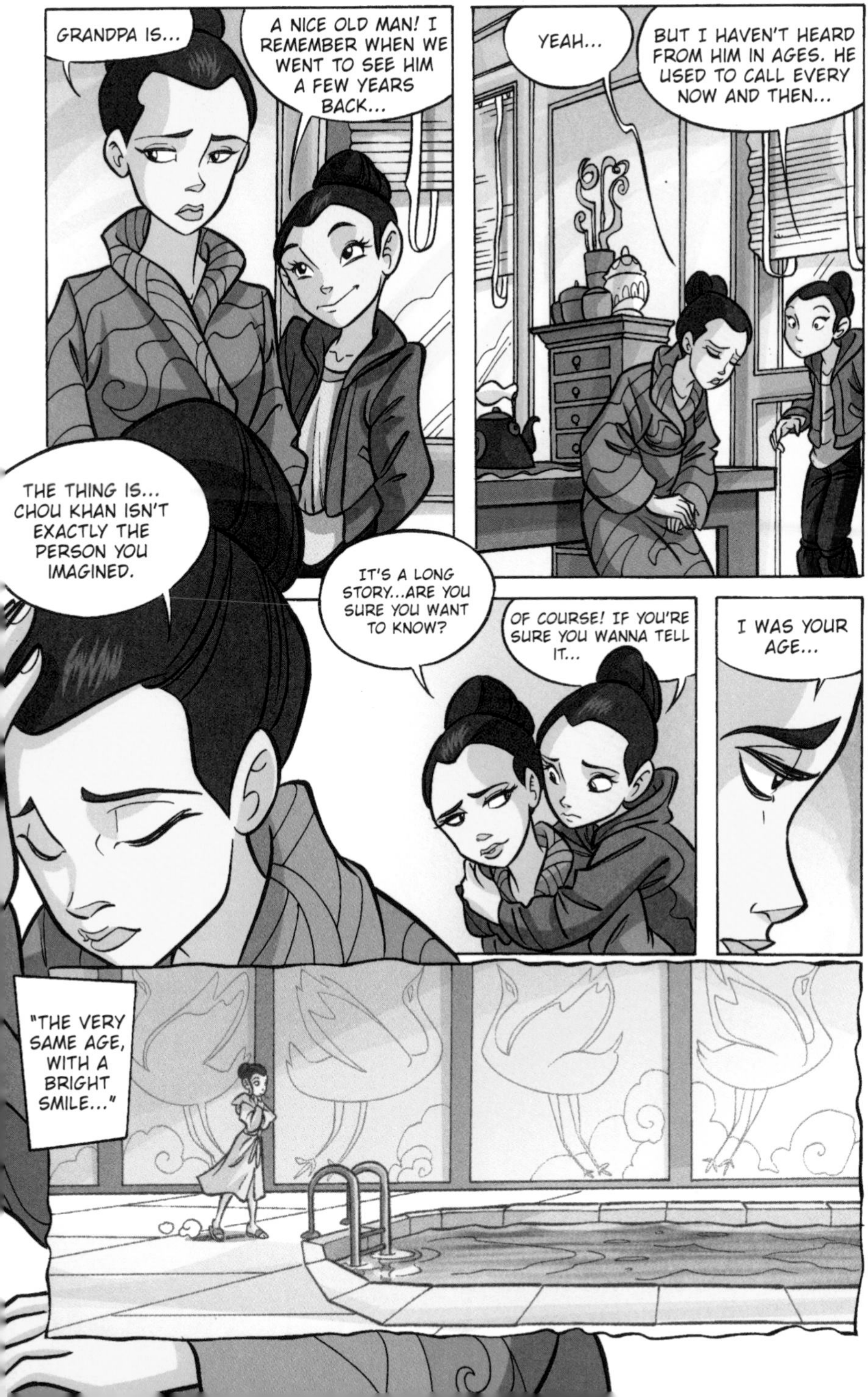
GRANDPA IS...
A NICE OLD MAN! I REMEMBER WHEN WE WENT TO SEE HIM A FEW YEARS BACK...
YEAH...
BUT I HAVEN'T HEARD FROM HIM IN AGES. HE USED TO CALL EVERY NOW AND THEN...
THE THING IS... CHOU KHAN ISN'T EXACTLY THE PERSON YOU IMAGINED.
IT'S A LONG STORY...ARE YOU SURE YOU WANT TO KNOW?
OF COURSE! IF YOU'RE SURE YOU WANNA TELL IT...
I WAS YOUR AGE...
"THE VERY SAME AGE, WITH A BRIGHT SMILE..."

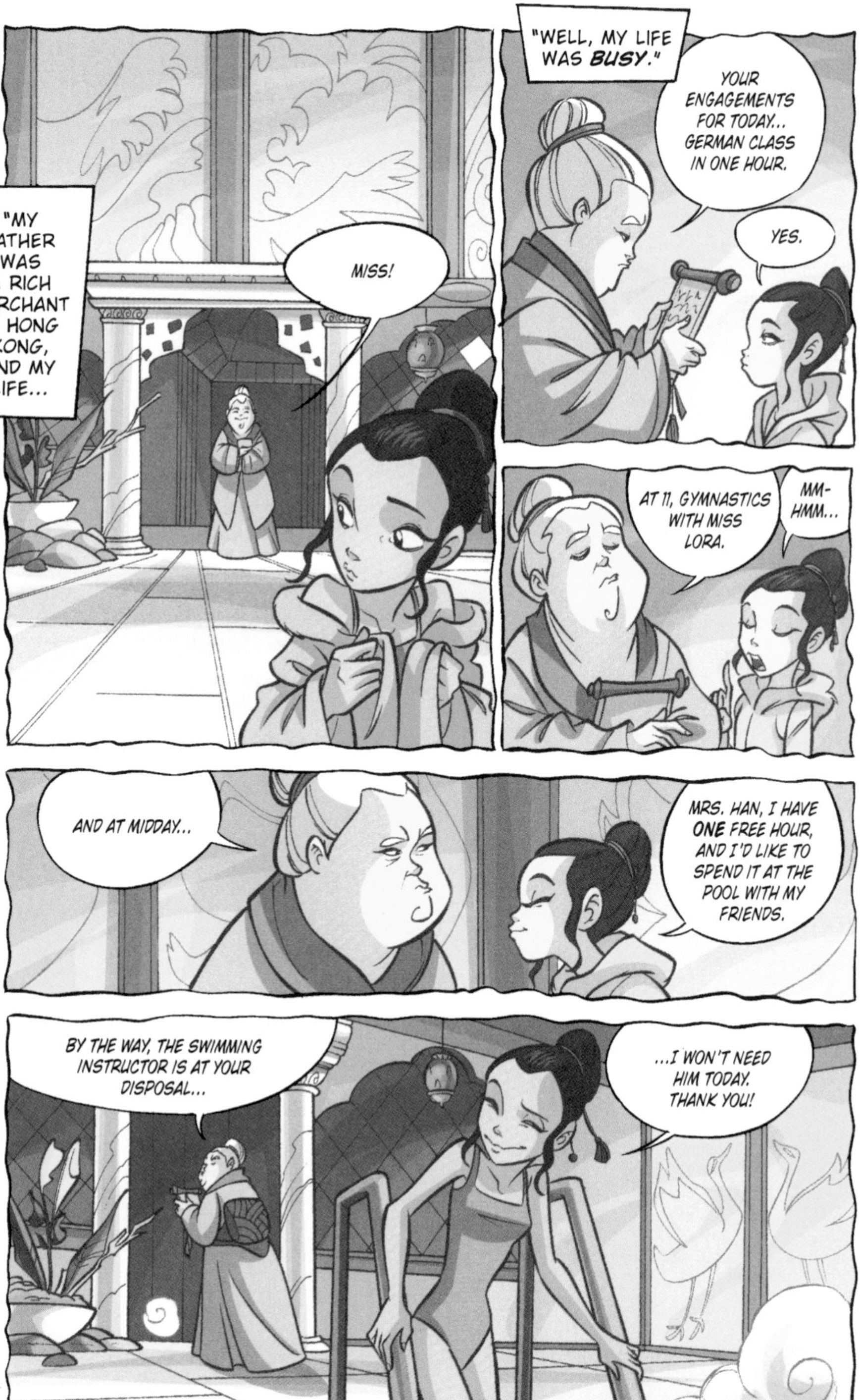
"MY FATHER WAS A RICH MERCHANT IN HONG KONG, AND MY LIFE...
MISS!
"WELL, MY LIFE WAS BUSY."
YOUR ENGAGEMENTS FOR TODAY... GERMAN CLASS IN ONE HOUR.
YES.
AT 11, GYMNASTICS WITH MISS LORA.
MM-HMM...
AND AT MIDDAY...
MRS. HAN, I HAVE ONE FREE HOUR, AND I'D LIKE TO SPEND IT AT THE POOL WITH MY FRIENDS.
BY THE WAY, THE SWIMMING INSTRUCTOR IS AT YOUR DISPOSAL...
...I WON'T NEED HIM TODAY. THANK YOU!

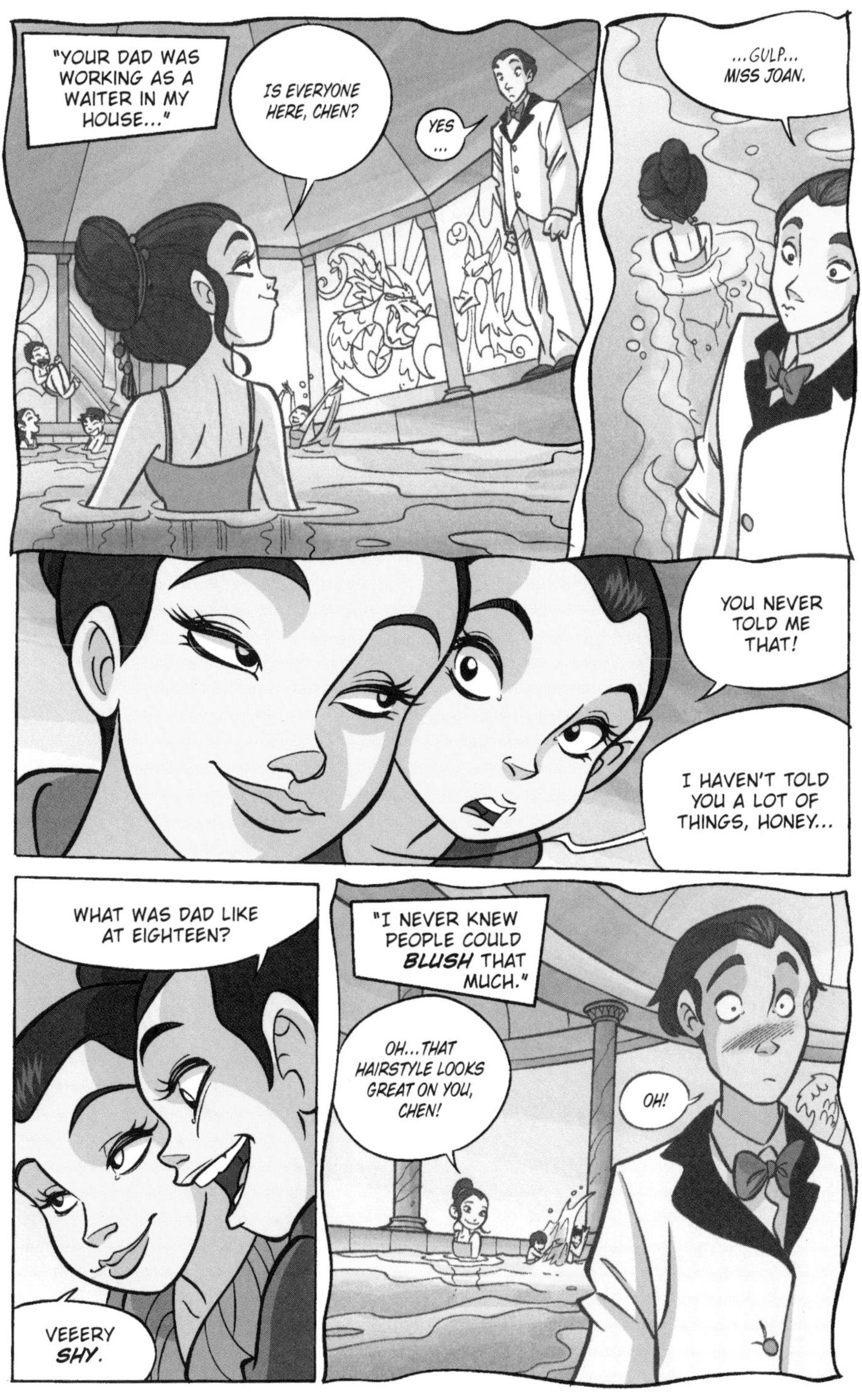
"YOUR DAD WAS WORKING AS A WAITER IN MY HOUSE..."
IS EVERYONE HERE, CHEN?
YES ...
...GULP... MISS JOAN.
YOU NEVER TOLD ME THAT!
I HAVEN'T TOLD YOU A LOT OF THINGS, HONEY...
WHAT WAS DAD LIKE AT EIGHTEEN?
VEEERY ***SHY***.
"I NEVER KNEW PEOPLE COULD ***BLUSH*** THAT MUCH."
OH...THAT HAIRSTYLE LOOKS GREAT ON YOU, CHEN!
OH!

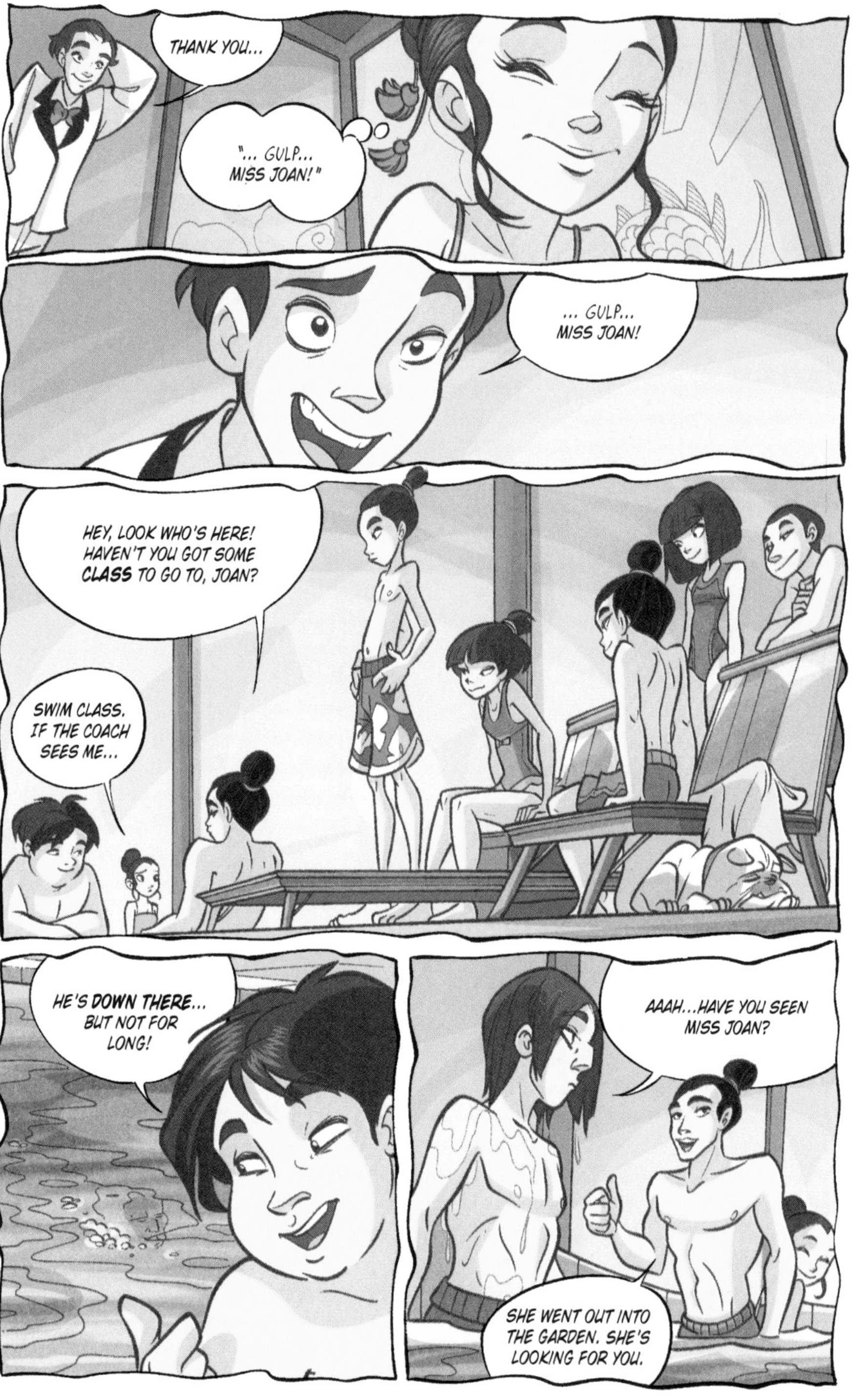
THANK YOU...
"... GULP...
MISS JOAN!"
... GULP...
MISS JOAN!
HEY, LOOK WHO'S HERE!
HAVEN'T YOU GOT SOME
CLASS TO GO TO, JOAN?
SWIM CLASS.
IF THE COACH
SEES ME...
HE'S **DOWN THERE**...
BUT NOT FOR
LONG!
AAAH...HAVE YOU SEEN
MISS JOAN?
SHE WENT OUT INTO
THE GARDEN. SHE'S
LOOKING FOR YOU.

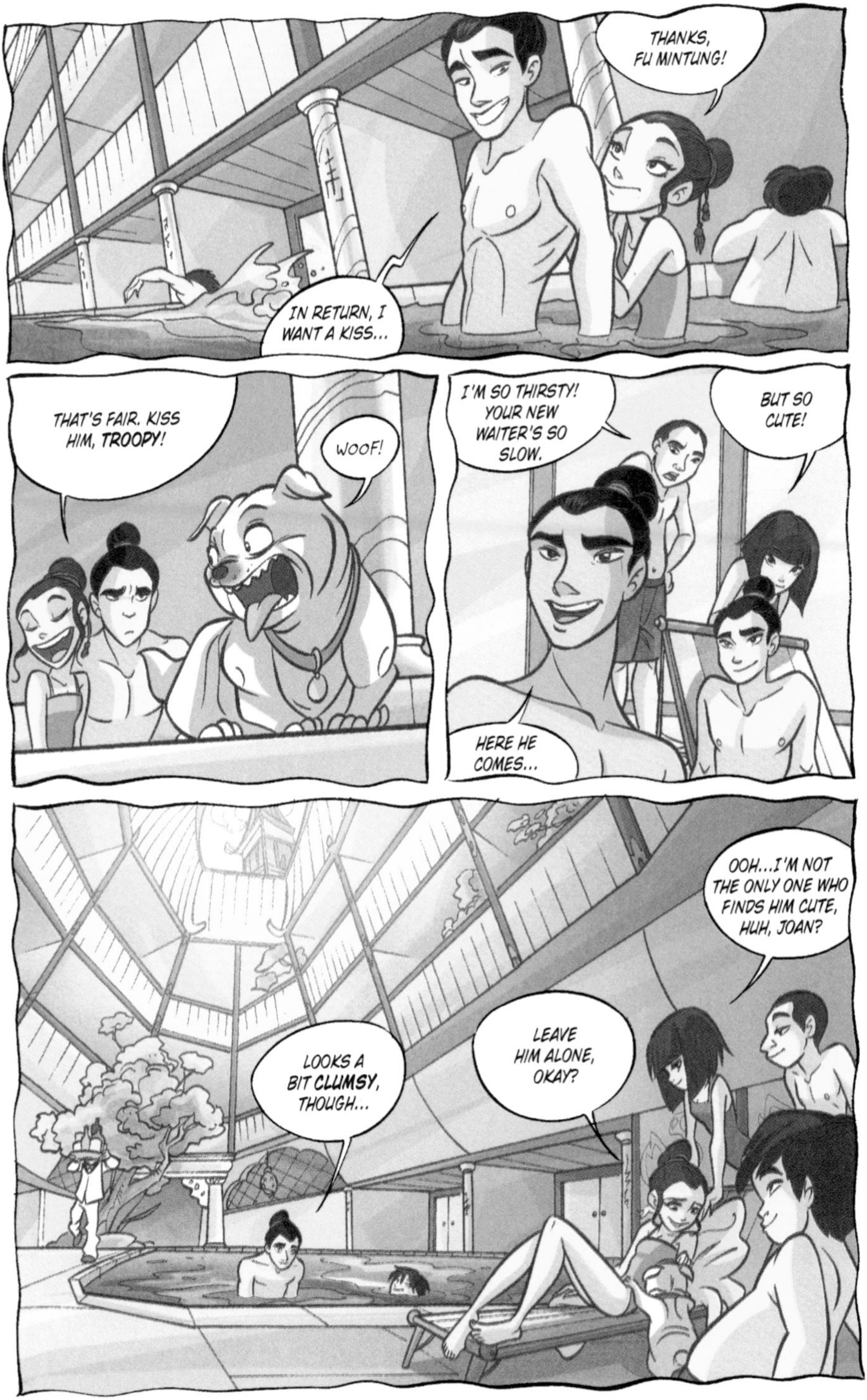
THANKS, FU MINTUNG!
IN RETURN, I WANT A KISS...
THAT'S FAIR. KISS HIM, TROOPY!
WOOF!
I'M SO THIRSTY! YOUR NEW WAITER'S SO SLOW.
BUT SO CUTE!
HERE HE COMES...
OOH...I'M NOT THE ONLY ONE WHO FINDS HIM CUTE, HUH, JOAN?
LEAVE HIM ALONE, OKAY?
LOOKS A BIT CLUMSY, THOUGH...

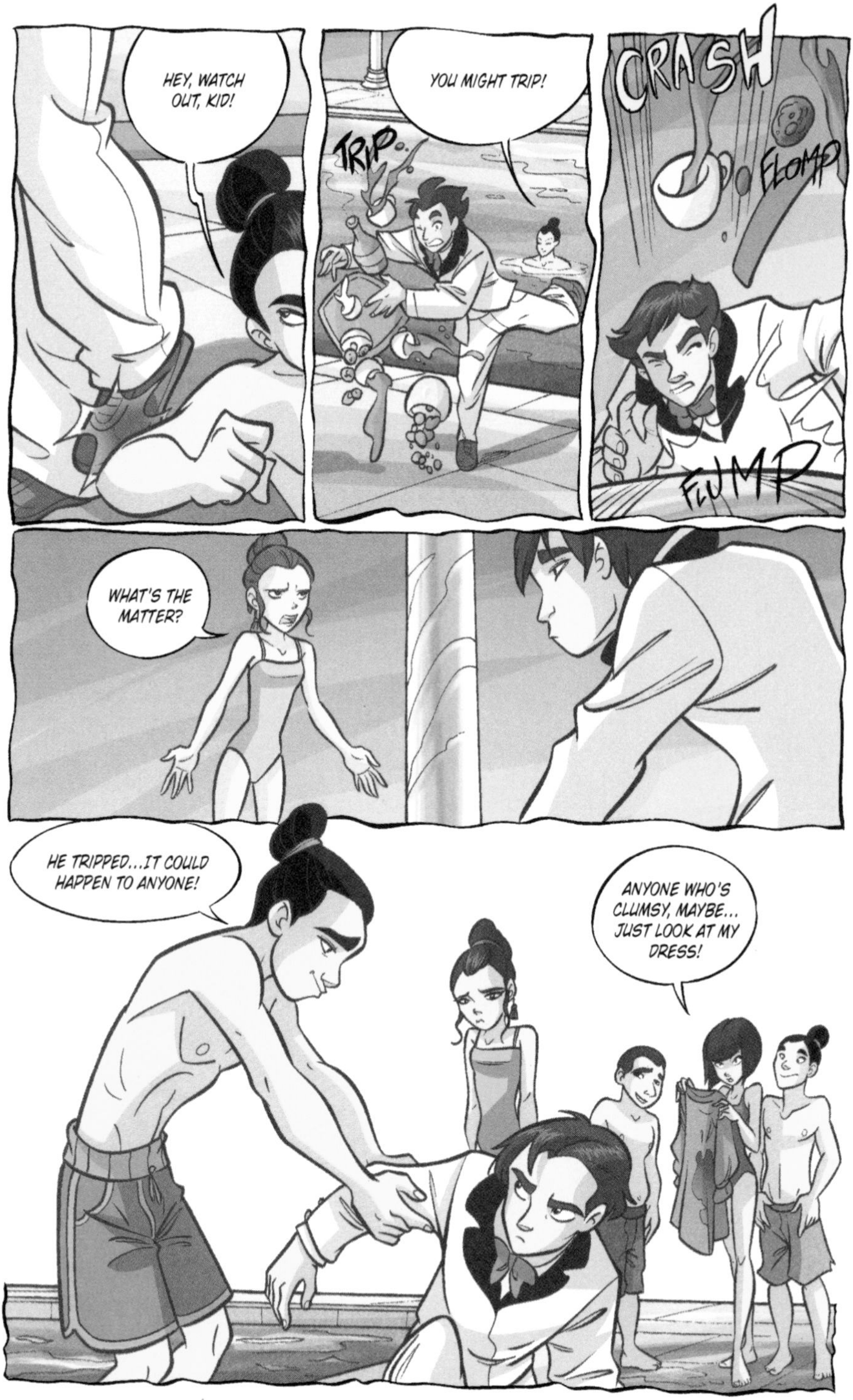
HEY, WATCH OUT, KID!
YOU MIGHT TRIP!
TRIP
CRASH
FLOMP
FLUMP
WHAT'S THE MATTER?
HE TRIPPED...IT COULD HAPPEN TO ANYONE!
ANYONE WHO'S CLUMSY, MAYBE... JUST LOOK AT MY DRESS!

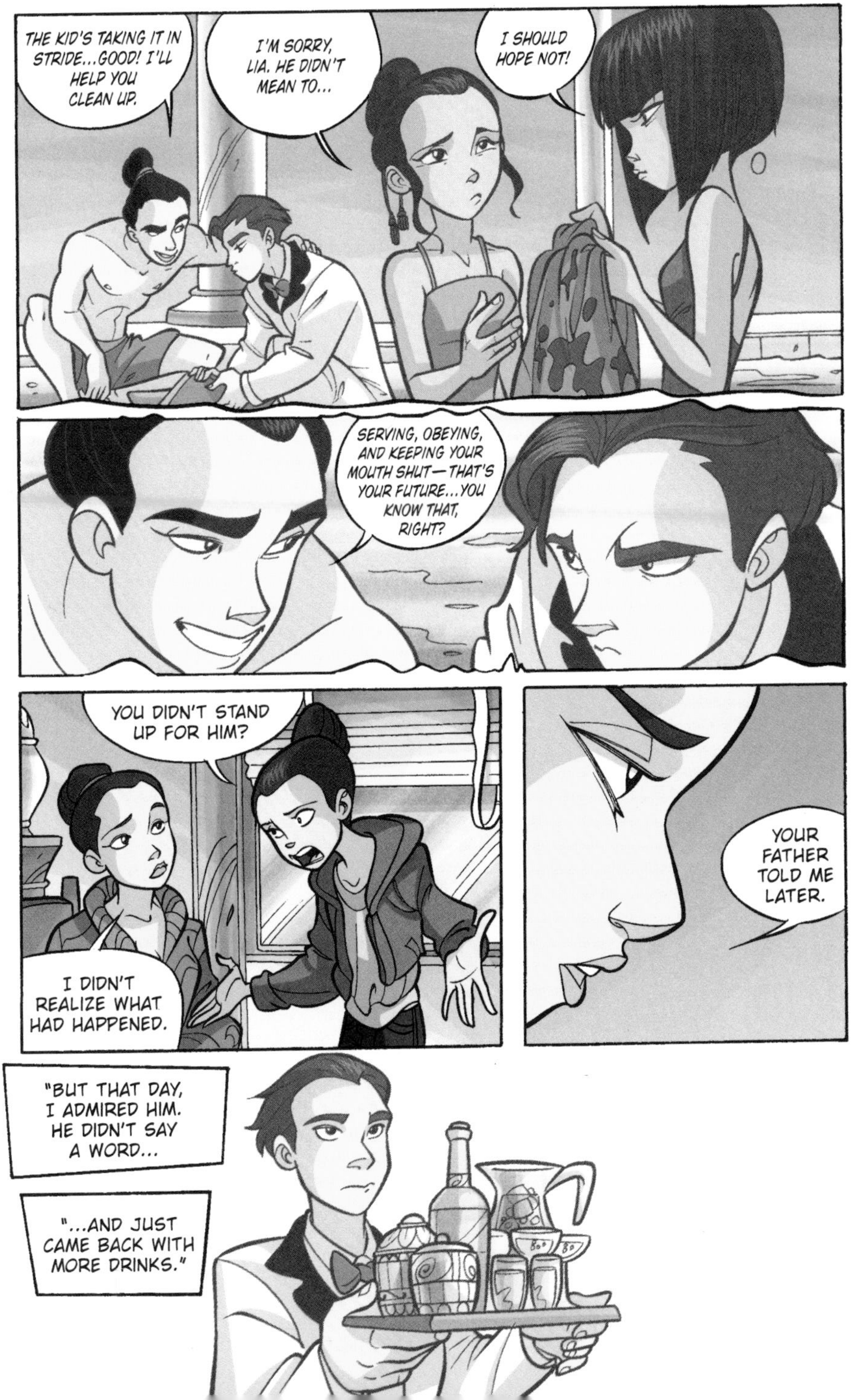
THE KID'S TAKING IT IN STRIDE...GOOD! I'LL HELP YOU CLEAN UP.
I'M SORRY, LIA. HE DIDN'T MEAN TO...
I SHOULD HOPE NOT!
SERVING, OBEYING, AND KEEPING YOUR MOUTH SHUT—THAT'S YOUR FUTURE...YOU KNOW THAT, RIGHT?
YOU DIDN'T STAND UP FOR HIM?
I DIDN'T REALIZE WHAT HAD HAPPENED.
YOUR FATHER TOLD ME LATER.
"BUT THAT DAY, I ADMIRED HIM. HE DIDN'T SAY A WORD...
"...AND JUST CAME BACK WITH MORE DRINKS."

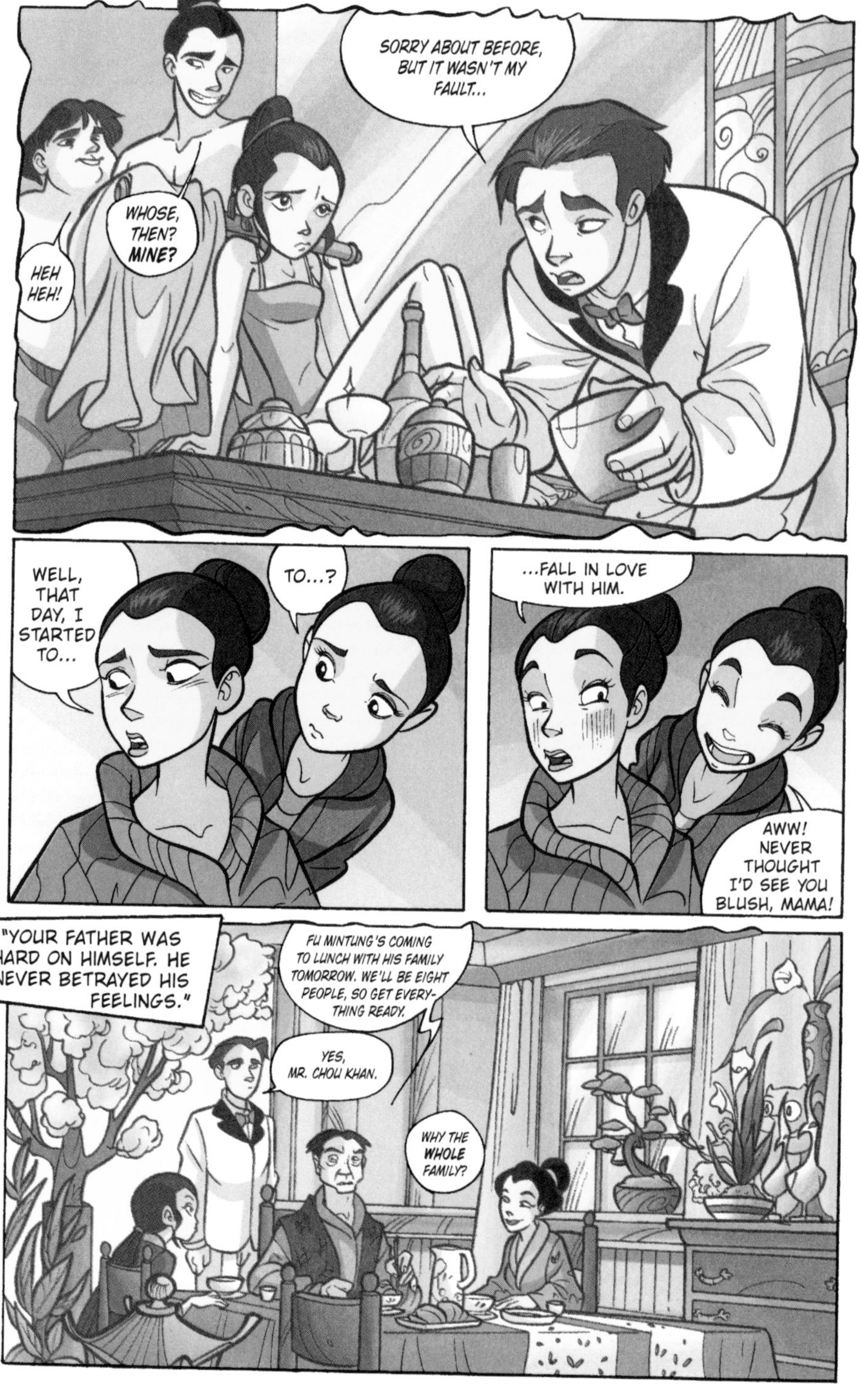
SORRY ABOUT BEFORE, BUT IT WASN'T MY FAULT...
WHOSE, THEN? **MINE?**
HEH HEH!
WELL, THAT DAY, I STARTED TO...
TO...?
...FALL IN LOVE WITH HIM.
AWW! NEVER THOUGHT I'D SEE YOU BLUSH, MAMA!
"YOUR FATHER WAS HARD ON HIMSELF. HE NEVER BETRAYED HIS FEELINGS."
FU MINTUNG'S COMING TO LUNCH WITH HIS FAMILY TOMORROW. WE'LL BE EIGHT PEOPLE, SO GET EVERYTHING READY.
YES, MR. CHOU KHAN.
WHY THE **WHOLE** FAMILY?

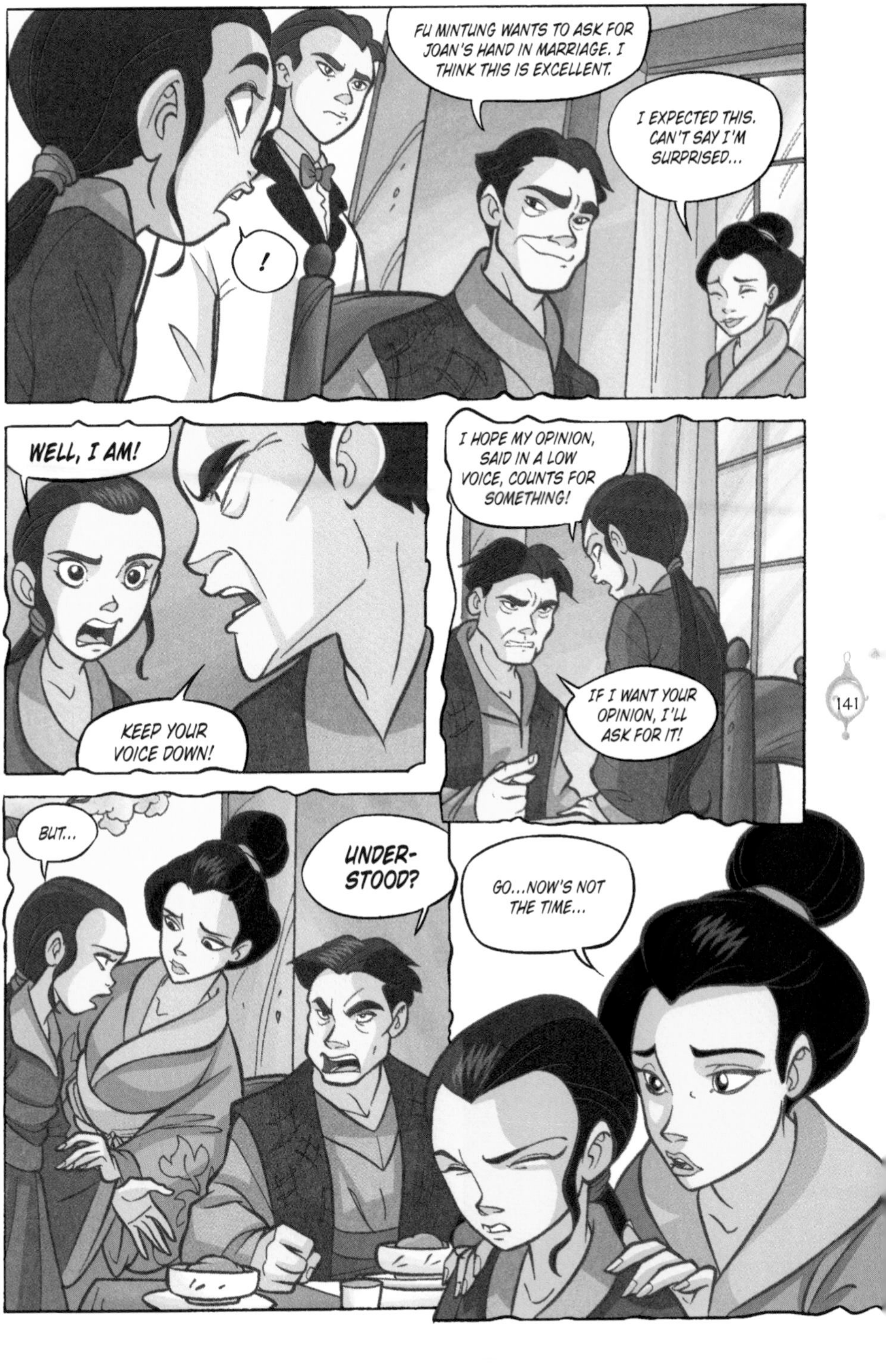
FU MINTUNG WANTS TO ASK FOR JOAN'S HAND IN MARRIAGE. I THINK THIS IS EXCELLENT.
I EXPECTED THIS. CAN'T SAY I'M SURPRISED...
!
WELL, I AM!
KEEP YOUR VOICE DOWN!
I HOPE MY OPINION, SAID IN A LOW VOICE, COUNTS FOR SOMETHING!
IF I WANT YOUR OPINION, I'LL ASK FOR IT!
BUT...
UNDER-STOOD?
GO...NOW'S NOT THE TIME...

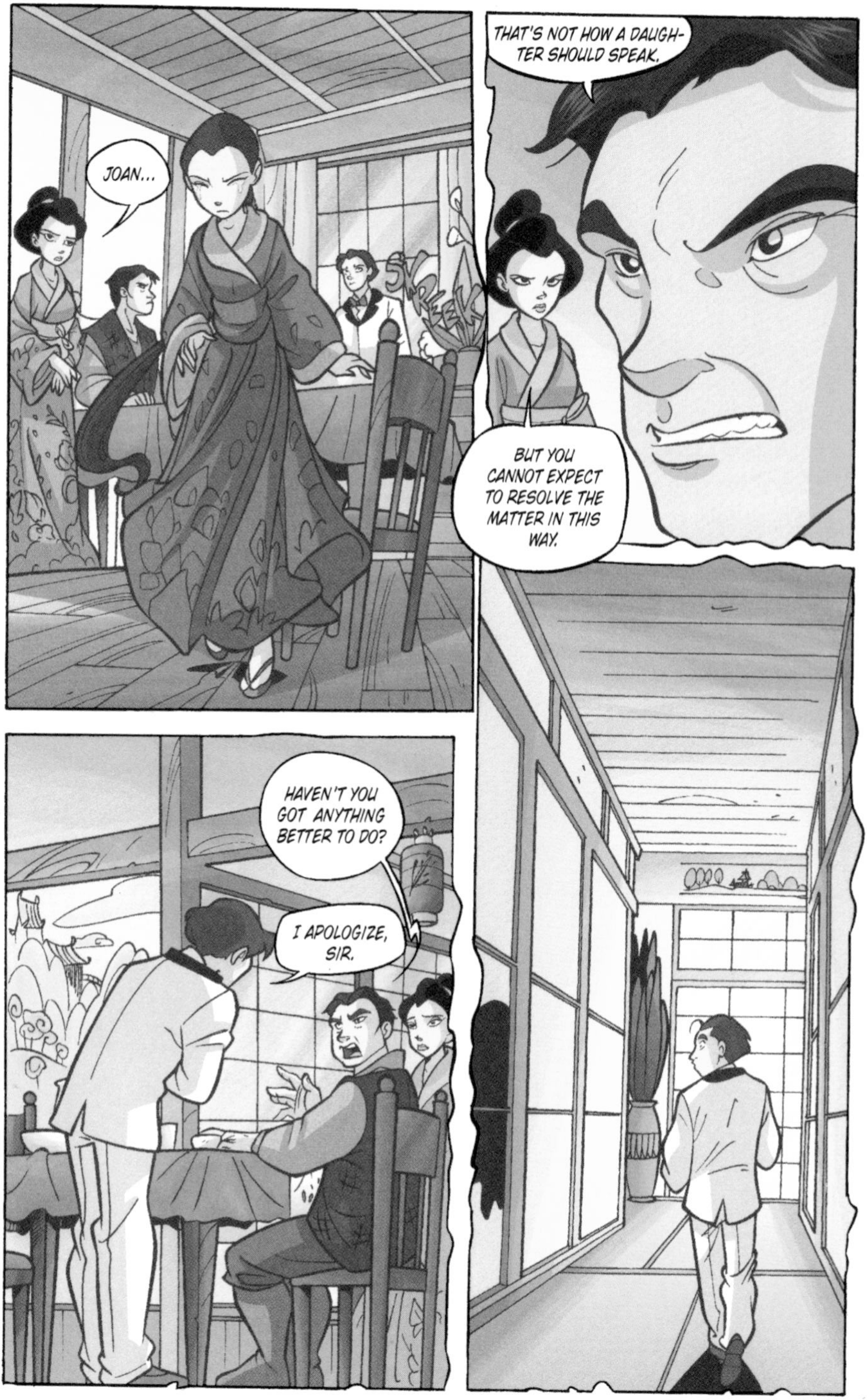
JOAN...
SKREEK
THAT'S NOT HOW A DAUGHTER SHOULD SPEAK.
BUT YOU CANNOT EXPECT TO RESOLVE THE MATTER IN THIS WAY.
HAVEN'T YOU GOT ANYTHING BETTER TO DO?
I APOLOGIZE, SIR.

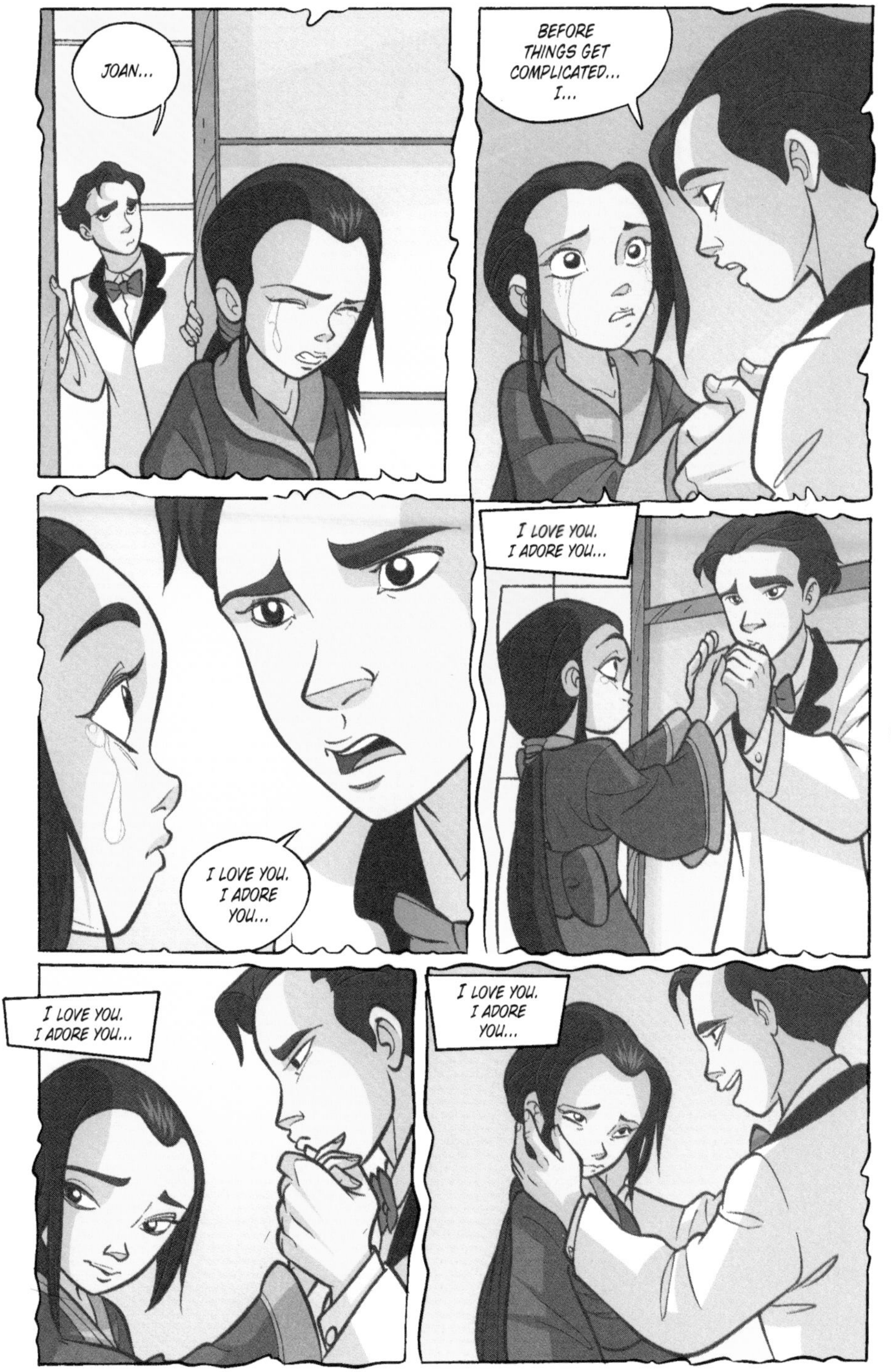
JOAN...
BEFORE THINGS GET COMPLICATED... I...
I LOVE YOU. I ADORE YOU...
I LOVE YOU. I ADORE YOU...
I LOVE YOU. I ADORE YOU...
I LOVE YOU. I ADORE YOU...

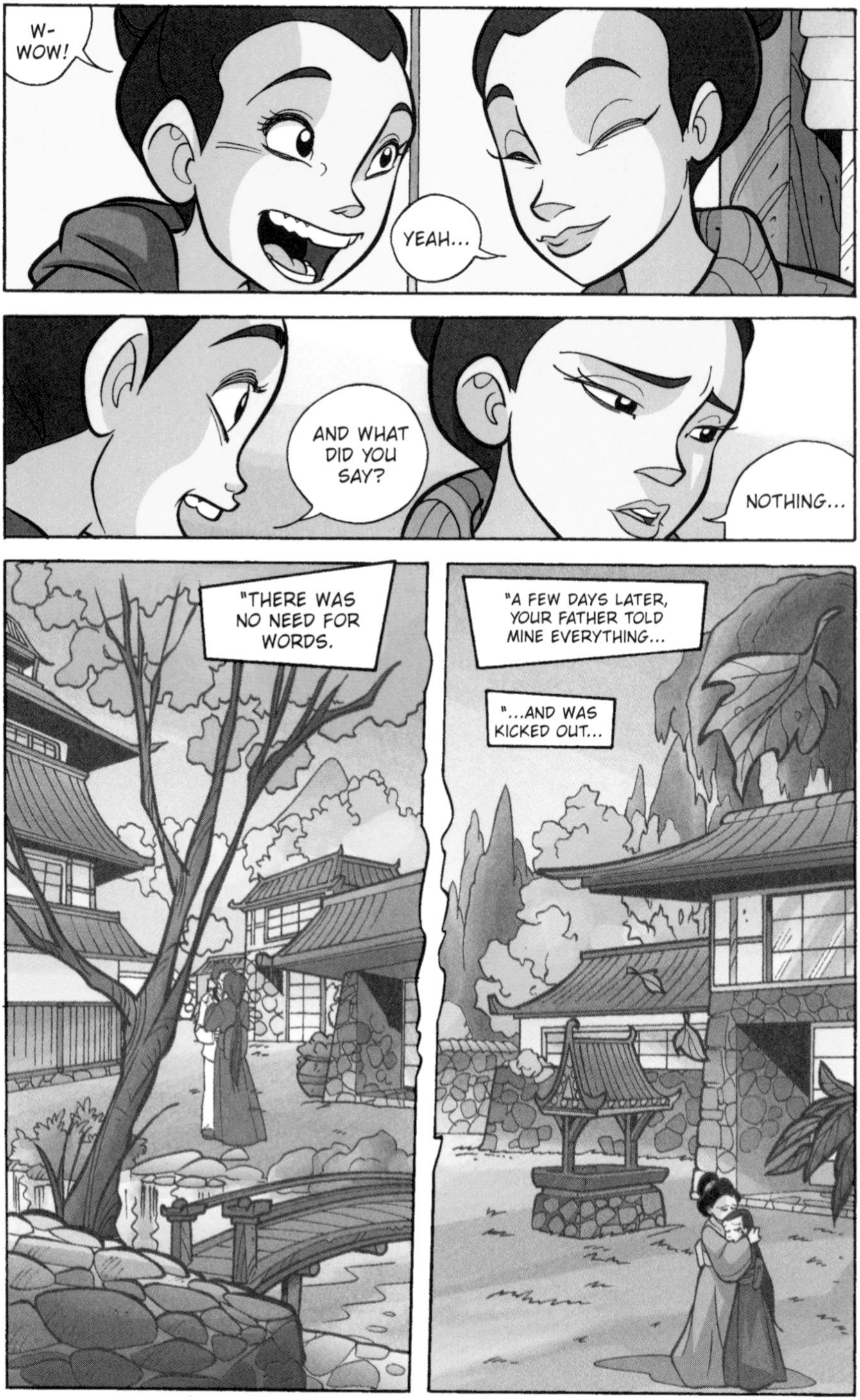
W-WOW!
YEAH...
AND WHAT DID YOU SAY?
NOTHING...
"THERE WAS NO NEED FOR WORDS.
"A FEW DAYS LATER, YOUR FATHER TOLD MINE EVERYTHING...
"...AND WAS KICKED OUT...

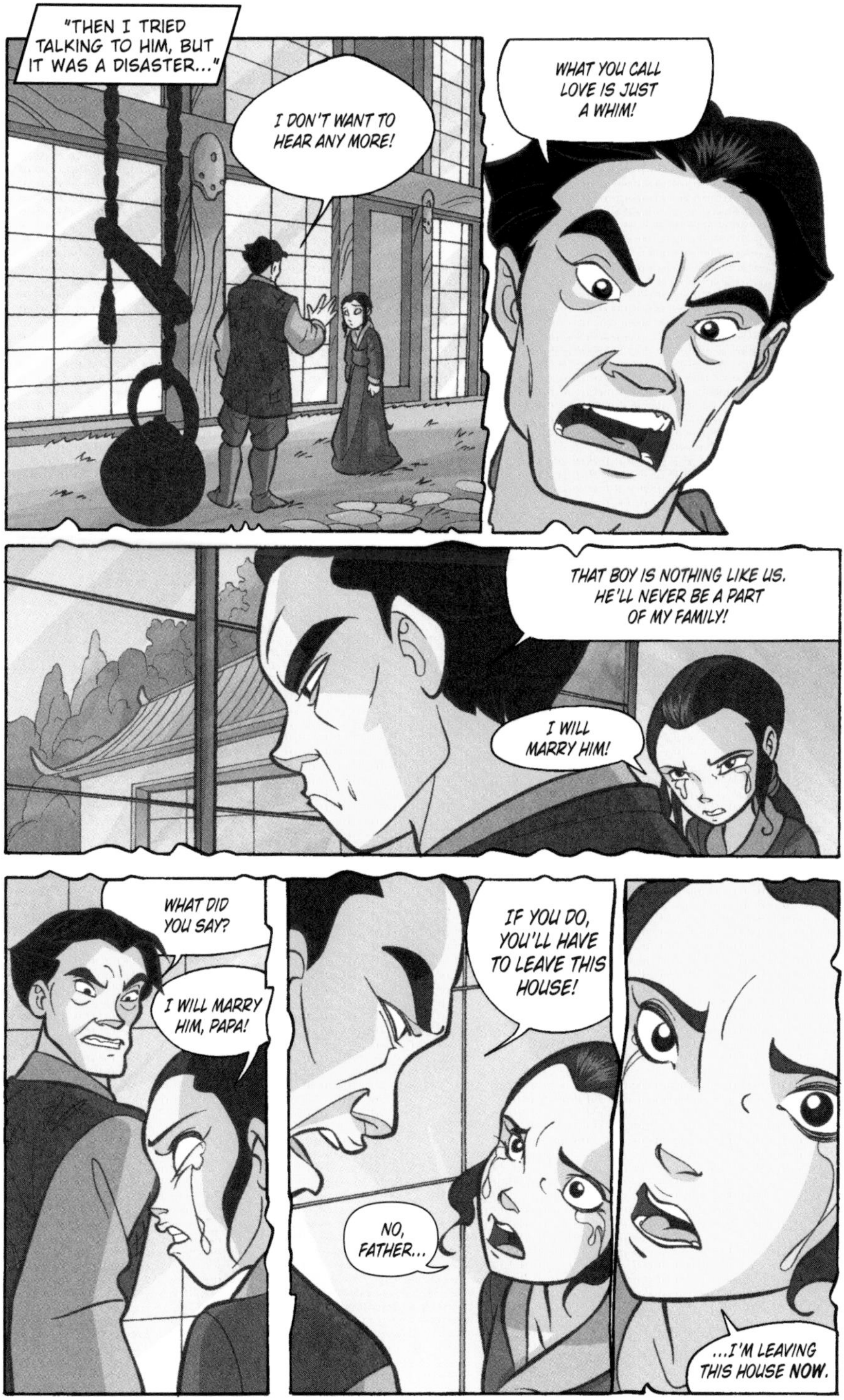
"THEN I TRIED TALKING TO HIM, BUT IT WAS A DISASTER..."
I DON'T WANT TO HEAR ANY MORE!
WHAT YOU CALL LOVE IS JUST A WHIM!
THAT BOY IS NOTHING LIKE US. HE'LL NEVER BE A PART OF MY FAMILY!
I WILL MARRY HIM!
WHAT DID YOU SAY?
I WILL MARRY HIM, PAPA!
IF YOU DO, YOU'LL HAVE TO LEAVE THIS HOUSE!
NO, FATHER...
...I'M LEAVING THIS HOUSE **NOW**.

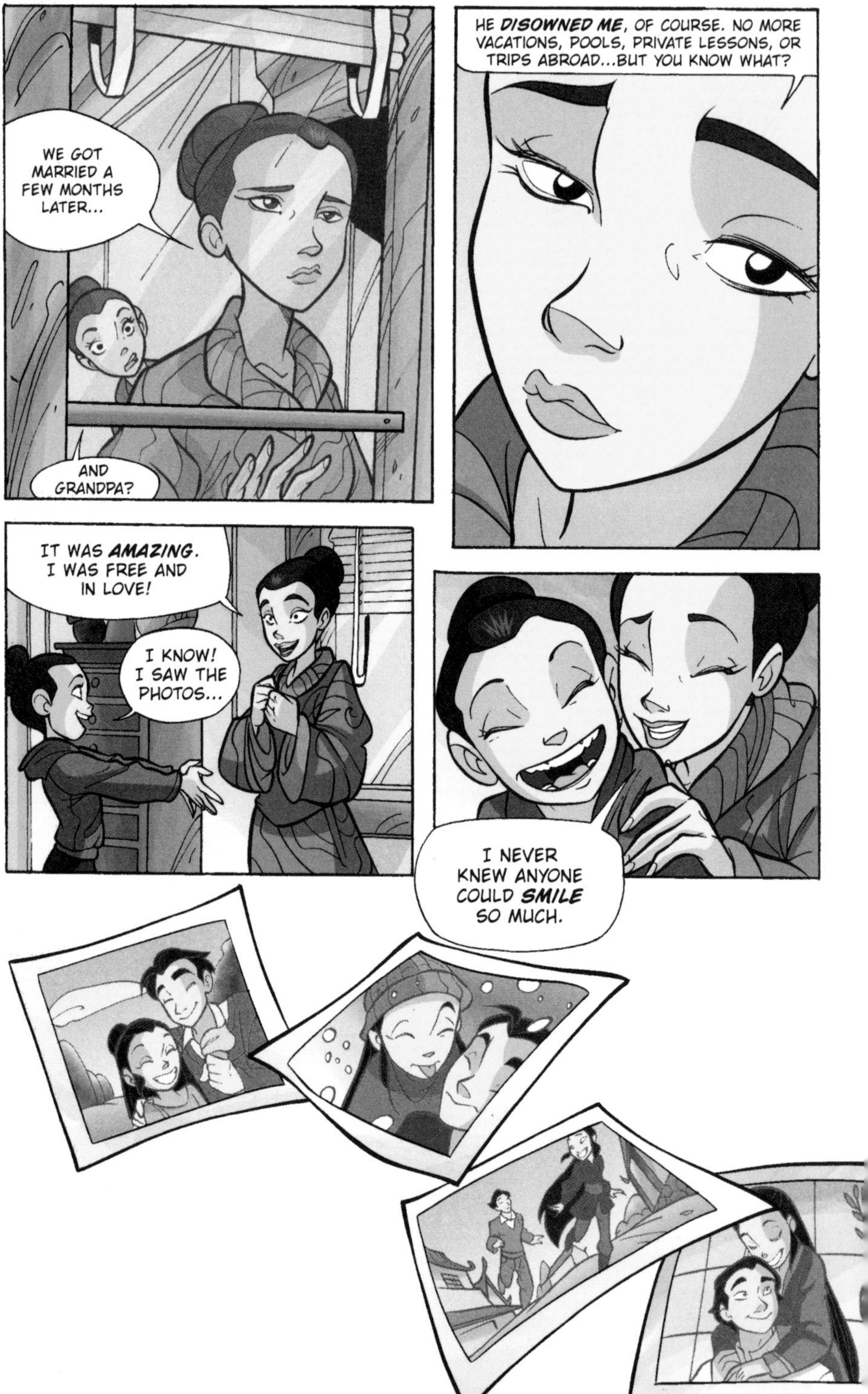
WE GOT MARRIED A FEW MONTHS LATER...
AND GRANDPA?
HE **DISOWNED ME**, OF COURSE. NO MORE VACATIONS, POOLS, PRIVATE LESSONS, OR TRIPS ABROAD...BUT YOU KNOW WHAT?
IT WAS **AMAZING**. I WAS FREE AND IN LOVE!
I KNOW! I SAW THE PHOTOS...
I NEVER KNEW ANYONE COULD **SMILE** SO MUCH.

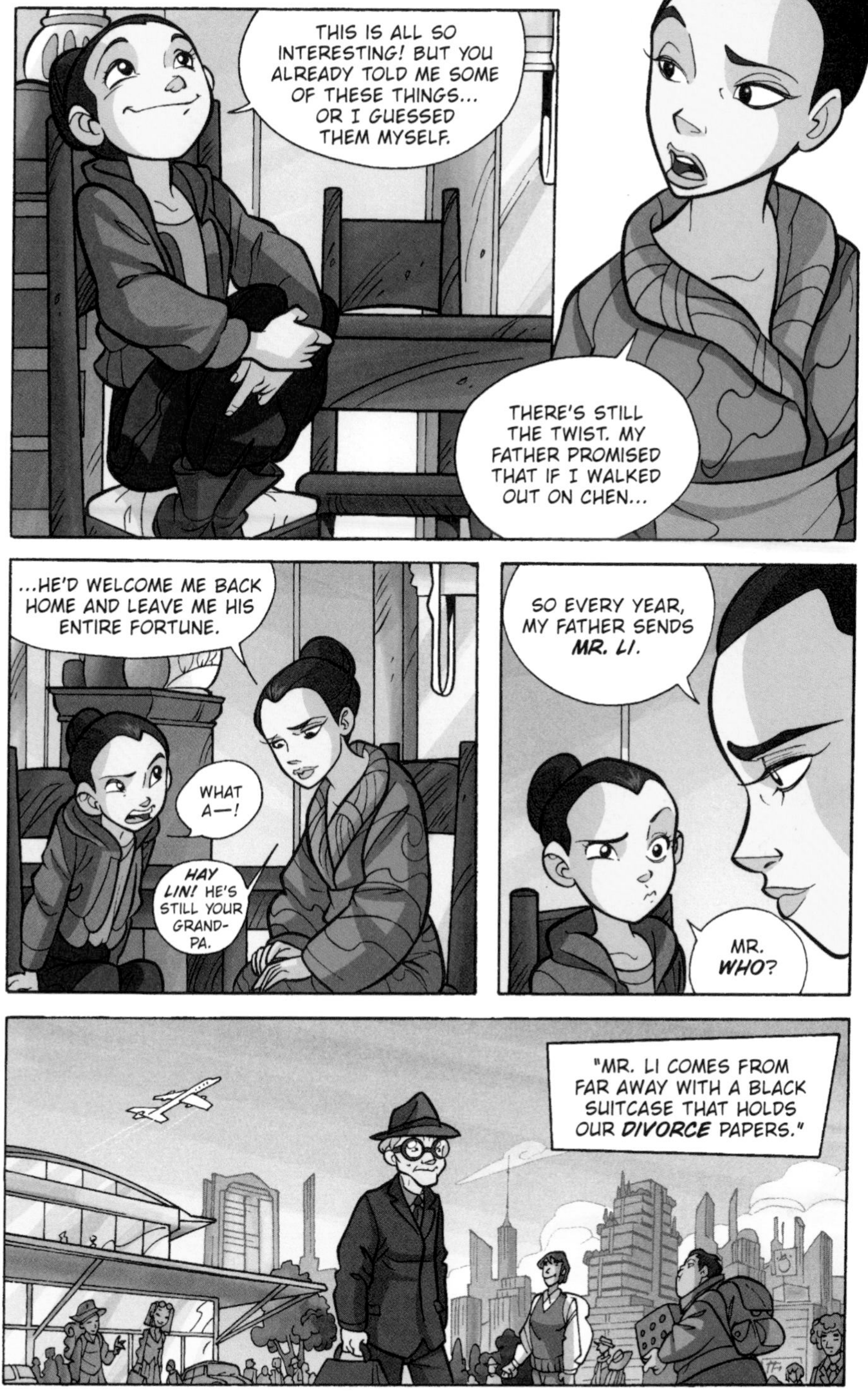
THIS IS ALL SO INTERESTING! BUT YOU ALREADY TOLD ME SOME OF THESE THINGS... OR I GUESSED THEM MYSELF.
THERE'S STILL THE TWIST. MY FATHER PROMISED THAT IF I WALKED OUT ON CHEN...
...HE'D WELCOME ME BACK HOME AND LEAVE ME HIS ENTIRE FORTUNE.
WHAT A—!
HAY LIN! HE'S STILL YOUR GRAND-PA.
SO EVERY YEAR, MY FATHER SENDS MR. LI.
MR. WHO?
"MR. LI COMES FROM FAR AWAY WITH A BLACK SUITCASE THAT HOLDS OUR DIVORCE PAPERS."

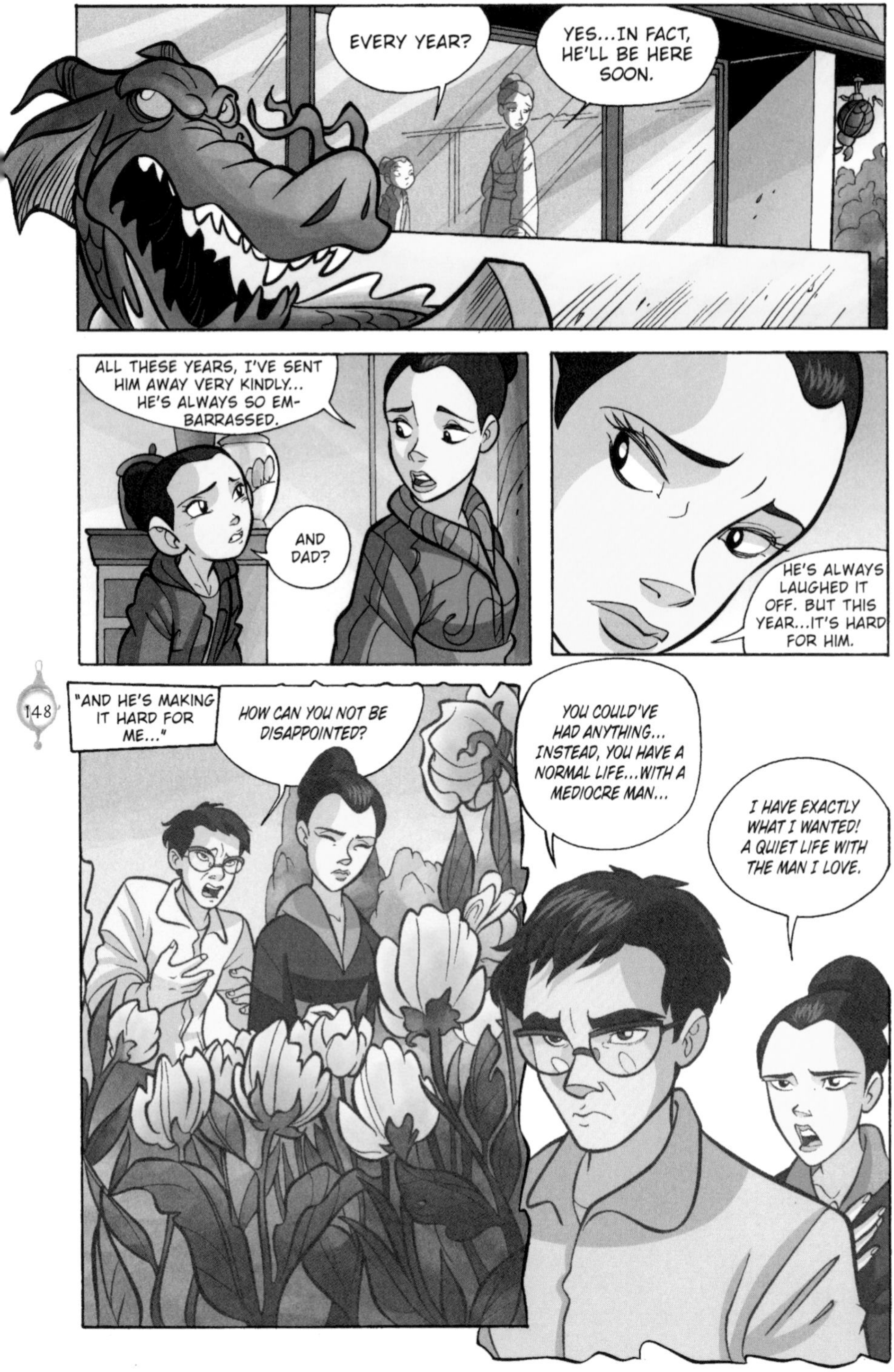
EVERY YEAR?
YES...IN FACT, HE'LL BE HERE SOON.
ALL THESE YEARS, I'VE SENT HIM AWAY VERY KINDLY... HE'S ALWAYS SO EMBARRASSED.
AND DAD?
HE'S ALWAYS LAUGHED IT OFF. BUT THIS YEAR...IT'S HARD FOR HIM.
"AND HE'S MAKING IT HARD FOR ME..."
HOW CAN YOU NOT BE DISAPPOINTED?
YOU COULD'VE HAD ANYTHING... INSTEAD, YOU HAVE A NORMAL LIFE...WITH A MEDIOCRE MAN...
I HAVE EXACTLY WHAT I WANTED! A QUIET LIFE WITH THE MAN I LOVE.

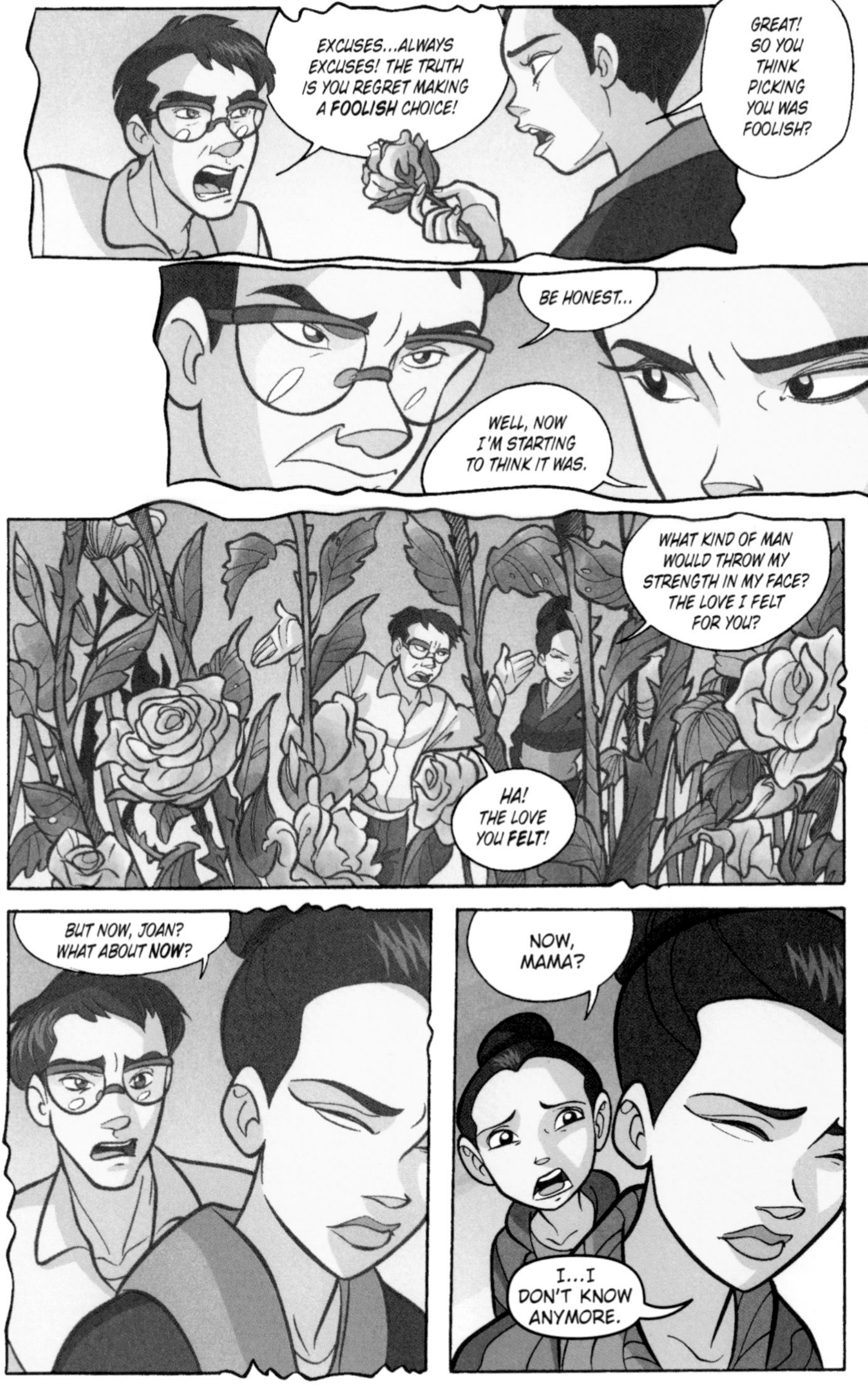
EXCUSES...ALWAYS EXCUSES! THE TRUTH IS YOU REGRET MAKING A **FOOLISH** CHOICE!
GREAT! SO YOU THINK PICKING YOU WAS FOOLISH?
BE HONEST...
WELL, NOW I'M STARTING TO THINK IT WAS.
WHAT KIND OF MAN WOULD THROW MY STRENGTH IN MY FACE? THE LOVE I FELT FOR YOU?
HA! THE LOVE YOU **FELT**!
BUT NOW, JOAN? WHAT ABOUT **NOW**?
NOW, MAMA?
I...I DON'T KNOW ANYMORE.

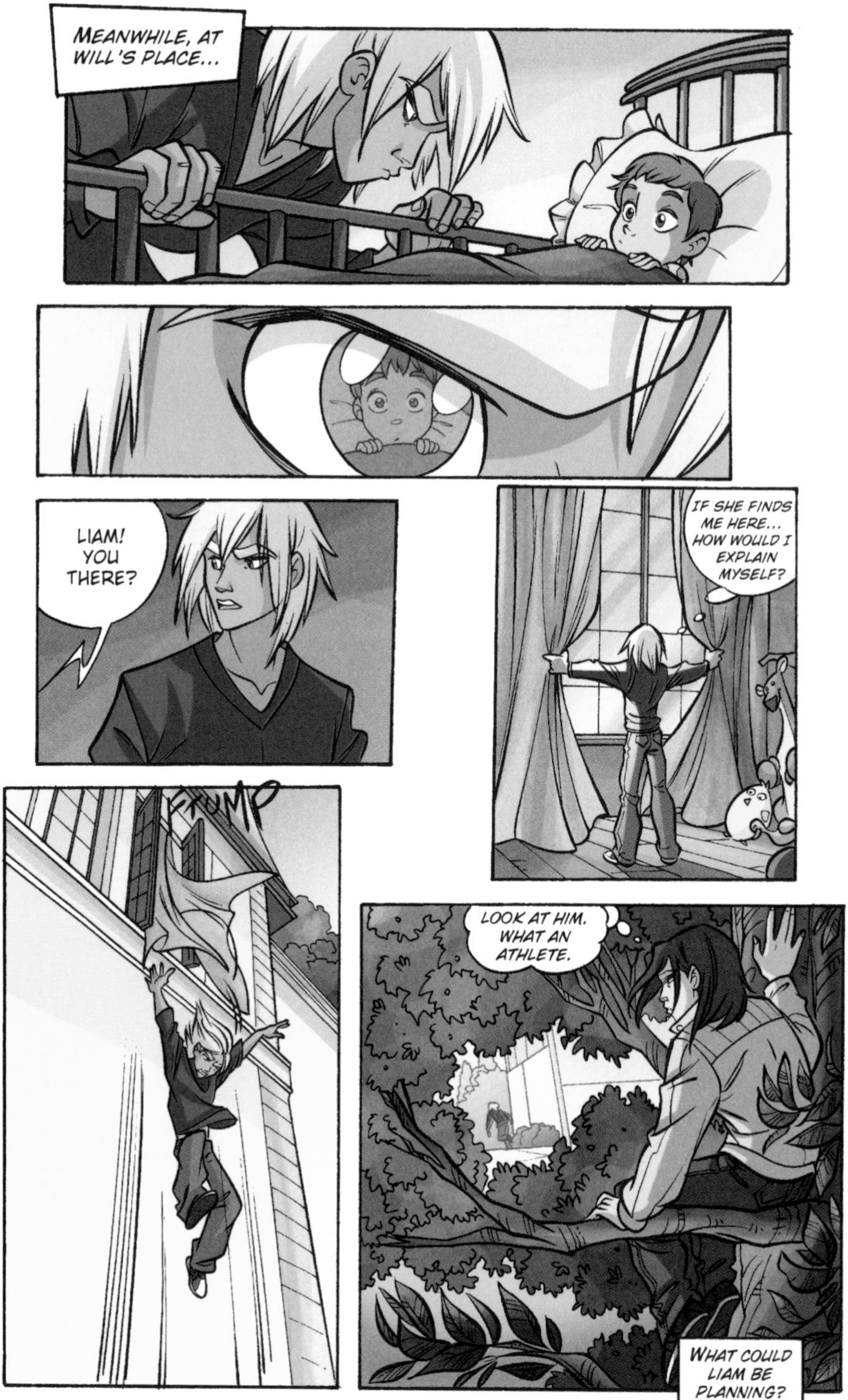
MEANWHILE, AT WILL'S PLACE...
LIAM! YOU THERE?
IF SHE FINDS ME HERE... HOW WOULD I EXPLAIN MYSELF?
FRUMP
LOOK AT HIM. WHAT AN ATHLETE.
WHAT COULD LIAM BE PLANNING?

W.i.t.c.h.

Will Irma Taranee Cornelia Hay Lin

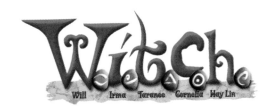

W.i.t.c.h.

Will Irma Taranee Cornelia Hay Lin

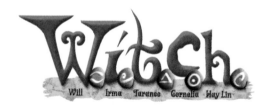

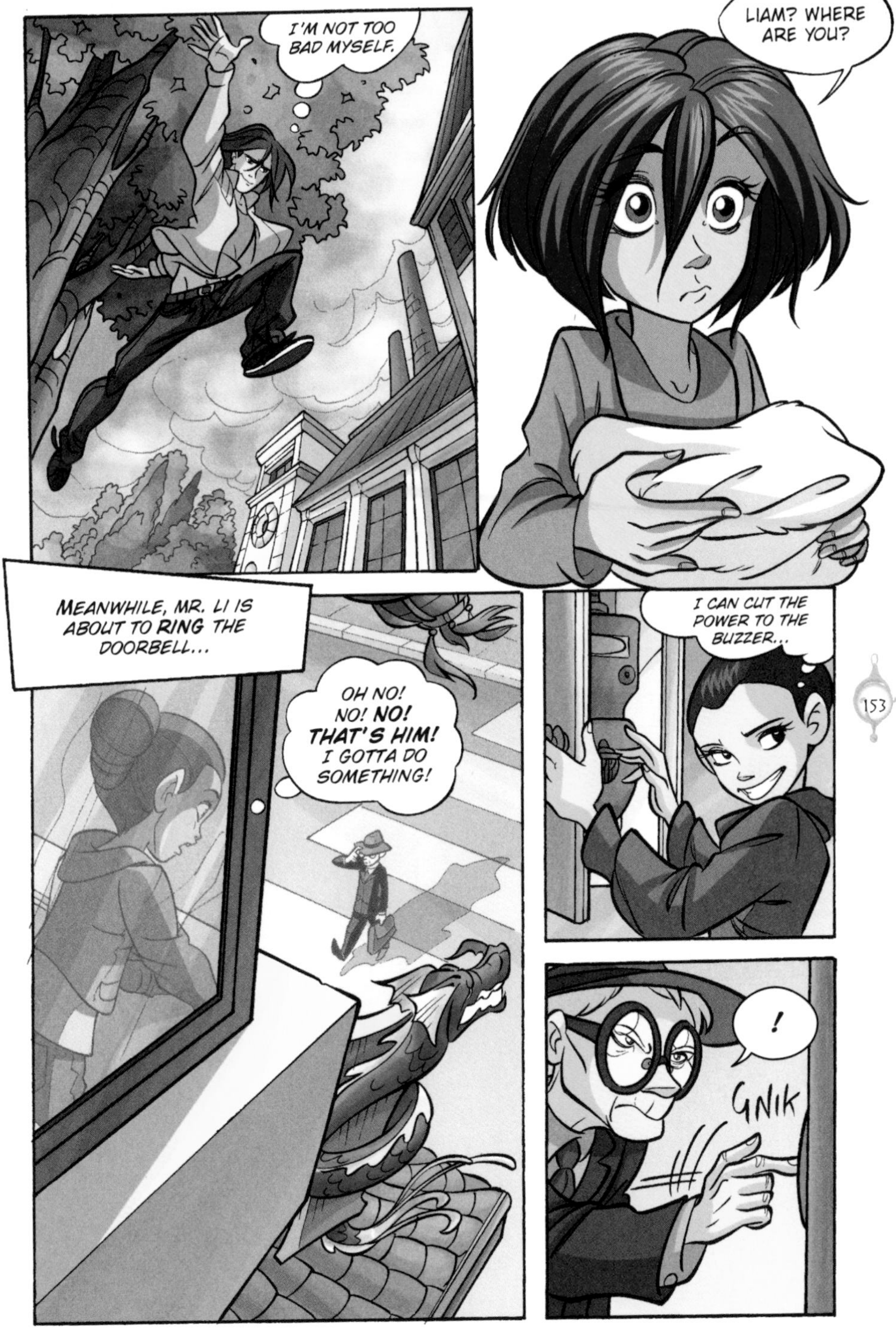
I'M NOT TOO BAD MYSELF.
LIAM? WHERE ARE YOU?
MEANWHILE, MR. LI IS ABOUT TO **RING** THE DOORBELL...
OH NO! NO! **NO! THAT'S HIM!** I GOTTA DO SOMETHING!
I CAN CUT THE POWER TO THE BUZZER...
!
GNIK

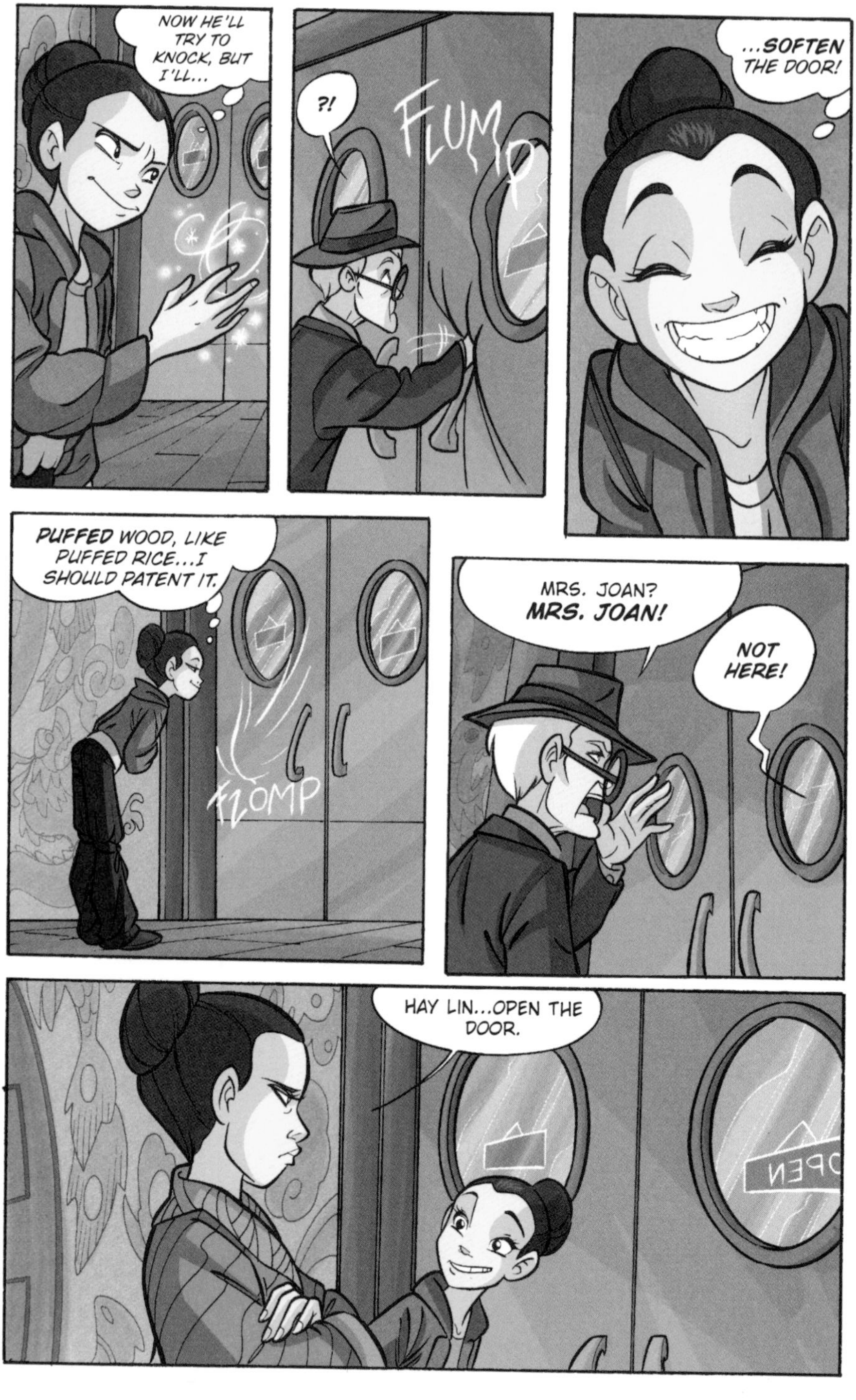

NOW HE'LL TRY TO KNOCK, BUT I'LL...
?!
FLUMP
...SOFTEN THE DOOR!
PUFFED WOOD, LIKE PUFFED RICE...I SHOULD PATENT IT.
FLOMP
MRS. JOAN? MRS. JOAN!
NOT HERE!
HAY LIN...OPEN THE DOOR.
OPEN

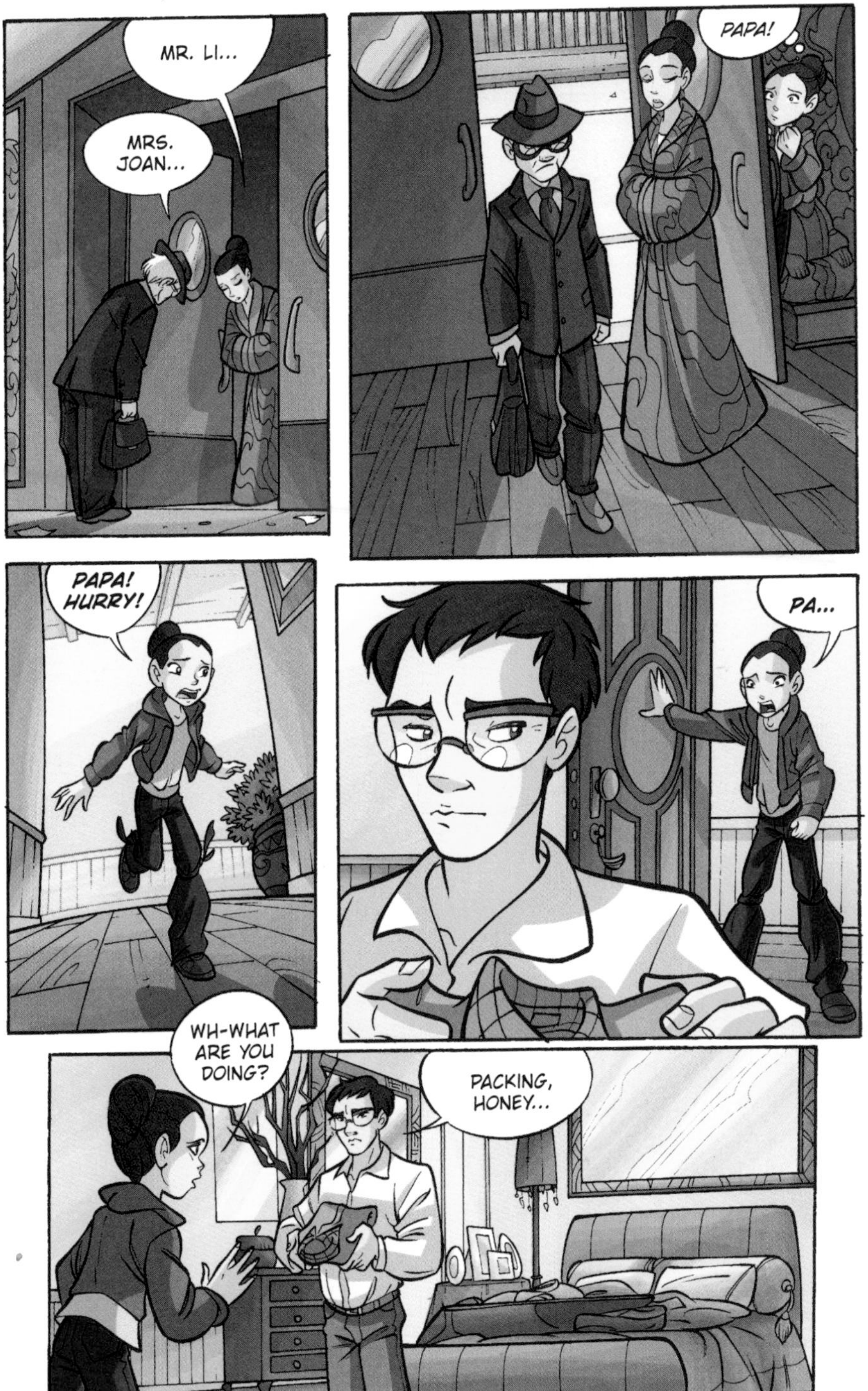
MR. LI...
MRS. JOAN...
PAPA!
PAPA! HURRY!
PA...
WH-WHAT ARE YOU DOING?
PACKING, HONEY...

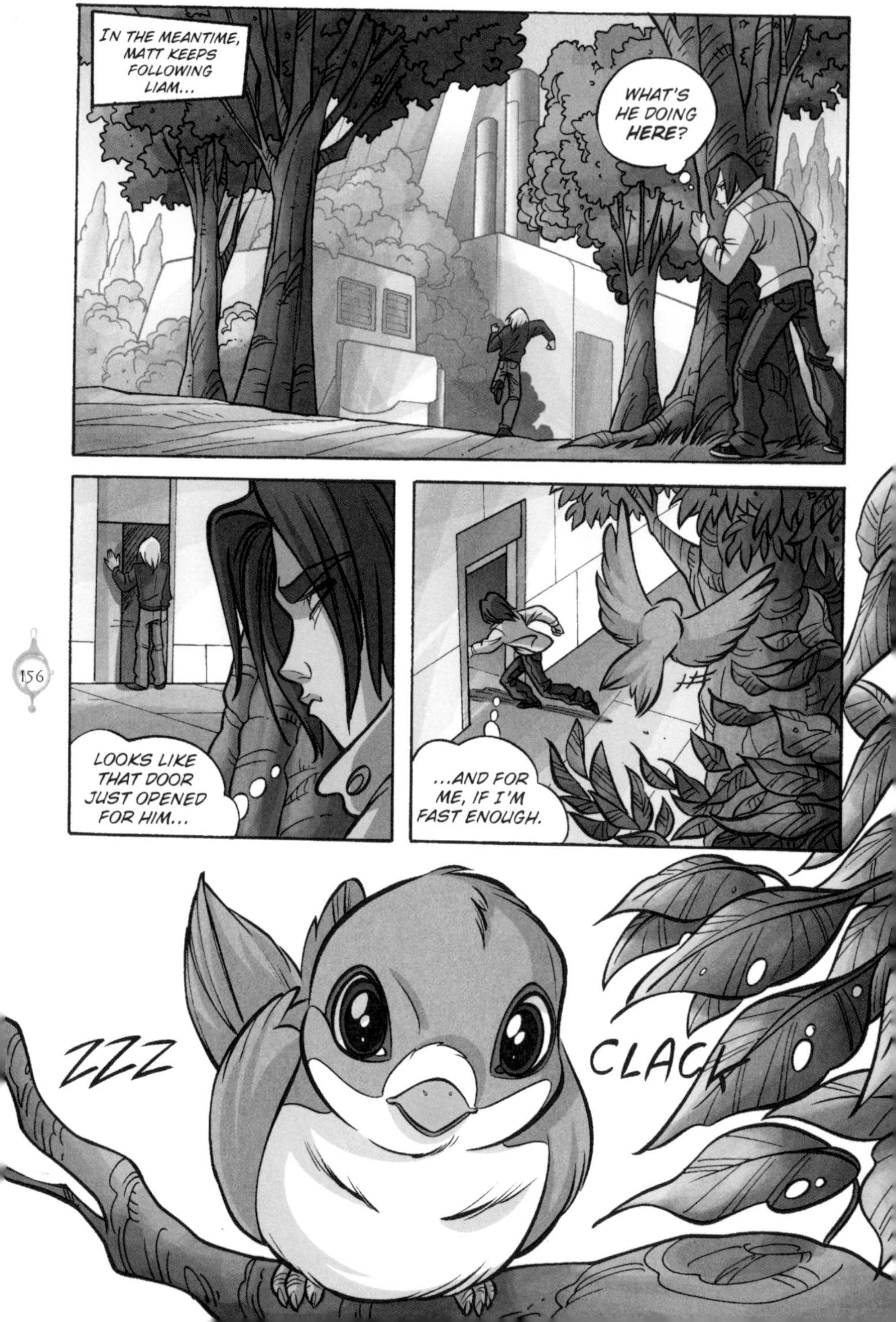
IN THE MEANTIME, MATT KEEPS FOLLOWING LIAM...
WHAT'S HE DOING **HERE**?
LOOKS LIKE THAT DOOR JUST OPENED FOR HIM...
...AND FOR ME, IF I'M FAST ENOUGH.
ZZZ
CLACK

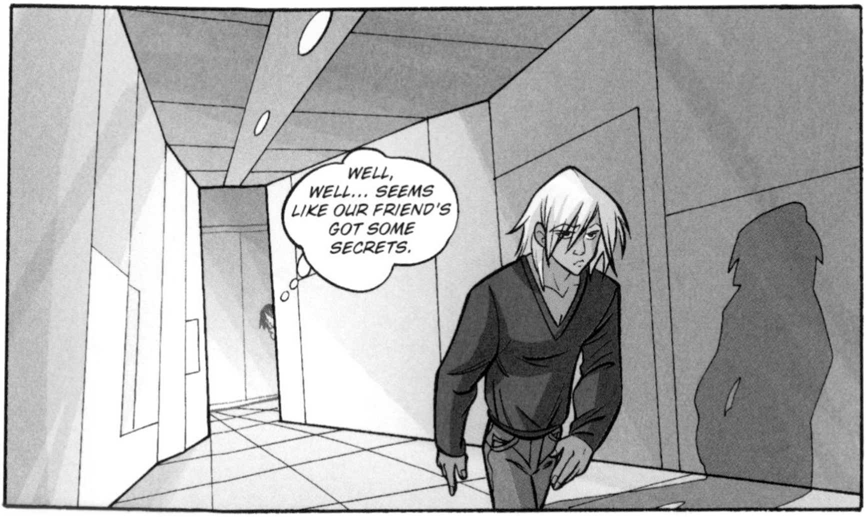
WELL, WELL... SEEMS LIKE OUR FRIEND'S GOT SOME SECRETS.

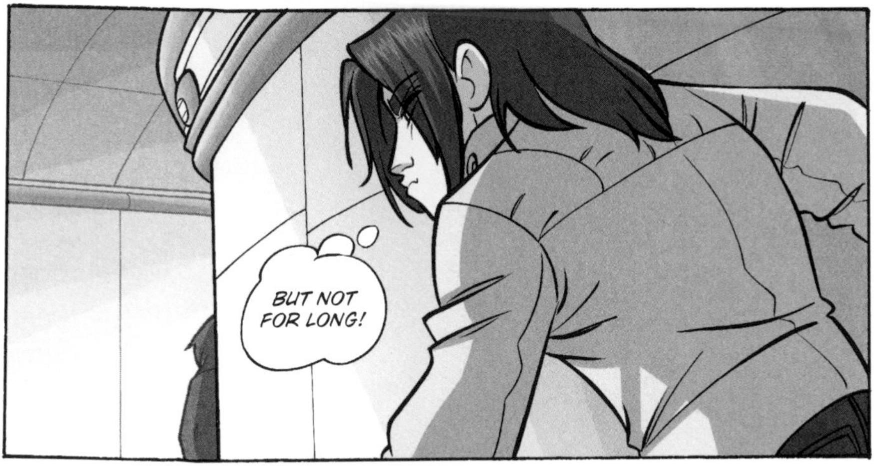
BUT NOT FOR LONG!

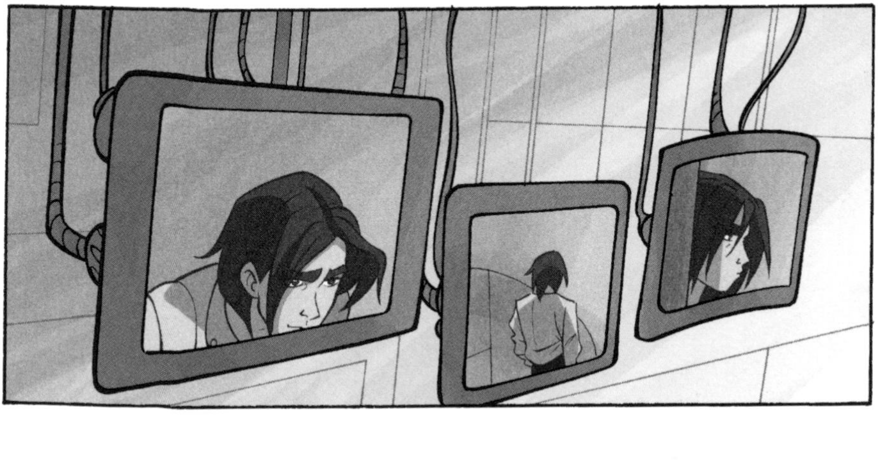

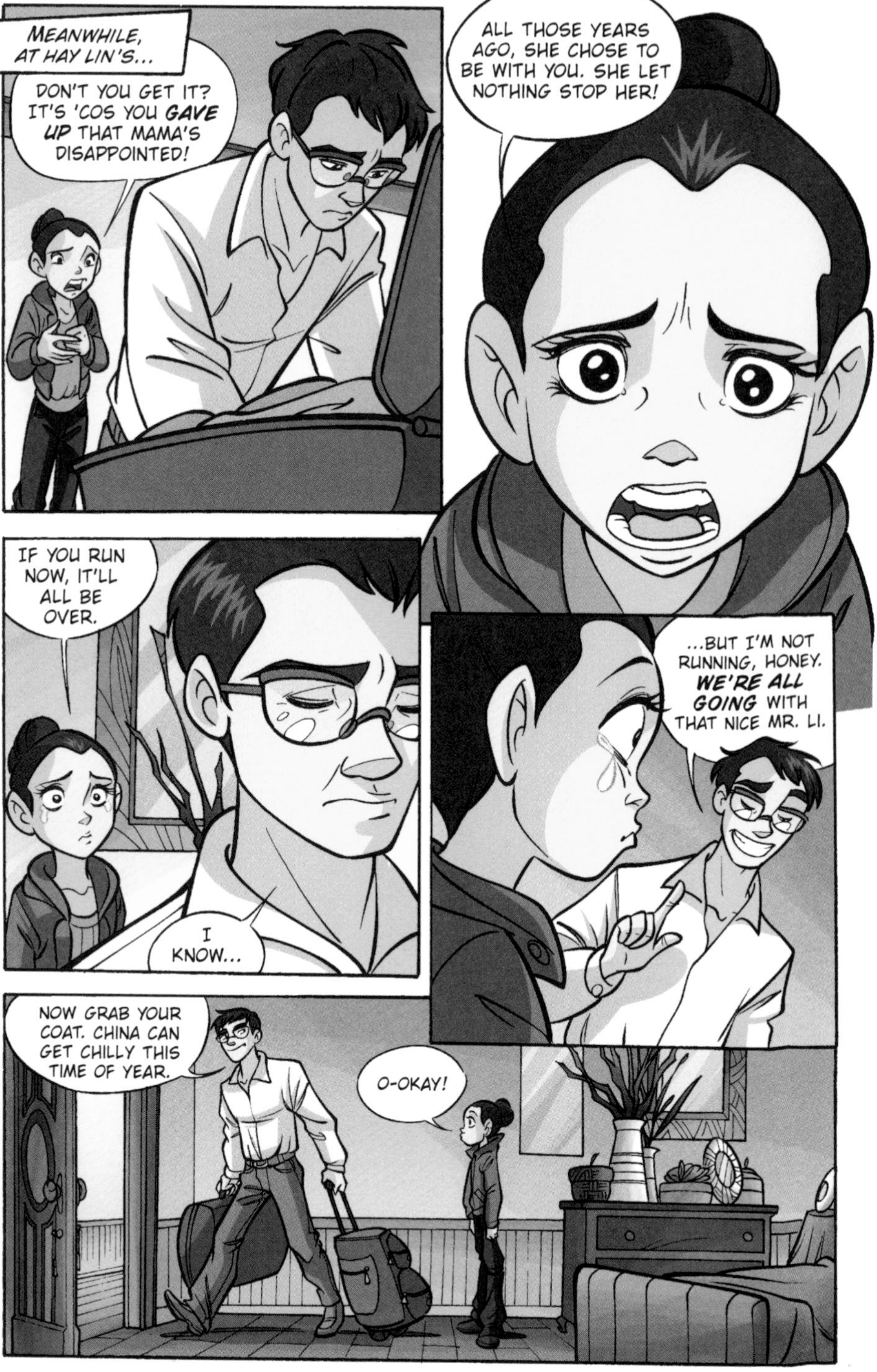
MEANWHILE, AT HAY LIN'S...
DON'T YOU GET IT? IT'S 'COS YOU GAVE UP THAT MAMA'S DISAPPOINTED!
ALL THOSE YEARS AGO, SHE CHOSE TO BE WITH YOU. SHE LET NOTHING STOP HER!
IF YOU RUN NOW, IT'LL ALL BE OVER.
I KNOW...
...BUT I'M NOT RUNNING, HONEY. WE'RE ALL GOING WITH THAT NICE MR. LI.
NOW GRAB YOUR COAT. CHINA CAN GET CHILLY THIS TIME OF YEAR.
O-OKAY!

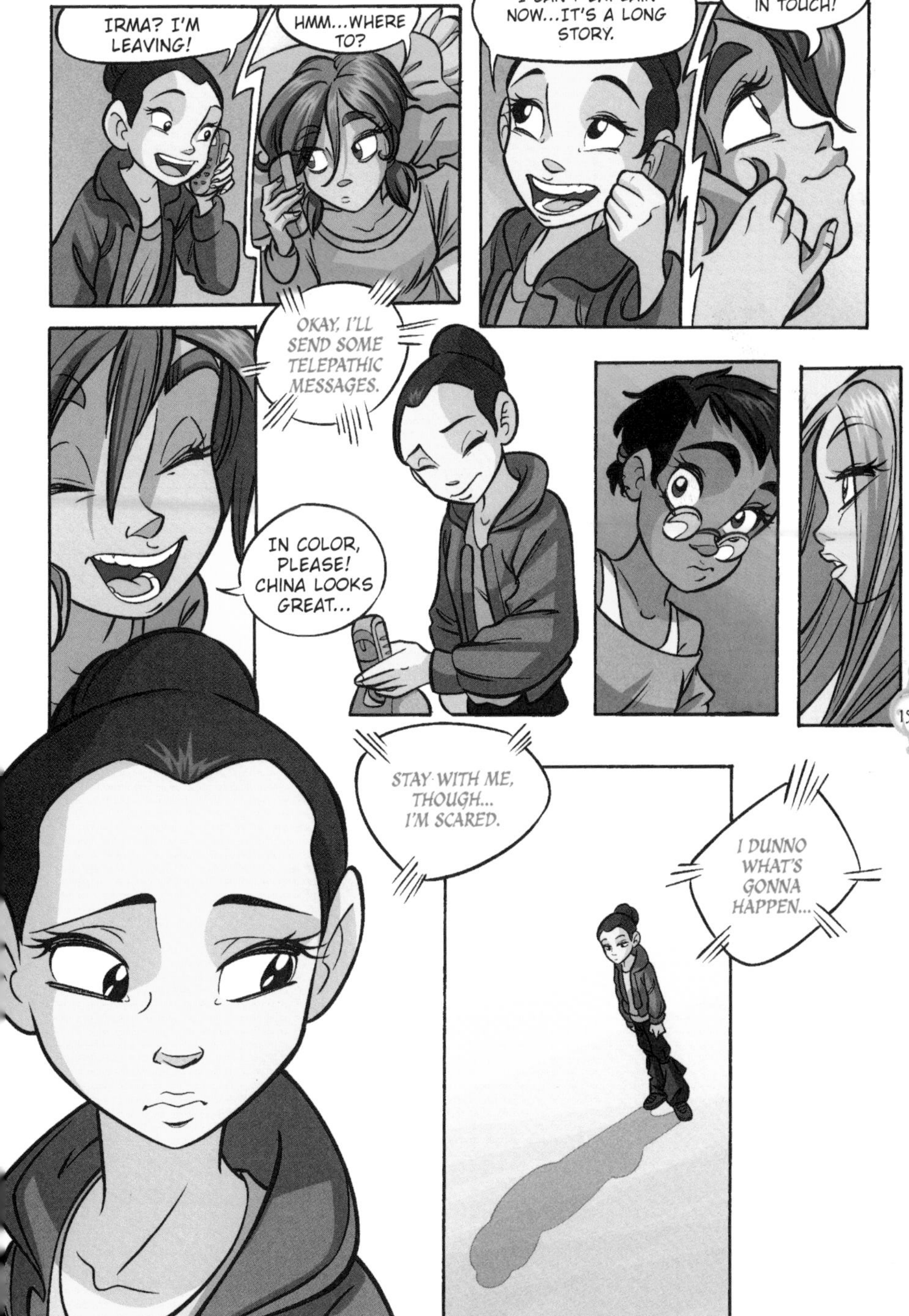
IRMA? I'M LEAVING!
HMM...WHERE TO?
I CAN'T EXPLAIN NOW...IT'S A LONG STORY.
THEN KEEP IN TOUCH!
OKAY, I'LL SEND SOME TELEPATHIC MESSAGES.
IN COLOR, PLEASE! CHINA LOOKS GREAT...
STAY WITH ME, THOUGH... I'M SCARED.
I DUNNO WHAT'S GONNA HAPPEN...

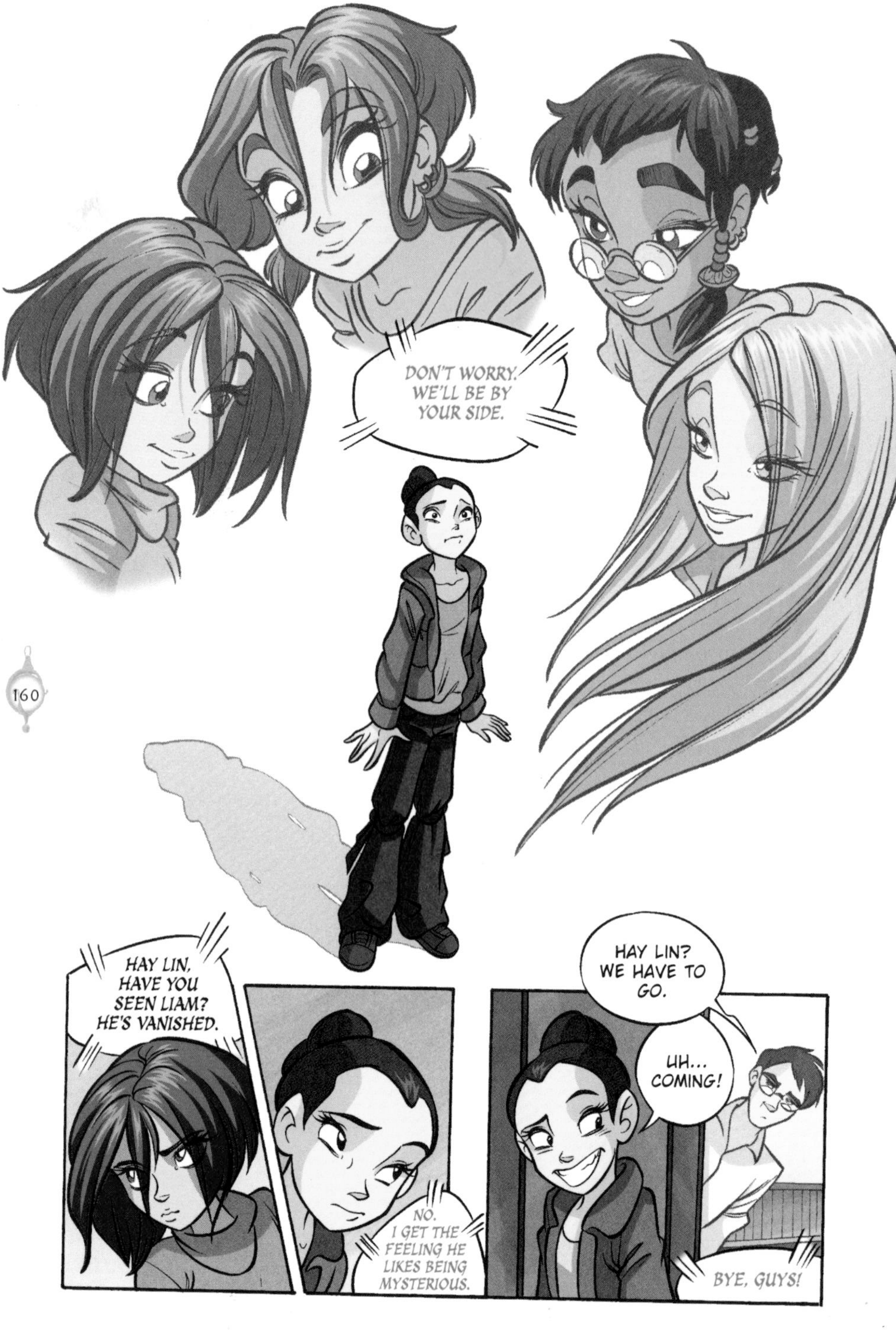
DON'T WORRY. WE'LL BE BY YOUR SIDE.
HAY LIN, HAVE YOU SEEN LIAM? HE'S VANISHED.
NO. I GET THE FEELING HE LIKES BEING MYSTERIOUS.
HAY LIN? WE HAVE TO GO.
UH... COMING!
BYE, GUYS!

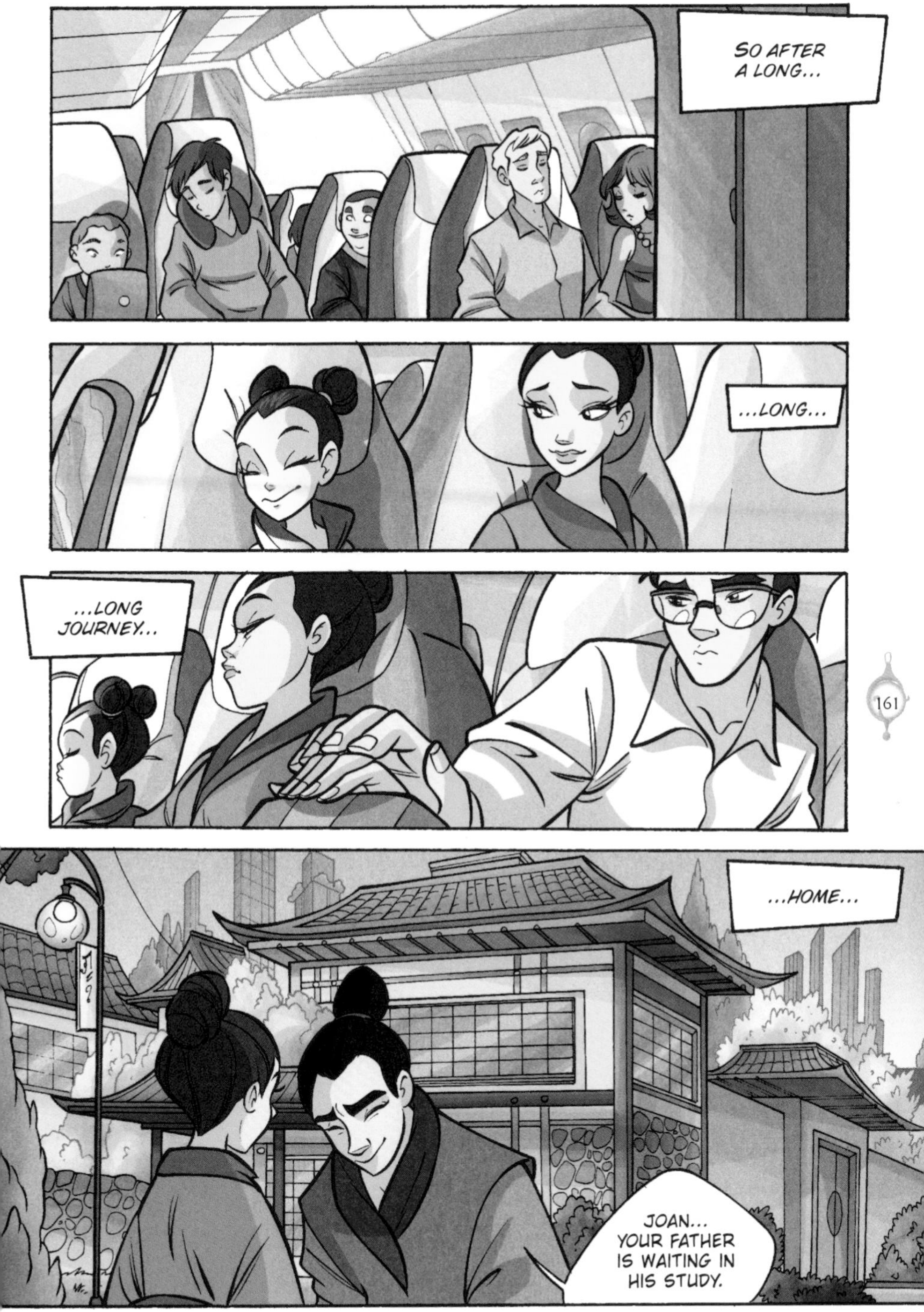
SO AFTER A LONG...
...LONG...
...LONG JOURNEY...
...HOME...
JOAN... YOUR FATHER IS WAITING IN HIS STUDY.

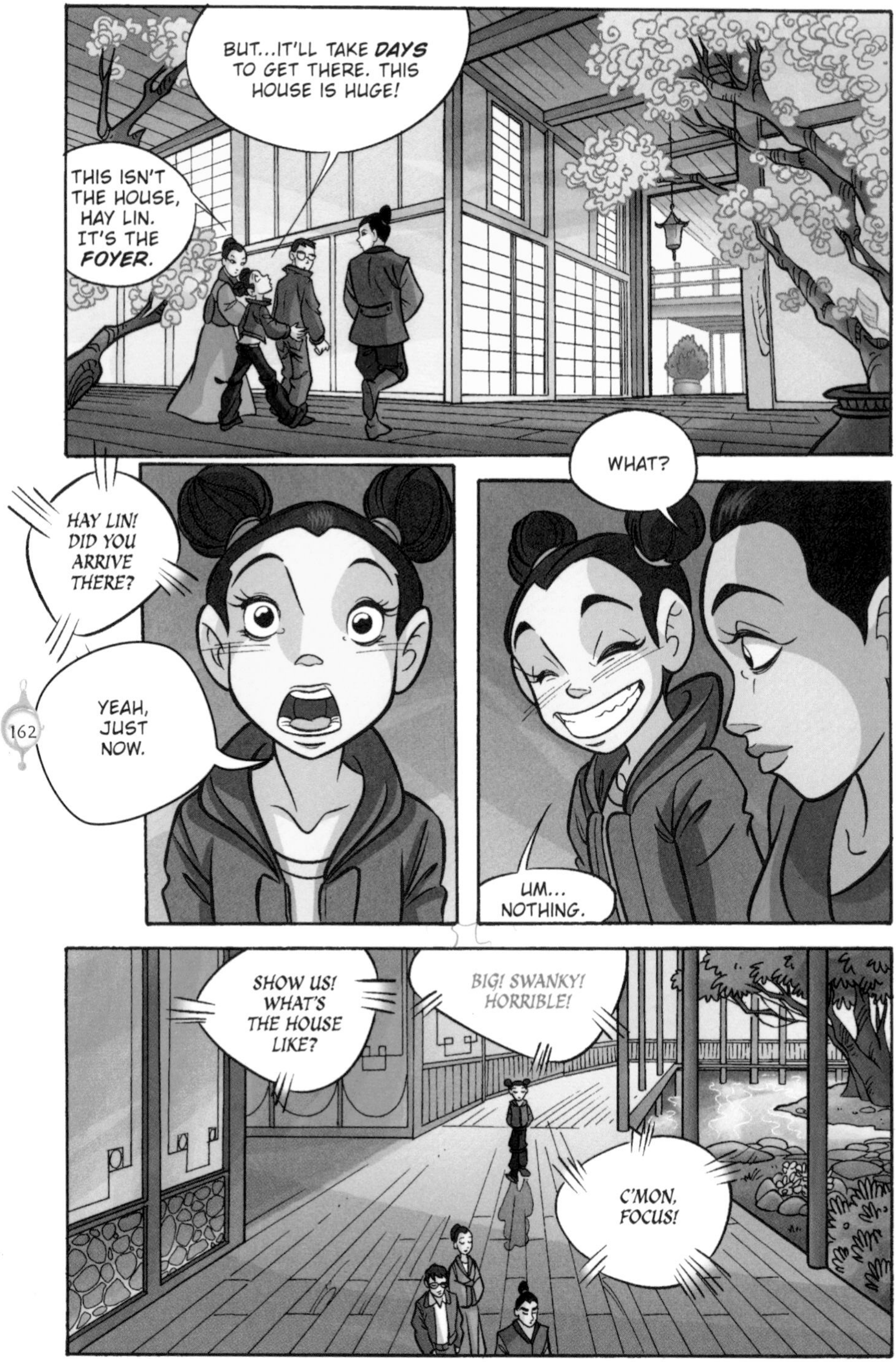
THIS ISN'T THE HOUSE, HAY LIN. IT'S THE FOYER.
BUT...IT'LL TAKE DAYS TO GET THERE. THIS HOUSE IS HUGE!
HAY LIN! DID YOU ARRIVE THERE?
YEAH, JUST NOW.
WHAT?
UM... NOTHING.
SHOW US! WHAT'S THE HOUSE LIKE?
BIG! SWANKY! HORRIBLE!
C'MON, FOCUS!

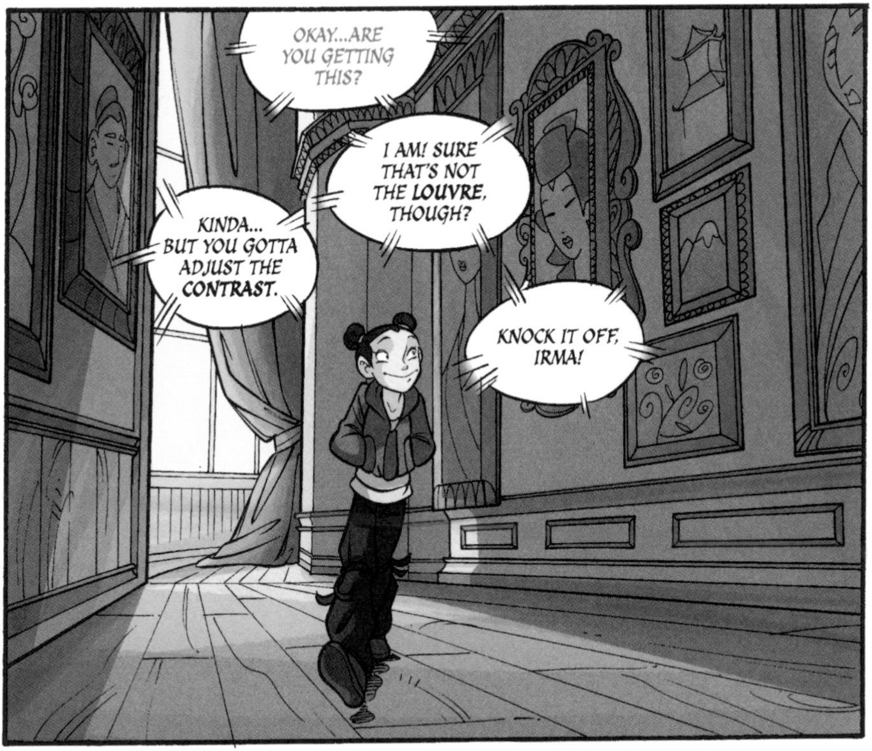
OKAY...ARE YOU GETTING THIS?
I AM! SURE THAT'S NOT THE LOUVRE, THOUGH?
KINDA... BUT YOU GOTTA ADJUST THE CONTRAST.
KNOCK IT OFF, IRMA!

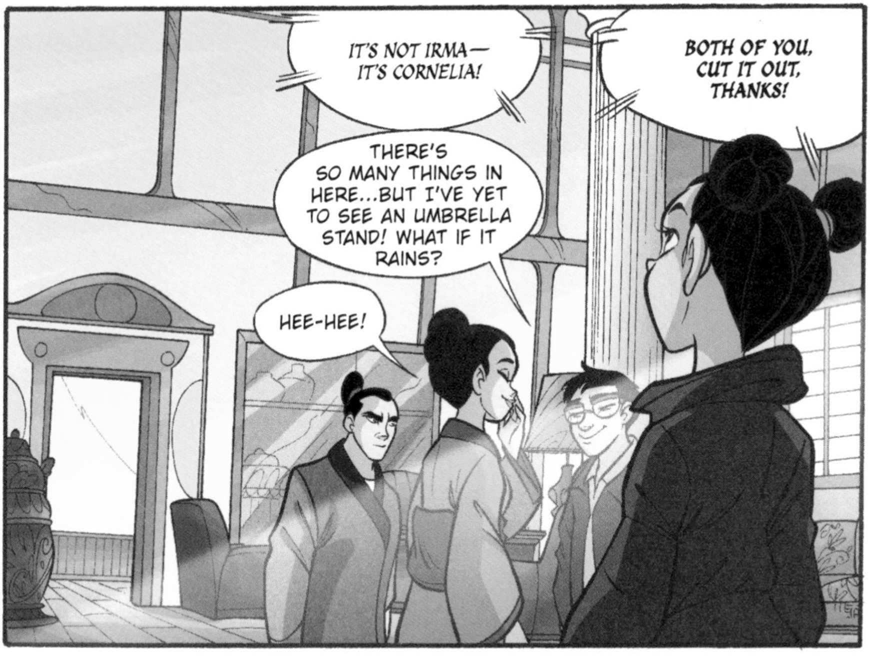
IT'S NOT IRMA— IT'S CORNELIA!
BOTH OF YOU, CUT IT OUT, THANKS!
THERE'S SO MANY THINGS IN HERE...BUT I'VE YET TO SEE AN UMBRELLA STAND! WHAT IF IT RAINS?
HEE-HEE!

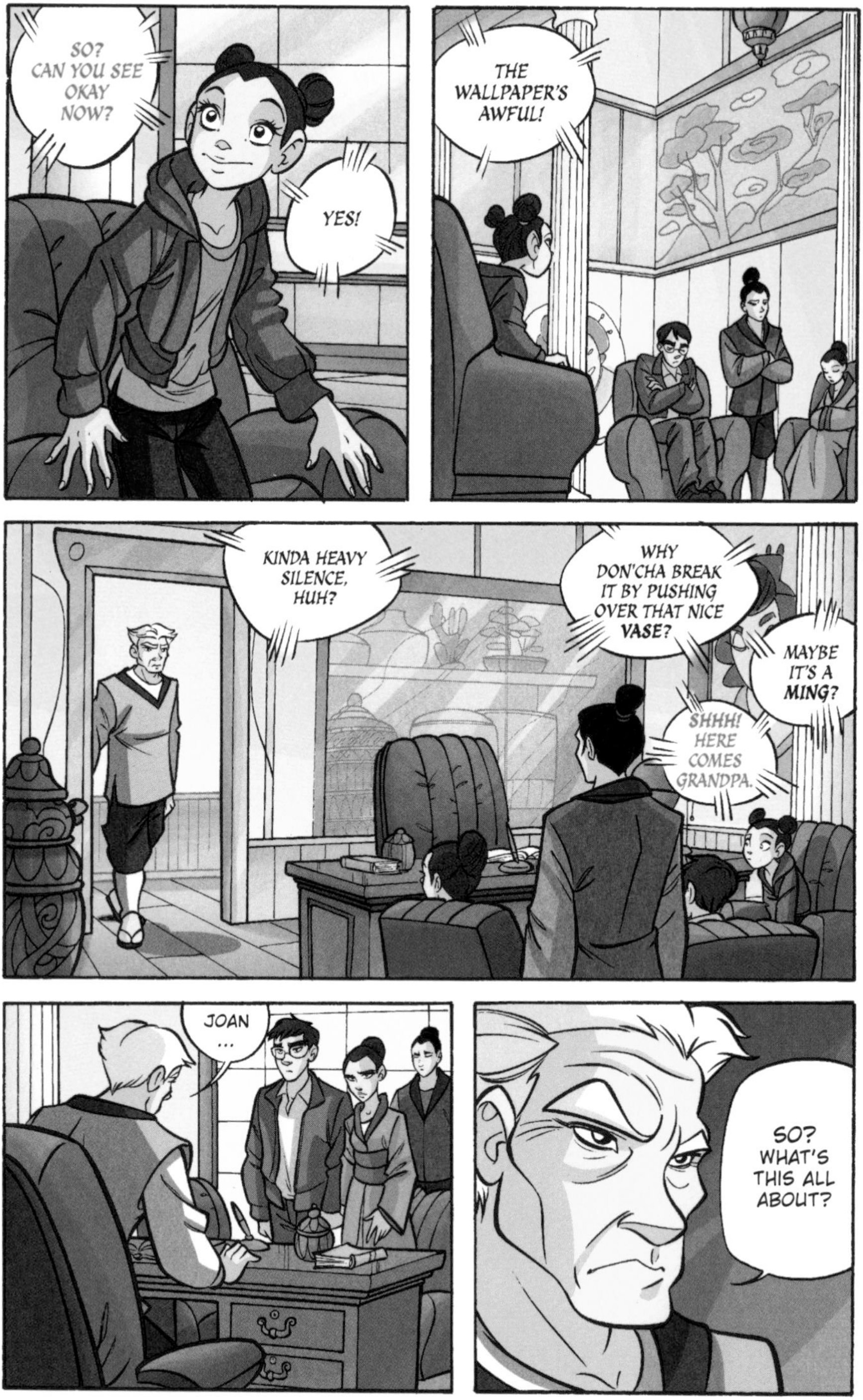

SO? CAN YOU SEE OKAY NOW?
YES!
THE WALLPAPER'S AWFUL!
KINDA HEAVY SILENCE, HUH?
WHY DON'CHA BREAK IT BY PUSHING OVER THAT NICE **VASE**?
MAYBE IT'S A **MING**?
SHHH! HERE COMES GRANDPA.
JOAN ...
SO? WHAT'S THIS ALL ABOUT?

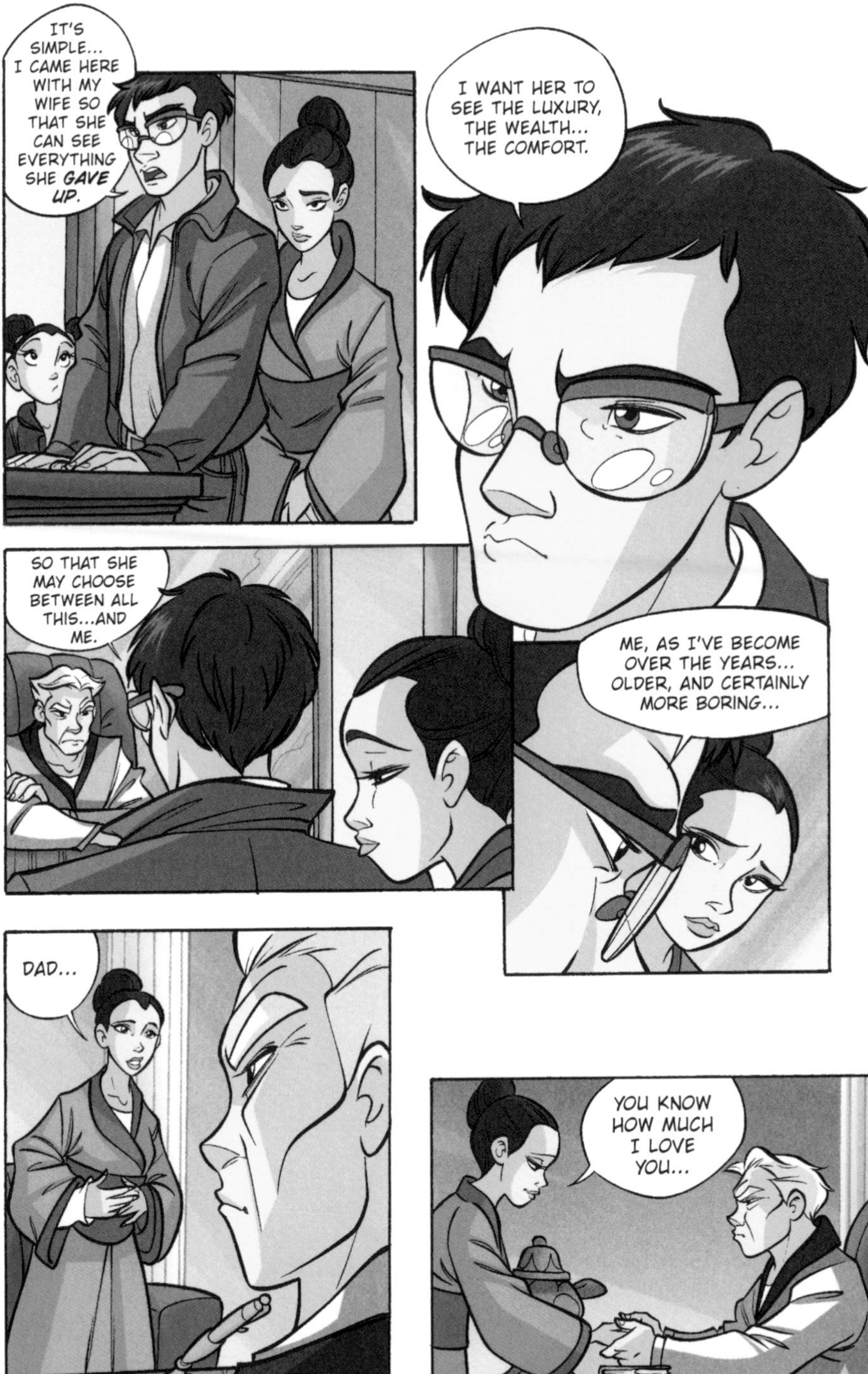
IT'S SIMPLE... I CAME HERE WITH MY WIFE SO THAT SHE CAN SEE EVERYTHING SHE *GAVE UP*.
I WANT HER TO SEE THE LUXURY, THE WEALTH... THE COMFORT.
SO THAT SHE MAY CHOOSE BETWEEN ALL THIS...AND ME.
ME, AS I'VE BECOME OVER THE YEARS... OLDER, AND CERTAINLY MORE BORING...
DAD...
YOU KNOW HOW MUCH I LOVE YOU...

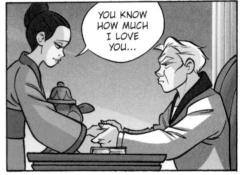

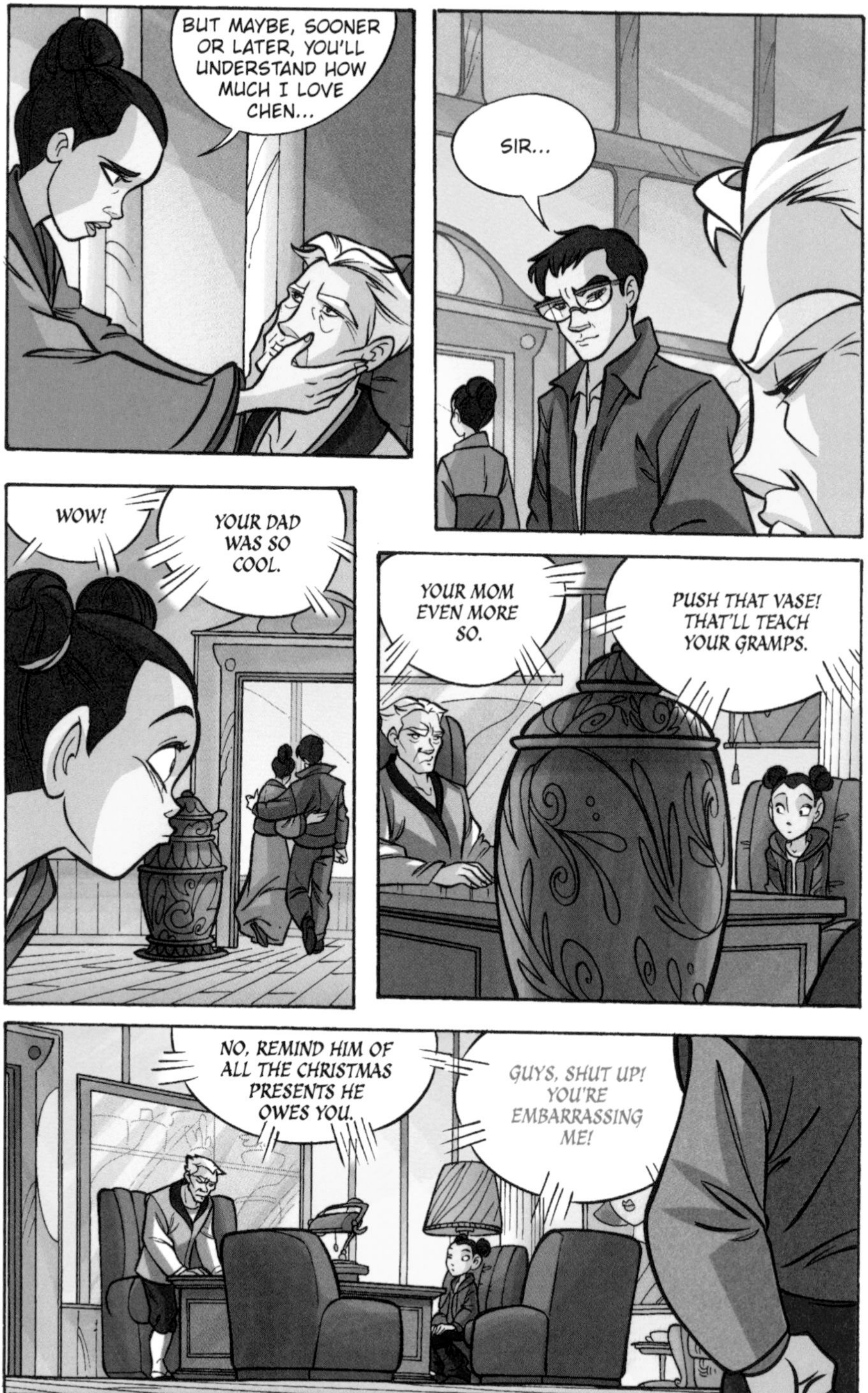
BUT MAYBE, SOONER OR LATER, YOU'LL UNDERSTAND HOW MUCH I LOVE CHEN...
SIR...
WOW!
YOUR DAD WAS SO COOL.
YOUR MOM EVEN MORE SO.
PUSH THAT VASE! THAT'LL TEACH YOUR GRAMPS.
NO, REMIND HIM OF ALL THE CHRISTMAS PRESENTS HE OWES YOU.
GUYS, SHUT UP! YOU'RE EMBARRASSING ME!

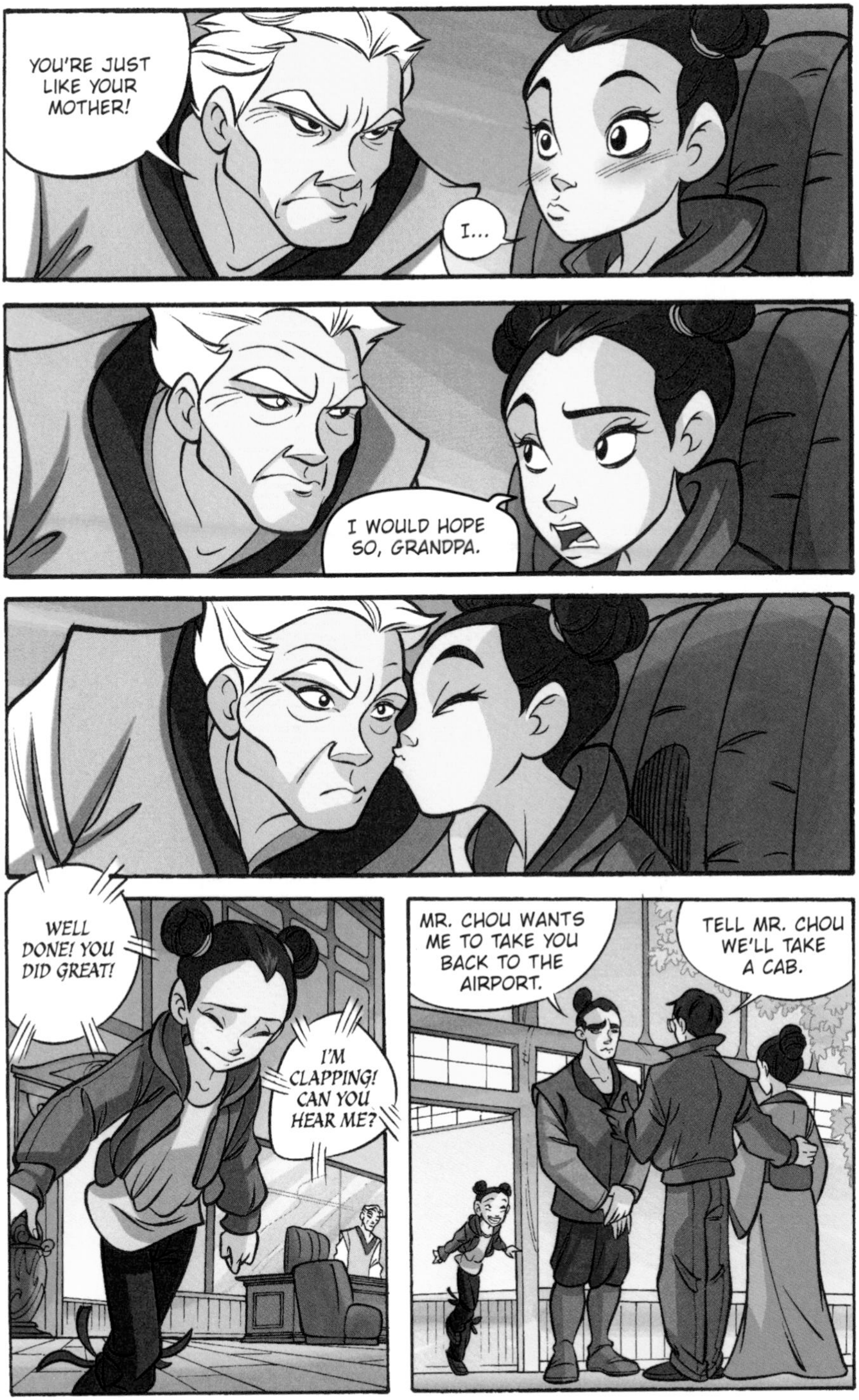
YOU'RE JUST LIKE YOUR MOTHER!
I...
I WOULD HOPE SO, GRANDPA.
WELL DONE! YOU DID GREAT!
I'M CLAPPING! CAN YOU HEAR ME?
MR. CHOU WANTS ME TO TAKE YOU BACK TO THE AIRPORT.
TELL MR. CHOU WE'LL TAKE A CAB.

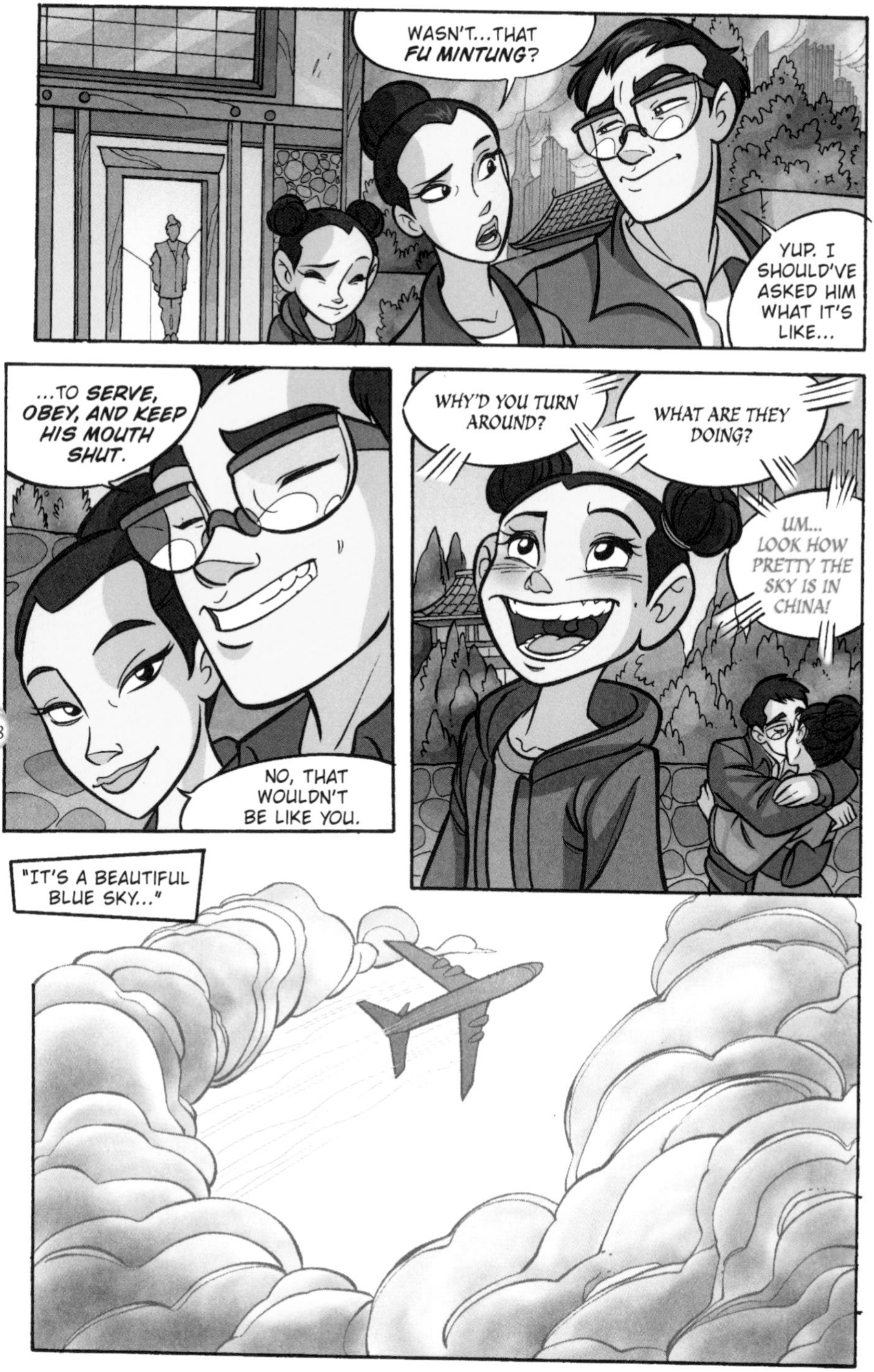
WASN'T...THAT FU MINTUNG?
YUP. I SHOULD'VE ASKED HIM WHAT IT'S LIKE...
...TO SERVE, OBEY, AND KEEP HIS MOUTH SHUT.
NO, THAT WOULDN'T BE LIKE YOU.
WHY'D YOU TURN AROUND?
WHAT ARE THEY DOING?
UM... LOOK HOW PRETTY THE SKY IS IN CHINA!
"IT'S A BEAUTIFUL BLUE SKY..."

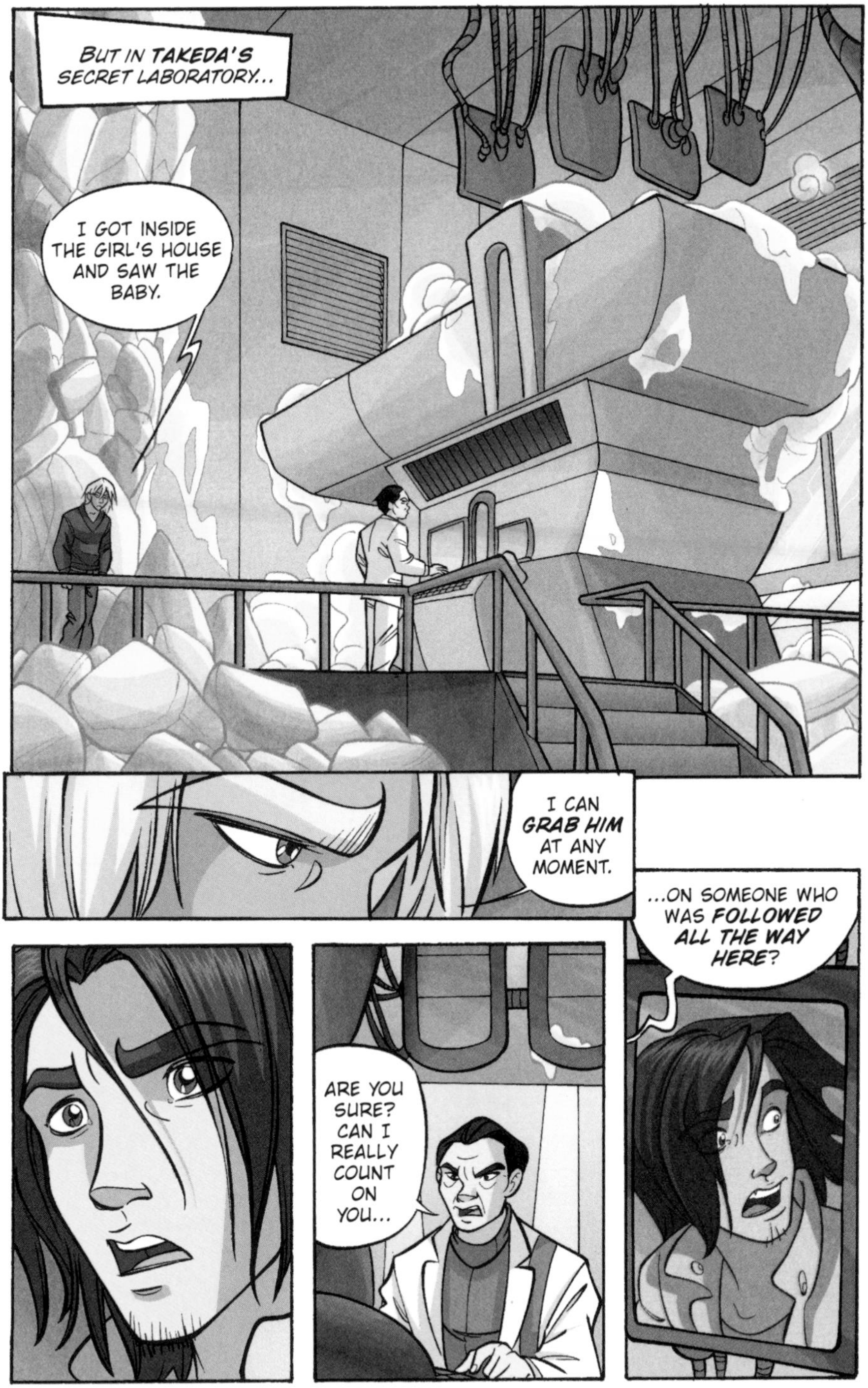
BUT IN TAKEDA'S SECRET LABORATORY...
I GOT INSIDE THE GIRL'S HOUSE AND SAW THE BABY.
I CAN GRAB HIM AT ANY MOMENT.
...ON SOMEONE WHO WAS FOLLOWED ALL THE WAY HERE?
ARE YOU SURE? CAN I REALLY COUNT ON YOU...

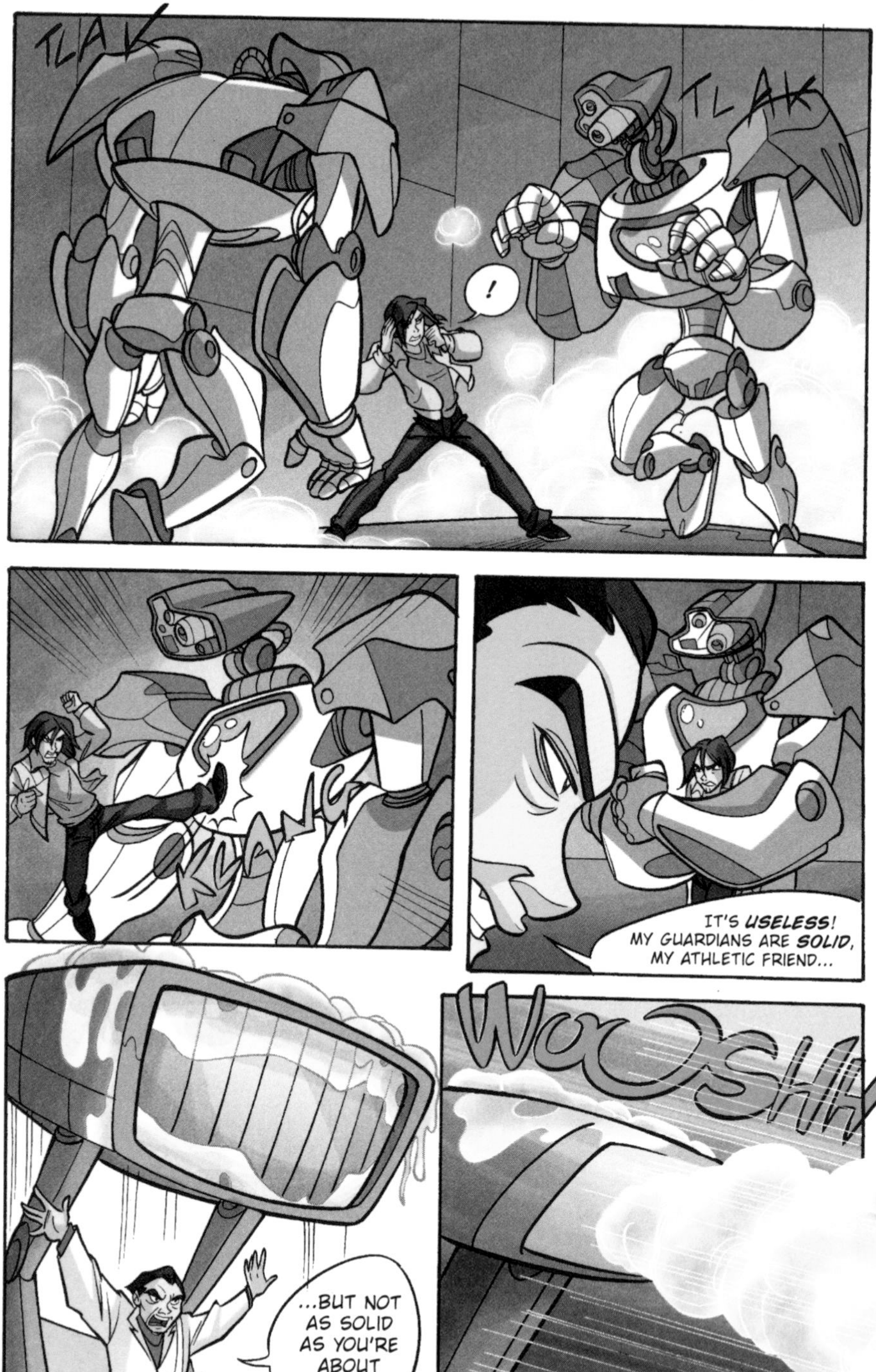
TLAK
TLAK
!
IT'S ***USELESS***! MY GUARDIANS ARE ***SOLID***, MY ATHLETIC FRIEND...
...BUT NOT AS SOLID AS YOU'RE ABOUT TO BE!
WOOSH

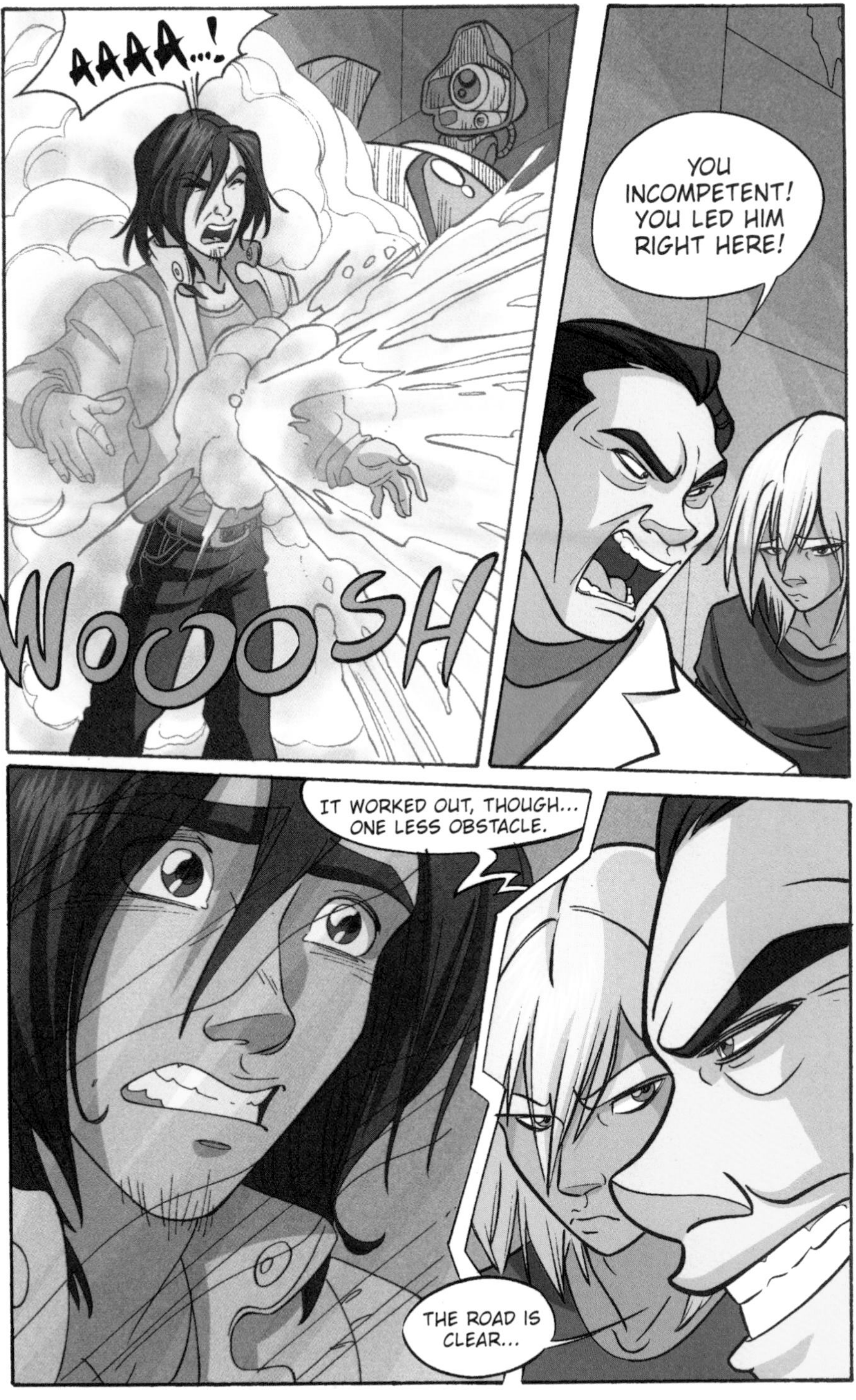
AAAA...!
WOOOSH
YOU INCOMPETENT! YOU LED HIM RIGHT HERE!
IT WORKED OUT, THOUGH... ONE LESS OBSTACLE.
THE ROAD IS CLEAR...

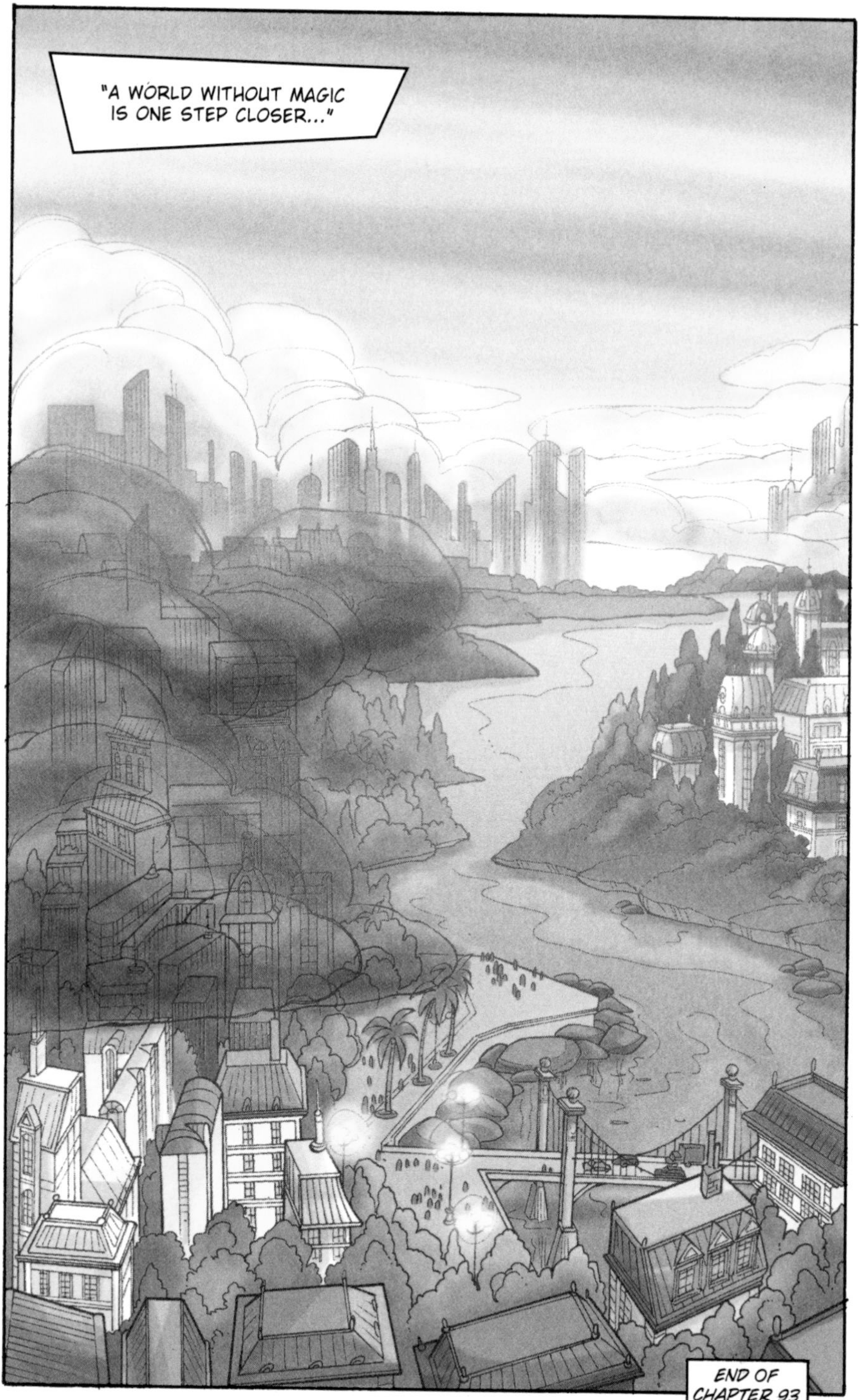
"A WORLD WITHOUT MAGIC IS ONE STEP CLOSER..."
END OF CHAPTER 93

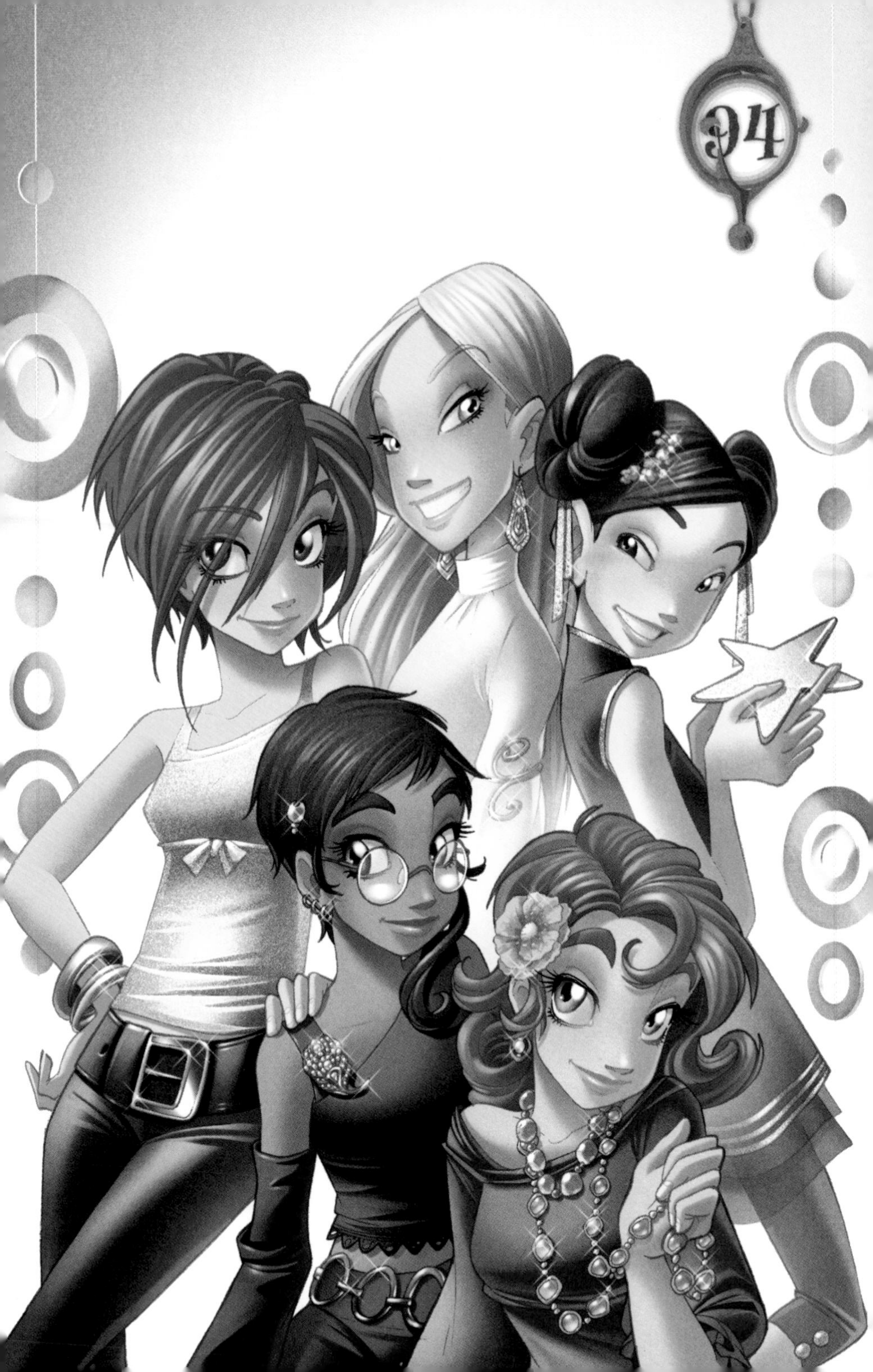
04

The Reckoning

"I could fool her only because her heart was pure!"

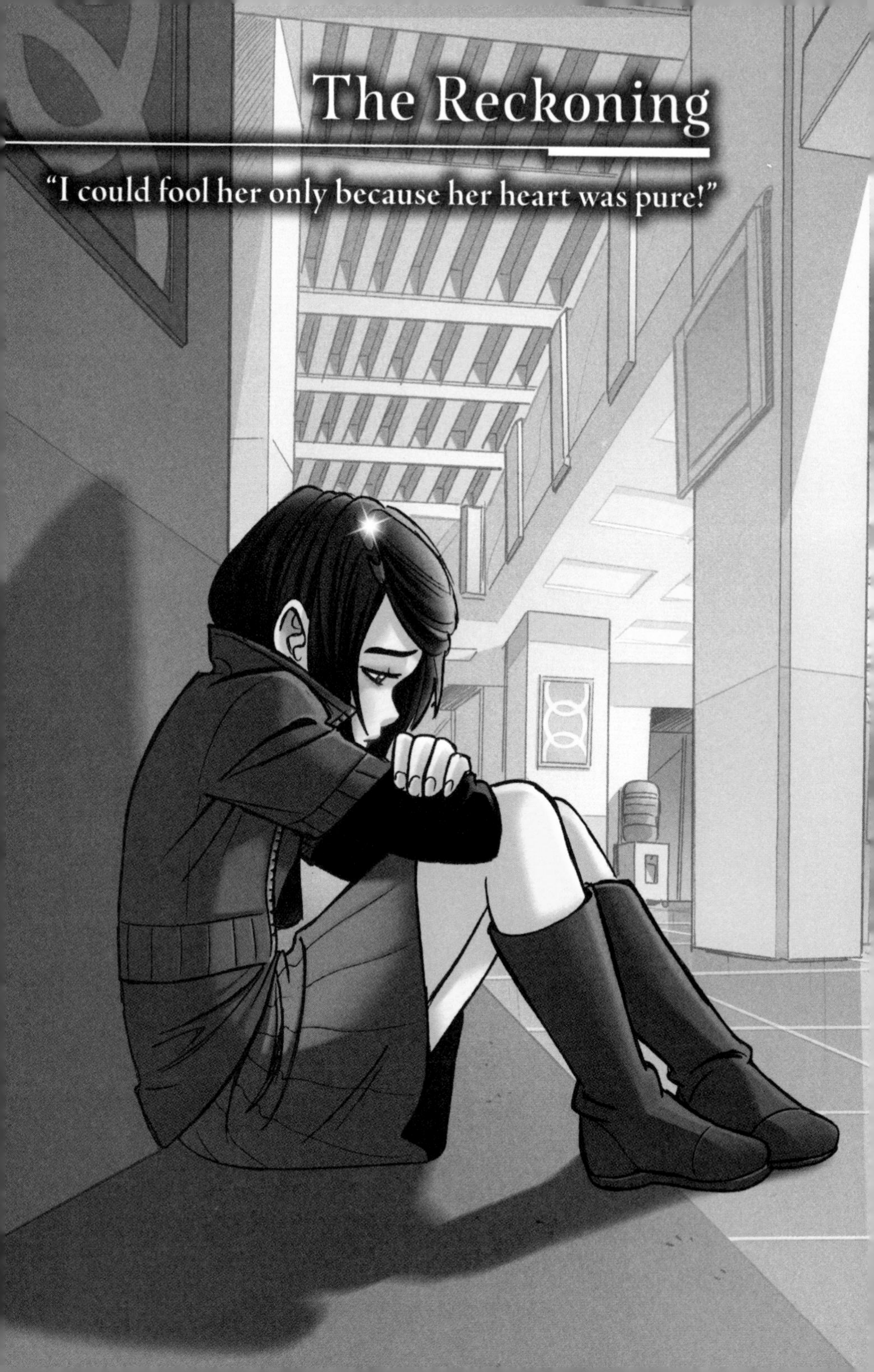

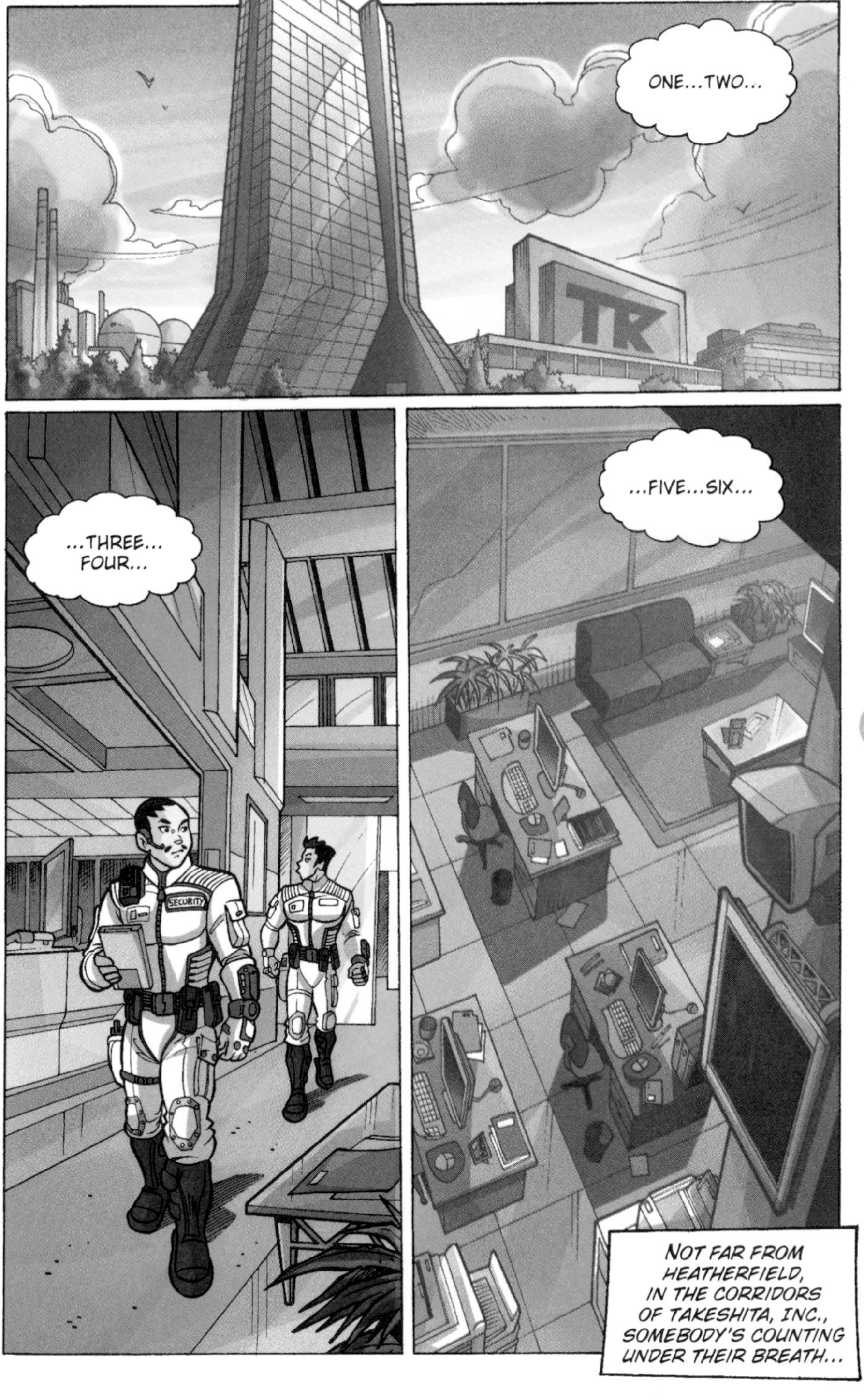
ONE...TWO...
...THREE...
FOUR...
...FIVE...SIX...
NOT FAR FROM HEATHERFIELD, IN THE CORRIDORS OF TAKESHITA, INC., SOMEBODY'S COUNTING UNDER THEIR BREATH...

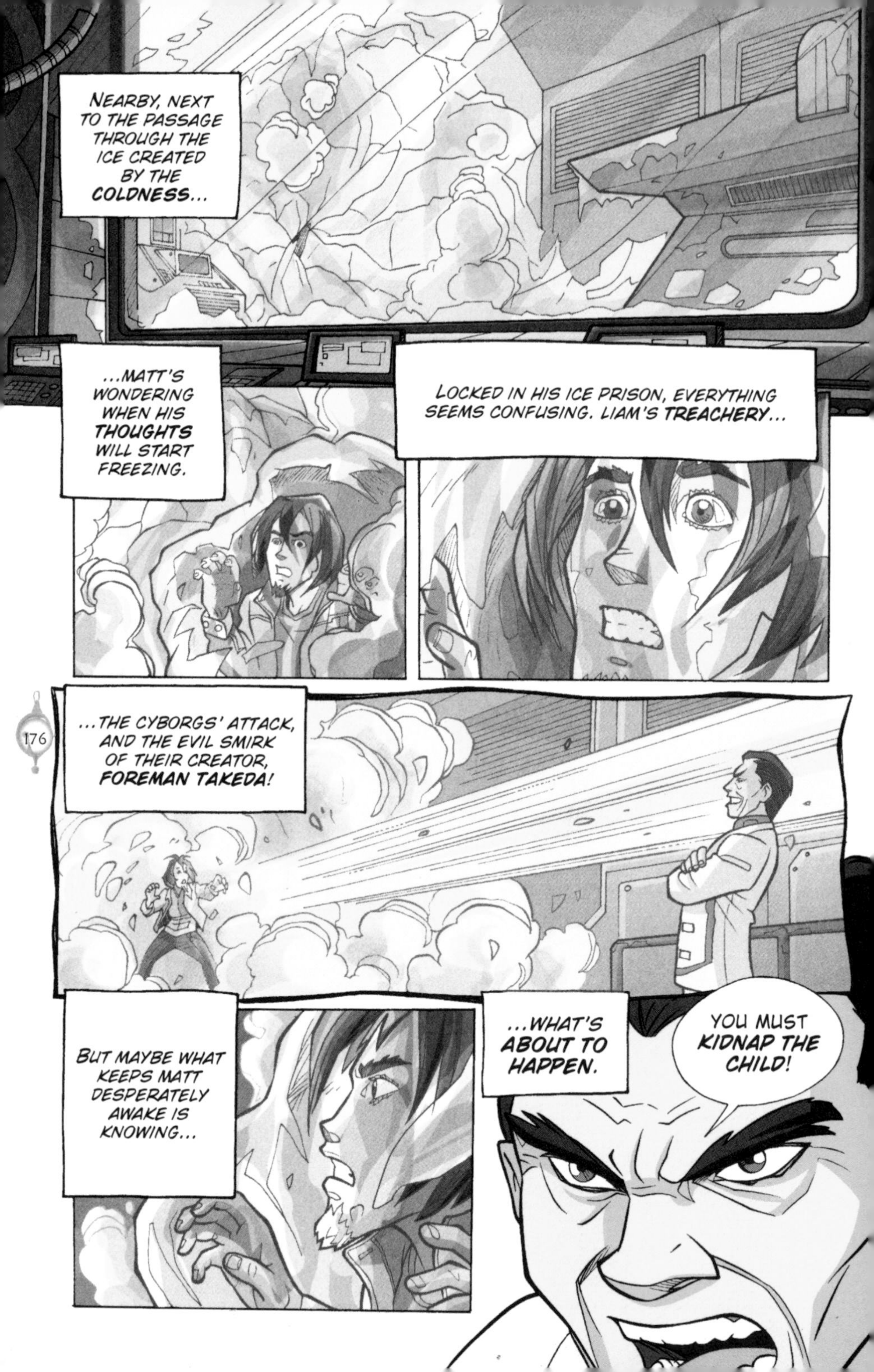

NEARBY, NEXT TO THE PASSAGE THROUGH THE ICE CREATED BY THE **COLDNESS**...
...MATT'S WONDERING WHEN HIS **THOUGHTS** WILL START FREEZING.
LOCKED IN HIS ICE PRISON, EVERYTHING SEEMS CONFUSING. LIAM'S **TREACHERY**...
...THE CYBORGS' ATTACK, AND THE EVIL SMIRK OF THEIR CREATOR, **FOREMAN TAKEDA!**
BUT MAYBE WHAT KEEPS MATT DESPERATELY AWAKE IS KNOWING...
...WHAT'S **ABOUT TO HAPPEN.**
YOU MUST **KIDNAP THE CHILD!**

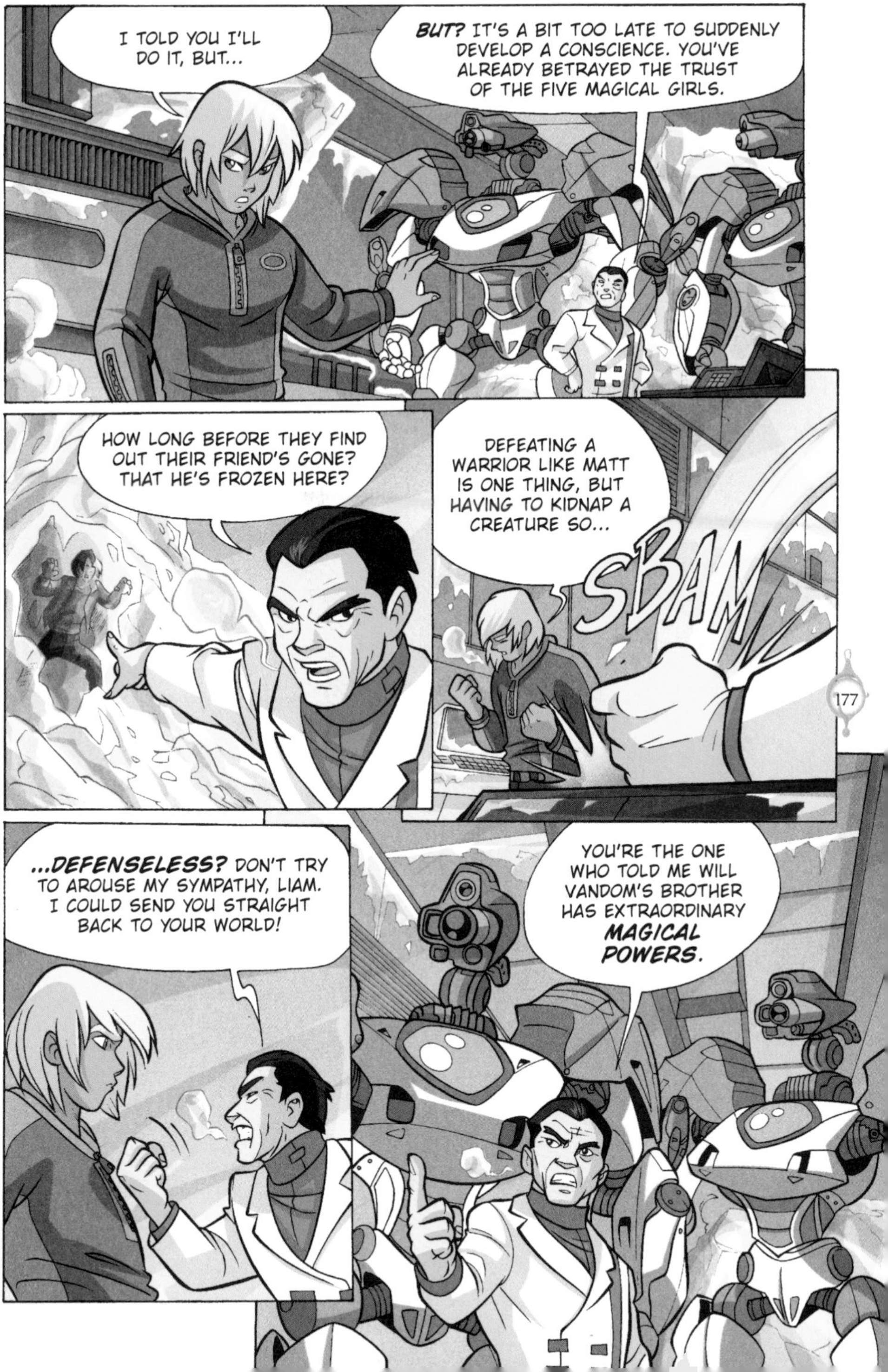
I TOLD YOU I'LL DO IT, BUT...
BUT? IT'S A BIT TOO LATE TO SUDDENLY DEVELOP A CONSCIENCE. YOU'VE ALREADY BETRAYED THE TRUST OF THE FIVE MAGICAL GIRLS.
HOW LONG BEFORE THEY FIND OUT THEIR FRIEND'S GONE? THAT HE'S FROZEN HERE?
DEFEATING A WARRIOR LIKE MATT IS ONE THING, BUT HAVING TO KIDNAP A CREATURE SO...
SBAM
...DEFENSELESS? DON'T TRY TO AROUSE MY SYMPATHY, LIAM. I COULD SEND YOU STRAIGHT BACK TO YOUR WORLD!
YOU'RE THE ONE WHO TOLD ME WILL VANDOM'S BROTHER HAS EXTRAORDINARY MAGICAL POWERS.

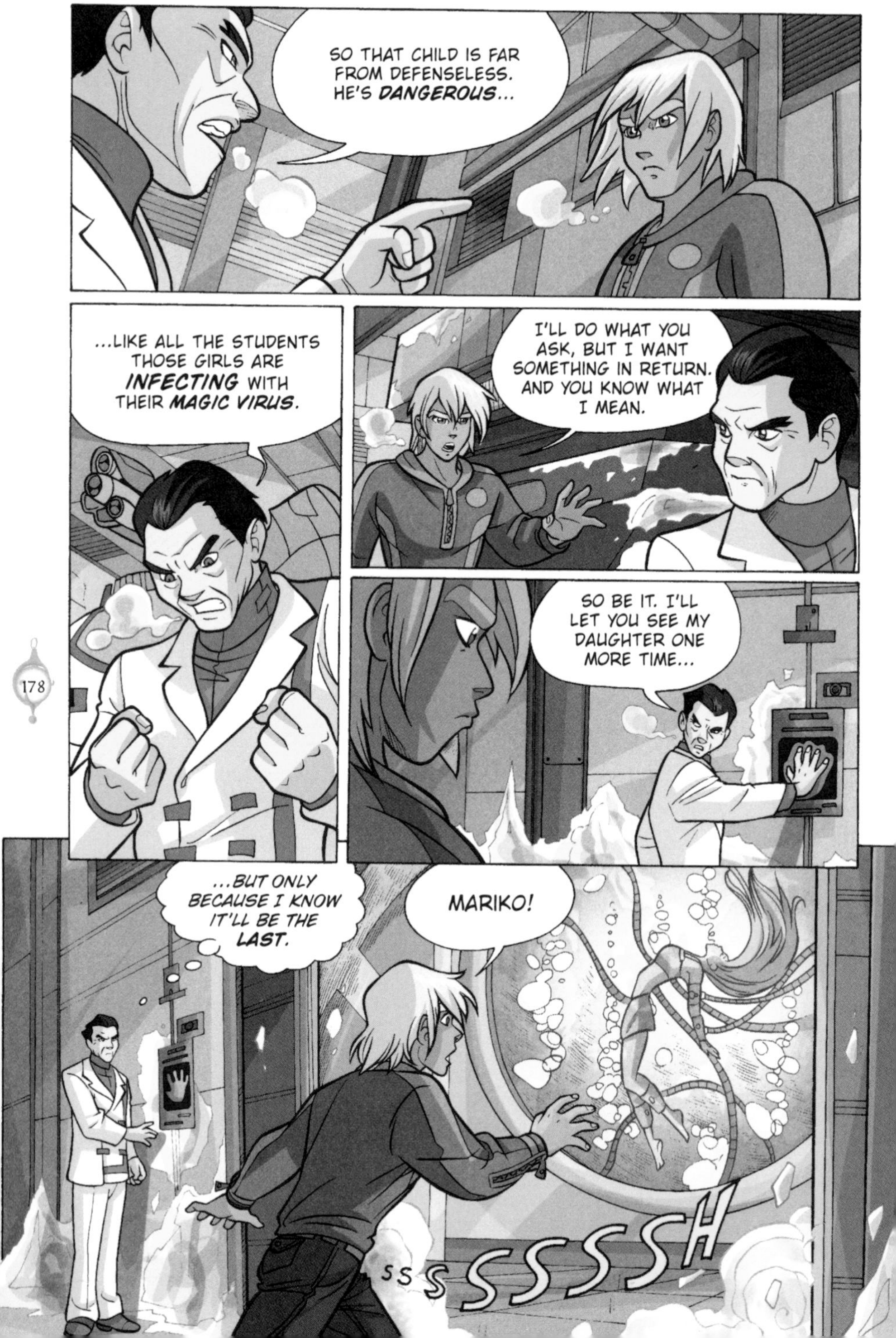
SO THAT CHILD IS FAR FROM DEFENSELESS. HE'S *DANGEROUS*...
...LIKE ALL THE STUDENTS THOSE GIRLS ARE *INFECTING* WITH THEIR *MAGIC VIRUS*.
I'LL DO WHAT YOU ASK, BUT I WANT SOMETHING IN RETURN. AND YOU KNOW WHAT I MEAN.
SO BE IT. I'LL LET YOU SEE MY DAUGHTER ONE MORE TIME...
...BUT ONLY BECAUSE I KNOW IT'LL BE THE *LAST*.
MARIKO!
SSSSSSSSH

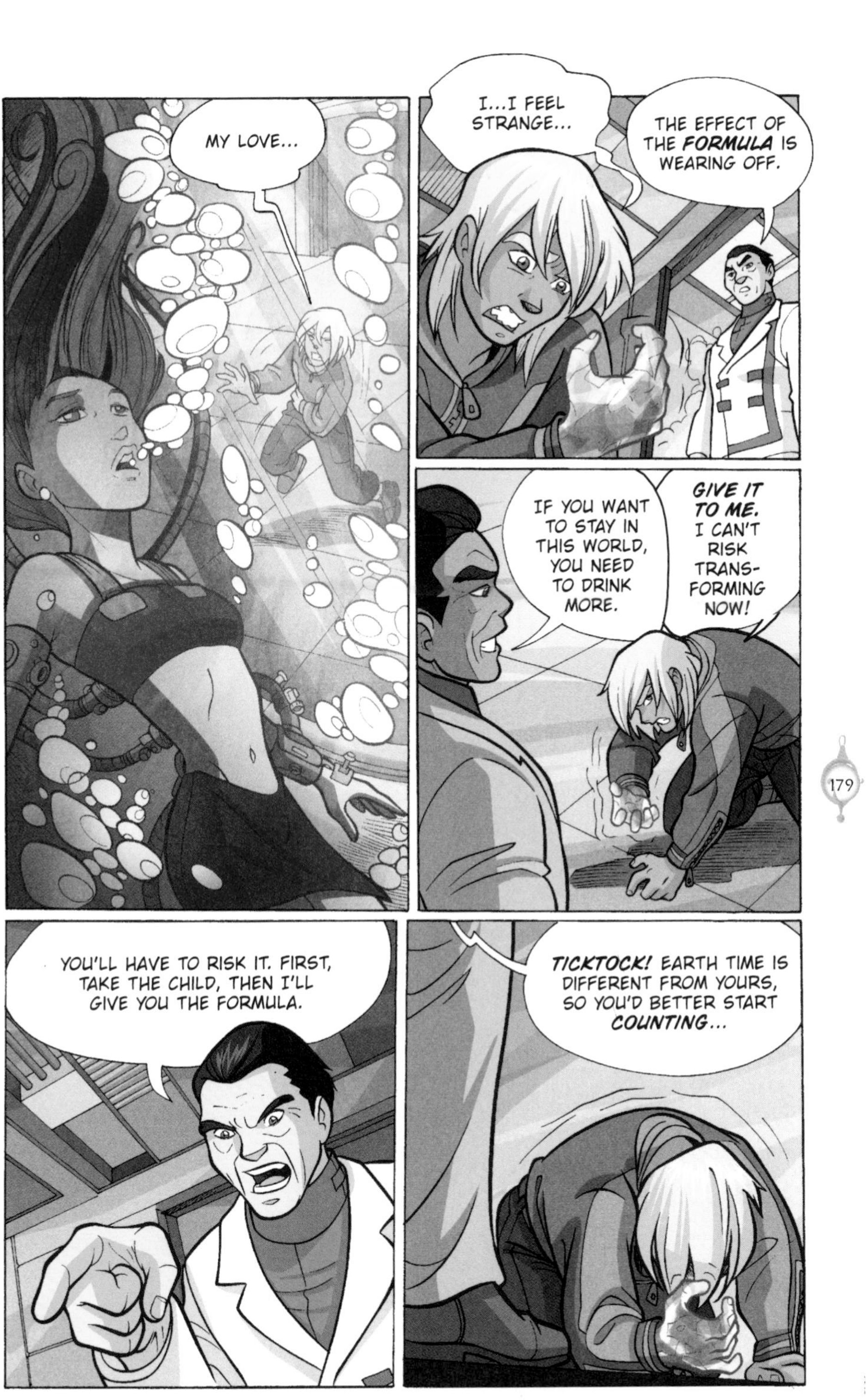
MY LOVE...
I...I FEEL STRANGE...
THE EFFECT OF THE ***FORMULA*** IS WEARING OFF.
IF YOU WANT TO STAY IN THIS WORLD, YOU NEED TO DRINK MORE.
GIVE IT TO ME. I CAN'T RISK TRANS-FORMING NOW!
YOU'LL HAVE TO RISK IT. FIRST, TAKE THE CHILD, THEN I'LL GIVE YOU THE FORMULA.
TICKTOCK! EARTH TIME IS DIFFERENT FROM YOURS, SO YOU'D BETTER START ***COUNTING***...

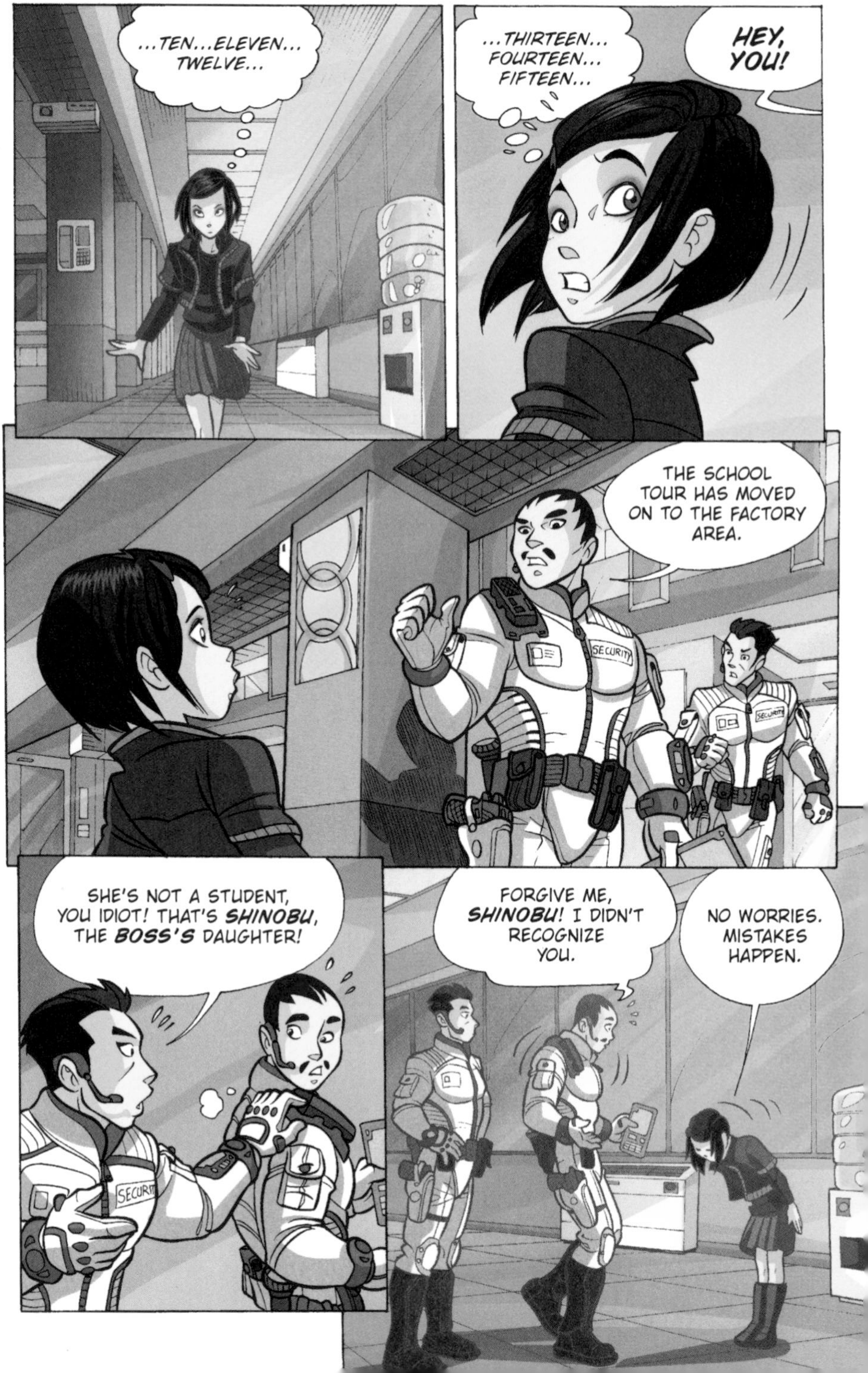
...TEN...ELEVEN... TWELVE...
...THIRTEEN... FOURTEEN... FIFTEEN...
HEY, YOU!
THE SCHOOL TOUR HAS MOVED ON TO THE FACTORY AREA.
SECURITY
SECURITY
SHE'S NOT A STUDENT, YOU IDIOT! THAT'S SHINOBU, THE BOSS'S DAUGHTER!
SECURIT
FORGIVE ME, SHINOBU! I DIDN'T RECOGNIZE YOU.
NO WORRIES. MISTAKES HAPPEN.

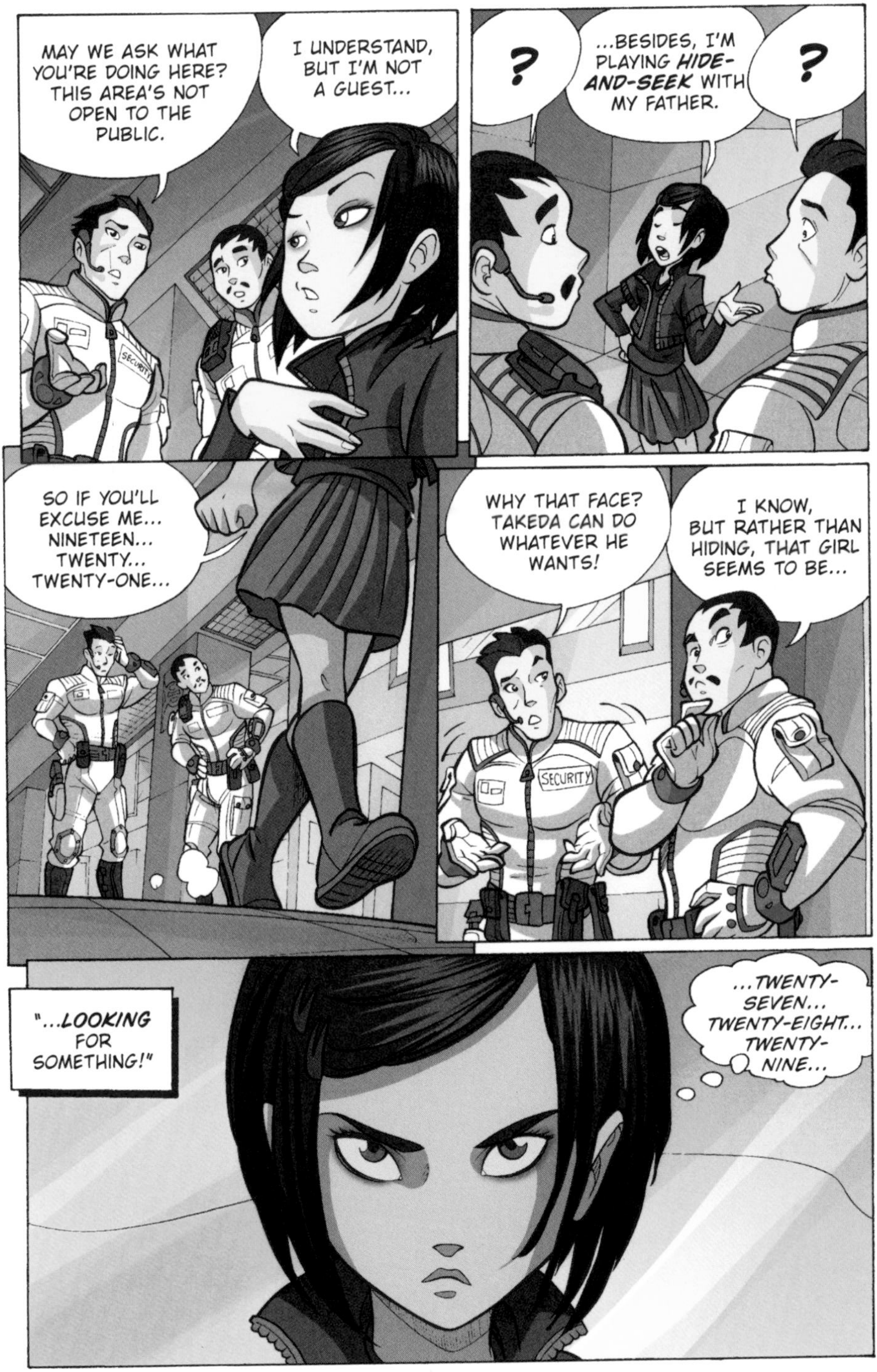
MAY WE ASK WHAT YOU'RE DOING HERE? THIS AREA'S NOT OPEN TO THE PUBLIC.
I UNDERSTAND, BUT I'M NOT A GUEST...
?
...BESIDES, I'M PLAYING HIDE-AND-SEEK WITH MY FATHER.
?
SECURITY
SO IF YOU'LL EXCUSE ME... NINETEEN... TWENTY... TWENTY-ONE...
WHY THAT FACE? TAKEDA CAN DO WHATEVER HE WANTS!
I KNOW, BUT RATHER THAN HIDING, THAT GIRL SEEMS TO BE...
SECURITY
"...LOOKING FOR SOMETHING!"
...TWENTY-SEVEN... TWENTY-EIGHT... TWENTY-NINE...

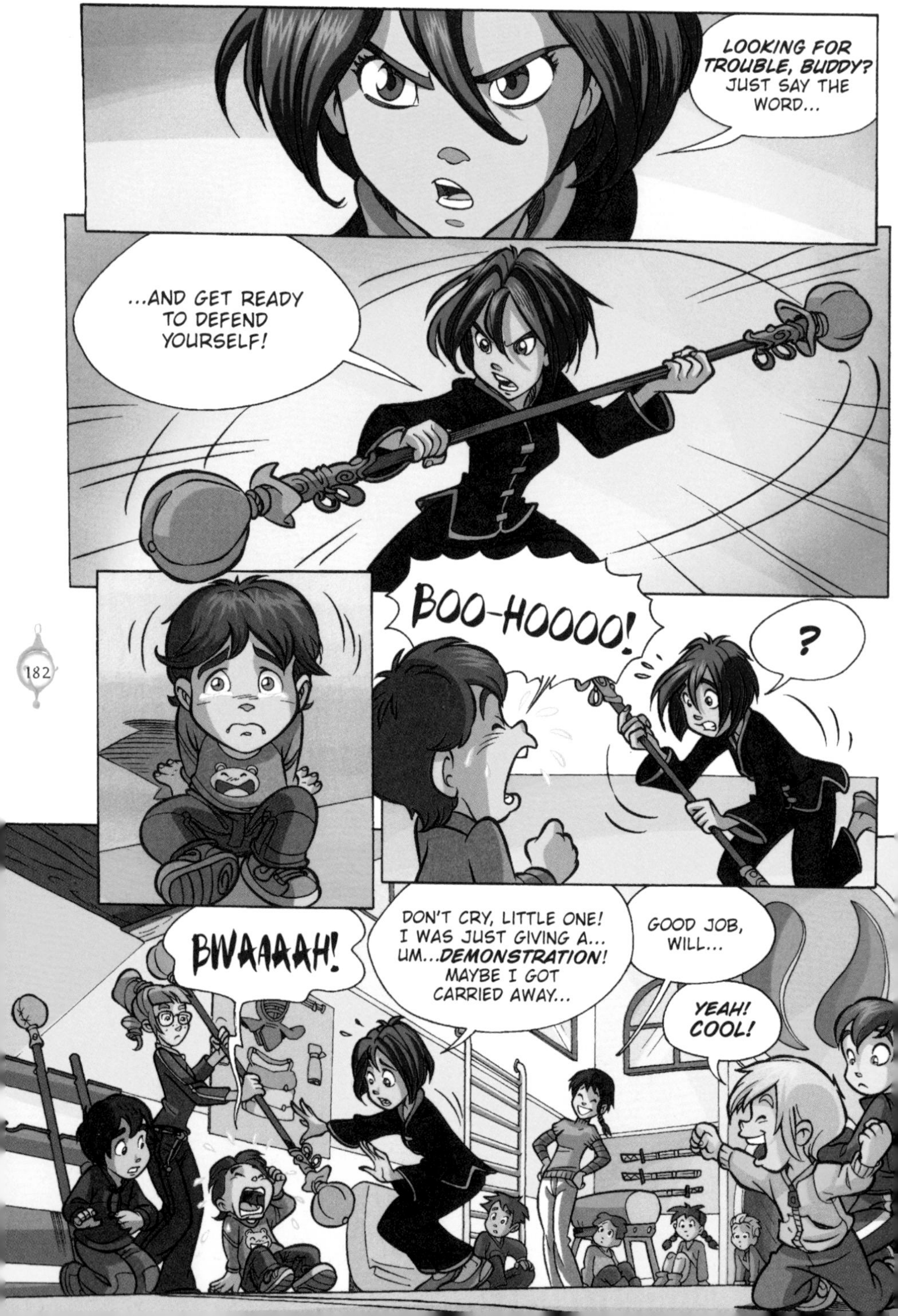
LOOKING FOR TROUBLE, BUDDY? JUST SAY THE WORD...
...AND GET READY TO DEFEND YOURSELF!
BOO-HOOOOO!
?
BWAAAAH!
DON'T CRY, LITTLE ONE! I WAS JUST GIVING A... UM...DEMONSTRATION! MAYBE I GOT CARRIED AWAY...
GOOD JOB, WILL...
YEAH! COOL!

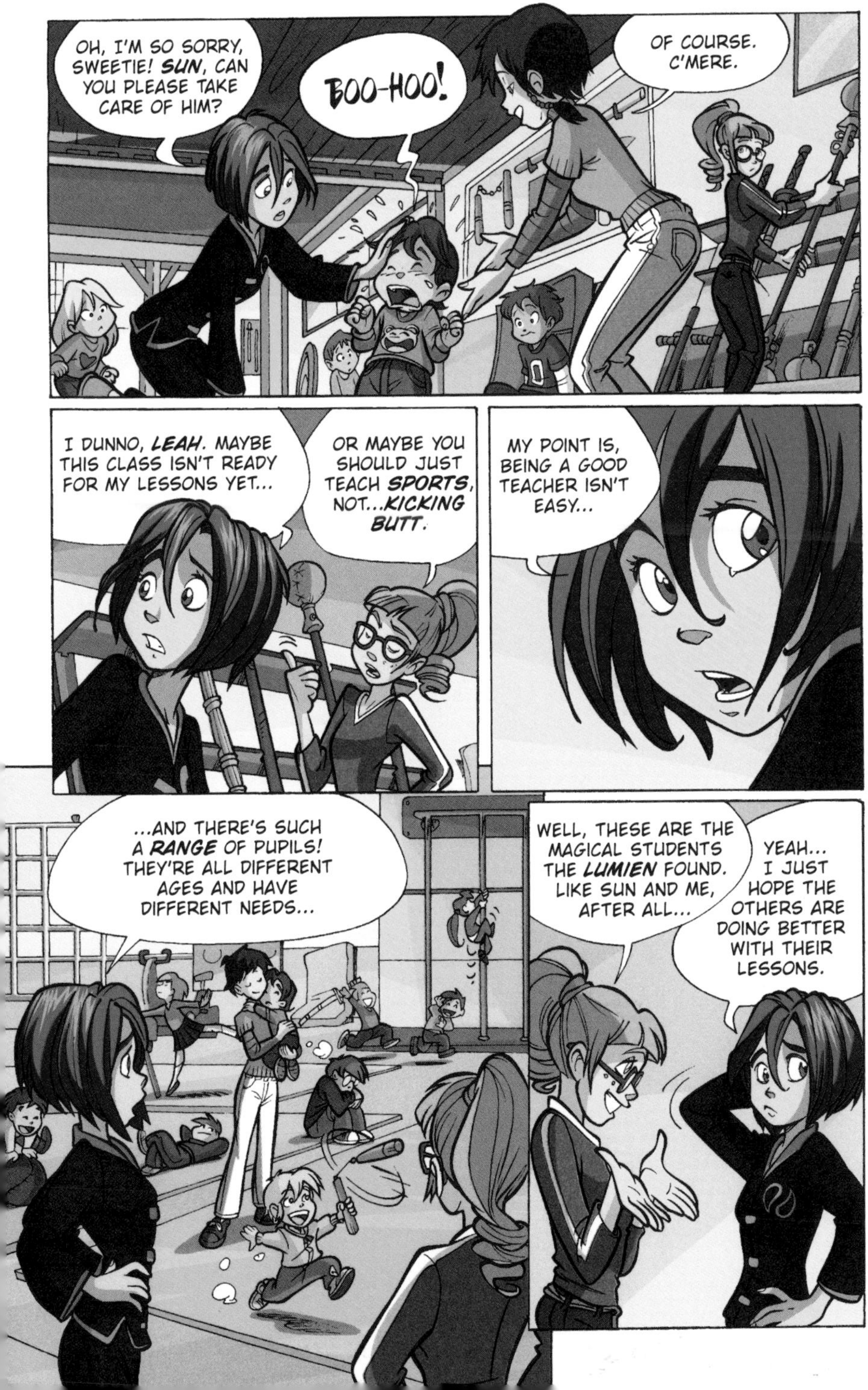
OH, I'M SO SORRY, SWEETIE! SUN, CAN YOU PLEASE TAKE CARE OF HIM?
BOO-HOO!
OF COURSE. C'MERE.
I DUNNO, LEAH. MAYBE THIS CLASS ISN'T READY FOR MY LESSONS YET...
OR MAYBE YOU SHOULD JUST TEACH SPORTS, NOT...KICKING BUTT.
MY POINT IS, BEING A GOOD TEACHER ISN'T EASY...
...AND THERE'S SUCH A RANGE OF PUPILS! THEY'RE ALL DIFFERENT AGES AND HAVE DIFFERENT NEEDS...
WELL, THESE ARE THE MAGICAL STUDENTS THE LUMIEN FOUND. LIKE SUN AND ME, AFTER ALL...
YEAH... I JUST HOPE THE OTHERS ARE DOING BETTER WITH THEIR LESSONS.

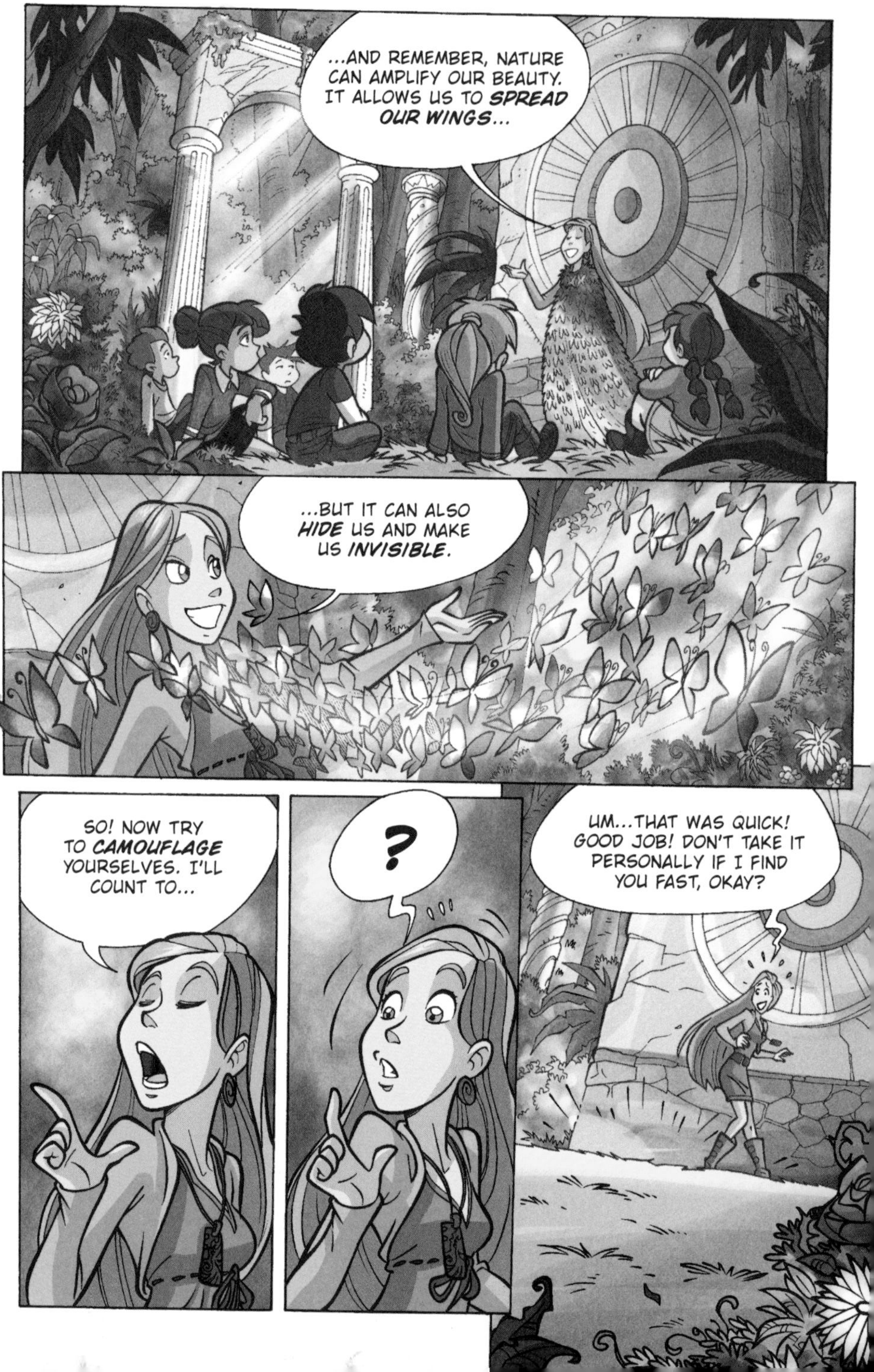
...AND REMEMBER, NATURE CAN AMPLIFY OUR BEAUTY. IT ALLOWS US TO SPREAD OUR WINGS...
...BUT IT CAN ALSO HIDE US AND MAKE US INVISIBLE.
SO! NOW TRY TO CAMOUFLAGE YOURSELVES. I'LL COUNT TO...
?
UM...THAT WAS QUICK! GOOD JOB! DON'T TAKE IT PERSONALLY IF I FIND YOU FAST, OKAY?

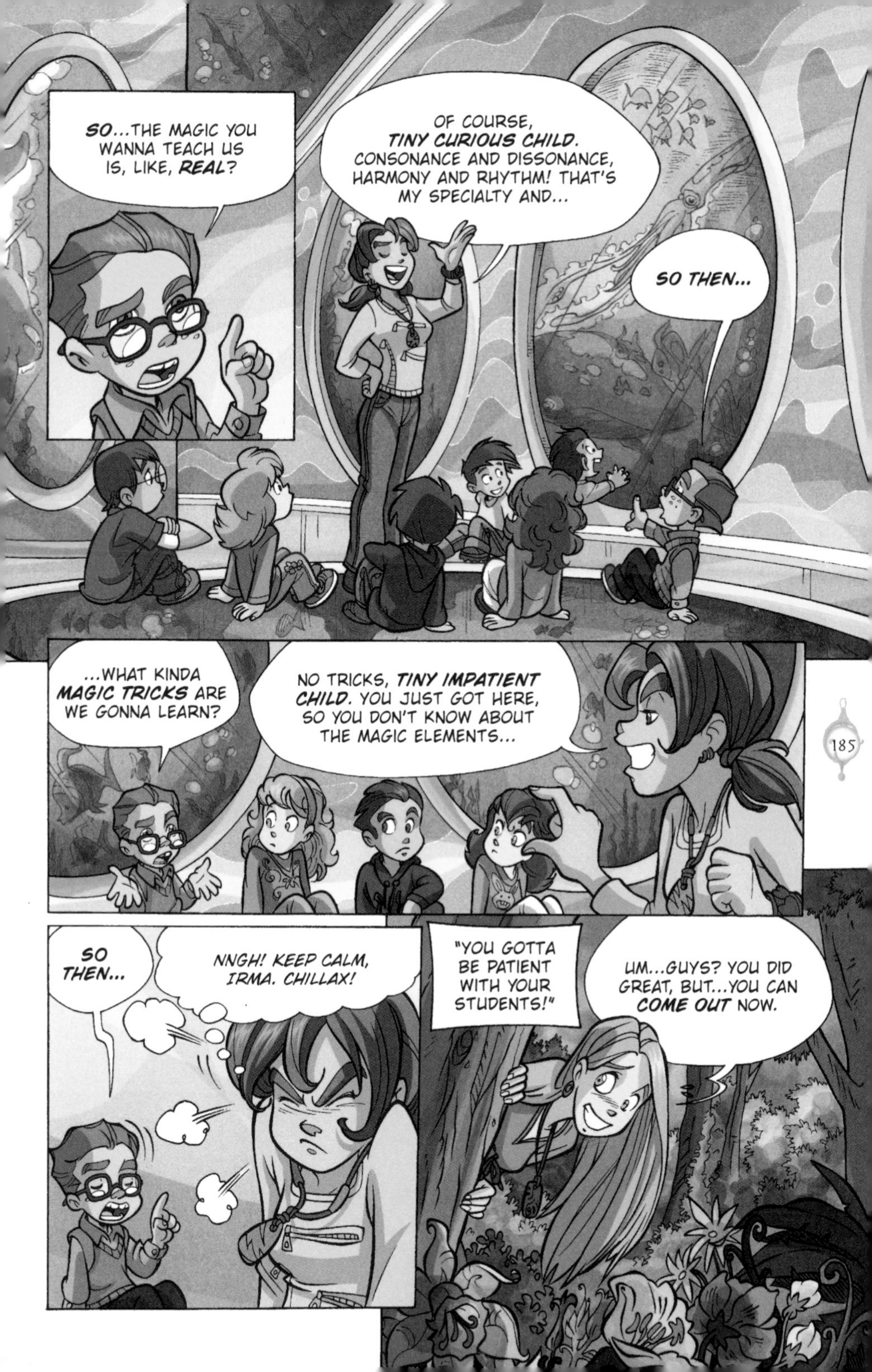

SO...THE MAGIC YOU WANNA TEACH US IS, LIKE, REAL?
OF COURSE, TINY CURIOUS CHILD. CONSONANCE AND DISSONANCE, HARMONY AND RHYTHM! THAT'S MY SPECIALTY AND...
SO THEN...
...WHAT KINDA MAGIC TRICKS ARE WE GONNA LEARN?
NO TRICKS, TINY IMPATIENT CHILD. YOU JUST GOT HERE, SO YOU DON'T KNOW ABOUT THE MAGIC ELEMENTS...
SO THEN...
NNGH! KEEP CALM, IRMA. CHILLAX!
"YOU GOTTA BE PATIENT WITH YOUR STUDENTS!"
UM...GUYS? YOU DID GREAT, BUT...YOU CAN COME OUT NOW.

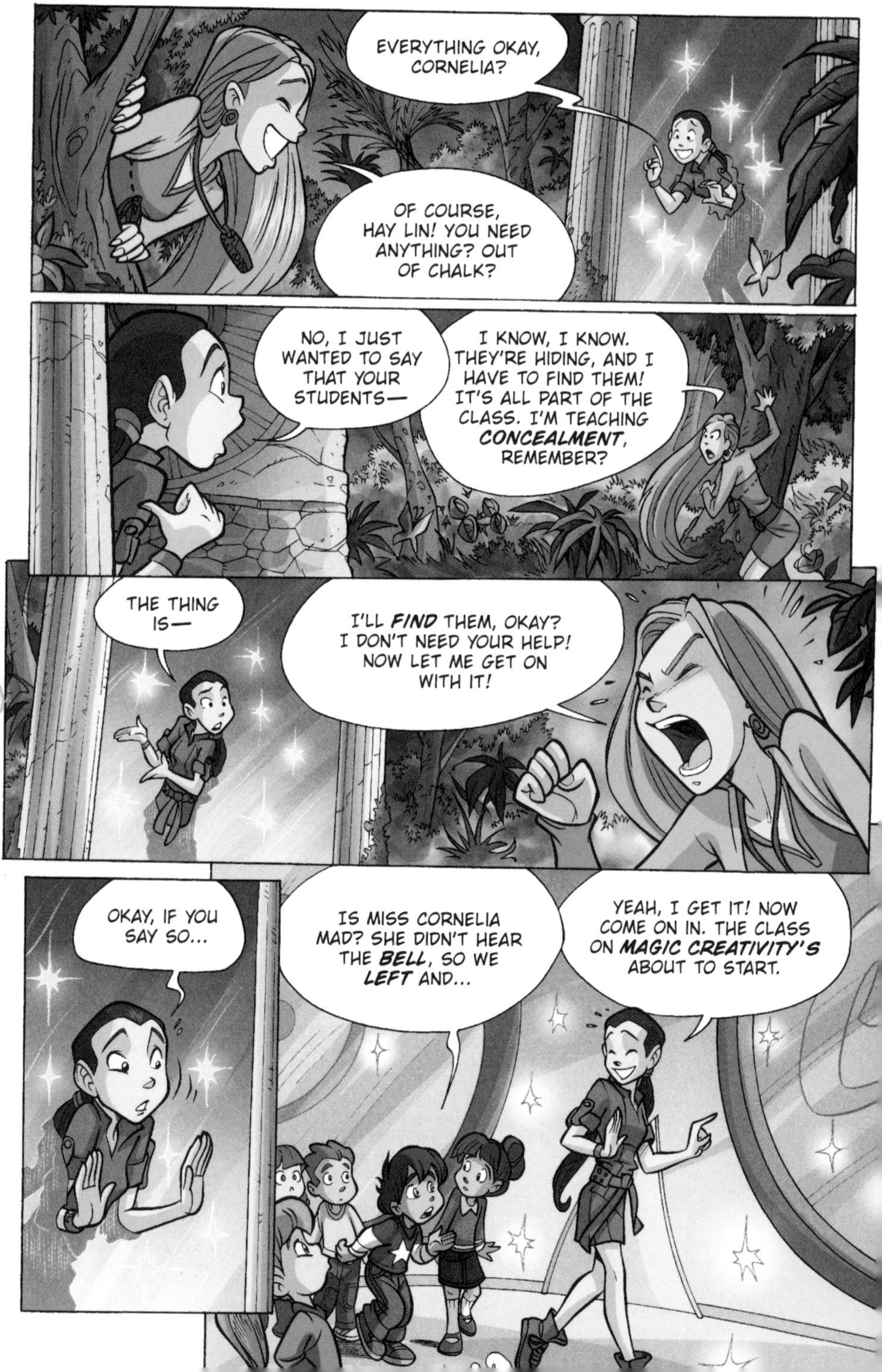
EVERYTHING OKAY, CORNELIA?
OF COURSE, HAY LIN! YOU NEED ANYTHING? OUT OF CHALK?
NO, I JUST WANTED TO SAY THAT YOUR STUDENTS—
I KNOW, I KNOW. THEY'RE HIDING, AND I HAVE TO FIND THEM! IT'S ALL PART OF THE CLASS. I'M TEACHING CONCEALMENT, REMEMBER?
THE THING IS—
I'LL FIND THEM, OKAY? I DON'T NEED YOUR HELP! NOW LET ME GET ON WITH IT!
OKAY, IF YOU SAY SO...
IS MISS CORNELIA MAD? SHE DIDN'T HEAR THE BELL, SO WE LEFT AND...
YEAH, I GET IT! NOW COME ON IN. THE CLASS ON MAGIC CREATIVITY'S ABOUT TO START.

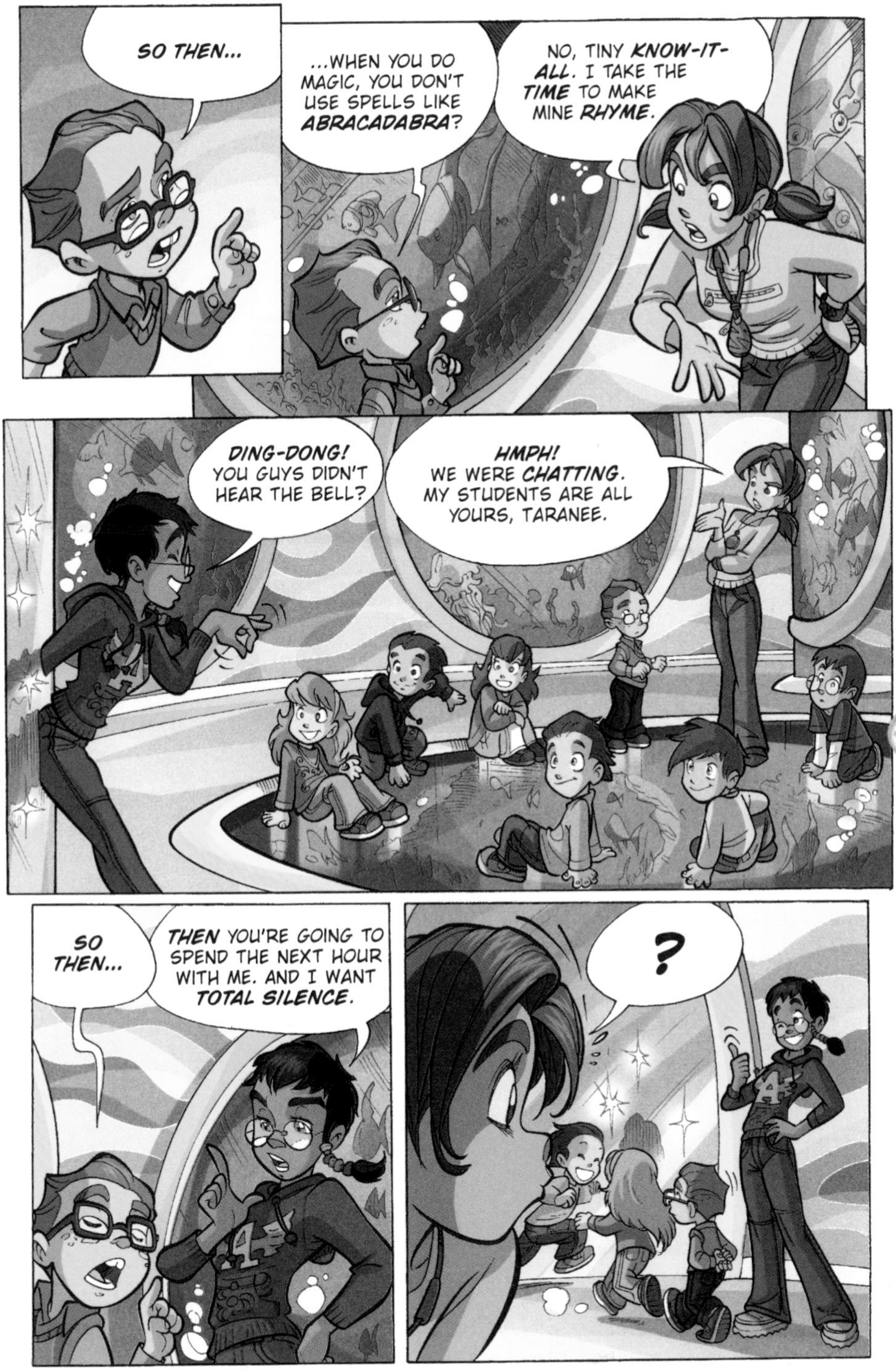
SO THEN...
...WHEN YOU DO MAGIC, YOU DON'T USE SPELLS LIKE ABRACADABRA?
NO, TINY KNOW-IT-ALL. I TAKE THE TIME TO MAKE MINE RHYME.
DING-DONG! YOU GUYS DIDN'T HEAR THE BELL?
HMPH! WE WERE CHATTING. MY STUDENTS ARE ALL YOURS, TARANEE.
SO THEN...
THEN YOU'RE GOING TO SPEND THE NEXT HOUR WITH ME. AND I WANT TOTAL SILENCE.
?

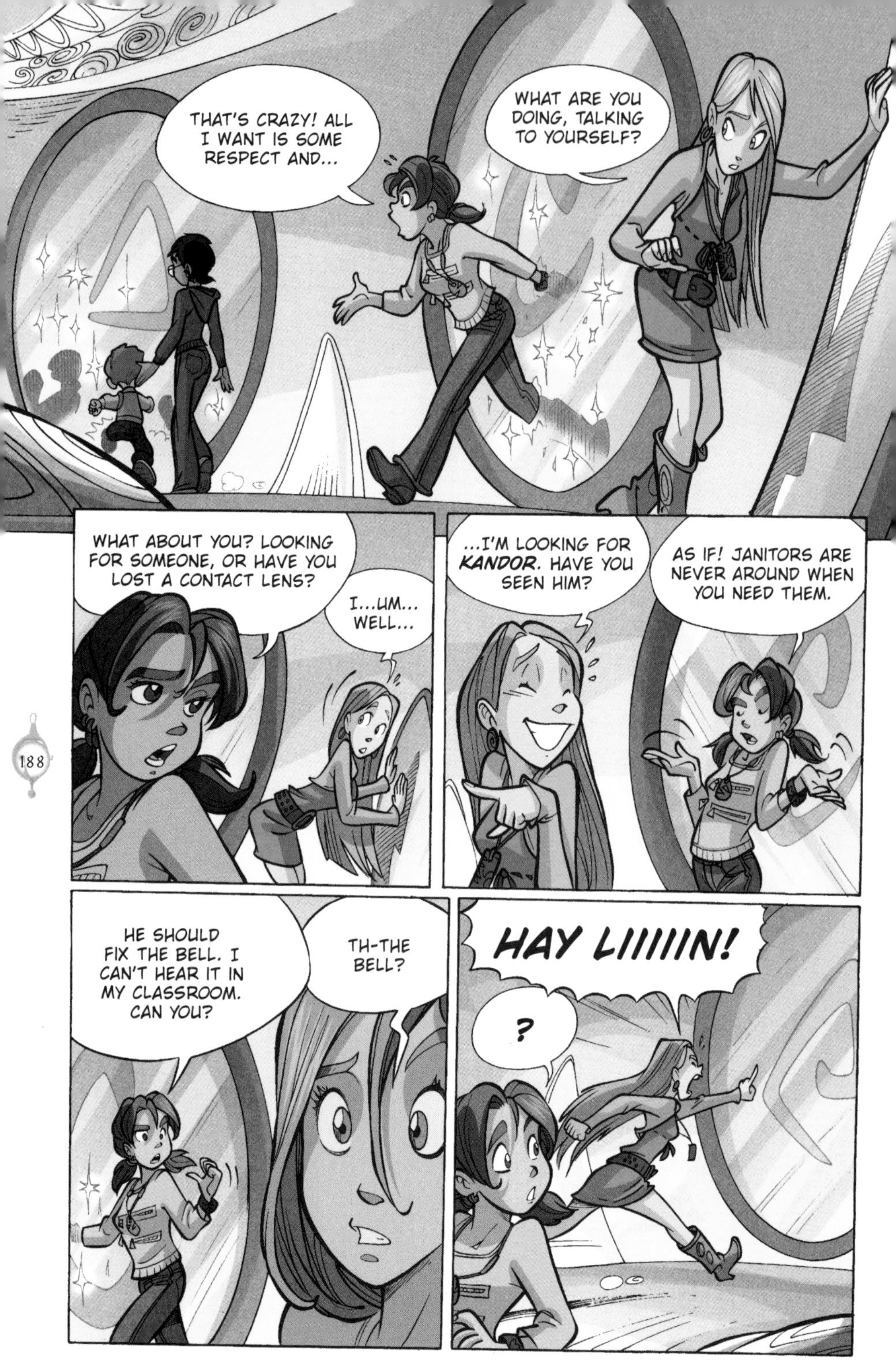
THAT'S CRAZY! ALL I WANT IS SOME RESPECT AND...
WHAT ARE YOU DOING, TALKING TO YOURSELF?
WHAT ABOUT YOU? LOOKING FOR SOMEONE, OR HAVE YOU LOST A CONTACT LENS?
I...UM... WELL...
...I'M LOOKING FOR KANDOR. HAVE YOU SEEN HIM?
AS IF! JANITORS ARE NEVER AROUND WHEN YOU NEED THEM.
HE SHOULD FIX THE BELL. I CAN'T HEAR IT IN MY CLASSROOM. CAN YOU?
TH-THE BELL?
HAY LIIIIIN!
?

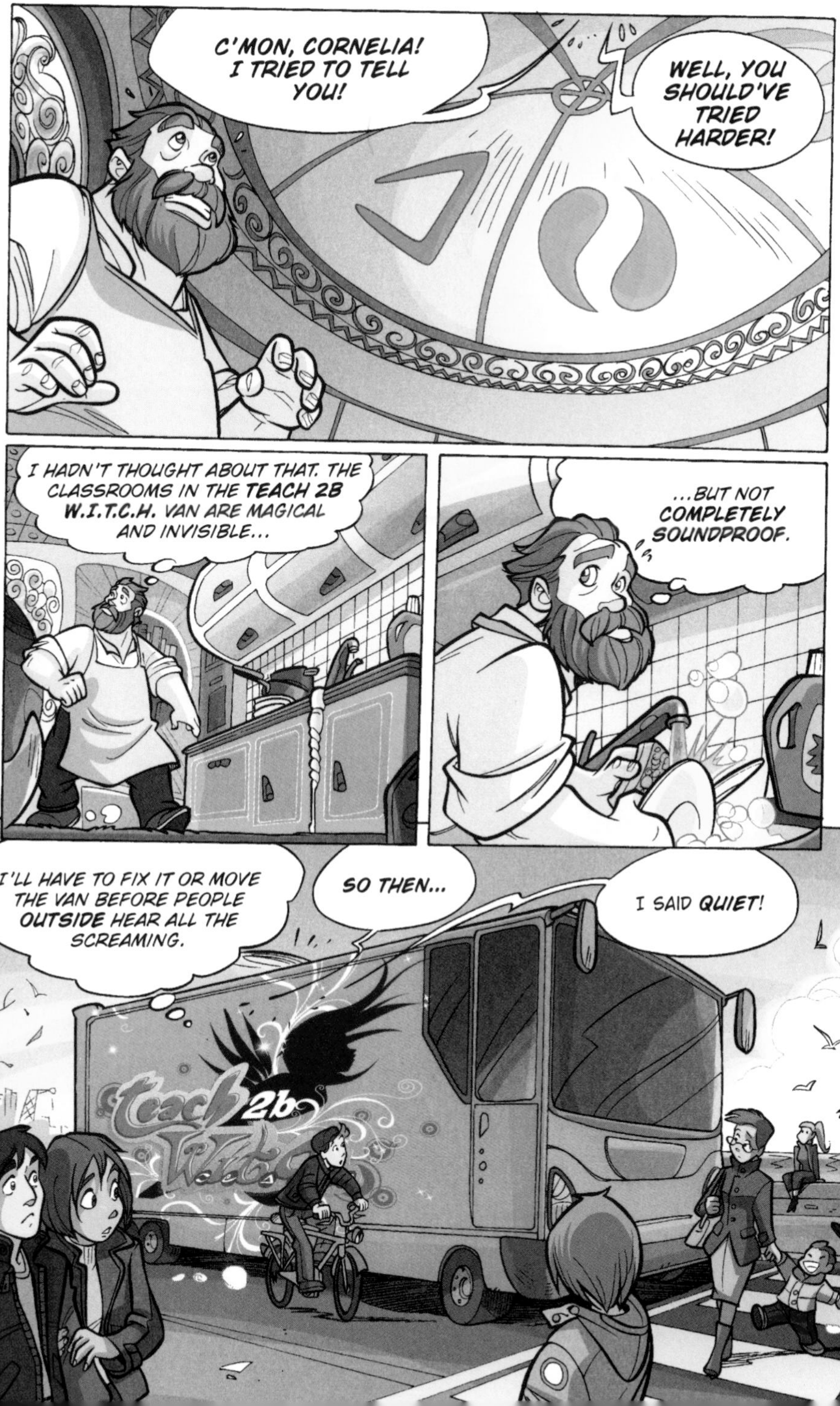
C'MON, CORNELIA! I TRIED TO TELL YOU!
WELL, YOU SHOULD'VE TRIED HARDER!
I HADN'T THOUGHT ABOUT THAT. THE CLASSROOMS IN THE **TEACH 2B W.I.T.C.H.** VAN ARE MAGICAL AND INVISIBLE...
...BUT NOT **COMPLETELY SOUNDPROOF.**
I'LL HAVE TO FIX IT OR MOVE THE VAN BEFORE PEOPLE **OUTSIDE** HEAR ALL THE SCREAMING.
SO THEN...
I SAID **QUIET!**
teach 2b

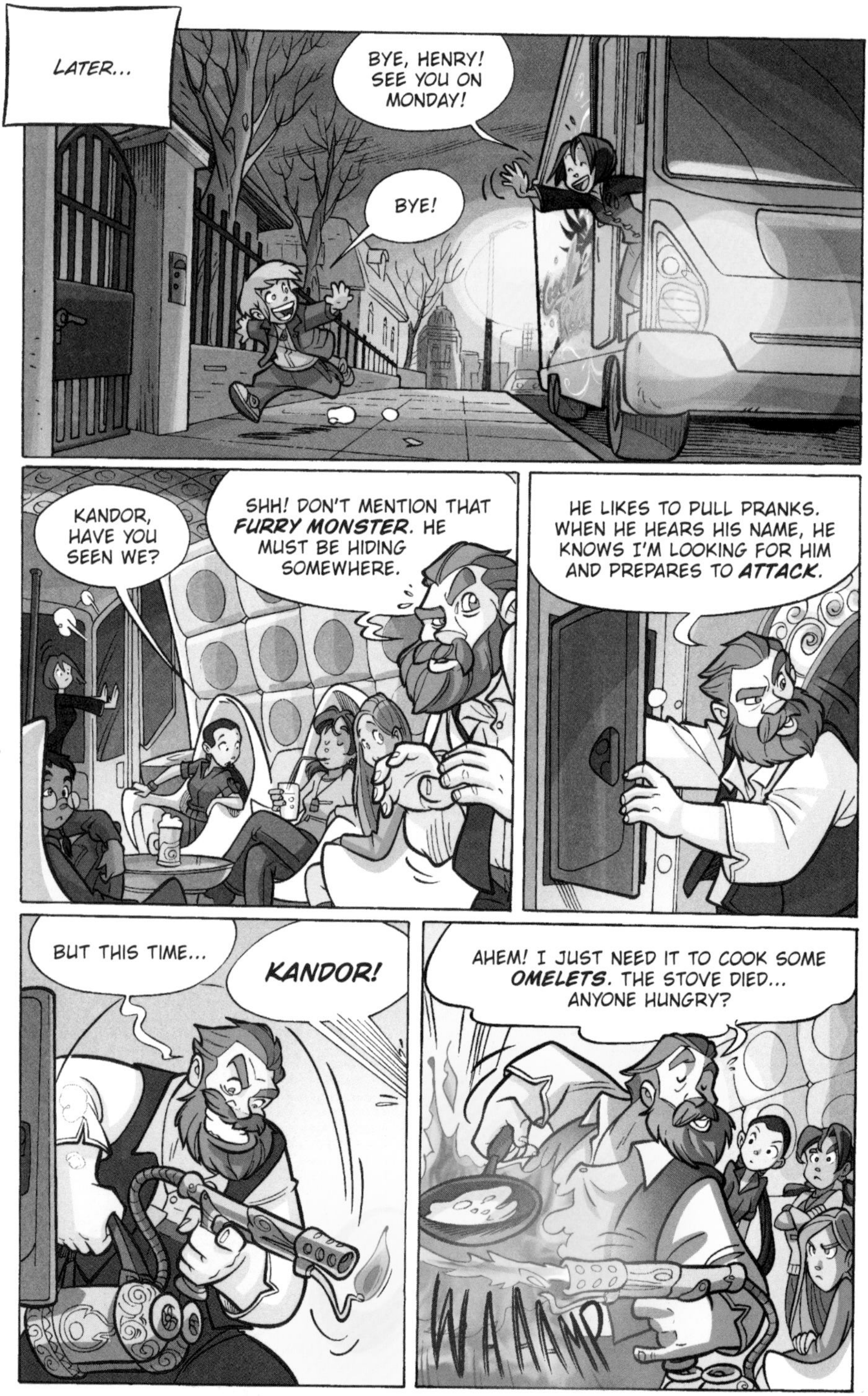
LATER...
BYE, HENRY! SEE YOU ON MONDAY!
BYE!
KANDOR, HAVE YOU SEEN WE?
SHH! DON'T MENTION THAT FURRY MONSTER. HE MUST BE HIDING SOMEWHERE.
HE LIKES TO PULL PRANKS. WHEN HE HEARS HIS NAME, HE KNOWS I'M LOOKING FOR HIM AND PREPARES TO ATTACK.
BUT THIS TIME...
KANDOR!
AHEM! I JUST NEED IT TO COOK SOME OMELETS. THE STOVE DIED... ANYONE HUNGRY?
WAAAMP

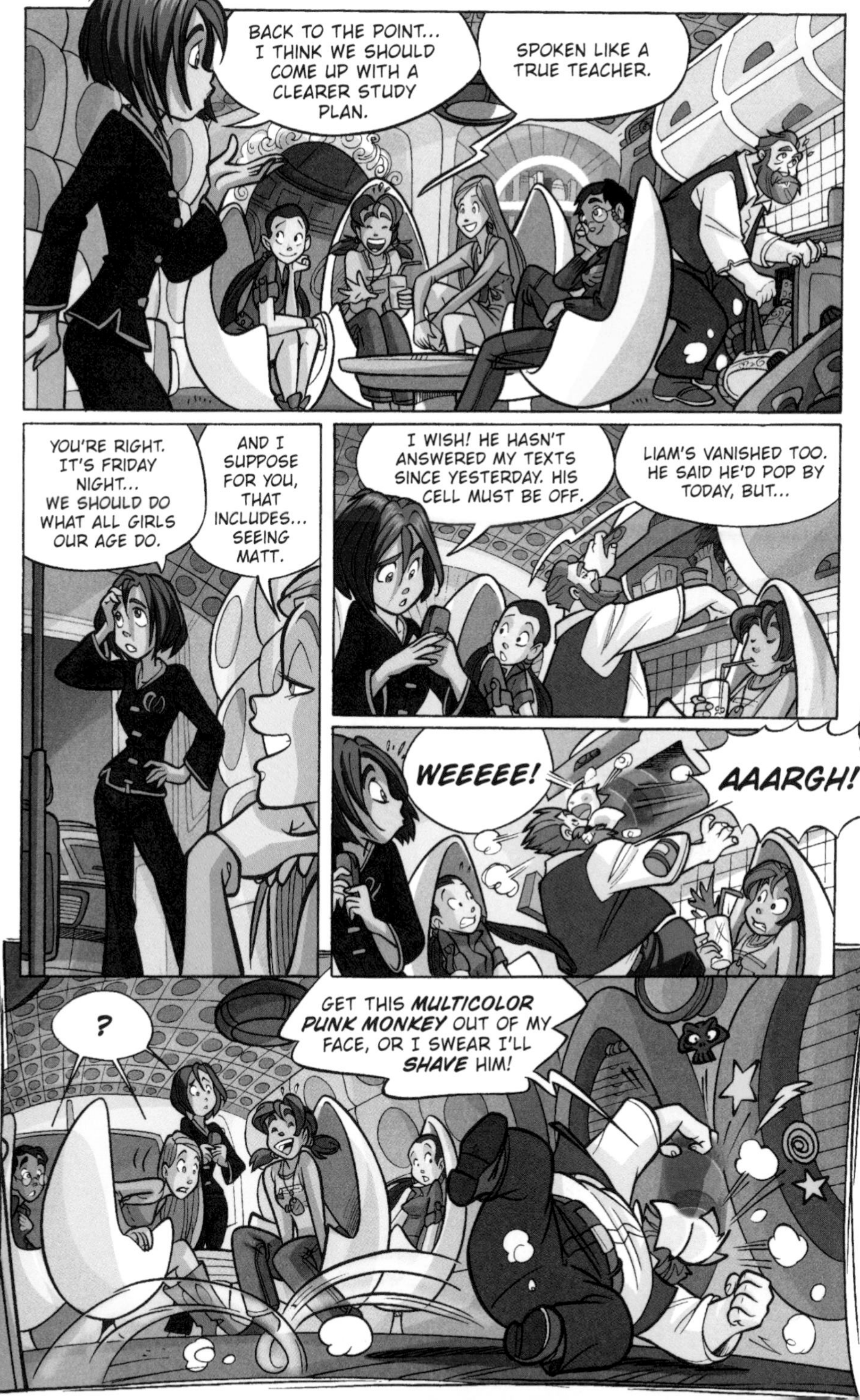

BACK TO THE POINT... I THINK WE SHOULD COME UP WITH A CLEARER STUDY PLAN.
SPOKEN LIKE A TRUE TEACHER.
YOU'RE RIGHT. IT'S FRIDAY NIGHT... WE SHOULD DO WHAT ALL GIRLS OUR AGE DO.
AND I SUPPOSE FOR YOU, THAT INCLUDES... SEEING MATT.
I WISH! HE HASN'T ANSWERED MY TEXTS SINCE YESTERDAY. HIS CELL MUST BE OFF.
LIAM'S VANISHED TOO. HE SAID HE'D POP BY TODAY, BUT...
WEEEEE!
AAARGH!
?
GET THIS MULTICOLOR PUNK MONKEY OUT OF MY FACE, OR I SWEAR I'LL SHAVE HIM!

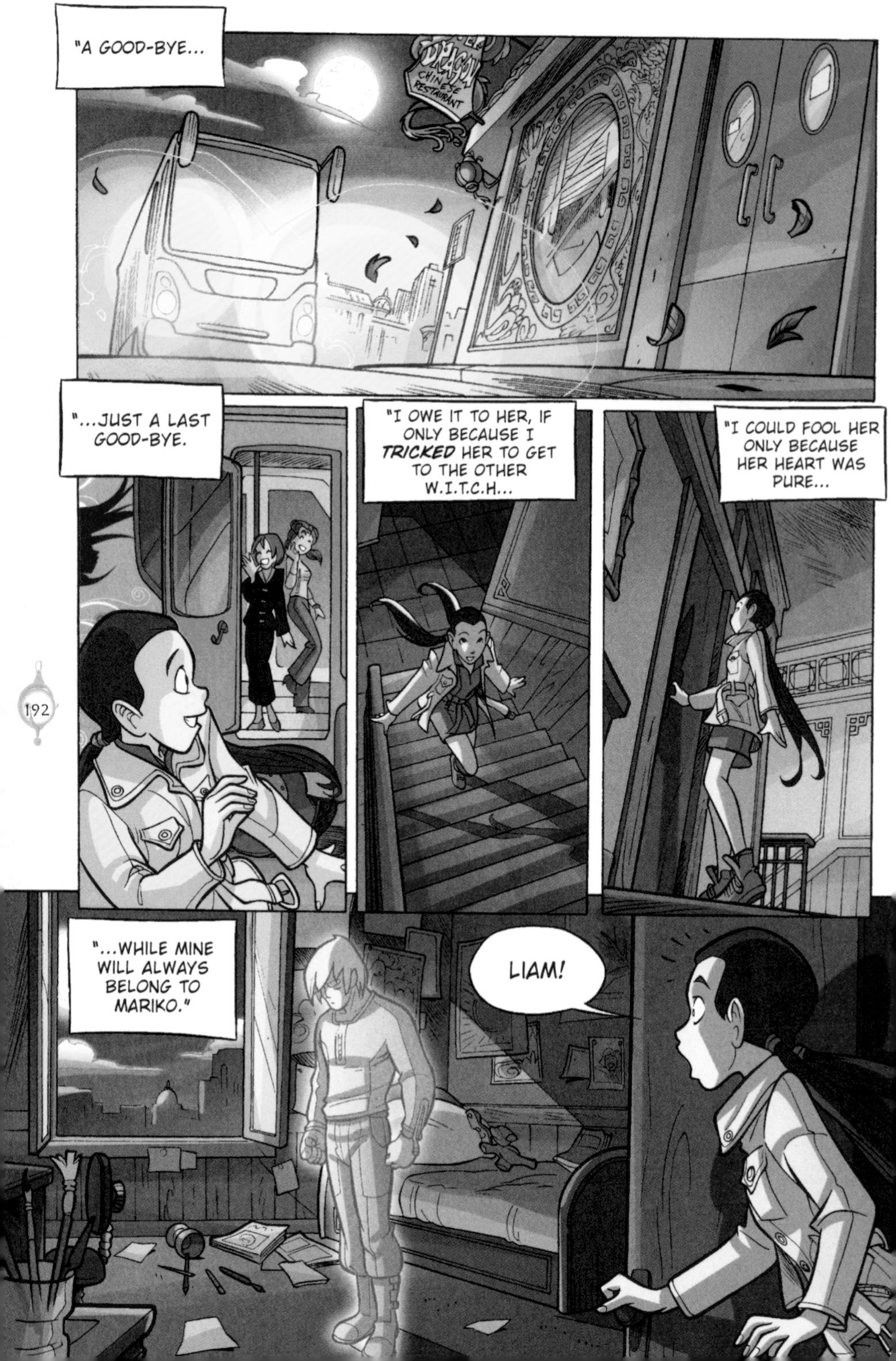
"A GOOD-BYE...
DRAGON CHINESE RESTAURANT
"...JUST A LAST GOOD-BYE.
"I OWE IT TO HER, IF ONLY BECAUSE I TRICKED HER TO GET TO THE OTHER W.I.T.C.H...
"I COULD FOOL HER ONLY BECAUSE HER HEART WAS PURE...
"...WHILE MINE WILL ALWAYS BELONG TO MARIKO."
LIAM!

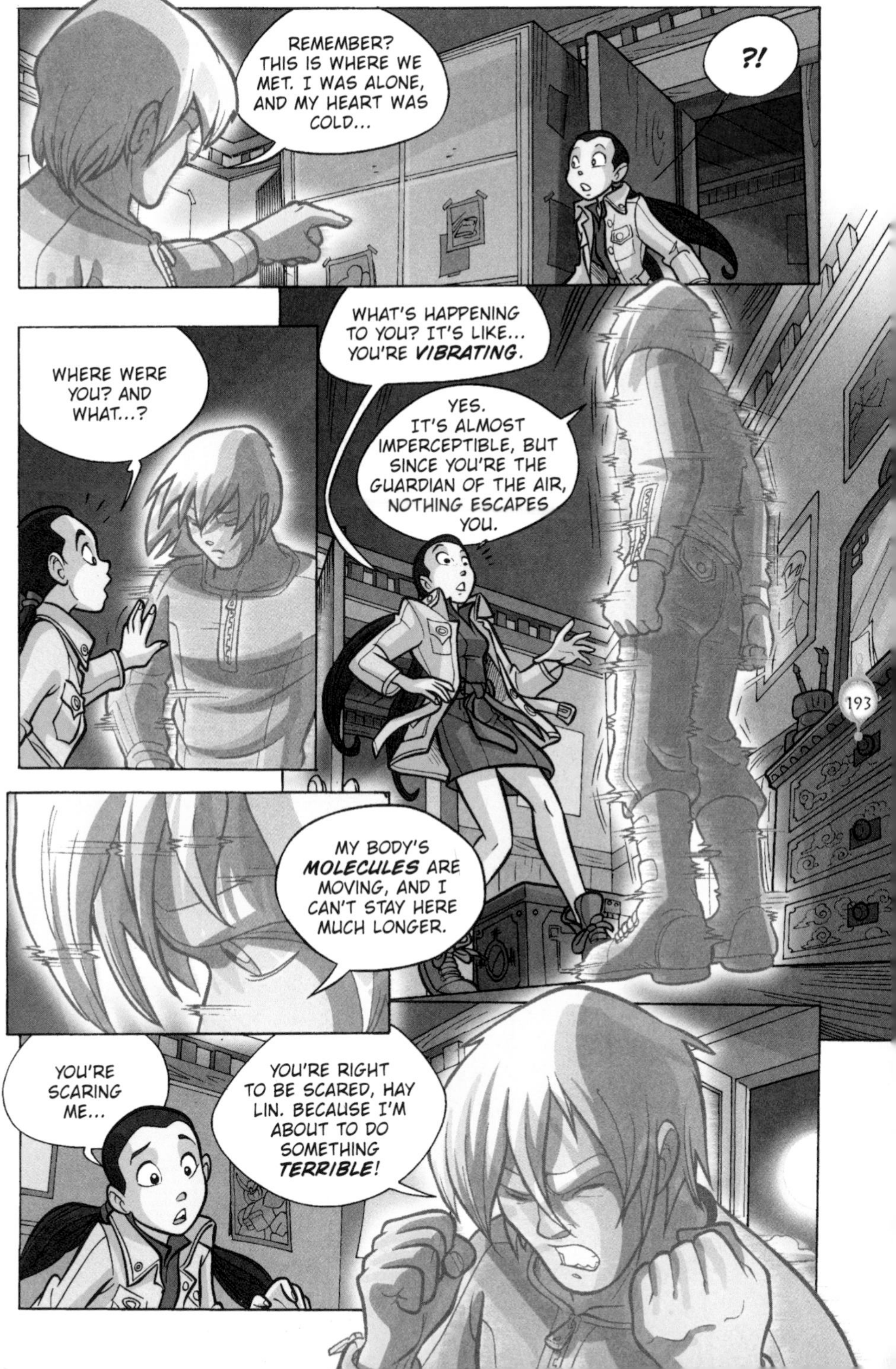
REMEMBER? THIS IS WHERE WE MET. I WAS ALONE, AND MY HEART WAS COLD...
?!
WHERE WERE YOU? AND WHAT...?
WHAT'S HAPPENING TO YOU? IT'S LIKE... YOU'RE VIBRATING.
YES. IT'S ALMOST IMPERCEPTIBLE, BUT SINCE YOU'RE THE GUARDIAN OF THE AIR, NOTHING ESCAPES YOU.
MY BODY'S MOLECULES ARE MOVING, AND I CAN'T STAY HERE MUCH LONGER.
YOU'RE SCARING ME...
YOU'RE RIGHT TO BE SCARED, HAY LIN. BECAUSE I'M ABOUT TO DO SOMETHING TERRIBLE!

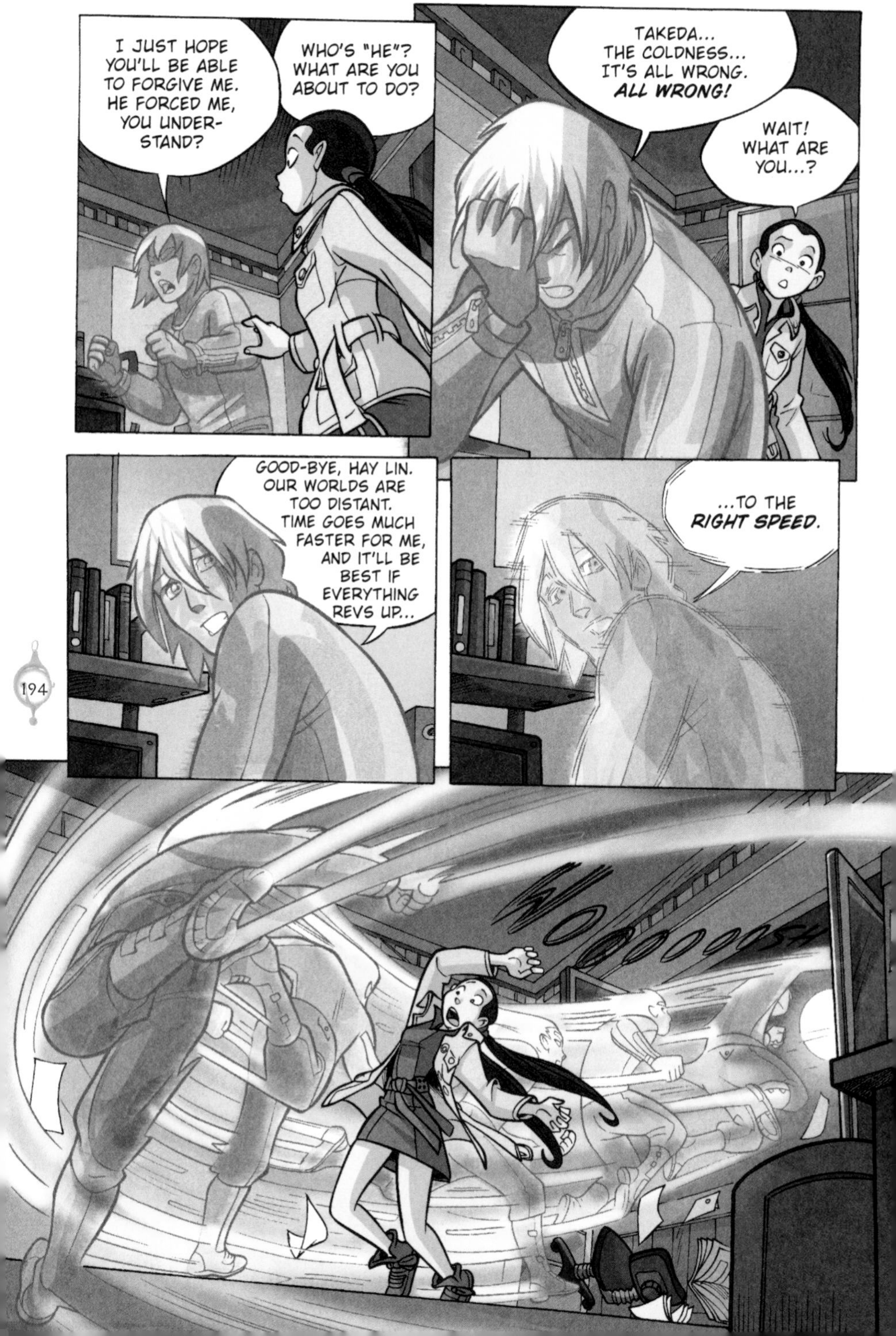
I JUST HOPE YOU'LL BE ABLE TO FORGIVE ME. HE FORCED ME, YOU UNDER-STAND?
WHO'S "HE"? WHAT ARE YOU ABOUT TO DO?
TAKEDA... THE COLDNESS... IT'S ALL WRONG. ***ALL WRONG!***
WAIT! WHAT ARE YOU...?
GOOD-BYE, HAY LIN. OUR WORLDS ARE TOO DISTANT. TIME GOES MUCH FASTER FOR ME, AND IT'LL BE BEST IF EVERYTHING REVS UP...
...TO THE ***RIGHT SPEED.***
WOOOOOOOOOSH

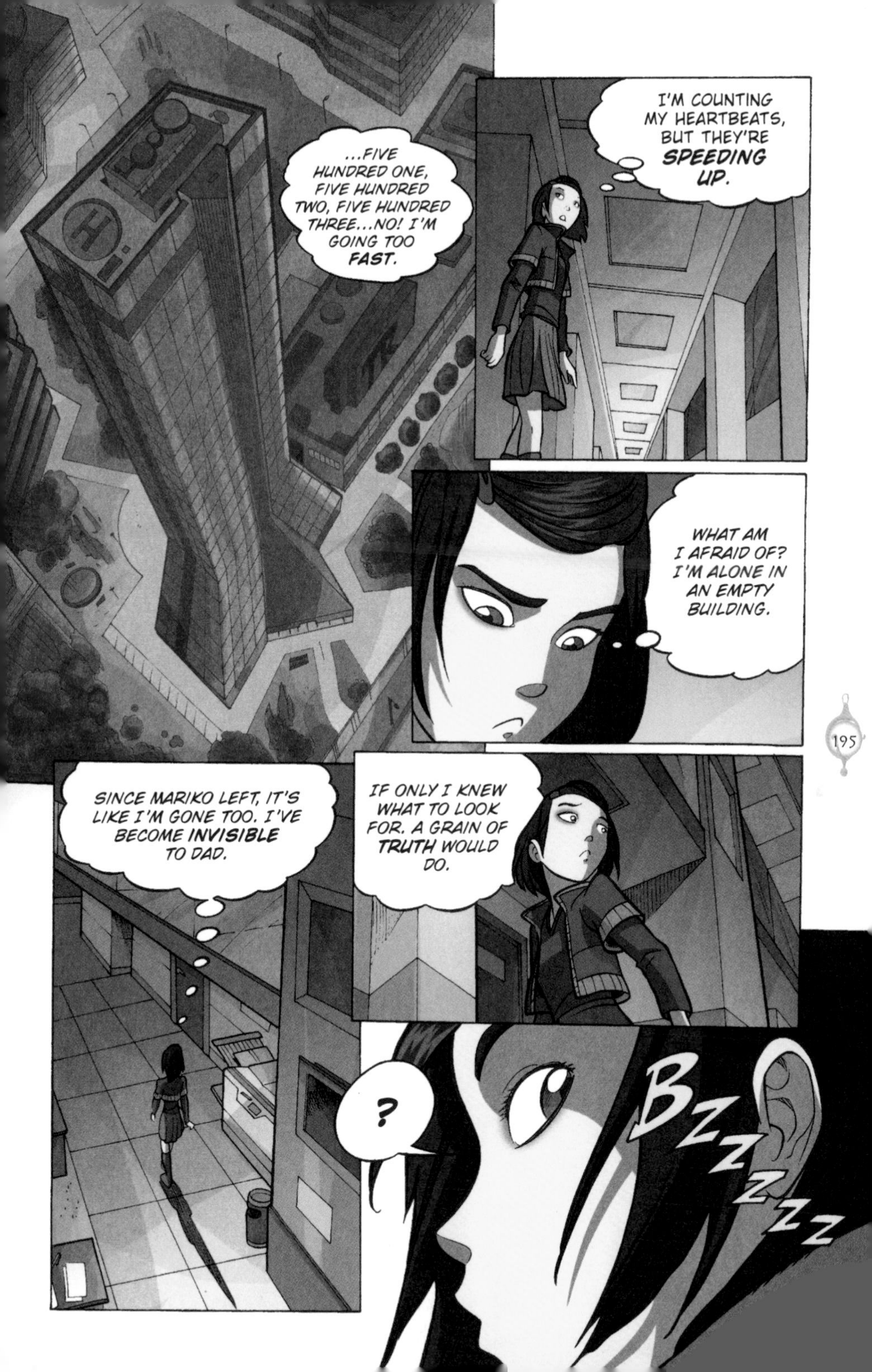
...FIVE HUNDRED ONE, FIVE HUNDRED TWO, FIVE HUNDRED THREE...NO! I'M GOING TOO FAST.
I'M COUNTING MY HEARTBEATS, BUT THEY'RE SPEEDING UP.
WHAT AM I AFRAID OF? I'M ALONE IN AN EMPTY BUILDING.
SINCE MARIKO LEFT, IT'S LIKE I'M GONE TOO. I'VE BECOME INVISIBLE TO DAD.
IF ONLY I KNEW WHAT TO LOOK FOR. A GRAIN OF TRUTH WOULD DO.
?
BZZZZZZ

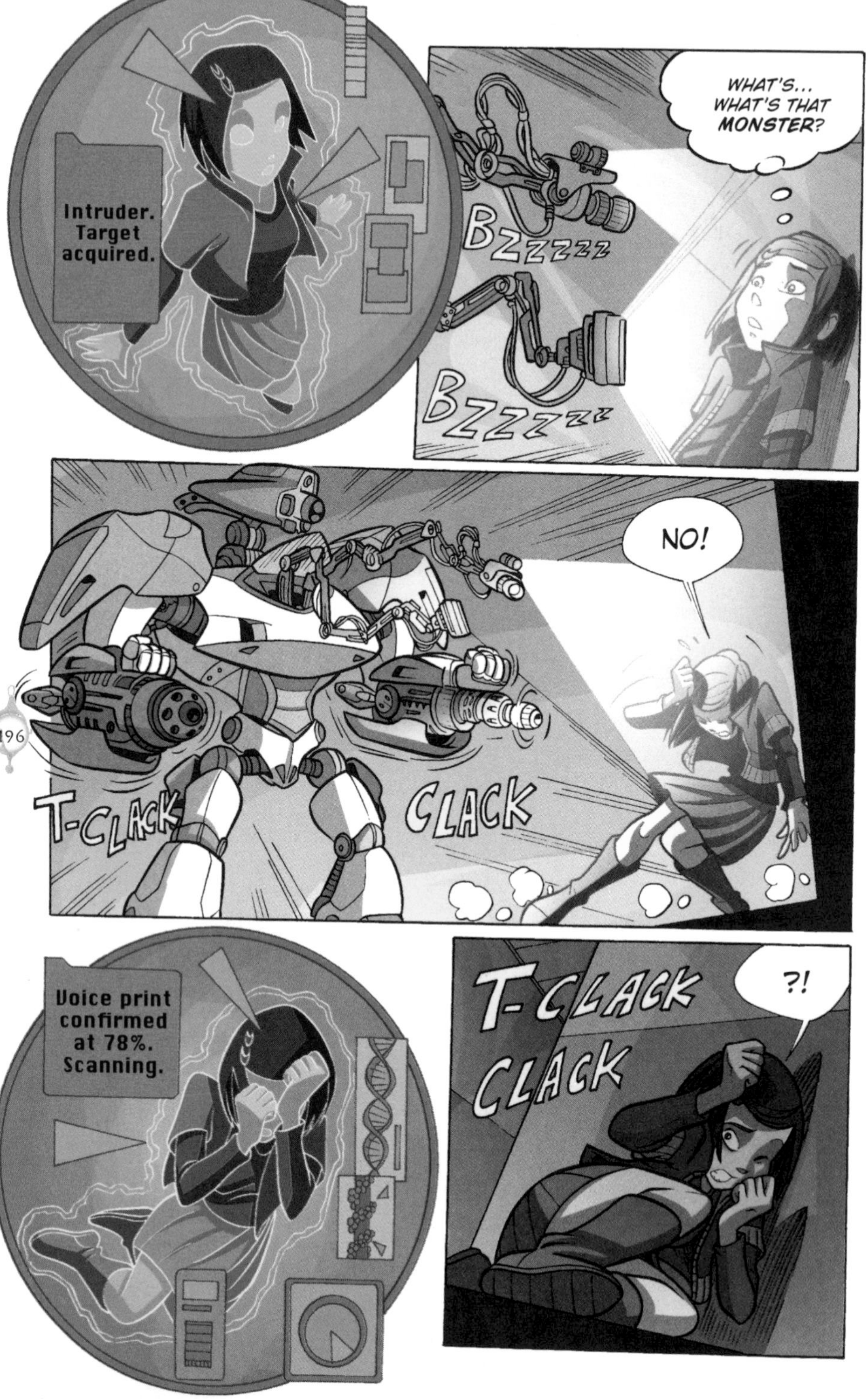
Intruder. Target acquired.
WHAT'S... WHAT'S THAT MONSTER?
BZZZZZ
BZZZZZ
NO!
T-CLACK
CLACK
Voice print confirmed at 78%. Scanning.
T-CLACK
CLACK
?!

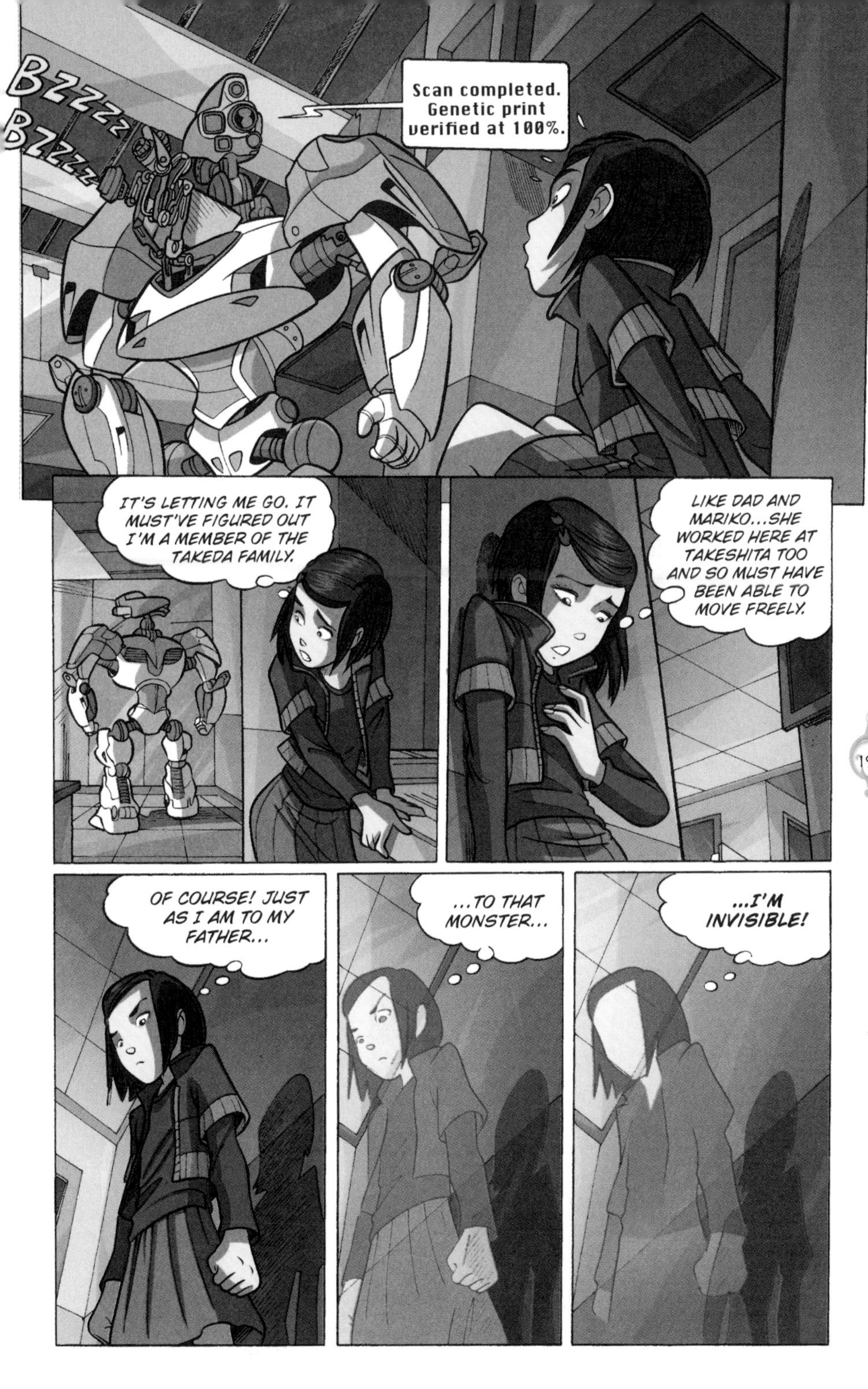
BZZZZZ
BZZZZZ
Scan completed. Genetic print verified at 100%.
IT'S LETTING ME GO. IT MUST'VE FIGURED OUT I'M A MEMBER OF THE TAKEDA FAMILY.
LIKE DAD AND MARIKO...SHE WORKED HERE AT TAKESHITA TOO AND SO MUST HAVE BEEN ABLE TO MOVE FREELY.
OF COURSE! JUST AS I AM TO MY FATHER...
...TO THAT MONSTER...
...I'M INVISIBLE!

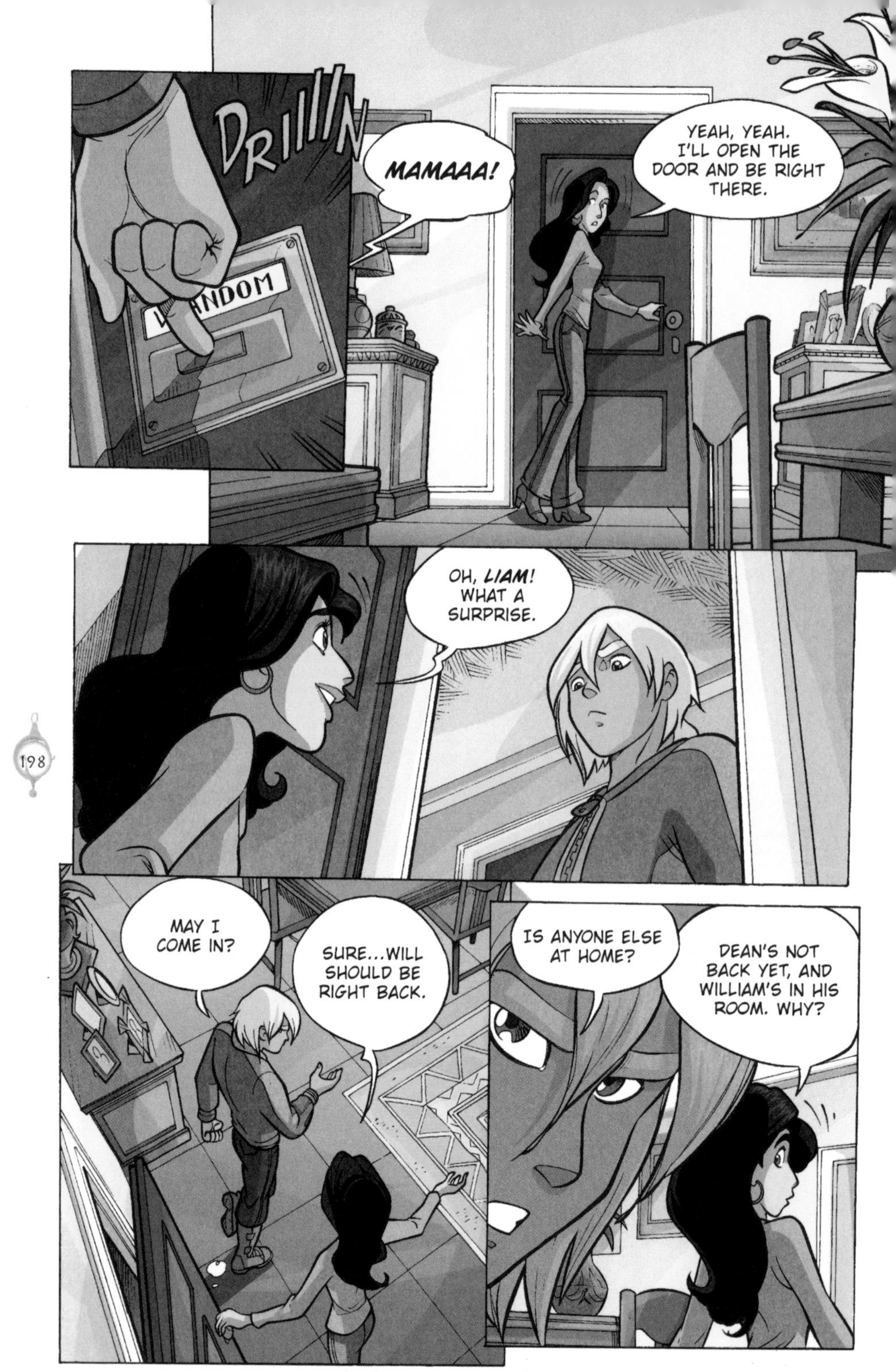
DRIIIN
MAMAAA!
YEAH, YEAH. I'LL OPEN THE DOOR AND BE RIGHT THERE.
OH, *LIAM*! WHAT A SURPRISE.
MAY I COME IN?
SURE...WILL SHOULD BE RIGHT BACK.
IS ANYONE ELSE AT HOME?
DEAN'S NOT BACK YET, AND WILLIAM'S IN HIS ROOM. WHY?

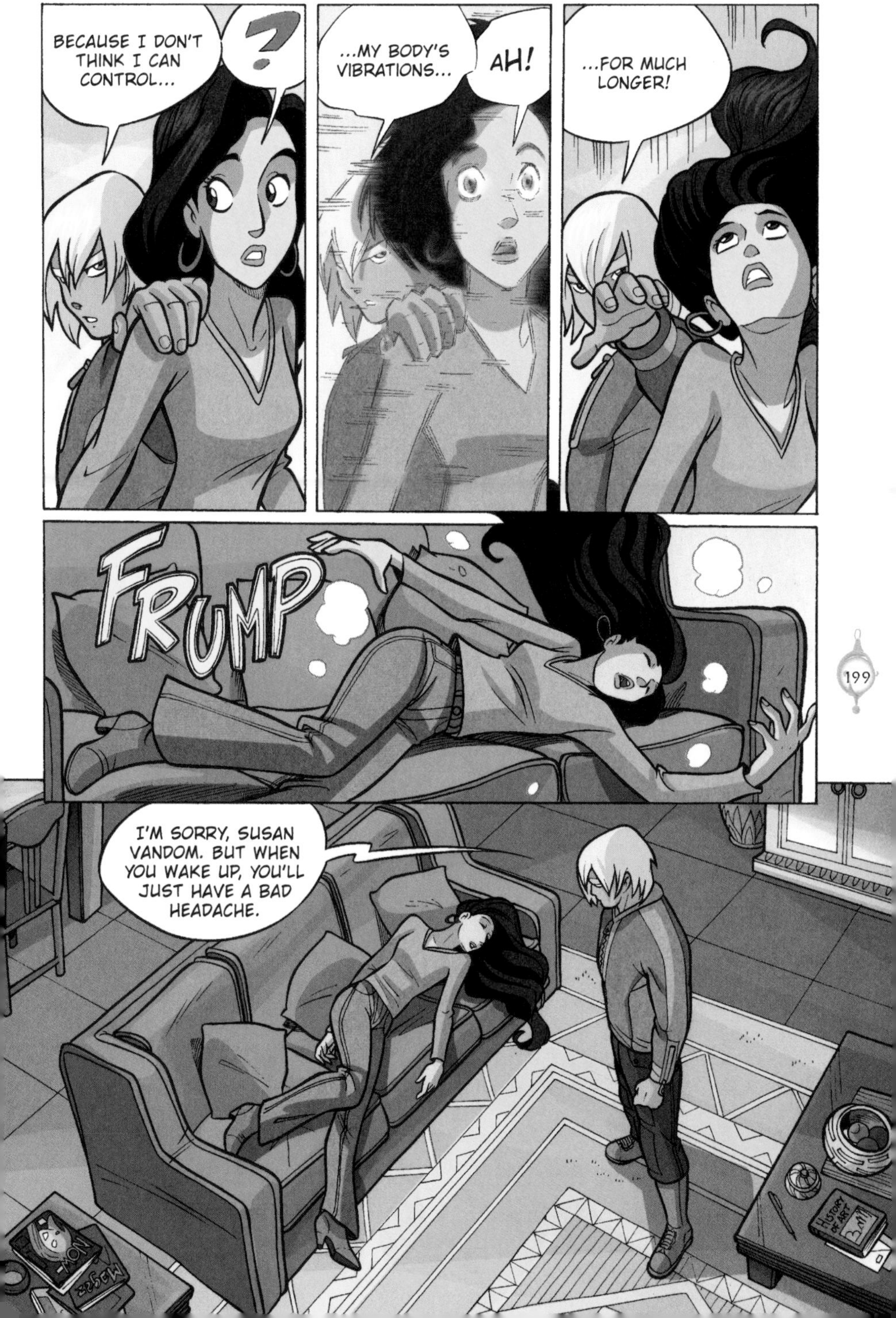
BECAUSE I DON'T THINK I CAN CONTROL...
?
...MY BODY'S VIBRATIONS...
AH!
...FOR MUCH LONGER!
FRUMP
I'M SORRY, SUSAN VANDOM. BUT WHEN YOU WAKE UP, YOU'LL JUST HAVE A BAD HEADACHE.
HISTORY OF ART

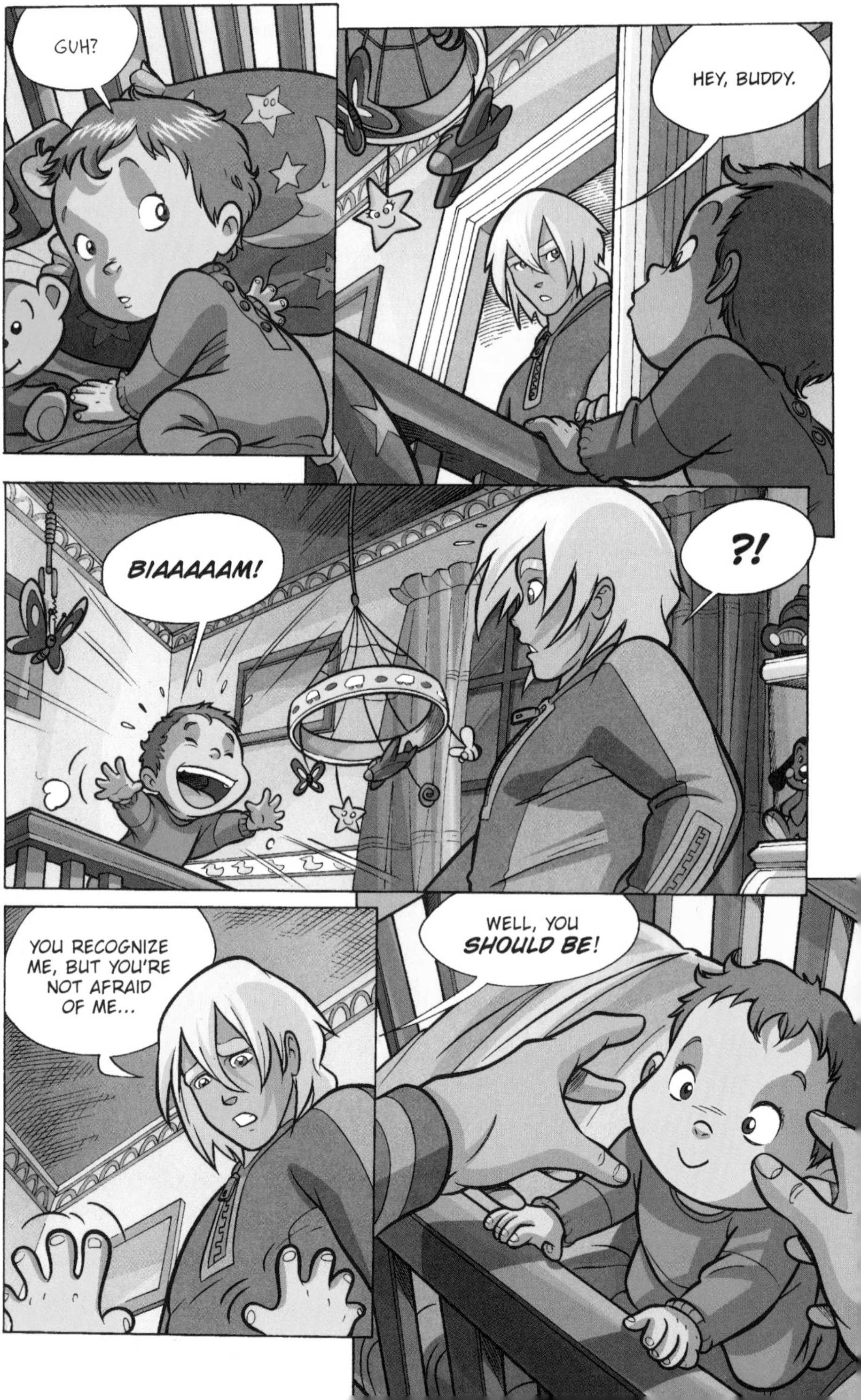
GUH?
HEY, BUDDY.
BIAAAAAM!
?!
YOU RECOGNIZE ME, BUT YOU'RE NOT AFRAID OF ME...
WELL, YOU SHOULD BE!

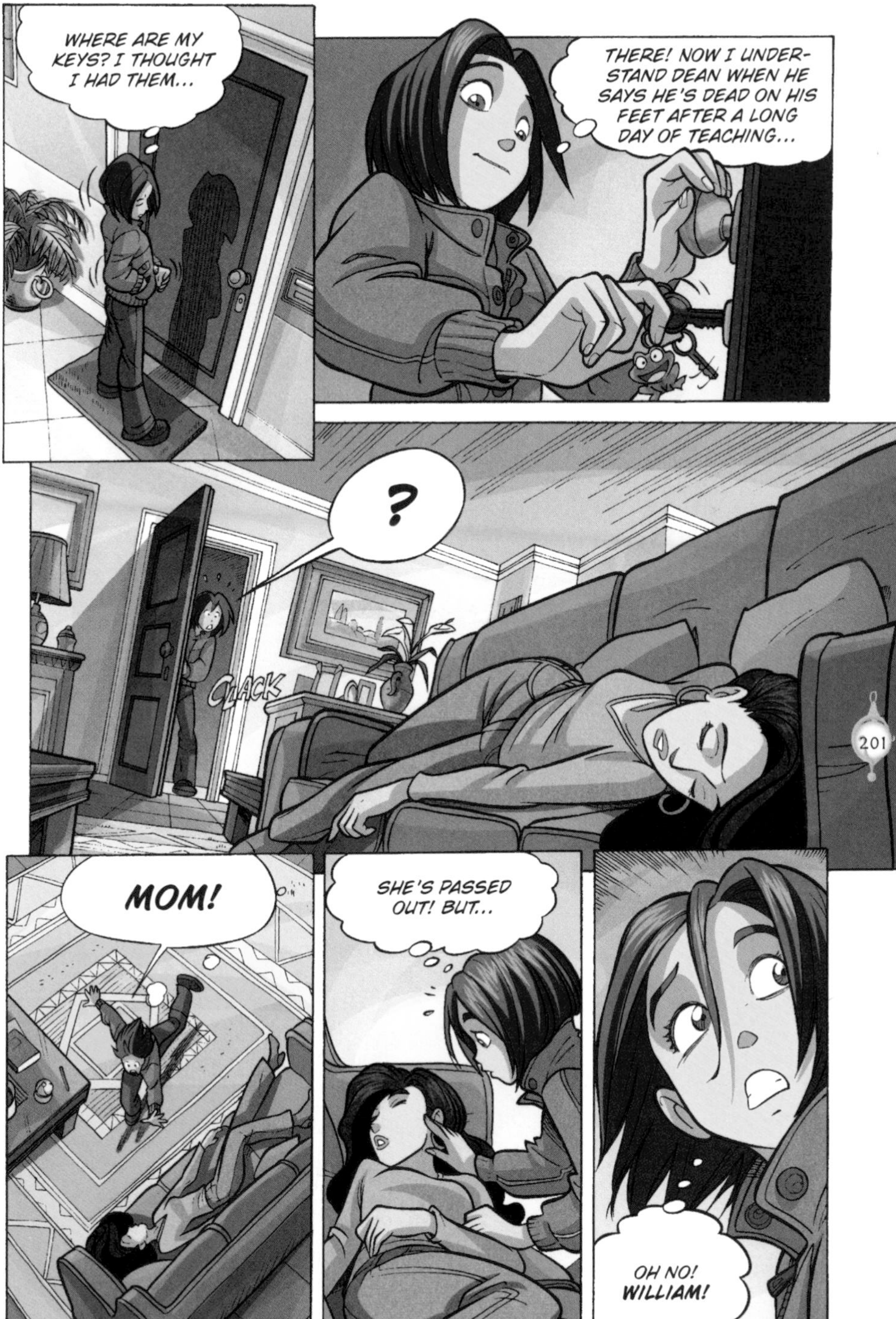
WHERE ARE MY KEYS? I THOUGHT I HAD THEM...
THERE! NOW I UNDERSTAND DEAN WHEN HE SAYS HE'S DEAD ON HIS FEET AFTER A LONG DAY OF TEACHING...
?
CLACK
MOM!
SHE'S PASSED OUT! BUT...
OH NO! WILLIAM!

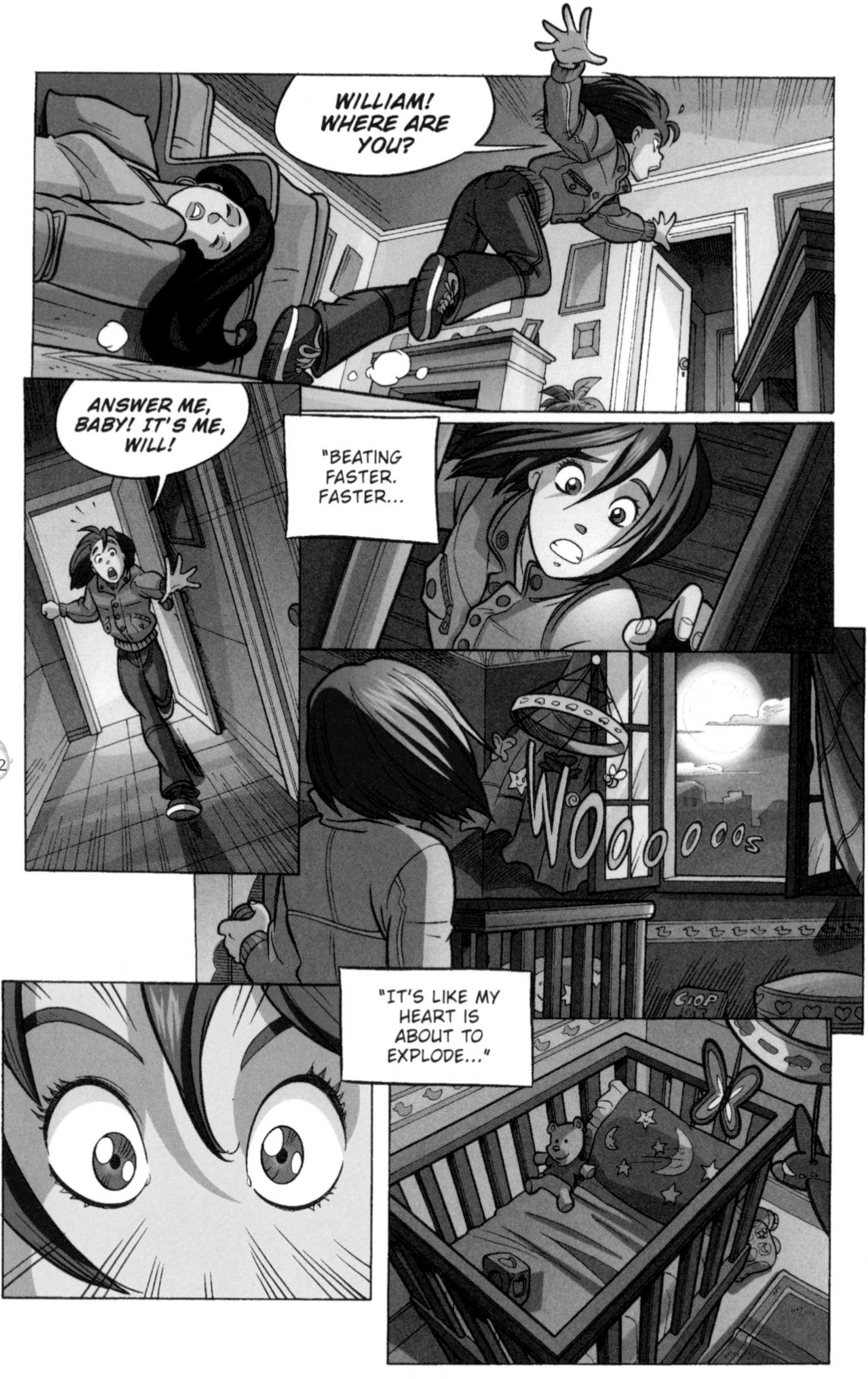
WILLIAM! WHERE ARE YOU?
ANSWER ME, BABY! IT'S ME, WILL!
"BEATING FASTER. FASTER...
WOOOOOOOS
"IT'S LIKE MY HEART IS ABOUT TO EXPLODE..."

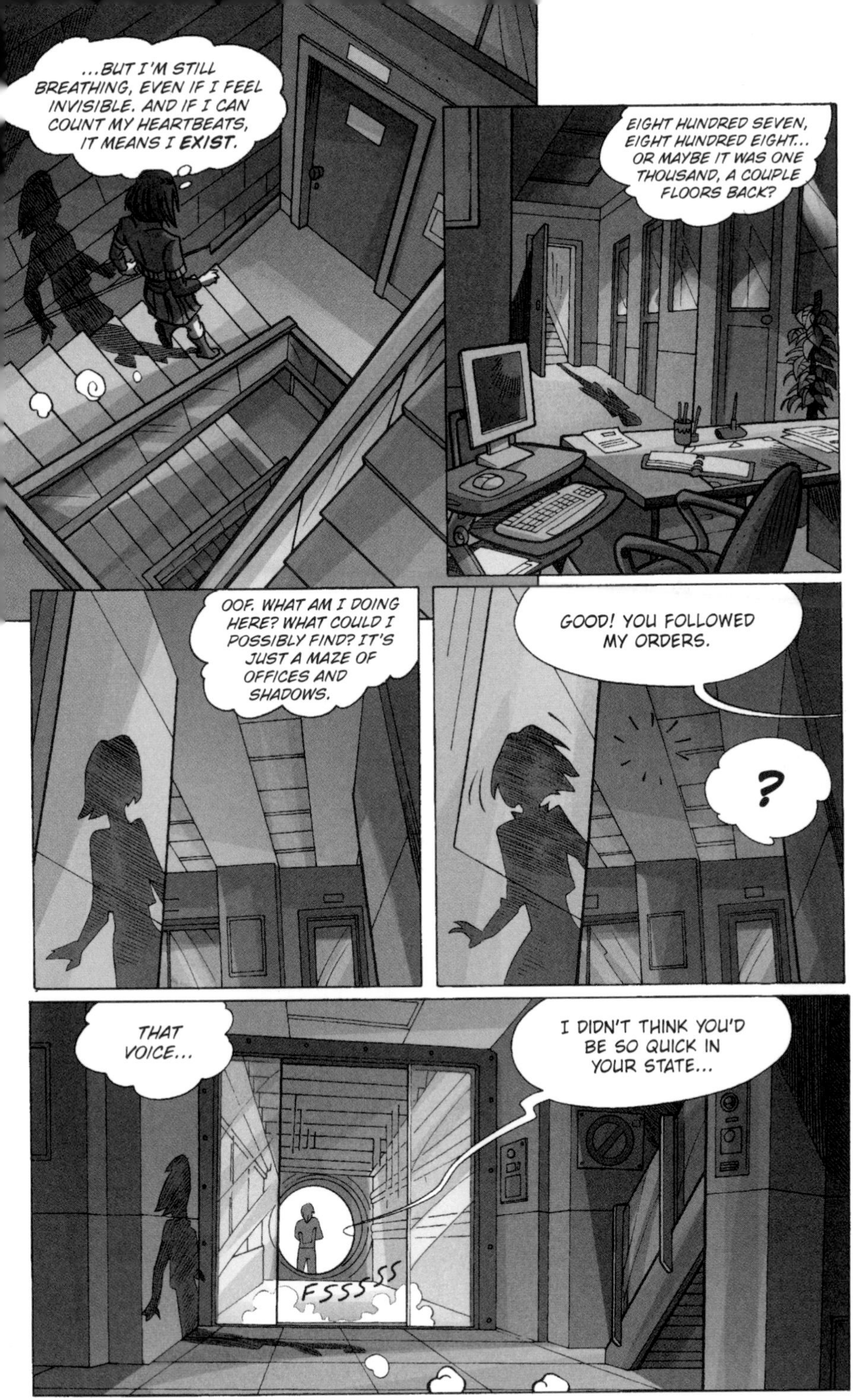
...BUT I'M STILL BREATHING, EVEN IF I FEEL INVISIBLE. AND IF I CAN COUNT MY HEARTBEATS, IT MEANS I EXIST.
EIGHT HUNDRED SEVEN, EIGHT HUNDRED EIGHT... OR MAYBE IT WAS ONE THOUSAND, A COUPLE FLOORS BACK?
OOF. WHAT AM I DOING HERE? WHAT COULD I POSSIBLY FIND? IT'S JUST A MAZE OF OFFICES AND SHADOWS.
GOOD! YOU FOLLOWED MY ORDERS.
?
THAT VOICE...
I DIDN'T THINK YOU'D BE SO QUICK IN YOUR STATE...
FSSSSSS

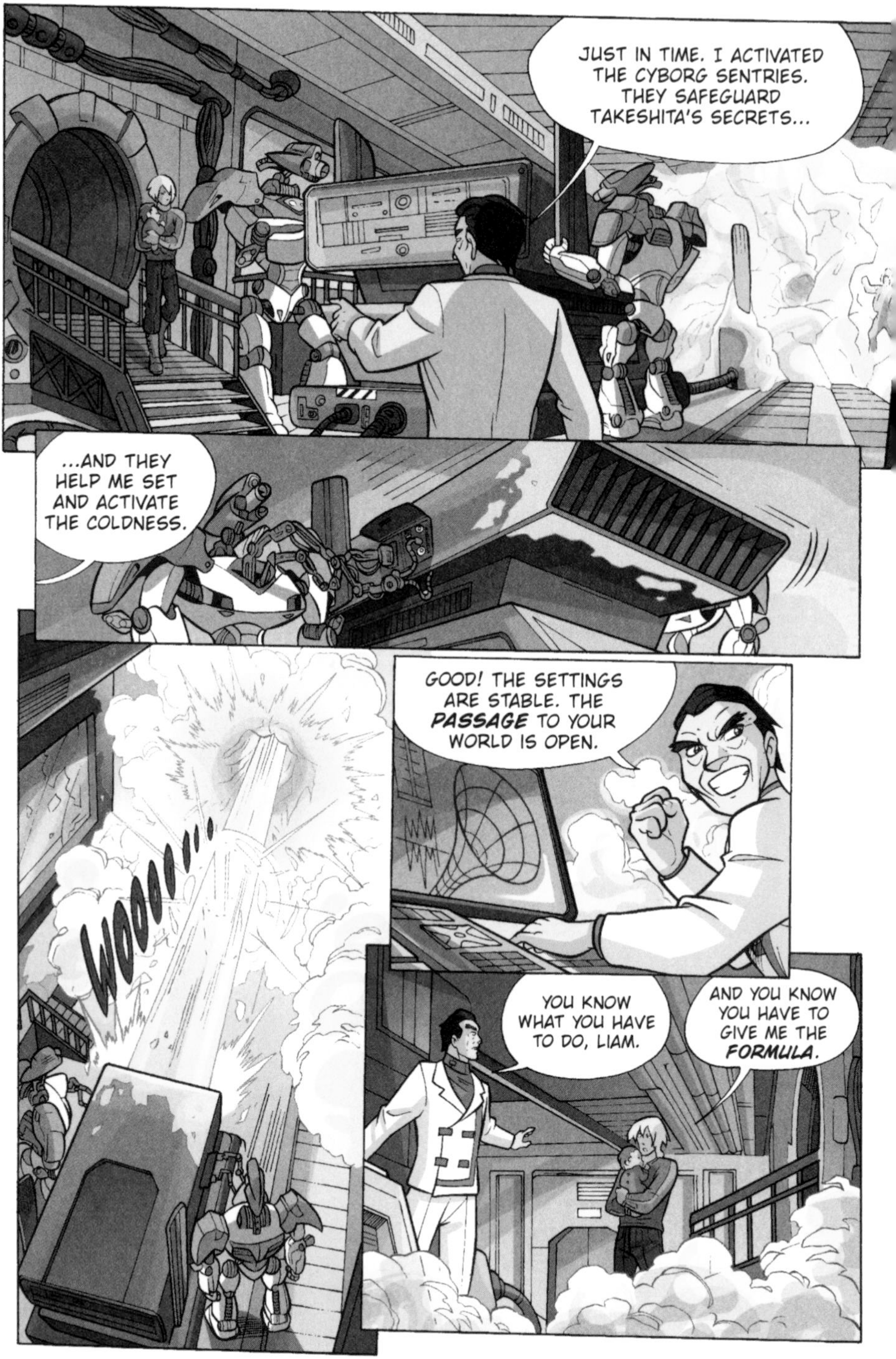
JUST IN TIME. I ACTIVATED THE CYBORG SENTRIES. THEY SAFEGUARD TAKESHITA'S SECRETS...
...AND THEY HELP ME SET AND ACTIVATE THE COLDNESS.
GOOD! THE SETTINGS ARE STABLE. THE PASSAGE TO YOUR WORLD IS OPEN.
WOOO...
YOU KNOW WHAT YOU HAVE TO DO, LIAM.
AND YOU KNOW YOU HAVE TO GIVE ME THE FORMULA.

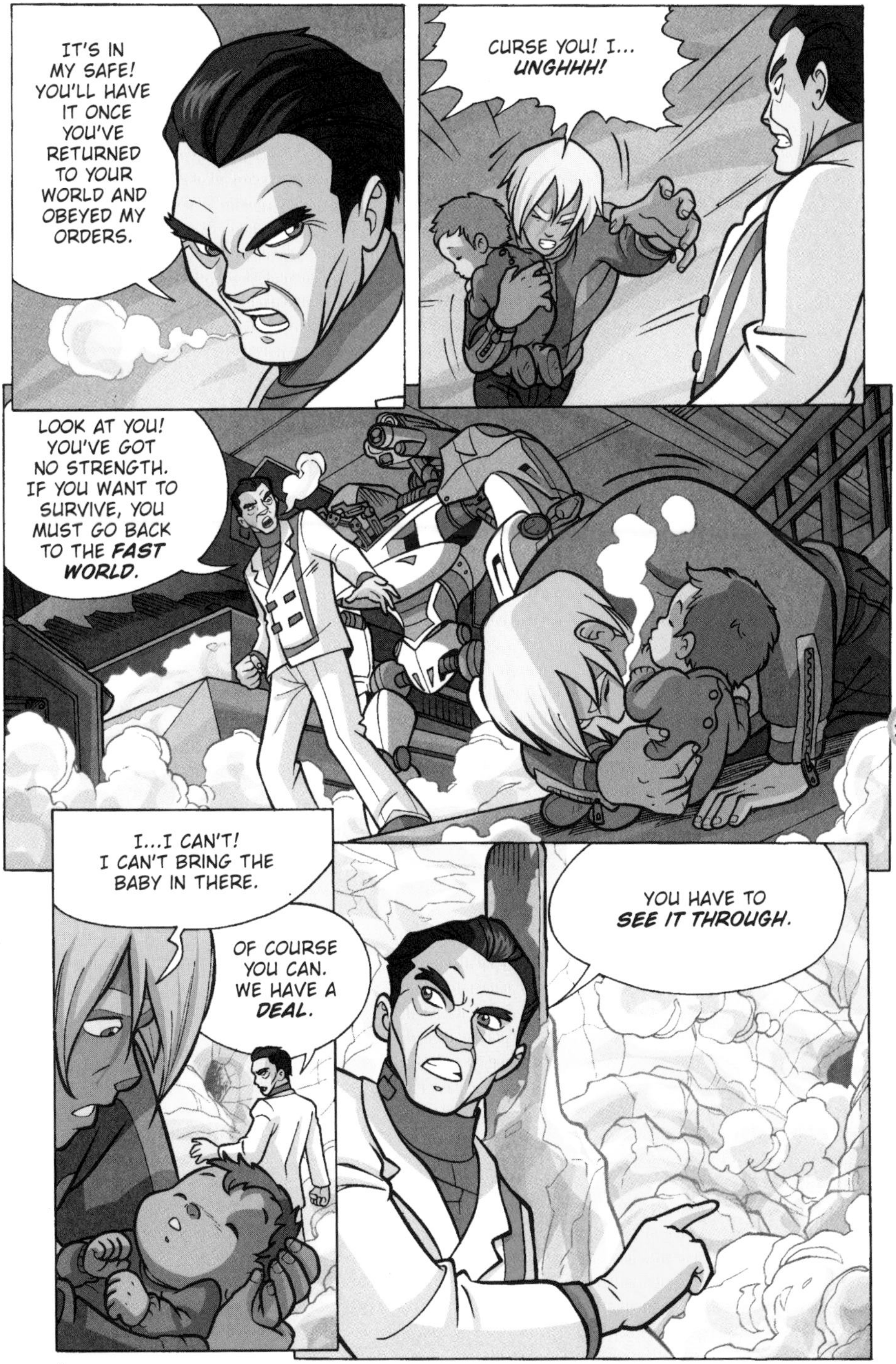
IT'S IN MY SAFE! YOU'LL HAVE IT ONCE YOU'VE RETURNED TO YOUR WORLD AND OBEYED MY ORDERS.
CURSE YOU! I... UNGHHH!
LOOK AT YOU! YOU'VE GOT NO STRENGTH. IF YOU WANT TO SURVIVE, YOU MUST GO BACK TO THE FAST WORLD.
I...I CAN'T! I CAN'T BRING THE BABY IN THERE.
OF COURSE YOU CAN. WE HAVE A DEAL.
YOU HAVE TO SEE IT THROUGH.

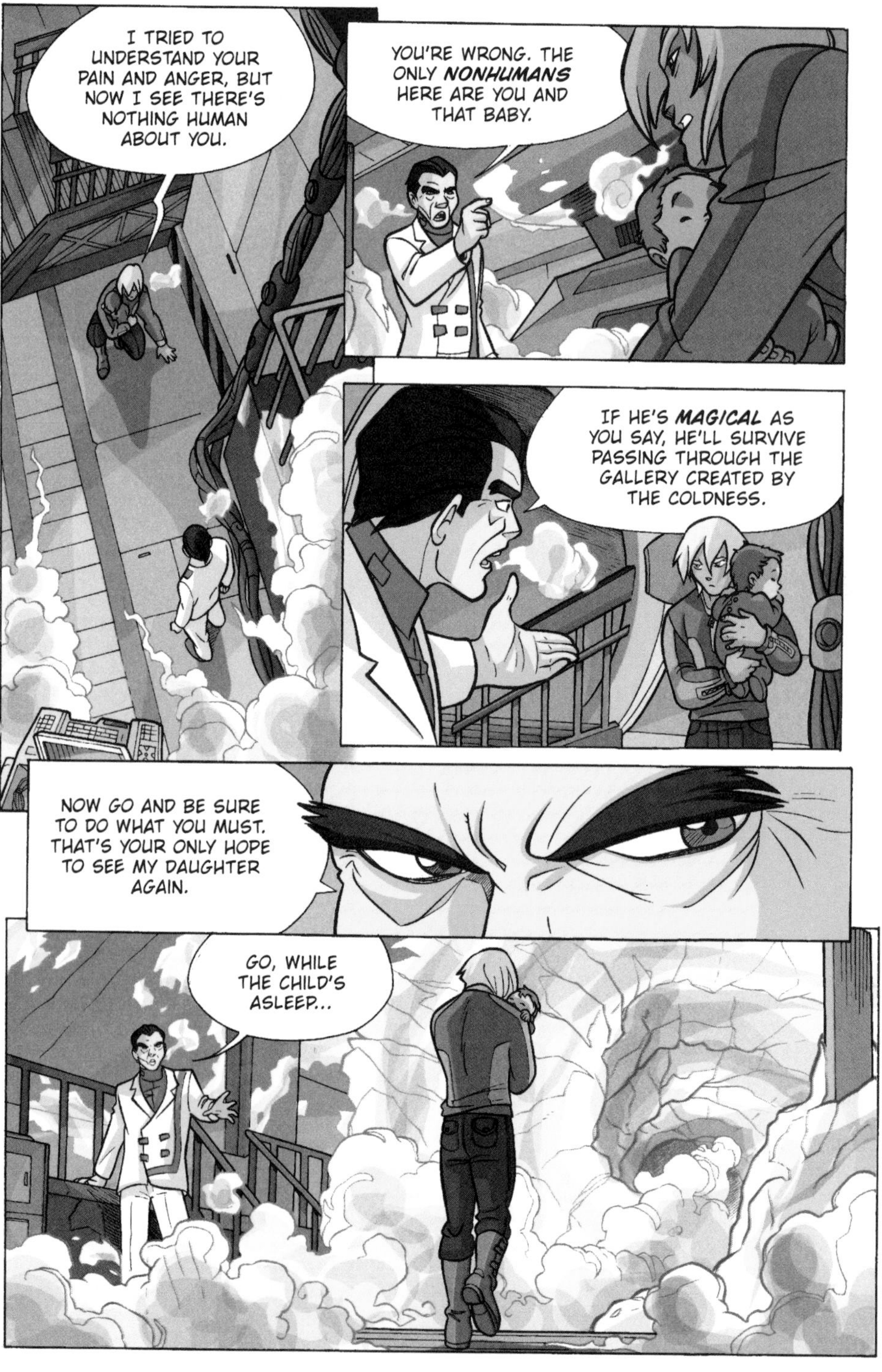
I TRIED TO UNDERSTAND YOUR PAIN AND ANGER, BUT NOW I SEE THERE'S NOTHING HUMAN ABOUT YOU.
YOU'RE WRONG. THE ONLY NONHUMANS HERE ARE YOU AND THAT BABY.
IF HE'S MAGICAL AS YOU SAY, HE'LL SURVIVE PASSING THROUGH THE GALLERY CREATED BY THE COLDNESS.
NOW GO AND BE SURE TO DO WHAT YOU MUST. THAT'S YOUR ONLY HOPE TO SEE MY DAUGHTER AGAIN.
GO, WHILE THE CHILD'S ASLEEP...

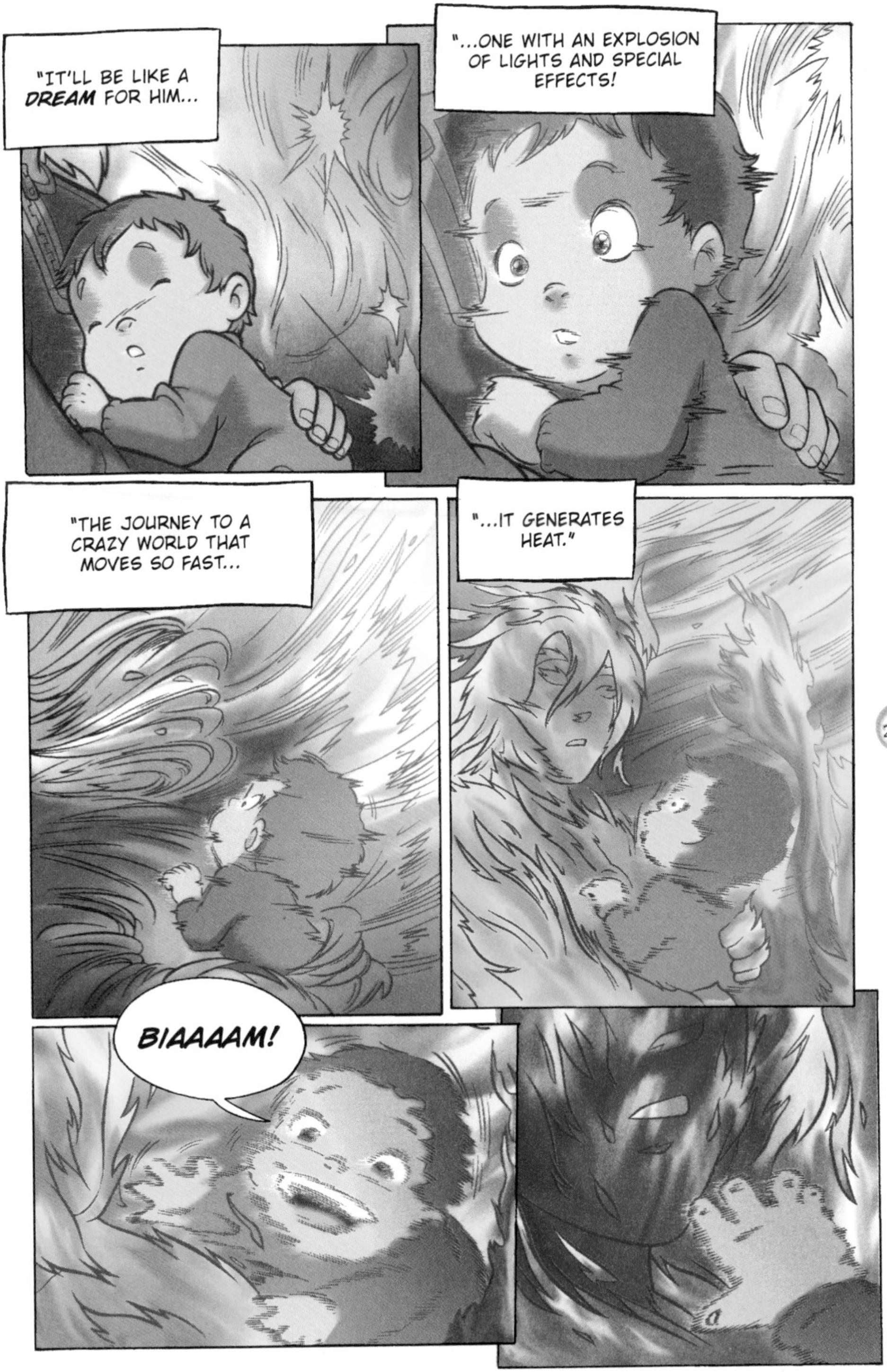
"IT'LL BE LIKE A *DREAM* FOR HIM...
"...ONE WITH AN EXPLOSION OF LIGHTS AND SPECIAL EFFECTS!
"THE JOURNEY TO A CRAZY WORLD THAT MOVES SO FAST...
"...IT GENERATES HEAT."
BIAAAAM!

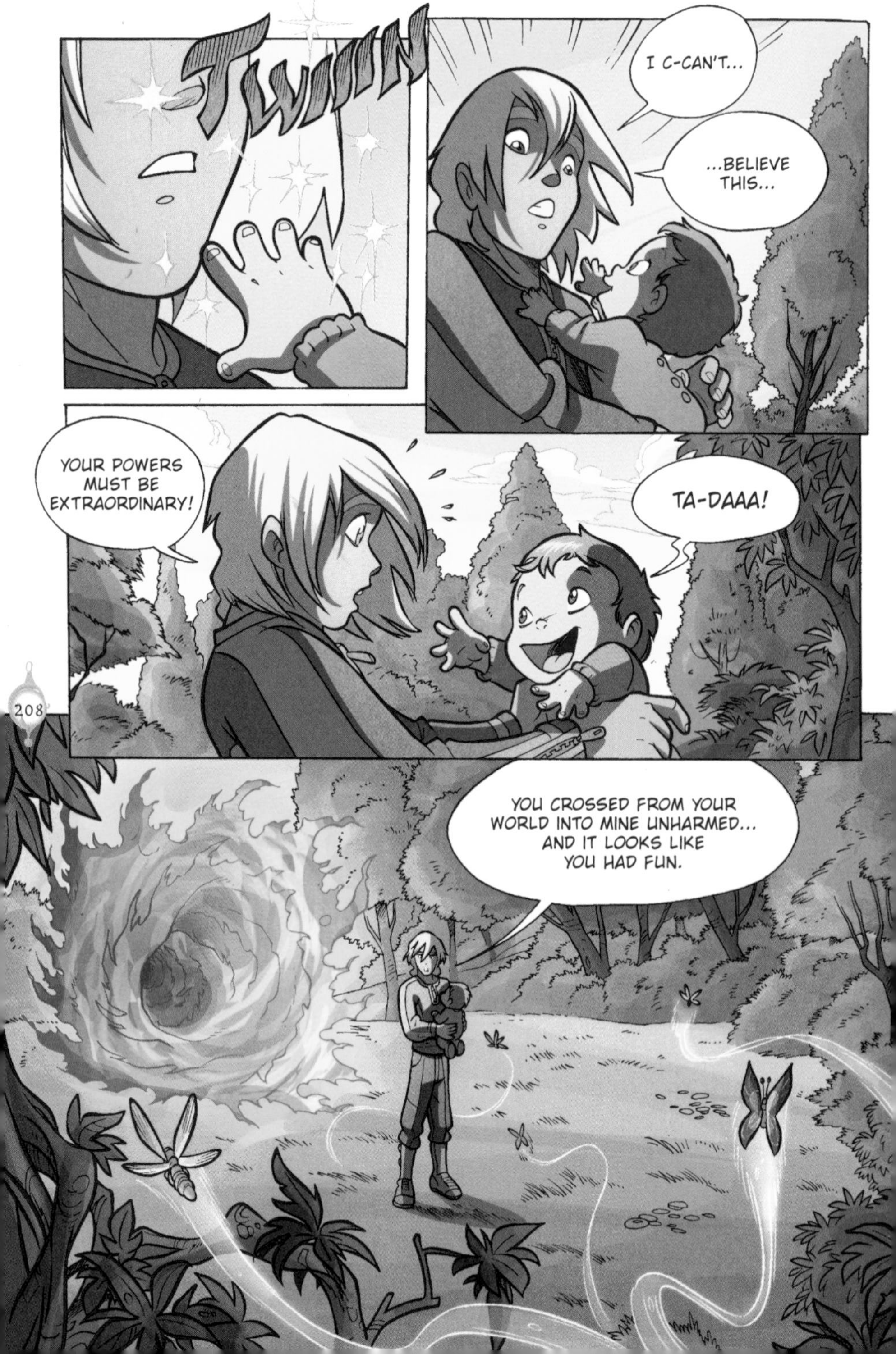
TWIIIN
I C-CAN'T...
...BELIEVE THIS...
YOUR POWERS MUST BE EXTRAORDINARY!
TA-DAAA!
YOU CROSSED FROM YOUR WORLD INTO MINE UNHARMED... AND IT LOOKS LIKE YOU HAD FUN.